DEATH WATCH

By the same author

Orchestrated Death

DEATH WATCH

Cynthia Harrod-Eagles

Charles Scribner's Sons
New York

Maxwell Macmillan International
New York Oxford Singapore Sydney

First United States Edition 1993
Copyright © 1992 by Cynthia Harrod-Eagles

Charles Scribner's Sons
Macmillan Publishing Company
866 Third Avenue
New York, NY 10022

Macmillan Publishing Company is part
of the Maxwell Communication Group of Companies.

Library of Congress Cataloging-in-Publication Data
Harrod-Eagles, Cynthia.
    Death watch/Cynthia Harrod-Eagles.—1st U.S. ed.
       p.   cm.
    ISBN 0-684-19519-4
    I. Title.
PR6058.A6945D4   1993   92–30924   CIP
                   823'.914—dc20

Macmillan books are available at special discounts for bulk purchases for sales promotions, premiums, fund-raising, or educational use. For details, contact:

Special Sales Director
Macmillan Publishing Company
866 Third Avenue
New York, NY 10022

10 9 8 7 6 5 4 3 2 1

Printed in the United States of America

This book is dedicated to Gordon Barker, for all his kindness and patience in putting me straight about The Job.

Gawd bless yer, sarge. The Met are wonderful!

Author's Note

I WAS BORN AND BROUGHT up in Shepherd's Bush. Most of the places mentioned in this book are real, but all the characters are fictitious.

There is, of course, a real Shepherd's Bush Police Station, but I think I ought to explain that I have never set foot in it. This is not out of any disrespect for the men and women who work there, but purely so that no-one could possibly say that any of my characters was based on a real person.

I could have invented a police station and its ground, but I've never felt the Bloggs Lane, Anytown convention was very convincing; and besides, it's much more fun this way.

I have done my research at quite a different police station. If anyone feels they recognise a policeman of their acquaintance in these pages, it can only be because coppers after all really are much the same the Met over – thank God!

CHAPTER ONE

London's Noblest

IT WAS A GREY AND dismal day, arriving, after the manner of London buses, immediately behind two others precisely similar. The last thing Slider felt he needed on such a morning was a fire.

A fire when it was alight and glowing in a fireplace was a delightful thing, of course. Slider's memory immediately offered him a beguiling image of Joanna, naked and rosy on the hearthrug, and he put it sadly aside. A fire when it was out, and had been where it shouldn't be, was an entirely different thing. It was nasty and depressing, and probably the dirtiest thing in the known universe, with the possible exception of Dirty Donald, the vagrant drunk who lived under the railway bridge in Sulgrave Road.

Atherton was on the spot already – of course – exquisite as a cat, in pale grey trousers and grey suede shoes, his long bony hands thrust into his pockets in a way that would make a tailor feel faint. He was singing under his breath, a sad little policeman's ditty entitled *If This is Life, My Prick's a Bloater*. He managed to make it sound quite cheerful.

'I don't know why you're so happy,' Slider said. 'Those trousers are going to be ruined.'

'That's all right – I never liked them,' Atherton said easily. ''Orrible morning, isn't it, Guv?'

'I hate fires,' said Slider. A nosegay of disgusting odours assailed him, and he shivered like a horse that smells pigs. Every man has his particular vulnerability: Atherton, for

1

instance, couldn't bear the dirty-bodies-and-old-piss stink of winos, and since his first day in the Job had gone to extreme lengths to avoid having to arrest them. As a matter of fact, he'd never really liked having to arrest anyone, and during his brief time in uniform he'd earned the nickname of The Gurkha, because he took no prisoners.

For Slider, anathema was the smell of carbonised everyday life. He stared resentfully at the sodden ruin before him. 'Why on earth would anyone want to open a motel in the Goldhawk Road?' he demanded of the morning.

'I suppose it isn't that far from the M4,' Atherton said helpfully, though he knew it wasn't really a question.

The main building was an Edwardian pub/hotel, built on the site, it was said, of an old coaching inn called the Crown and Sumpter. A natural phonic confusion, aided perhaps by the prevalence of tuberculosis in the area between the wars, had blighted its popularity and it had never thrived.

In the late sixties a single-storey extension in the New Brutalist style had been added on a bomb-site at the back, and the Crown Motel had been born. Since then it had changed hands several times with ever-declining fortunes, gaining no very savoury reputation on the way.

Then in eighty-five it had been bought by a chain, completely refurbished, renamed The Master Baker Motor Lodge, and apparently settled down into moderate respectability, despite the inevitable popular corruption of its name to The Masturbator.

The ancient history Slider had from Sergeant Paxman, a grizzled thirty-year veteran who had served his whole career at Shepherd's Bush nick, and knew every inch of the ground. Paxman – known inevitably as Pacman because of the way he chewed the heads off erring PCs – had been on duty last night when the fire was reported, and had not yet gone off when Slider came in.

'Of course, when I say respectable, that's not to guarantee anything,' Paxman added. He had a large, handsome face, round, rather blank eyes, and tightly curling hair, and needed only a pair of horns and a ring through his nose to complete the resemblance to a Hereford bull.

'A fair amount of naughtiness still goes on. The local toms use the annexe, and the better class of queers meet each other there. You know, the respectable married men on their way home from the office, popping in for a spot of illegal parking before they go home to the wife.'

'I suppose it is quite handy for the tube,' Slider said absently.

Paxman's brown eyes became stationary as he wondered how far that was a joke. He had never really got to grips with Slider, whom he thought a strange man. 'But we don't get any trouble from them, as you know,' he resumed, giving it up. 'The management runs a tight house, and we've never had so much as a disturbance there in two years.'

'What about this fire?'

'I've heard nothing yet. They did have a dodgy fire back in seventy-five or 'six. Insurance scam. But the present owners are making ends meet all right, and they've not long done it all up inside, so there'd be no reason for them to torch it.'

Thus forearmed, Slider faced Atherton. 'So what have we got?'

'The fire started some time before two this morning. A passer-by saw the flames and raised the alarm at ten to two, but it had taken a good hold by then. You can see it started in the end cabin – number one – and by the time the FS got here they couldn't get near it. It wasn't until the fire was out that they were able to get inside, and then they found the body. That was about half past six.'

'Perfect timing,' said Slider. The CID's night shift ended at six in the morning, and the early shift didn't come on until eight. Between six and eight, the Department was unmanned. 'Who was on last night? Hunt, wasn't it? He'll be sorry to have missed the fun.'

DC Hunt, having passed his sergeant's exam – *mirabile*

dictu – was deeply anxious to catch top brass eyes, to secure himself a posting.

Atherton grinned. 'Oh, but he didn't! When the word went out that there was a corpus, Hunt was still in the canteen having breakfast. He volunteered, the twonk!'

Slider shook his head disbelievingly. 'The man's sick. Sick. Well, we'd better go and take a look, I suppose. I'll talk to Hunt later.' A cruel thought occurred to him. 'I could make him exhibits officer. That'd keep him out of trouble.'

Atherton smiled approval. Ensuring 'continuity of evidence' was a painstaking, time-consuming and largely boring part of an investigation. Just what he'd have wished for Hunt himself. Trouble was, Hunt'd probably like it.

The annexe stuck out at right-angles from the back of the hotel, a single-storey building divided into ten cabins in back-to-back pairs. Numbers one and two, the furthest away from the main block, were almost completely destroyed; those nearer the hotel were progressively less damaged, ending with nine and ten, smoke-damaged and wet but intact.

The senior fire officer on the spot was the Divisional Commander, Carlton by name. He was waiting for them in front of cabin number one in the manner of the mountain not coming to two very minor Mahomets. He was a big man, standing square and capable amid the destruction in his yellow helmet and unshakeable boots.

'. . . And summoned the Immediate Aid, of London's Noble Fire Brigade,' Atherton chanted appreciatively. 'God, those uniforms are sexy! Who'd be a copper?'

'Morning,' Carlton said with a spare smile as they reached him. There was sometimes a faint hostility between firemen and policemen – more especially since their pay structures had parted company to the former's disadvantage. Carlton had often been vocal on the unpalatable fact that the police were nominally in charge of any multiple-service incident, which could theoretically

4

mean a two-year PC giving orders to a twenty-year fireman. On the other hand, members of the CID deplored the way firemen burst onto a scene with their axes, boots and hoses and utterly fucked up the evidence before they could get at it. It was as long as it was broad.

'Hullo Gordon,' Slider said pleasantly. 'Rotten start to the day – though I suppose it's all routine to you. What've you got for me? It looks as though it was a pretty fierce blaze.'

Carlton's face took on animation. 'This place was a death trap. It was an inferno waiting to happen. I've been saying so for years.'

'It's got its fire certificate, hasn't it?'

'Oh yes – for what that's worth! It's got the right number of exits and extinguishers. It's also got about eighteen layers of paint on everything, inflammable furniture, ceiling tiles, insulation – you name it. We tell them, but they won't listen. And while the Government won't move to ban these materials, what can we do?'

Slider nodded deferentially. 'Is it all right to have a look now?'

'It's safe enough,' Carlton conceded, half unwilling to be charmed, even by Slider, whom he almost liked. He glanced at Atherton's trousers and shoes and brightened. 'You're not dressed for it, lad. Those'll be ruined.'

Atherton gave him a smile of piercing sweetness. 'A policeman's lot, I'm afraid,' he said with dainty ruefulness.

Carlton shot him a suspicious look and led the way in.

'Don't you know better than to torment a man with a large chopper?' Slider murmured as he and Atherton followed.

'Whoops. Sorry.'

'Have you ever done a fire before?'

'Not a fire with a body,' Atherton admitted.

'You won't enjoy it,' Slider promised.

Slider had been with the old C Division at the time of the Spanish Club fire in Denmark Place, where thirty-seven people had died.

'Which was the worst fire I've ever seen or ever want to

see. The bodies were lying in heaps. It took us weeks to identity them all. Anything else is a picnic by comparison.'

'Baptism of fire?' Atherton suggested.

Slider didn't smile. He looked around him with distaste. The cabin had been virtually destroyed. The roof had fallen in, too, which made it harder to recognise any of the component parts. A lovely job for the boys from The Lab.

'The body's over here,' said Carlton. 'From the layout of the other cabins – they're all identical – we know this was where the armchair was. You can see some fragments of it. Part of the frame, you see, here, and a castor, and this looks like a bit of webbing. He was probably sitting watching the telly – that's over there. Having a last cigarette perhaps. Maybe dropped off, set light to the chair with the stub, and – voom.'

It must have been a pretty comprehensive voom, Atherton thought. He was no tyro when it came to bodies, but even he had to pause for a moment or two to get used to the sight of this one. There was a whole range of unpleasant smells, too. He was reminded of the story of The Legend of Roast Pork. It gave you a whole new perspective, he thought, on the barbecue.

The victim was male, naked, and badly charred, particularly in the lower half – the feet and lower legs were burned through to the bone. Atherton knew from his reading that the action of fire on the extensor muscles sometimes caused the body to contract into what was called the 'pugilist position', a grotesque parody of an old-fashioned prize-fighter's pose, like Popeye squaring up to Bluto.

The legs of this body were drawn up into a crouch, but the arms did not seem to be so affected: they were twisted, one under the body and one out to the side, but not contracted. The upper front part of the body was less badly burned than the rest, which perhaps was what you'd expect if he was sitting up in the chair; and probably his mother might have recognised him, but Atherton wouldn't have cared to have to ask her.

'Has it been moved?' Slider asked.

6

'No. That's the position we found it in, but of course we shifted a lot of stuff off it,' Carlton said. 'It was pretty well buried when the ceiling came down. By the time we got here, the place was an inferno. Fortunately the other cabins were empty, bar seven and nine at the other end, and the occupants of those were accounted for.'

Slider crouched down and stared at the body in silence, his forearms resting on his knees, his hands relaxed; still as a countryman, he might have been watching for badgers for anything he showed. Carlton regarded him for a moment, and then said, 'Well, duty calls. If you need me, I'll be outside.'

'Yes, thanks Gordon,' Slider said absently, without looking up. He was puzzled by the arms, firstly that they had not contracted like the legs, and secondly that the underside – soft side – of the forearms was more badly burned than the topside, which was the opposite to what he would have expected. In most normal postures the underside of the forearms rested against the body and was therefore partly protected.

And there was something else. 'What do you make of this?' he asked Atherton at last.

It was a brownish mark around the front of the neck, just below the Adam's apple. 'You see the way the head falling forward has protected this part of the neck from the fire. Round the back the skin is too badly burned to see anything.'

'A ligature mark?' Atherton said. 'Possibly, I suppose. Couldn't be the mark of his collar, could it, Guv?'

'I don't think so. See the texture of it, with these diagonal ridges? Rope, more likely. We may find some of it amongst the debris they moved off him. Pity the ceiling's come down. There must have been some sort of pipe up there, or an air duct or something.'

'You think he hanged himself?' Atherton frowned.

'I don't think he was watching telly.'

'Suicide, then? But what about the fire – an accident? The condemned man enjoyed – no, that doesn't work, does it? I can't see anyone putting a rope round his neck

7

with a fag still on. Perhaps he'd put it down half smoked, and then kicked the ashtray over in his convulsions. But would anyone hang themselves *before* finishing their cigarette?' He had never been a smoker, and therefore couldn't judge the niceties of the ritual.

'The fire worries me,' Slider admitted. 'But look, d'you see here?'

He took a biro out of his pocket and pointed at the side of the head. Atherton stooped. There was a shred of something adhering to the charred and brittle hair. Several shreds of something.

'It looks like melted plastic.'

'Yes. A melted plastic bag, wouldn't you say?'

Atherton straightened. 'Belt and braces, you mean. Well, they do, don't they, suicides, like to make sure?'

'Hmm.' Slider got up carefully and straightened himself, and stood looking down at the body with an unseeing frown. 'I don't like it,' he said at last.

'I don't think you're meant to,' Atherton said gently.

'Is the photo team on the way?'

'Yes, and Doc Cameron, and forensic. I don't expect they'll be here for at least an hour, though, given the traffic.'

Slider smiled suddenly.

'Then we might as well go and have some breakfast. I could do serious structural damage to a sausage sandwich.'

Atherton turned his eyes resolutely from the body. 'Fine by me. D'you want to talk to Hunt first?'

That at least made Slider shudder.

'Not on an empty stomach,' he said.

Hunt, despite having been up all night and at the scene since six forty-five, still looked perfectly neat and tidy, as if his clothes had been painted on; and since he had lately grown a beard, he didn't even appear unshaven. He had always been a great one for going by the book, a spit-and-polish man, and as nearly stupid as it was possible to be and still get into the Department; but since passing his exam, he had added keenness to his other vices.

As Atherton put it in technical language to WDC Swilley, 'He was always a paper-tearing prat, but now he's a total pain in the arse.'

'Bound to get on, then,' said Swilley, nodding wisely. 'Next thing you know, he'll be rolling up the leg of his John Collier and doing funny handshakes.'

Hunt was in the motel manager's office, which they had requisitioned, when Slider and Atherton got back from breakfast.

'I interviewed the night clerk, sir,' he told Slider smartly. 'Deceased arrived last night at eleven fifty-five, and signed the register in the name of John Smith. I think that was probably a false name, though.'

With anyone else, it would have been either a joke, or cheek. Slider had the depressing certainty that Hunt meant it. 'Alone?'

'Yes, sir. He paid cash, and the address he gave was a company one – Taylor Woodrow at Hanger Lane – but I've called their personnel department, and they don't have a John Smith working there.'

'What about his car?'

'I thought of that,' Hunt said proudly. 'Apparently he didn't put down a car registration number, and the clerk didn't ask. There's no car outside the cabin, but he could have parked out on the street somewhere. There are plenty of parked cars around. Or of course he might have arrived on foot, or from the tube station, or by taxi. Just because it's called a motor lodge, doesn't mean you've got to come in a car.'

'Really? I would never have thought of that,' said Slider. Hunt didn't blush. 'So we have no idea who he is?'

'No, sir.'

'Nobody recognised him? What about the people staying in seven and nine?'

'The clerk says he'd never seen him before. The other guests were woken by the hotel staff telling them to get out because of the fire. They both say they didn't see deceased at any point, but I haven't taken detailed statements from them yet.'

'All right, you can get someone started on that now. Who else is here?'

'PC D'Arblay – he was first on the scene. It's his beat. And Jablowski's just arrived, and Mackay's on his way.'

'All right, you and Jablowski can make a start, and Mackay can help when he gets here. Get on with it, then.'

It was the mark of the man that he almost saluted. 'Yes sir,' he said, departing. D'Arblay passed him in the doorway.

'Photographer's here, sir,' he said.

'Right, I'm coming,' said Slider. He turned to Atherton. 'When you've a minute, you might ask the night clerk whether our man asked for number one, or was given it.'

'Righto, Guv.' It was a small point, but it might be telling. A man bent on self-destruction might well seek the privacy of the furthest cabin from the main building.

'I hope we find his wallet in there somewhere,' Slider said as he turned away. 'Otherwise we may end up having to do a PNC on every parked car in the Bush.'

Joanna came into his office at a quarter to two.

'Just got back?' Slider asked astutely, seeing she was carrying her violin case. His powers of detection were razor sharp today. 'How was your rehearsal?'

'Awful. More than ever I ask myself if it can be a coincidence that conductors and blind men both use white sticks.' She leaned across the desk and kissed him. 'How has your day been? I gather you've been having some excitement.'

'How do you gather that?'

'I've just been talking to Flatulent Fergus downstairs. You lucky mugs! A fire and a corpus already, and it's still only lunchtime!'

'You've missed out the best bit,' said Slider bitterly. 'We had a flying visiting from Detective Chief Superintendent Richard Head.'

'Yes, O'Flaherty told me. Known to his friends as God. *Deus ex machina* was what Fergus said.'

10

'I suppose he came in a car.'

'And what did he want?'

'What do brass always want? To make trouble, of course. And with Dickson not here, that dropped him straight onto my neck.'

'Was it a routine roust, or something to do with the fire?'

'Oh, the fire. He wanted to make sure I understood he'd like it to be a suicide.'

Joanna wrinkled her brow. 'Why would he want that?'

'Because suicide isn't a crime, and we're getting near the end of the budget period, and murder enquiries are very expensive.'

She stared. 'You're not serious?'

'Top brass have to worry about things like that. It's one of the reasons I never wanted higher promotion.'

'But – he's not asking you to fabricate the evidence?'

'No, of course not. He doesn't really know what he's asking. He's like a kid saying "I wish I had a train set," on the off-chance that there really is a Father Christmas. Perhaps if he says he'd like it to be suicide, it might just turn out to be that way.'

'You don't like him, do you?' she said shrewdly.

'Oh—' He began automatically to shrug it off, and then paused, realising that it didn't matter what he said to Joanna about a senior officer. Head was tall, well-built, handsome in a thick sort of way, with curly hair and blue eyes and the sort of firm-featured looks that simply cry out for the stern glamour of uniform. He was younger than Slider, by far less experienced, several ranks above him, and thought he knew best. But it wasn't even any or all of that. There was just something about the way he didn't listen, the way he made it known that he knew he didn't *have* to listen, that got up Slider's nose.

'I don't like being loomed over,' was all he said, however.

Joanna looked at the puckered brow under the soft, untidy hair, and said, 'You don't think it is suicide?'

The brow cleared and he smiled at her ruefully. 'I don't think anything yet.'

'Open mind and closed mouth?'

'Until Freddie does the post, and I get the forensic report, I've got nothing to think with.'

She knew him better than that. 'Just a vague feeling of unease, then?'

'I don't like fires,' he admitted. 'We haven't even ID'd the poor bastard yet.'

'How will you go about that?'

'Oh, we've got various lines to try. We've started the house-to-house, and Atherton's downstairs with the night porter from the motel, putting together a photofit. We'll match that up against Missing Persons for a start, and if that doesn't yield anything we can circulate it in various ways. As a last resort we can go on the telly. But ten to one someone'll report him missing, if they haven't already. Most people have a slot they fit into, and it's noticed when they go astray. And we can check on all the parked cars in the immediate vicinity, to see if there's one unaccounted for.'

'It looks as though you'll be pretty busy, then?' she asked carefully. Slider felt the habitual stillness of caution creep into his bones.

'I'm afraid I won't be able to come to your concert tonight,' he said, watching her mouth. With a woman it was from the line of the lips that you could best judge how close you were to critical mass. 'There'll be too much to do.'

'What time d'you think you'll finish?'

He shrugged. 'It could be any time. Two, three in the morning. Maybe not at all.' She was taking it very well. He offered her the consolation prize. 'I've already told Irene I won't be back at all tonight, so if I do find I can knock off for an hour or two, can I come and wake you up?'

When she smiled, her face lit up like Harrods on Christmas Eve. She was his own personal Santa's Grotto – and full of goodies with his name on them. 'Yes please,' she said.

The night clerk from the motel looked haggard. He was Roger Pascoe, an Australian, twenty-three years old, travelling round the world by working in hotels, bars and restaurants – anywhere they were desperate for staff. He'd just

12

had a hectic season as a barman in Miami: Canadians, down for the winter, drank like sinks when released from their own draconian liquor-laws. He'd come to London for a rest before going to Europe for the summer.

He'd deliberately chosen a quiet job in an out-of-the-way spot, and expected to be reading a lot of novels through the nights, sleeping through the days, and saving a great deal of money. What he hadn't expected was strife of this order. A registration clerk who allowed a suicidal guest in to torch himself and destroy the entire building would be about as popular with future potential employers as a fart in a phone box.

'No, he asked for number one,' he said to Atherton. 'At least, he said could he have the end cabin, the furthest away one.'

'You didn't find that surprising?'

Pascoe rubbed his eyes wearily. 'Why should I? I didn't know he was going to top himself. He could have any one he wanted. He could have 'em all, for all I cared, as long as he paid.'

'Was that before or after he signed in as John Smith?'

'Christ, I don't know! After, I think. What does it matter? You think I should have asked him for his ID, asked him what he was up to? My bosses wouldn't agree with you. He paid cash up front, he could do what he liked in there.'

'Your bosses wouldn't want their premises to be used for illegal purposes,' Atherton suggested mildly.

'Going with a prozzie isn't illegal.'

'Is that what he was doing?' Atherton said, interested.

Pascoe looked wild. 'Oh look mate, I been up all night. Don't lay traps for me. A lot of blokes bring tarts back there, and mostly they don't want anyone to know. Married blokes, you know? It's not my business. I'm not the Archbishop of Canterbury.'

'But you said this man was alone?'

'He came in alone. I don't know who he might have had waiting for him outside, do I?'

'True.' Atherton smiled a little. 'Take it easy, guy. I just

13

want to know what you know. Did he seem as though he might have a girl waiting for him outside? Did he seem excited, nervous – what?'

Pascoe looked away, remembering. 'He'd been drinking. He wasn't drunk, but I could smell it on him. He was – I don't know how you'd put it. Happy? A bit lit up? Not sad or depressed, anyway. Yeah, he could have had a girl waiting for him. Or a bloke.' He gave Atherton a serious look. 'We get a lot of the other sort in, you know.'

'Yes, I know. Did he seem that way to you?'

Pascoe shrugged. 'You can't tell. I wouldn't have said so, but, Christ, a bender can seem like Joe Normal nowadays. He didn't mince in and call me duckie, for what it's worth. He was just a middle-aged bloke in a suit. If I'd known he was gonna fry himself I'd have taken more notice.'

'All right. And you don't know if he had a car? You didn't hear a car pull up? He didn't mention a motor at all?'

Pascoe shook his head numbly. 'You can't see outside from my desk. I already told your mate all this, the one with the beard. Why can't you get it from him?'

'Because I want you to tell me. You might just remember something else, something you didn't tell him.'

'What, like the bloke had a wooden leg, or one eye missing?' Pascoe sneered, and then he stopped, his jaw sagging ludicrously. 'Blimey, you're right! I've just remembered something – he had a scar on the back of his hand.'

'Which one?'

'His right hand. When he was signing the register. An old scar – a strip of shiny skin, about an inch wide, from his wrist right up to his knuckles.' He looked at Atherton, pleased, expecting praise. 'I never told your mate that. It's only just come to me.'

'You say it looked old? It wasn't puffy, or puckered, or red?'

'No. Smooth, pale pink and shiny. Years old. You'd hardly notice it, if you weren't looking. It wasn't ugly.'

'It sounds as though it could have been a skin graft.'

14

'Yeah. Like that. Maybe he'd had a bad burn—' Pascoe's smile came slowly to pieces. 'Christ, the poor bastard. Did you see that cabin? What a way to go.'

'He would probably have been overwhelmed by the smoke in the first few minutes,' Atherton offered him, for comfort. 'Do you think you could help us put together a photofit of him? Do you remember what he looked like?'

'Remember?' Pascoe stared, putting two and two together, and going slightly green. 'Yeah, I could give it a shot. He was a good-looking bloke. He was—'

He closed his mouth tightly.

'Don't think about it,' Atherton advised.

CHAPTER TWO

Dutch Courage, French Leave

FORENSIC PATHOLOGISTS WERE AS DIFFERENT from each other as God makes all men, but they generally had two things in common: they smelled of peppermints, and they didn't wear ties.

Freddie Cameron wore a bow-tie. Today's was navy-blue silk with a tiny crimson spot, to match the remote-crimson stripe in his dark blue suit. His wife Martha chose his clothes, and he sometimes felt her taste was too conservative. Spending most of his life in morgues, he could have fancied something a touch more cheerful from time to time. He'd once had a yellow waistcoat, when he was much younger. Now that'd be the thing to brighten up the place! But he'd thrown it away when Martha said it made him look like a bookie. Not that he had anything against bookies, of course. Some of his best friends were bookies. But at the time he'd been trying to make his way in his profession, and what he really wanted to look like was a top-class pathologist.

His old friend Bill Slider would never look like anything but a policeman, he thought. He did at least seem a lot more cheerful these days. There'd been a time – during that Austen case – when Cameron had been worried old Bill was going to have a breakdown. He'd got extremely twitchy, and did some very strange things, but he seemed to be back to his old self now, thank God.

'Well old chum, how are you?' Cameron greeted him breezily. 'You're looking fit. Are you getting enough?'

16

'I'm getting so much I'm thinking of taking on a lad,' Slider said inscrutably.

Cameron made the obvious connection. He had never liked Irene, and felt that Joanna was much more the thing, but since Bill was apparently still living with his Madam, it made things a little awkward. In the normal course of events he and Martha would invite Bill and Irene over from time to time, but Cameron didn't feel able either to do that, or to tell Martha about the new circumstances. Martha was a bit old-fashioned about that sort of thing. Well, women were, weren't they? They felt threatened by it. So he'd had to make excuses both ways.

'How is your young woman?' he said politely.

Slider had a fair idea of what was going through Cameron's mind, and said blandly, 'You must meet her, Freddie. Perhaps the four of us could go out for a meal sometime.'

Cameron's eyes bulged a little. 'Ha! Yes, why not, why not? Good idea! Well, perhaps we should get on.'

He led the way, a dapper figure looking to Slider's eyes strangely out of place in this modern chrome and steel setting. They had finally closed down the old morgue of glazed bricks, porcelain sinks and enamelled herringbone tables with which Slider always associated Cameron, and the posts were all done in the hospital's path department now.

Inside was the usual merry throng of onlookers, known in the Department as the Football Crowd – Lab liaison officer, Coroner's officer, photographers, Hunt as exhibits officer to oversee the sealing and labelling, and D'Arblay, as first officer on the scene, to identify the body as the one from the motel. The morgue attendants hovered in the background like mothers at a ballet exam, and there were a couple of white-coated hospital researchers and some medical students along for the ride.

At least at the old morgue, Cameron had confided to Slider once, it was too cold and uncomfortable to attract the crowds. It was Freddie's custom to pass round the extra-strong mints before beginning. 'This new place is costing me a packet,' he said.

17

When the preliminaries were over, he picked up his long scalpel with the nine-inch blade, ventured a little pathologists' joke – 'Shall I carve?' – and shaped up to the body. 'Have we got a name yet?' he asked after a moment.

'Not yet,' said Slider.

'Just as well,' said Atherton. 'It isn't etiquette to cut anyone you've been introduced to.'

'Eh?' said Cameron.

'Alice – Mutton; Mutton – Alice.'

The 'Alice' gave Slider the clue, and he shook his head at his colleague sadly. One of these days he must get round to reading that damned book. When Atherton and Joanna got together it was like being the only person at a dinner-party who'd never heard of Salman Rushdie.

'So, we're looking for a suicide, are we?' Cameron said.

'Head's looking for a suicide. Or an accident will do. As long as we can crash the case. He's got our clear-up rate to worry about.'

'Thank God we don't earn his salary, eh?' said Cameron.

He whistled almost soundlessly as he worked. Atherton realised, with an inward smile at the massive incongruity, that the tune was *The Deadwood Stage*.

'Your ligature mark's coming out very nicely, Bill,' Cameron remarked. 'I've no doubt about it, but I'll take some sections for slides, make a few nice piccies for the Coroner and his chums. Now let's see . . .'

He worked on, interrupting himself with comments from time to time. 'Well, I don't know. Very little bruising here. Windpipe intact, no rupture of the large veins and arteries. Cricoid, arytenoids intact. I'll take the hyoid, see if there's any fracture to be seen under the microscope, but it doesn't look like a very serious attempt at hanging, old chum . . .'

'No carbon traces in the nostrils, and the exterior burns are all post mortem. We'll take some sections of lung. Looks like anoxia caused by occlusion – the plastic bag over the head to you and me and the Coroner's jury. These suicides like to make sure, don't they? Let's see if he poisoned himself as well . . .'

18

As he opened the stomach, even Atherton, standing back and sucking hard at the Trebor's, caught the smell of alcohol.

'Dutch courage. A brandy man, too,' Cameron said with a mixture of approval and regret. 'Must have drunk the whole bottle. Precious little to eat, though. I wouldn't say he hadn't had a pint or two, as well, earlier on.'

'How drunk would he have been on that lot?' asked Slider.

'As a sack, old boy. Legless. If he hadn't hanged himself, he'd have probably died of alcoholic poisoning. We'll send this off to the Lab for analysis, just in case.'

Slider exchanged a glance with Atherton. It was beginning to look better. A man as drunk as that could have set fire to the place by accident. 'Perhaps it's going to be Head's lucky day.'

But a little later Cameron said in a quite different voice, 'Hullo-ullo-ullo. Now here's a thing. This is a bit nasty. Come and have a look, Bill.'

He had plunged a pair of forceps into the area of the groin, and as Slider stepped closer he saw something which gleamed dully between the jaws.

'It looks like wire,' Slider said.

'Plastic covered wire. The plastic's melted, look, here and here,' said Cameron. 'You see how it was twisted right around the scrotum, too?'

Slider felt his own balls trying to creep for safety up into his pelvis. 'What about the wrists and ankles, Freddie?'

'It's hard to tell,' Cameron said at last. 'You see here and here where the skin's intact? It could be a ligature mark. I can't be sure without microscopical examination. The sub-cutaneous layers aren't entirely destroyed, fortunately. I'll take some sections: there could be hemp fibres amongst the tissue. But I'd say the arms could well have been tied. It might account for the arms not having contracted as the legs did.'

'I suppose you won't get anything from the ankles, they're so badly burned.' There was virtually nothing left of the feet but bones. 'Was there something wrong with his feet, d'you think? The bones look funny.'

'So would you if you'd been roasted in the fiery furnace,' Freddie said. He bent closer, went in again with his forceps and lifted something triumphantly. 'Ha! A fibre. Carpet or rope? We shall see.' He looked over the top of his half-glasses at Slider. 'Trussed up like the Christmas turkey, and a bag over his head. You know what this begins to look like, don't you, Bill?'

'Sexual strangulation,' Slider said reluctantly.

'Come again?' said Atherton.

Slider turned to him. 'Hanging perversion. Haven't you come across it? Well, it's not all that common, I suppose.'

'Bill and I have met a couple of cases in our time,' Cameron said. 'One of the pleasures of working Central. The victim brings himself to orgasm by strangling or suffocating himself. Sometimes both, as it would appear in this case. They like to tie themselves up, too, with particular attention to the arms and genitals. And of course, sometimes they go too far, and find they can't release themselves in time. That's when they usually come to my attention.'

'What some people will do for pleasure,' said Atherton.

'The odd thing is, they so often seem to be quiet, respectable men,' Cameron went on, taking tissue sections of the wrists. 'Their families never have the slightest idea of what they get up to, despite the fact that they must have a suitcase full of equipment hidden somewhere in the house.'

'Equipment? You mean the ropes?' Atherton asked.

'And hoods,' Slider said neutrally. 'And strop magazines. And women's underwear, sometimes. It takes a number of forms.' He sighed. 'It begins to look, then, like an accident rather than suicide. I don't know if that will make it any easier to tell the next-of-kin.'

'When you find out who he is, of course. Or was,' said Cameron.

Atherton looked at his superior's sad frown. 'Has it ever occurred to you, Guv, that Earth may be some other planet's Hell?' he said comfortingly.

*

20

Beevers burst into the CID room, his moustache bristling with excitement like a sexually aroused caterpillar.

'I think we've got him!'

Everyone looked up. There were a lot of empty desks, but it was still a gratifying audience. DC Tony Anderson was just back off leave from having moved house. He had shown photographs of his new semi taken from twenty-two different artistic angles to everyone, even the patient Andy Mackay, despite the fact that since Mackay had helped him move, he already knew what it looked like.

WDC Kathleen 'Norma' Swilley was conversing in a low voice with WPC Polly Jablowski, who was known, largely for onomatopoeic reasons, as The Polish Plonk – plonk being the current slang for policewoman. Polish was doing a tour with the Department, which she hoped to join. Norma, in anticipation, had been advising her on how to cope with the differing advances of 'Gentleman' Jim Atherton and Phil 'The Pill' Hunt – equally persistent but far from equally tiresome.

And most gratifying of all, Slider was there, consulting in an undertone with Atherton, who was already deeply distracted by having caught the sound of his own name on Norma's lips, which had made it difficult for him to concentrate on what Slider was saying.

Slider straightened. 'The motel corpse?'

'Yes sir,' Beevers said smartly. It was quite a coup, he felt, and his inward gratification was so great that his left leg jiggled all by itself even while he stood to semi-attention. 'It was one of the cars parked in Rylett Road, a red Escort XR3—'

'Ah, a prat car,' Anderson murmured knowledgeably. Hunt's customised XR3 was what he spent most of his salary on, and Beevers longed for one just like it.

Beevers didn't even break stride. 'The registered owner's a Richard Neal, address in Pinner. His wife says he's supposed to be away on business for a few days, up north – left Sunday evening. She doesn't know of any friends or business acquaintances or any reason he'd be parked in Rylett Road. We've checked the hotels he's

21

supposed to be staying at, and they haven't seen him; and her description of him fits, as far as age and height.'

'She hadn't reported him missing?' Norma said. 'Wouldn't she have expected him to ring home by now?'

'I don't know,' Beevers admitted reluctantly. 'Perhaps he didn't usually.'

'All right,' Slider interposed, 'we'd better look into it.' It sounded promising, but he wasn't going to send Beevers, who despite his cosy looks was as soothing as an attack of piles, to tell Mrs Neal she might be a widow. This looked like a job for Superman. 'Atherton, you'd better go and talk to her. Take the photofit, see if she recognises it. Norma, I think you'd better go too, just in case, to give her the option.'

'What about giving Polish a chance, sir?' Norma said generously. 'Good experience for her.'

'Yes, all right, why not. Let us know straight away if she gives us a positive ID, and we'll bring the car in and let forensic go over it.'

'How much should we tell her about how he died?' Atherton asked.

'As little as possible. I'll tell her the rest myself, once we're sure. See if she's got a recent photograph of him, and we can try it on Pascoe. If he confirms, we'll have to arrange a formal identification at the morgue, but I don't want to put her through that unnecessarily.'

'Right, Guv.' Atherton unfolded his Viking length and projected it at the door. 'Come on, Polish. We're off to strange foreign parts, so keep your harpoon handy. I'll steer, you keep watch for sharks.'

'I thought she lived in Pinner?'

Atherton favoured her with a bolting look. 'Have you ever *been* to Pinner?'

Pinner was typical Metroland, a tiny rural village untouched by time until the coming of the railway, and now just part of the anonymous sprawl of Greater London. The original village was still visible in a high

22

street of crooked half-timbered houses and a pretty church with a clock-tower, but the architecture grew increasingly bungaloid as you headed outwards from the historic centre. It was the kind of suburban landscape that made Atherton shiver: he liked town or country, one or the other – not the bleakness of this compromise which lacked the advantages of either. It was one of the reasons he never went back to his own birthplace of Weybridge. That, too, had been quite rural when he was a child . . .

'You've just passed it,' said Polish suddenly. 'That was Cranley Gardens on the left.'

'Was it?' Atherton glanced in his mirrors, then stood on everything and did a violent U-turn, and turned right. Polish, accustomed to squad cars, didn't bat an eyelid. 'What number?'

'Nineteen. There it is.'

Atherton pulled up. 'Blimey! Imitation Georgian front door, Tudor windows, and Swiss chalet-style false shutters. It's a good job the Governor's not here.'

'Why, wouldn't he like it?'

'He's very sensitive about architecture. You might say he has an edifice complex.'

She missed that one. 'Well, I think it's very nice.'

Atherton sighed. 'Polish, you have no discrimination.'

'Discrimination's a luxury. You should live where I live, in a room in a house, not even a nice room, and the kitchen's always full of other people's washing up.'

'Don't, you're making me cry. All right, I take it back, and I'll cook you dinner at my house to make it up to you.'

'Okay.' She smiled. 'It's a funny logic, but okay.'

Mrs Neal was a good-looking woman, forty-nine passing forty-five; well preserved and smartly dressed, but with a discontented look about her mouth and a certain puffiness around her eyes which Atherton, of his vast experience, believed came from not making love often enough.

She looked at the photofit for a long time, her face working between doubt and fear. 'It looks a bit like him. It

23

could be him. I don't know – how can I tell?' She looked up, tracking between Atherton and Polish and settling finally on Atherton. Her voice rose half an octave. 'What's happened to him? Where is he? Where did you get this picture?'

'Mrs Neal—' Atherton began, but she cut him off.

'What's he done? Why can't I see him? He's my husband, you can't stop me seeing him. I know my rights!'

'Mrs Neal, we don't know yet that the man we've found is your husband. That's what we're trying to establish—'

'What do you mean, found? He's dead, isn't he? That's what you're trying to tell me.'

Atherton eyed her in the manner of a barman judging whether a customer could safely take one more.

'The man in question is dead, but we don't know whether or not it was your husband. There was nothing on him to identify him.'

'But you've found his car, you said?'

'His car has been found near the scene. That's what led us to you. If you can't account for its presence there, it may be—'

'Oh God.' She sat down abruptly, crushing the photofit in her hands. Her face was suddenly haggard, as though she'd gained five years, but her mind still seemed to be working.

'It's that woman – she's killed him. What was it, drugs? Or his heart?' She laughed mirthlessly. 'I always thought his heart would give up one of these days if he carried on the way he did. I told him, I said you'll be found dead in bed with one of your whores one day. I said you're fifty, not twenty-five, but you carry on like—' She stopped abruptly and bit her lip.

Polish sat down on the chair next to her and leaned forward sympathetically. 'Whores, Mrs Neal?'

She looked up with a flash of her eyes. 'What else would you call them? Girls young enough to be his daughters, most of them, just after a good time. No morals, no manners. He splashed his money about. What did they care if he was married? And this latest one – red-haired

24

trollop! I saw her getting out of his car at the station, with a skirt right up to her ears, the little bitch. Leaning in to kiss him goodbye, showing her knickers to the world. The wonder of it was she was even wearing any!'

Atherton sat down very carefully. 'Your husband was having an affair, was he?'

'He was always having an affair,' she said bitterly. 'Ever since we first met. We've been married sixteen years, and he's been having affairs for fifteen of them. He doesn't even bother to hide it any more. All these business trips! Does he think I'm stupid? I told him last year, after I tried to phone him at the Dragonara in Leeds and they'd never heard of him, I told him not to bother lying to me any more. He used to phone up and pretend he was at some stupid hotel, when all the time he was in some little tart's flat having a—' She gasped as the tears began to rise. 'I told him not to bother to lie any more.' Her face crumpled. 'And he didn't. The bastard didn't.'

She wept, noisily and angrily. Atherton sat quietly, waiting for her to go on. Out of the corner of his eye he could see Polish looking embarrassed and trying not to, and he caught her eye and shook his head just slightly. Mrs Neal wanted to talk, and at the moment she didn't see either of them as real people. They were just someone to spill it all out to.

After a moment she stopped crying enough to go on, dragging her breath in tearing sobs between phrases. 'I should have known better than to marry him. I mean, it goes with the job. Oh, they gave him a fancy name, but when it came down to it he was just a rep. A travelling salesman. Well, it's a joke, isn't it? Like a long – a long distance—'

She stopped and fumbled in her sleeve for a handkerchief and blew her nose heartily. Atherton waited until she'd finished, and then put in another question, anxious to keep her talking before she recovered a normal degree of self-consciousness.

'What did he sell?'

'Fire detection systems and security systems, for offices

and factories and hotels, places like that. He used to be a security guard when I first met him, but he gave it up after we got married. He said it was too dangerous, it wasn't fair on me to take the risk. Fair on me!' She gave a bark of ironic laughter, and then suddenly seemed to see them again, and to hear her own voice. She pulled her lip in under her teeth with embarrassment. She had exposed herself to strangers. 'Well,' she muttered, 'you know all about it, don't you.'

'Mrs Neal,' Atherton said, 'does your husband have any distinguishing marks? A mole or a scar or anything like that?'

Her face sharpened as she remembered suddenly what this visit was all about. She'd gained ten years now. Atherton doubted if she'd ever look forty-five again.

'Yes,' she said unwillingly, as though she'd been asked to incriminate her husband. 'He had a scar on the back of his hand, here. An old scar, from before I ever met him.'

She searched Atherton's face, and a dead look came into her eyes, a look of hope ending. There would never now be that reconciliation scene, the dream of which had sustained her for years, in which he repudiated all the other women and told her that he realised it was her he loved, only her. This time he wasn't coming back.

'It is him isn't it?' she said in a flat voice. 'He's dead.'

'The man we've found does have a scar in that place,' Atherton said gently.

'Oh my God.' She said it quite automatically, her bruised mind still functioning. 'But I don't understand – he had business cards in his wallet, and his credit cards. And there was his driving licence – he always carried that with him. Why didn't you know his name?'

'We didn't find any of those documents.' Atherson was aware of Polish looking at him, a brief, keen look of mingled enquiry and alarm.

'His wallet wasn't there? What, did she steal it? Did she – or was it – was he robbed? Mugged?' Realisation caught up with her, about what she didn't yet know. 'How did he die?'

Now was the time to be very careful indeed. 'There was a fire at a motel, Mrs Neal. It seems your husband had booked into a room there—'

'Oh my God. Oh my God. Oh my God.' She hardly seemed to know she was saying it. 'Oh my God. Oh my God.' Atherton thought she might go on repeating it for ever, but after a bit she stopped.

When they finally left, Polish sat looking straight ahead through the windscreen.

'Well, there you have it,' Atherton said lightly. 'Unfortunate that it fell to us. Usually we leave that sort of thing to the woodentops.'

'Yes, I know. I am one, remember.' She frowned a little. 'She didn't want to talk to me. She hardly really knew I was there at all. It was you she wanted, for comfort.'

'Yes.' It was received opinion in the Job that a distressed woman, who'd been raped or attacked or bereaved or whatever, needed another woman to confide in, but in Slider's experience women would always far sooner unburden themselves to a man – provided it was a kind, sympathetic man – and Atherton agreed with him. 'I suppose it's like girls never being able to discuss their periods with their mothers,' he said after a moment.

'Really? Was that your experience too?'

'Bugger off. I suppose women don't really trust each other, that's what it comes down to.'

Polish reached out and patted his knee, briefly and electrically. 'Daft. Women don't trust men, either. They just know how to manipulate 'em.'

Dickson was back, to Slider's profound relief. He might be an impossible bastard – anyone above the rank of inspector was, by definition – but as least he was a proper CID impossible bastard, with whom one could therefore do business.

Slider looked at him almost with affection as he entered

27

the Bells-and-Marlboro-scented bower. Dickson had done his probationary two years on the beat, transferred to CID as soon as he could, and spent the entire rest of his career in the Department. He was CID right through the entire vulcanised thickness of his being.

Head, on the other hand, had been in the uniform branch all the way up, and had only recently made a sideways career move to speed his upward passage to the stars. He'd be going back into uniform as soon as a Commander's post became vacant, probably hoping to forget the undisciplined nightmare of the Department as if it had never happened.

Dickson's vast bulk was penned, palpitating, in his swivel chair, his ash-strewn suit barely able to contain the stuff of him. His huge hands rested on the desk top as if they were so heavy he'd needed to put them down somewhere for a minute, and the nicotine stains on his fingers seemed to have spread lately, heading, like gangrene, for his heart.

Yet to Slider's keen eye, there was a change in the old bull. He appeared – could it be? – to have lost weight. The wide, bottled face seemed fractionally less wide, the veined red cheeks the merest shade paler. He looked like a man who had been ill – not very, but unexpectedly. And the boiled boot eyes were perhaps just slightly less impenetrable than usual.

'Yes, Bill,' he greeted Slider perfunctorily. 'What's the SP on this motel fire? You had a set-to over it with Detective Chief Superintendent Head, I understand.'

'Hardly a set-to, sir,' Slider began, but Dickson rode over him like twenty thousand head of cattle.

'He doesn't like you. Mark you, he doesn't like any of us. But he seemed to get it into his head that you were lacking in respect. *Dumb insolence* – would that be the phrase?'

'His phrase, sir?'

Dickson didn't answer what he didn't care to. 'Sit down. Tell me what you've got.'

Slider told him.

'Looks like accidental death. So what's the problem with it?'

'There are a number of things, sir. According to Neal's wife, he was a noted cocksman – girl in every port. Is it likely, then, that he'd need to resort to ropes and wires to get his gratification?'

'Maybe he wasn't. Maybe she was lying. Or maybe he'd lied to her about his prowess.'

'Yes sir. But I'd like to know, all the same. Then there's the fact that he didn't have his wallet and credit cards with him. We thought at first they'd been stolen, but when we brought the car in, we found his wallet with everything in it intact in the dashboard compartment.'

'How did he pay for the motel room?'

'Cash.'

'Then he didn't need his credit cards, did he?'

'No, sir. But why leave them in the car? It's not natural. And we didn't find his car keys.'

Dickson looked restless. 'Well. Is that all?'

'Not quite. There's the fire. I was never happy about that. The dropped cigarette theory didn't go with the hanging perversion motif, to my mind; and now forensic have come up with traces of candle-wax on the floor and on fragments of the fabric of the chair.'

'Candle wax.' Dickson eyes were flatter than a bootsole now. They were as flat as the half-used bottle of tonic you find in the back of the fridge when you come back from holiday. The only thing in the universe flatter was his voice. 'That's it, is it? Candle wax?'

Slider kept his peace.

'I don't have to tell you, do I, how many things a man can do with a lighted candle? Besides immolating himself, that is. That cabin was a favoured resort of toms and turd-burglars and God knows what other slags. There are even those, it's rumoured, who use candles in connection with the illegal insertion into their bodies of well-known recreational drugs.'

'Sir—'

'So what you've got, to set against all Mr Head's well-reasoned logic, is surprise that the man was a pervert, surprise he left his wallet in his car, surprise that his car keys haven't been found, and suspicion over the presence in what amounts to a trick-pad of some candle-wax?'

All coppers are actors, convincing actors: they have to be, to survive. But they don't always manage to convince each other – and of course they don't always intend to. Slider surveyed the broad range of genial irony, withering scorn, and righteous anger he had been offered, and didn't believe any of it.

'It doesn't feel right to me,' he said, acting the part of baffled but stubborn probity. 'I think there was someone else there.'

'Well so do I,' Dickson said, lighting another cigarette. 'I trust your instincts. And I trust the feeling I get up here—' He tapped himself just behind the ear, perilously, with the forefinger that was supporting the glowing fag – 'when someone's handing me a parcel of shit and passing it off as profiteroles. So you can look into it. I'll tell the Coroner to give us an adjournment, and we'll treat this as suspicious circumstances.'

'Thank you,' said Slider.

Dickson leaned forward slightly, and a look frighteningly close to human appeal came into his eyes. 'But for fucksake, Bill, get me something soon. Head isn't going to like this drain on the budget. He's going to take a bit of persuading. And if the wheel comes off and I get dropped on from a great height, I don't need to tell you who'll be underneath me, do I?'

'No, sir,' said Slider.

Of all the threats he'd been at the sharp end of in twenty years in the Job, this last one was somehow the least convincing. Dickson, he thought, as he made his puzzled way back to his own office, seemed in danger of turning into a pussy-cat.

CHAPTER THREE

Stolen Tarts

THE CANTEEN DID A GOOD fry-up: full house, all the
business including fried bread, for which Slider had a
lamentable passion. There was a separate room where the
'governors' could eat apart from the 'troops', but Slider sat
with Joanna in a secluded corner of the main canteen. He
disliked the whole idea of segregation. How would you
ever hear the gossip if you dined apart? There was a
separate governors' lav, too, but he did use that. It was the
closest to his room, and it had proper soap.

'So where do you go from here?' Joanna asked, carefully
stripping the rinds off her bacon.

'We start the hard slog of old-fashioned police work.
Find out where he was that evening, who he was with. Who
were his friends? Did he have any enemies? Any secrets,
any debts, any vices?'

'I thought you knew about those.'

'I'm more than ever convinced that was a set-up. Now
I've spoken to his wife—'

'God, that must have been hard! No wonder you look
pale.'

'Do I? She was upset, of course. But at least I could offer
her the comfort that it wasn't being left at that, that we
were investigating the suspicious circumstances.'

'Would that be a comfort? I wonder,' Joanna mused.
'But does anyone except you think it was supicious?'

'Freddie Cameron's come round to my way of thinking.
He came back to me on the tissue sections of the wrists and

ankles, and confirmed that they had been bound. He also confirmed what I noticed when I examined the body, that the insides of the wrists were more badly burned than the backs, which is the opposite to what you'd expect.'

'Is it?'

'Think about it. If you tied your own wrists, for what ever reason, you'd have to tie them in front of you – yes? So that you could pull the knot tight with our teeth, or by gripping the end between your knees.'

'Yes.'

'And if you tie them in front of you, it's much more natural to tie them inside to inside.'

Joanna's face grew intent as she tried it for herself under the level of the table. 'Yes,' she agreed.

'On the other hand, if you tie someone else's hands behind them, it's easier to tie them back to back, because that's the way the elbows bend.'

'Yes, I see. So if Neal's hands were tied back to back, they were probably tied behind him, so someone else must have done it. There must have been someone else there.'

'Exactly. Whoever it was probably took Neal's car keys, too. Picked them up by mistake, perhaps – it's easily done. Or maybe he intended to drive Neal's car away, and then thought better of it.'

She considered. 'But his death still could have been an accident. I mean, whoever it was might have tied him up for fun, or at his own request, and then got in a panic and run away when he suddenly upped and died on him.'

'It's possible,' Slider said, 'but not likely. If Neal really was a hanging fetishist, he wouldn't have had anyone else there. It's a thing they do strictly alone, and they'll usually go to any lengths to hide what they are from the world.'

'Couldn't it have been ordinary old ten-a-penny bondage?'

'I don't think so. The style's all wrong. I think he was murdered, and it was meant to look like accidental death through sexual asphyxiation.'

'But then what about the fire? It doesn't make sense for someone to murder this bloke, go to all the trouble to make him look like a particular kind of pervert, and then destroy their handiwork by setting fire to him. I mean, if they just wanted him dead, what's wrong with simply whacking him on the head with the good old traditional Blunt Instrument?'

Slider smiled. 'Some murderers have no sense of our heritage. I don't know about the fire. Maybe it was just an accident. Or maybe the murderer was trying to make absolutely sure – second and third lines of defence.'

She sighed. 'It's ridiculously over-elaborate. Like something in a novel.'

'Yes. Just like that. Nature imitating art.'

'So what you're looking for is a crime fiction aficionado. Or a television cop-show addict,' she said. He didn't respond, and she glanced up and saw from his face that he had gone away. It was something she'd had to get used to in the time she'd known him.

She shrugged and turned her attention to the sausage she'd saved until last. Why was it, she wondered, that catering sausages were always so much nicer than the ones you had at home? Perhaps it was because they consisted entirely of fat and rusk, making them, in effect, a kind of tubular fried bread. She shared Slider's unwholesome passion for fried bread.

She reached for the tomato sauce. Foreigners, she thought, would never understand the British aversion to the horrid Continental practice of putting meat in sausages. It was one of the things that made them foreign, of course, poor things.

The widow Neal had become quite expansive with Slider over a large, medicinal whisky on the brocade sofa in the pink-shaded living-room. There was a Barbara Cartland sort of opulence to the decor which he thought Irene would really have liked in their house if she'd had the social courage. And if he'd had the salary, of course: chandeliers, white fur rugs and reproduction mahogany Queen-Anne-chiffonier TV-and-video cabinets didn't grow on trees.

'It's ironic that he should die in a fire like that, when he spent his entire life trying to prevent them,' she said.

Slider could tell from her voice that it hadn't really come home to her yet that he was dead. Part of the time she was hearing herself speak; half expecting the appropriate emotions to arrive on their own, part of the package, as it were, of bereavement. The rest of the time, though she spoke in the past tense, the words were still being driven by her feelings towards the living man, whose echo and after-image would linger in her mind and her days long after she had accepted intellectually that he was not coming back.

'A friend of his was killed in a fire once. That's when he got that scar. That was before he met me, of course. But he did actually care about fire prevention – I mean, really care. He felt his job was important. It was about the only thing he did care about,' she added bitterly. 'But I suppose that's why he did well at it.'

'Did he?'

She looked up quickly. 'Oh yes. His firm thought the world of him. They used to say he could have sold a fridge to an eskimo. I suppose he was a good salesman in a way. I mean, he could always sell himself – to women, at least.' The bitterness again. 'But it wasn't that, so much, more that he really believed in what he was selling. I think people can always tell, don't you?'

'Yes,' said Slider comfortably. 'Did it pay well?'

For answer she made a curious flat gesture around the room. 'It brought all this. And his car, and his suits – he liked to dress.' The heavy gold bangle on her wrist seemed to catch her attention. 'I never wanted for anything. Jewellery, clothes. Anything money could buy. He was always generous.'

Slider's roving gaze gathered in the pink and white expensiveness of the room. It had a curiously static quality, as if it had been put together for an exhibition at the V and A: Home Decor Through the Ages. This was in the Post-Contemporary Harrow and Wealdstone section.

'You never had any children?' he hazarded.

34

'I couldn't.' She took a gulp at her whisky to fortify the baring of All. 'We'd have liked some, at first anyway, when we were still – when things were all right. Maybe if we'd had a kiddie . . . I've sometimes wondered whether that was why Dick ran after other women. A sort of compensation. Because he was disappointed in me.'

'Have you any reason to think he was?'

She didn't answer at once. Her eyes were distant and there was a small smile on her lips. 'It was so good at first. We fell in love at first sight – really,' she added, as if Slider had protested at the platitude. 'He'd had lots of girlfriends, but he'd never asked anyone to marry him, even though he was thirty-three when I met him. Everyone said we were an ideal couple.' She sighed reminiscently. 'He was so attentive. He had lovely manners. Women like that.' She focused on him suddenly to deliver this useful piece of information, and Slider nodded gratefully. 'He could make you feel special. Perhaps if I'd had a kiddie, it would all have . . .'

She drifted away for a moment, and then sighed. 'I don't know. Maybe not. He was always, you know, very *active*.' She looked at Slider carefully to see if he did, in fact, know. 'That's all right for a time, but you can have enough of it, when it's every night. I don't think women feel the same way about that sort of thing as men. I mean, they don't sort of do it for its own sake, the way men do, and after a while, well—'

She hesitated, and Slider helped her out. 'His appetites grew too much for you?'

She looked at him sharply. 'Don't get me wrong. He was all man, my husband, but there was nothing funny about him. Nothing kinky. He just liked to do it a lot, that's all. And with his job, he had all the opportunities.'

'How did you find out?' Slider asked.

She shrugged. 'A woman always knows. Not necessarily who, but what.'

It wasn't the first time he'd heard that said, and he still begged leave to doubt it. But there seemed to be a special sealed compartment in women's minds where they could keep bunkum – intuition, astrology, telepathy, precognition and suchlike – without its contaminating the rest of their common sense.

'Anyway,' she went on, 'he wasn't exactly careful to hide it. Oh, I don't mean he paraded it, but he left things around. I could have found out everything if I'd wanted. And if I faced him with something, he usually admitted it. He didn't,' she added in a puzzled voice, 'seem to have any bad conscience about it. As if it was – just part of the job.'

Slider nodded. He knew coppers like that – several of them. And since Joanna, musicians too. Men whose jobs made them unaccountable . . . Was it something inherent in all men? Or was it an infection they caught from each other? Well, and now him, too. But it was different for him. He and Joanna were different – weren't they?

He pulled himself together. 'I believe you told my colleague that you actually saw your husband with a young woman—'

'Little tart!' she said explosively.

'Was that recently?'

'Oh yes. Well, three, maybe four weeks ago. She was his latest.'

'Did you know her?'

'I know who she is.' Her eyes narrowed in hatred. 'Her name's Lorraine or Debbie or one of those common names. She works in Dick's office – one of the backups for the salesmen. Every new girl that joins, he has to try out – if she's half-way decent-looking. Laughable, really, a man of his age chasing young girls like that. I said to him, you're too old for this sort of thing. I said you're going to die of a heart-attack one of these days—'

She stopped abruptly, snapping her mouth shut. Her eyes met Slider's in terrible, pitiful appeal. Under the expensive makeup her face had the nakedness, the unfinished look of the unloved child. 'When he left—' Her mouth worked. 'I didn't know I'd never see him again. I didn't tell him – I never even said goodbye. Not properly.'

Slider remembered a remorseful poem his mother used to recite, about a father sending his small son to bed in

36

anger 'with harsh words, and unkissed'.

'I'm sure he knew you loved him,' he said.

'Do you really think so?' The eyes fawned now, craving reassurance.

'Sure of it.' He had kept on coming home to her, hadn't he, through sixteen years of unfaithfulness, knowing that however much he hurt her, she would always forgive him.

Men may not always know what, he paraphrased her words inwardly, but they know who.

Joanna saw that he'd come back to her. He blinked a little in the sudden daylight at the end of his thought-tunnel.

'So we're going to Atherton's for dinner tonight,' she said, by way of landing him gently.

'Hmm? Oh – yes. Unless something comes up.'

'Always unless something comes up,' she agreed. 'His dinners are becoming famous, you know. Norma told me that last time she was invited he had real truffles in his pâté.'

'I don't think I've ever even seen a truffle,' Slider said vaguely. 'Have you?'

'Nobody knows the truffles I've seen. I wonder about Atherton, though. Do you think he's trying to build himself a persona, or is he really like that? Oddly enough, he seems to get more intensively the same the longer I know him. Is it an elaborate mask to hide his quiveringly naked soul from the harsh winds of reality, or is Time eroding the topsoil from him and revealing the bedrock of his genuine character underneath?'

Slider gave the propositions his weightiest consideration. 'Dunno,' he said at last.

'Thanks,' she smiled. 'I love you, Inspector.'

The lines around his mouth softened a little. 'I love you too.'

'Who else is going to be there, anyway?'

'Only Polly Jablowski.'

'Oh. Is he having a crack at her? That's quick work.'

'I like Polish,' he said, as if it had been a criticism. 'I think she'll be an asset to the Department.'

'Yes, she seems a bright kid. I hope she doesn't mind sharing his favours, though. He was never one to confine himself to one woman.'

'Is he still seeing that solicitor from the magistrates' court?'

'He's seeing two, actually.'

'Why two?'

'Everest syndrome – because they were there.'

'Sooner him than me. All solicitors are as mad as gerbils,' he said automatically.

'Sometimes, Bill Slider, you're a typical copper,' she said, and he looked pleased. 'Well, if Atherton ever thinks of settling down, someone like Polish would be my choice for him.'

'And at least he'd be settling with a woman who understands his way of life,' Slider said unwarily.

'Thanks.' He saw her expression change as rapidly and completely as someone pulling off a mask. It was one of the things he loved about her, that she hid nothing from him, but it had its disadvantages sometimes.

'Bill, what's going to happen to us?' He didn't answer this in any case unanswerable question, and she went on, 'We haven't had any proper time together for God knows how long. It's always snatched moments in unsuitable places.'

'We could have had time together this evening. We didn't have to accept Atherton's invitation,' he pointed out.

'But I wanted to. I want to go places with you, to see you in company with other people, the way proper couples do. I don't want to be hidden away like a shameful secret.'

'You're not—'

'Don't say it! You know what I want. It was supposed to be what you want too. You said you wanted to be with me.'

Oh God, he thought, sadly but without rancour. He entered into her predicament far more completely than she could possibly realise. 'It's going to be difficult for a while. You know what it's like with a major case. You know how little time I have.'

'But what little there is you could spend with me. You're going back to Ruislip tonight, aren't you?'

She never talked about his going home now. The house where his wife lived was 'Ruislip' and her house was 'here' or 'Chiswick'.

'I have to,' he said helplessly.

'No, you don't have to, that's the whole point.'

'While I live there, I have to.'

'You wouldn't have had to, if you'd done what you were going to do.'

'I know,' he said. He was beginning to feel hollow. The situation was a bastard, and the full and frank admission that it was of his own making didn't help a bit. 'I did ask you to be patient—'

'I have been. I am. But for how long? I want a proper life with you, not this piecemeal business. I want us to live together. When are you going to move in with me?'

He looked at her helplessly. There was nothing he could say to her, no decision to give her, no excuse to offer for the lack of a decision. The fact was he simply hadn't been able to face up to the gross deed, the actual leaving of Irene. Leaving, nothing! What about the first step, what about *telling* Irene for a chilling start? How did any man ever do it? Even with the stoicism for facing unpleasant situations developed over twenty years in the Job, it was still a brown-trouser notion by any standard.

And here in the canteen, after the days and nights he had just spent, in this brief pause in a long period of sustained concentration, everything outside the Job seemed, in any case, a fantastic irrelevance. Life beyond the Department had all the gripping qualities of the repeat of an episode of a television soap you hadn't been following.

'Oh Jo, not now,' he said. 'I can't think about it now.'

He saw her cheek muscles tremble, with anger she was holding back because she wanted to discuss with him, not quarrel. A quarrel could never lead to a conclusion, and she wanted a conclusion. But despite herself, a little spurt of steam escaped. 'It's always not now, though, isn't it? There never is a good time.'

'There will be. We're on the same side. We want the same thing. It's just timing. There's no need for us to fight.'

He saw the last words, at least, make an impact. 'Let's fight until six, and then have dinner,' she suggested.

He didn't always understand her oblique references, but he knew the tone of her voice. He said, 'We will talk about it, I promise you, but not now. I know I've no right to ask you to go on being patient, but I do ask it. When I'm in the middle of something like this, it takes all my concentration. You've seen it before – you know.'

For a long moment she said nothing. He could see everything flitting with endearing visibility through her face, as she weighed her frustration against her understanding of his position, her hatred of the situation against her sense of fair play. She came down in the end, as it seemed she always did, on his side. It was that generosity which made women victims, he thought – like Mrs Neal. But he would never be a Richard Neal to Joanna. And then he thought, depressingly, that he was being a Richard Neal to Irene, wasn't he?

'Yes, I know,' she said. 'Well, just hurry up and get a result, then. What is it they say? You only get seventy-two hours to catch a murderer.'

The storm had passed over without breaking. He wished it made him feel better. 'You're beginning to sound like Dickson,' he said.

The red-haired trollop of Mrs Neal's anathema turned out to be a Miss Jacqueline Turner, and apart from the fact that she abbreviated her name to Jacqui, and dotted the 'i' with a little circle, Atherton found nothing to dislike about her.

He went to interview her at her place of work, the Omniflamme office in Coronation Road, Park Royal. The grim hinterland of the industrial estate stretched away forever in a vista of stained concrete, flat roofs, cheap flettons, plastic fascias and metal-frame windows: an

40

affront to the senses, relieved only by the determined reclamation attempts of ragwort and buddleia at the foot of every lamp-post; and the brave, rich odour of roasting hops in the air, drifting over from the Guinness brewery.

Atherton spent eight long minutes in the Omniflamme reception area, perched on the edge of a minimalist black leather sofa, reading the Omniflamme sales literature he found on the minimalist glass coffee-table. *Omniflamme for all your Detection and Protection needs,* he read. A cross between Phil Hunt and a Durex, then, he thought to himself. Though there really wasn't a lot of discernible difference between Phil Hunt and a Durex, not as far as intellect went, anyway.

Omniflamme, he learned with the appropriate amounts of surprise and pleasure, could interface with his existing systemised personnel alerting capacity, and extend and maximise its function; or on the other hand – if, indeed, it was another hand – could be personally tailored to his individual needs and requirements. At that point, and to his profound relief, he was accessed to Miss Turner on a prioritised one-to-one basis and advised that he could interface with her in the small conference room, which was momentarily in vacant standby mode.

She led him there in silence, and as soon as the door was shut behind them turned to him with the urgent question, 'Is it true?'

Jacqui Turner was extremely easy on the eye, although Atherton would have described her hair as strawberry blonde rather than red. She was wearing a mini-skirt, though not a terribly abbreviated one, and she had the legs to match, but to his keen eye she was on the borderline of being too old for it – twenty-five or thereabouts. She was wearing quite a lot of makeup, but it was skilfully applied, and there was nothing about her to invite the description of trollop – except, of course, from a wronged wife.

Under the makeup her face was drawn with anxiety. 'They've been saying – people have been saying – that Dick – Mr Neal – is – that he's been killed. It's not true, is it?'

'Yes, I'm afraid so,' Atherton said.

Her face quivered, and she went very white. 'Oh God,' she whispered.

'I think you'd better sit down,' he said, drawing out one of the chairs from the long table. She sat down abruptly and rested her forearms on the table, and stared blindly ahead of her. Atherton sat down cater-cornered to her and drew out his notebook.

'I can't believe it,' she said eventually. 'When Bob said it I thought it was a joke. A sick joke. He *can't* be dead. It must be a mistake.' She looked at him. 'Couldn't it be a mistake? Someone else, not Dick?'

'No mistake,' he said, holding her gaze steadily.

She searched his face for a moment, and then looked away and said bleakly, but in acceptance, 'Oh God.'

'I have to ask you a few questions,' Atherton went on. 'I understand you were very close to him.'

'I'm his sales backup,' she said automatically, not with him, her mind busy elsewhere. 'I make his appointments, type up his quotations, order his samples, all that sort of thing. A bit like a PA, you know, except that we have three Account Executives each to look after.'

'Didn't you have a more personal relationship with Mr Neal, though?'

She turned her head back to him slowly, catching up with the question. A look of bitterness came over her. 'I suppose there's no point in trying to keep it secret now. We were – lovers. He was – we were going to get married.'

'But you must have known he was already married?'

'When he got the divorce, I mean,' she said with dignity. 'His marriage had been over a long time, in all but name. He and his wife – well, they just shared the same house, that was all. They didn't sleep together or anything. And as soon as the divorce came through, we were going to get married.'

'Mrs Neal knew about you, then?' Atherton asked, fascinated, as always, by the lengths to which human self-deception could go. She *knew* none of that was true, he could see it in her face.

'Oh yes, of course. He'd told her all about it. It was all

42

out in the open as far as she was concerned. We tried to keep it a secret, otherwise, though. The company wouldn't have liked it, you see, if it had got back.'

'Did you ever meet Mrs Neal?'

'No, of course not.'

'Or speak to her?'

'No.'

'I see.' Atherton's voice was as neutral as magnolia matt emulsion.

She was stung by it. 'But I knew all about her. He'd told me all about her. He didn't hide anything from me.' She was desperate to convince him. 'He wanted children, you see, and she couldn't have any. She *told* him to find someone else. She did't mind. They were more like brother and sister. He told me she said he should marry someone who could—' The story was too thin to be jumped up and down on like that. He saw her foot go straight through it. Her face crumpled, and she put her hands over it. 'Now he's dead,' she gasped, 'and she'll be the widow, and I'll be *nothing*! They didn't even *tell* me. I won't even be allowed to go to the funeral.'

He waited while she cried, not feeling any inclination to laugh at her choice of words. She had put her finger, with the unerring aim of the interested, on the essential difference marriage made: the right to know, the right to ask, the right to be told. It was stronger than love, or even habit. It was self-evidently stronger than death. He remembered how, at the end of the Austen case, when Bill had been lying in hospital covered in bandages, it was Irene who went to visit him there. Joanna wasn't even allowed to enquire after him: if she had telephoned the hospital, they would have refused to tell her anything.

It was some time before Jacqui Turner had recovered enough for him to get her back to specifics. With the fourth tissue in her hand, she answered his questions dolefully and docilely, as if she had no more fight in her.

'When did you last see him?'

'On Friday. He came in to the office at about five to do his paperwork, and then we went to Crispin's for a drink and

43

something to eat.'

'That's the wine bar in Ealing, is it?'

She nodded. 'We went there a lot. I live at Ealing Common, so it was handy for my place. He lives in – lived in Pinner. Oh, well, I suppose you know that.'

'So you had a meal and some wine—?' He left a space for her, but she didn't correct him or add anything, so he went on, 'And after that, what?'

'He went back to my place.'

'For coffee and brandy?'

'Whisky, if you want to be particular. I don't have any brandy. Dick's a whisky drinker.'

'Did he smoke?' Atherton asked through natural association.

'Like a chimney. They all do.'

'They?'

'All the salesmen. It goes with the job.'

'I see. And after the coffee and the whisky—?'

She met his eye defiantly. 'We made love, of course.'

'Of course. And what time did he leave?'

'I don't know exactly. About ten, I think.'

'And when did you next expect to see him?'

'Well, normally it would have been on Saturday. We always had lunch together on Saturdays, unless he was away, and Sundays he spent at home. And Monday he was supposed to be in Bradford and Leeds for two days, so I suppose it would have been Wednesday. I'd have spoken to him, though – they have to ring in every day.'

'But you didn't, in fact, see him on Saturday?'

'He said he couldn't because he was meeting someone.'

'Did he say who?'

She shrugged, her lower lip drooping. He saw that they had quarrelled about it. 'He just said an old friend.'

'He didn't mention a name? Or where he knew him from? Anything about him at all?'

'He said he'd got to meet an old friend he hadn't seen for years, and that's all he said.'

'What was his manner when he told you that? Was he worried, apprehensive, disappointed, bored?'

'He sounded pleased,' she said sulkily, 'as if he was looking forward to it. He was sort of grinning to himself, as if he had some stupid secret he wasn't going to let *me* in on.'

'I see,' Atherton said sympathetically. 'So from that you gathered that it wasn't a business meeting?'

'If you want to know,' she said, turning her annoyance on him, 'I thought he was meeting some old mate of his and they were going on the piss together, to some stupid club or something, probably with topless waitresses or something pathetic like that. Or maybe it was a dirty film – some man-thing, anyway.'

'Did he often do that sort of thing?'

'Oh—!' Her anger ran out of places to go. She sighed and said, 'You know what men are like when they get together. They're just like little boys. All the salesmen are like it when they get together. They drink and tell dirty jokes and – oh, you know.'

'Was he particularly interested in blue movies?'

She looked faintly puzzled. 'What do you mean? All men are, aren't they, when they get the chance? He didn't have a collection of them, if that's what you mean. If you want to know, he'd always sooner be doing it than watching it.'

'Did he like doing unusual things?'

She actually blushed, though whether with embarrassment or anger he wasn't sure. 'That's not what I meant. No, he didn't. And why are you asking me questions like that? What's going on? What's it got to do with you how he spent his spare time?'

Spare time was the mot juste, Atherton thought. 'I assure you I'm not asking questions out of idle curiosity, Miss Turner,' he said with reassuring formality. 'You say that he normally telephoned the office when he was away on business. Do you know if he did, in fact, call on Monday?'

'No, he didn't. Well, he didn't call me and I'm his backup. I don't know if he called anyone else.'

'It was you he was meant to call?'

'Yes.'

'And you weren't worried when he didn't?'

45

'I *wondered* – I wasn't exactly worried.'

'What did you wonder?'

She bit her lip. 'I thought he might be skiving off. I was worried he'd get into trouble. They'd have told me if he'd rung in sick, you see, because I'd've had to call his customers, so I knew it wasn't that.'

'He'd done it before, had he? Skived off, I mean.'

'Yes, when he was out of Town. More than once. He sort of went out on the spree, and drunk too much, and then couldn't make it to his appointments the next day. He got a warning last time. I didn't want him to get into trouble.'

'He liked a drink, then?'

'He was a social drinker, that's all,' she said defensively. 'He had friends everywhere, people he'd worked with, or met through his work. Well, he'd been a salesman for years – he was in insurance before he joined Omniflamme – and when he met up with them, they'd go for a drink, and—' She let the end of the sentence hang for him.

'Yes, I see.' He was getting a very clear picture of Mr Richard Neal, the Rep with the Quick Dick and the All-England capacity. 'So there was nothing unusual in his telling you he was going to meet an old friend on Saturday?'

She shook her head. 'Except that he wouldn't say who it was. Even when I asked him.' She met his eyes urgently. 'They're saying he was killed in a hotel fire – is that true?'

'Yes,' said Atherton. He could see her thinking.

'But if it was just a fire, just an accident, you wouldn't be asking all these questions, would you? You think it was deliberate? That someone started it deliberately?'

'We don't know yet. Let's say there were suspicious circumstances.'

'What circumstances?'

'I'm not at liberty to tell you.'

She stared, thinking hard. 'This man he was meeting—?'

'If you think of anything, anything at all, that might help us to find out who he is, it would be very helpful. We know Mr Neal didn't go to Bradford, but we don't know where he *did* go. It's possible he said something to this friend of his.'

She shook her head slowly. 'I can't think of anything. But

it must have been an accident. It *must* have been. Nobody would want to hurt Dick. Everyone liked him. He had friends everywhere. *Everyone* liked him.'

Apart from his predilection for getting drunk, and nibbling on forbidden sweetmeats, Atherton thought, he seemed to have been a regular little Postman Pat. Mr Popularity. If only I could have got on with people like that, I might have been a Commissioner by now – or dead, of course.

CHAPTER FOUR

Talk to the Animals

JUST BEFORE THE UNIFORM SHIFT change at two o'clock, D'Arblay appeared politely in Slider's office.

'Sir – could I have a word?'

'Yes, of course.' Slider liked D'Arblay. There was a pleasant modesty about him, though he must have been tough enough underneath, having survived his first six years in the criminal hothouse of Central. 'What is it?'

He seemed hesitant. 'Well, sir, the Skipper said I should mention it to you, though I didn't want to presume.'

'Presume?' Slider savoured the word. It was like something Joanna would say.

D'Arblay looked uncomfortable. 'I didn't want it to look as if I was trying to tell you your job, sir.'

Slider smiled. 'Relax, lad. What's on your mind?'

'Well, sir, as the motel fire was on Sunday night, I wondered if you'd thought of asking Mrs Mason if she saw anything?'

'Mrs Mason?'

'Elsie Mason, the old bag lady, sir.'

'Oh, Very Little Else, you mean. I never knew she had a surname.'

'Yes sir,' D'Arblay said seriously. 'I always call her by it – she seems to like the bit of formality.'

They taught them that in Central, Slider remembered. It sometimes paid off, especially if some really scuzzy wino was shaping up to give you trouble, to address them with formal politeness. A kind of benign shock treatment. Not

48

that Very Little Else came into that category, of course.

'She's around that area on Sundays, is she?'

'Yes sir. She walks along Goldhawk Road and Askew Road on a Sunday. I didn't actually see her at the fire, but she'd be bound to have gone there once she heard the sirens – she's very curious about anything on her ground.'

'How reliable is she? I haven't spoken to her for quite a time.'

'Her memory's sound enough, sir. She acts a bit dotty, but she knows what's going on.' He looked at Slider hopefully.

'I see. Well, you did quite right to mention it.'

'Thank you, sir. But it was the Skipper said I should come and see you.'

Sergeant Paxman was not one to poach another man's credit. D'Arblay had had a good thought, and he'd let him run with it; and D'Arblay was handing the credit straight back to his skipper. It was touching about those two.

In fact, Slider had forgotten Very Little Else. She was one of the better known characters on their ground, a tiny creature, only four foot eight tall and thin as an adulterer's excuse. She dressed always, winter and summer, in a black coat, black boots, and a black felt hat, with, of course, the tastefully matching accessories of black teeth and black fingernails.

She was unusual for a bag lady in that she only ever toted one bag, whereas most female tramps collected more and more junk all the time. There was one in South Kensington, for instance, who now had to push a stolen supermarket trolley to carry all her bags; and another who lived under the bridge where the M4 crossed Syon Lane, who had accumulated so much stuff she could no longer move about at all. The last time Slider had passed she had even acquired a sofa and a matching armchair. He firmly expected to see a standard lamp and a sideboard next time he drove by.

Very Little Else, however, travelled light. She walked her ground in a methodical way, stumping along muttering to herself with her one bag clutched tightly in

49

her right hand, while her left gesticulated an accompaniment to her monologue. When Slider had first come to Shepherd's Bush, she'd had an old Turkish-patterned carpet bag, but that had gone the way of all flesh. Now it was just a plastic carrier, which only lasted a few weeks before having to be replaced. No-one had ever fathomed out where she slept, or what she lived on, but she was popular with the beat coppers because she was no trouble. Slider thought they probably all slipped her a few bob every time they met her.

Since D'Arblay evidently got on with her, perhaps he should get him to interview her about the motel fire. He glanced out of the window. On the other hand, the sun was shining out there, muted by the dust of ages on the window panes, but inviting. 'Any idea where she'd be today?'

'Somewhere between White City and East Acton, sir.'

'Ah. Thank you, D'Arblay.'

It was one of those sunny afternoons when suddenly the world slows down to continental pace. The pavements smelled like hot skin, the tar of the roads softened benignly, pigeons got serious about each other wherever there was a patch of balding urban grass. In the row of shops opposite the park in Bloemfontein Road, suddenly-genial shopkeepers propped their doors wide and dreamed of the subcontinent they'd left behind them. Windows stood open everywhere, and the air was exotic with the fragrance of spices and frying garlic. Outside the post office, two scrawny single mothers folded their arms and chatted, forgetting for once to slap and scold; and in a pushchair by the door a happy baby mugged old ladies for smiles.

It was here that Slider finally came upon Very Little Else. He spotted her turning the corner into Bryony Road, and going into the park through the gate by the bowling-green. He parked the car further up the road and went back to look for her, and found her sitting on a bench with her back to a warm privet hedge, blinking in the sunshine like a dusty black cat, and fumbling to open a packet of baby's rusks which she held in her lap.

The grass around her feet had bloomed as if by magic into a flock of hopeful pigeons, but she didn't seem to have noticed them, nor to care that her fingers slid again and again over the well-sealed packet-end without making any impression. She seemed to be quite happy just sitting there, and Slider felt it would have been a shame to disturb her, except that in the past he had found her not averse to a spot of company.

'Hello, Else,' he said, positioning himself so that his shadow fell across her face and she could see him clearly. He stood still to let her get a good look at him, and she examined him carefully, frowning as she sought through her mental files for recognition. 'Don't you remember me?' he said after a minute.

'Yore a pleeceman,' she said definitely, and then shook her head disappointedly. 'My memory's not what it was. I used to know you all once. But you keep changing every five minutes. Can't keep up with you no more. Which one are you, then?'

He sat down beside her, and she peered at him from closer quarters. The sun shone into her face. There was a bloom of age, like blue algae, over the brown of her irises, and it seemed to him that there was grey dust in the deep seams of her wrinkles. He wondered how old she was. Probably not more than sixty, though it was always hard to tell. Once people parted with the normal comforts and concerns of civilisation, they came to look both older and younger than their age.

'Yes, I know you now,' she announced. 'Mr Slider, ain't it? Yore the one who got his eyebrows burned off. I ain't seen you about lately.'

'I don't get out on the street as much as I'd like to. How are you, Else? You're looking fit.'

'Gotta keep fit, ain't I? No-one else'll look after me.' She examined him keenly. 'Yore puttin' weight on. See it round yer chin. Been on good grazin', aintcher?'

51

'I don't get the exercise you do, walking all day.'

'Got a girl, 'ave yer?' she asked astutely, and chuckled. 'Wass that advert they useter do, for evaporated milk? Comes from contented cows.'

He felt he should distract her from that train of logic. Her scrabbling fingers caught his eye. 'Here, let me open that for you.'

She looked down at the packet in her hand blankly, having evidently forgotten all about it. Like magic it disappeared, whisked into her bag as though it had never existed. Stolen, he thought. Did she actually steal it from a baby? Lifted it out of a pram, as like as not. But her need was probably greater than the baby's.

'Wanted a cuppa tea,' she complained, with a natural association of ideas, 'but the caffy's shut.'

'The cafe's been closed down for years, Else,' Slider said, wondering if D'Arblay was wrong about her memory.

But she looked indignant. 'I know that! Whadjer think, I'm going sealion?'

'No, not you, Else. You'll see us all out.'

'Sharp as a bell,' she said severely.

'I'm glad to hear it,' Slider said, 'because I wanted to ask you something.'

'Didn't think it was a social call,' she said, looking away from him across the grass. Girls were beginning to come out of the school, strolling across the park in pairs, all wearing short, tight skirts, white ankle socks, and black rowing-boat shoes. They all looked so alike, it made Slider feel dizzy, and he looked away.

'You want to know about the fire, I s'pose,' she said suddenly, without looking at him.

He was surprised. 'Why d'you say that?'

'Man got killed, didn't he? Pleece gotter investigate. You're The Man up Shepherd's Bush now, aintcher, now Mr Raisbrooke's gone. What happened to him, anyway?'

'He retired,' Slider said automatically. With her deductive powers, he thought, she should have been a detective. 'Did you see the fire, then?'

'I was there,' she agreed, between relish and pride. 'I

watched the firemen. Gor, it was a good one! Went up like a bombfire. They never had no chance of puttin' it out, I could see that 'fore they ever got there. I stopped all night, watchin'. It was lovely! Just like the war,' she said happily, 'and no bleedin' ARP wardens to tell you to clear off out of it, neether.'

'Were you round that way before the fire started? Did you see anyone going in, or coming out?'

Her gaze sharpened again. 'Which one you interested in?' Silently he gave her the photograph of Neal, blown up from a snapshot provided by Mrs Neal. She studied it. 'Is he the one what died?'

'Yes. Did you see him at the motel that night? Or parking his car, perhaps? He had a red car, sporty, parked it in Rylett Road and walked down. Maybe he had someone with him?'

'Na, I never see him there,' she said. She looked up from the photograph and eyed Slider speculatively, and then smacked her lips softly. 'I could go a cuppa tea, though. You got your car with yer, Mr Slider?'

He was wary. He had nothing but goodwill towards the old girl, but she wasn't what any man would choose for a travelling-companion. Even upwind he could smell her. 'What's this about, Else?'

'It's a dry sort a day,' she said dreamily. 'F'you could give me a ride up the Acropolis, they don't mind me there. Some places they won't serve the likes of me.' She handed the photograph back. 'Nice sort a face, ain't it? 'Ansome.'

'You didn't see him at the motel, you said?'

'Seen him somewhere else,' she said blandly. 'Can't think where, though.'

'If I give you a ride in my car, do you think you might remember?'

'Wasn't long ago, neether. Mighta been Satdy or Sundy,' she said with a sweet smile. 'Real thirsty sort a day, ain't it?'

'Come on then,' said Slider resignedly. If he was going to get rolled, at least it would only be for the price of a cup of tea.

She sat very upright in the bucket seat with her bag

clutched in her lap, and looked about her with evident delight on the short journey down Bloemfontein Road and along Uxbridge Road to the Acropolis Cafe. She loved riding in cars, and Slider found her pleasure rather touching. In the course of her long life she had been in so few of them that the experience still had all the childhood sharpness of novelty.

Outside the Acropolis he pulled up and went round to the passenger side to let her out. He delved into his pocket and pulled out a handful of loose change, saw there were a couple of pound coins amongst the silver, and held out the whole fistful to her. He knew from experience it would give her more satisfaction than a note.

She accepted the bounty gravely in her cupped hands, and then bestowed it into various pockets. Slider waited patiently until she looked up again.

'Satdy it was,' she said, suddenly business-like. 'Dinner-time. I see him go in the George and Two Dragons. He—'

'Where's that?'

'*You* know.' She seemed impatient of the interruption. 'Up the Seven Stars. I was sittin' on the wall oppsit. He was in there a long time. Havin' his dinner, most like. I could see the back of 'is 'ed through the winder. Noddin', like he was talkin' to someone. Then he comes out and I see him go up Gorgeous George's. He meets a girl there.'

'How d'you know? Did you see the girl? Could you describe her?'

But she only chuckled and turned away. 'You ask Gorgeous George,' she said, stumping towards the cafe door. 'He knows all about it.'

There was a complex road junction where Askew Road, Goldhawk Road and Paddenswick Road all met, which of late years had been turned into a free public bumper-car ride by the simple addition of two mini-roundabouts. A large pub called The Seven Stars and Half Moon dominated the scene, and had given its name to the whole area.

Gorgeous George was the local Arthur Daley, a blond and handsome South African who had a second-hand car lot in Paddenswick Road and conducted various slightly dubious business deals on the side. Slider had thus decoded two thirds of Else's cryptic message, but The George and Two Dragons eluded him. That had to wait until he got back to the factory and asked Bob Paxman. He was custody sergeant on the late relief, and Slider found him in the kitchen making himself a cup of Bovril.

'Oh, that's the pub, The Wellington, on the corner of Wellesley Road,' he answered Slider at once.

'Why on earth—?'

'It's only been called The Wellington since they tarted it up. That was in 1965 – 150th anniversary of the Battle of Waterloo. Some clever sod at the brewery noticed that Lord Wellington's name was Wellesley before he got made a duke, so they changed the pub name while they were refurbishing.'

'The things you know,' Slider said admiringly.

Paxman looked wary, wondering if he was being razzed. 'They had a grand reopening on June the whatever it was, day of the battle,' he went on, committed to his story now. 'Gave away free drinks. We got called out twice before nine o'clock – fights in both bars. Silly buggers.' He snorted and shook his head, and then remembered the point of the story. 'Anyway, before that it was called The George and Dragon. It was run for years and years by a little bloke called George Benson, with the aid of his large wife and his even larger mother-in-law. Hence—'

'Ah, I see!'

'Some of the older locals still call it The George and Two Dragons.' The round brown eyes rested on Slider with ruminative enquiry. 'Are you going to follow up what Little Else said?'

'Don't you think she's reliable?'

Paxman scratched the curly poll between his horns. 'She's given us some useful stuff in the past, but she's not getting any younger. And of course if it came to anything the CPS would never accept her as a witness.'

Slider shrugged. 'At the moment I've got nothing to lose. And circumstantially it sounds all right. It was sunny on Saturday round lunchtime, and there's a low wall opposite The Wellington – the wall of the park – where she might sit to enjoy the sunshine. And the second-hand car lot is just up the road, virtually next door to the pub. She could have seen him go in there without changing position.'

'So you'll be having a word with Gorgeous George, then.' Paxman smiled slowly. 'He's a funny bastard. You heard about his latest scam? He sells a clapped-out Japanese car to a black bloke and charges him a fancy price because he says it used to belong to Nelson Mandela. This bloke meets a friend, boasts about it – turns out the friend's also bought a car from Gorgeous George, same story. So they go round there to sort him out. A bit of a frackass ensues, and a neighbour calls us out. I send D'Arblay, who asks what's occurring, and Gorgeous George gives him a wide-eyed look and says, "I never said I got 'em from Nelson Mandela. I said I got 'em from the Nissan main dealer." What a funny bastard.' Paxman drew a beefy sigh. 'Almost makes you believe in God.'

Gorgeous George – Pieter George Verwoerd was the name on his well-worn passport – was in his office, for once, in his shirt sleeves, making a telephone call. It was one of those moments of sudden quiet that happen in London, when for perhaps five minutes it simply chances that no traffic passes, nor pedestrians, dogs or planes. Outside on the forecourt the used cars basked in the spring sunshine, innocent as seals on a rock; and a sparrow sitting on the roof gutter guarding a nest site said 'Chiswick, Chiswick,' over and over again like a demented estate agent.

Gorgeous George looked up as Slider came in. He said abruptly into the telephone 'I'll call you back,' put the receiver down, and thrust his chair back from the desk to look up at Slider from a position of complete apparent relaxation.

56

He was a larger-than-life character, giving an impression of great size, though he was neither tall nor fat. His light hair waved vigorously, like someone trying to attract the attention of a friend on the opposite platform of the Circle Line tube at Bayswater. His eyes were hazel and lazily feral, his lips full, his chin firm. He had a large, healthy laugh, which revealed an inordinate number of strong white teeth. Women found him irresistible. Men found him difficult to resist. His passage through life had been littered with broken hearts and broken limbs.

He had been a game warden in his youth, so legend had it, and had got himself out of trouble on one occasion by staring down a lion so that it gave up the idea of eating him and simply walked away. It was also said that he had worked in a slaughterhouse, where he had learned how both to subdue and to execute the unwilling with the least exertion or damage to himself.

Both legends were in their own way typical of the man and the effect he had on people. It was certain that he understood animals, and was suspiciously lucky on the ponies, and that even previously one-man dogs would go up to him with love in their eyes and lay their lives at his feet. The sniffer-dog handlers at Heathrow Airport knew him very well indeed, and viewed him with considerable jaundice.

Slider knew he had a weakness for the man, and that he wasn't alone in liking him, in spite of all suspicions. Gorgeous had so far got away with having some very disreputable acquaintances, and had never yet collected a record, though many visits had been paid him by various coppers, wanting to discuss cars with a tendency towards elective surgery, and orphaned consumer durables in search of a caring family environment.

'Well now, to what do I owe the honour of this visit?' he said at last.

'I just fancied a chat,' Slider said blandly, pulling a chair across and sitting down opposite him. 'How's it going, George?'

'When did you ever just want a chat? I hope this is not

57

going to be a roust,' Gorgeous said. He opened the box of twenty-five Wilhelms which was lying on the desk, extracted one, offered it to Slider, and then slipped it between his luscious lips. 'Because,' he went on, the cigarillo wagging with the words, 'I always think of you as the thinking man's copper, and I should hate to see you wasting your time and making a fool of yourself.'

He struck a match and drew the flame onto the tobacco. A blue wreath of smoke rose towards the ceiling.

'Your concern touches me deeply. But you should know better than me whether I've any reason to want to roust you,' Slider said.

'My conscience is clear,' he said, lazily smiling. 'Much to my relief. I couldn't fob you off like that blue-eyed boy of yours – what's his name?'

'Detective Sergeant Atherton.'

'Yeah, that's him. He came round here the other week asking me about funny money – as if I'd ever have to do with counterfeit! He took some convincing, too – *and* when I had a customer hanging around about to buy one of my specials. Lost me a perfectly good sale. They should use him on the recruitment posters,' he added with assumed disgust. 'He does for community relations what Icarus did for hang-gliding.'

'You shouldn't underestimate him,' Slider said. 'He's a good copper.'

George shrugged, removed the cigar from his lips, and inspected the burning end with interest. 'You shouldn't send a boy out to do a man's job,' he said. 'A boy with his mind on other things, as well – I saw him afterwards in The Wellington with his arm round a bird, looked like a plonk. Practically climbing inside her blouse, the eager little mountaineer.'

Slider laughed out loud, and George lifted his eyes to him. 'That's rich, coming from you!'

George grinned ferally. 'Ah, but I don't let it distract me from the real purpose of life.'

'Which is?'

'Making money,' he said simply. 'You got money, you

got power – and incidentally all the women you can eat. And, not to change the subject, what *do* you want?'

Slider produced the photograph of Neal. 'I believe you know this man.'

Gorgeous George looked at it and handed it back indifferently. 'Why should you think that?'

'He was seen going into your premises on Saturday afternoon.'

'Doesn't mean to say I know him, does it? My premises are open to the general public.'

'But he was here on Saturday afternoon?'

'You've just said he was seen going in. What do you want from me? Reassurance?'

'Did you see this man on Saturday afternoon?'

'Nope.'

'You're sure of that?'

'I couldn't have seen him, because I wasn't here on Saturday afternoon.'

'Where were you?'

'Well, as it happened, I had a business meeting with a financier in Newbury.'

'At what time?'

'Two o'clock, two-thirty, and three-fifteen.'

Slider grinned. 'Business, eh?'

'I came away fifteen hundred to the good. What would you call it?'

'You must have a system.'

'I have an infallible system, which I will divulge to you at no extra charge.' He leaned forward and lowered his voice conspiratorially. 'I always back the grey. And when there's no grey, I back the noseband.'

'And that works?' Slider asked with interest.

'It's as reliable as studying form, and much less like hard work.'

'I've heard it said,' Slider stared innocently at the ceiling, 'that you lean on the paddock rails and talk to the horses as they walk past. And that the horses tell you what they've decided amongst themselves.'

'You get a nice class of conversation from the English

59

thoroughbred racehorse,' he remarked. 'I'm a traditionalist. I love the simple things – English countryside, well-bred horses, and old-fashioned English coppers. God, what a country this is! You should never have let the Empire go.'

He looked expectantly at Slider, like someone facing a friend across a tennis-net, in anticipation of a challenging but good-natured game, and Slider squared his mental shoulders. It was a bit much, he thought, that he should have to perform for his living. This wasn't Broadway.

He tapped the photograph as it lay on the desk between them. 'We've been told that this man was seeing a woman on your premises.'

'And which of them do you want to know about – the man or the woman?'

'Let's start with the woman,' Slider said, hoping a new path might prove straighter. 'What's her name?'

George shrugged. 'The name she gave me was Helen Woodman. Whether that was her real name or not . . .' He let it hang.

'And what was she doing here?'

'She rented my small flat off me. You know I've got two flats over the showroom? Well, I have – the one I live in, and a small one, furnished – just one room plus kitchen and bathroom – which I let out sometimes.'

'Only sometimes?'

'When it suits me. Sometimes I want to use it myself, for friends or relations.'

Slider tried to marry up the notions of Gorgeous and friendship and failed. He put his money on relations. He remembered, irrelevantly, the story of the Irish couple who sat up all through their honeymoon night waiting for the carnal relations to arrive.

'Is she there now?'

'No. She quit on Sunday.'

'Oh? Did a bunk?'

George smiled. 'That's your nasty, suspicious police mentality asserting itself. No, she didn't do a bunk. She told me from the beginning she only wanted the place for

60

three weeks. She said she had some research to do in London, and she needed a pied-à-terre for three weeks, that's all.'

'What sort of research?'

'Didn't say.'

'Where did she come from? Did she give you a permanent address?'

'Nope.'

'Didn't you ask her for one? That was rather trusting of you, wasn't it, George?'

Gorgeous George turned his hands palm upwards. 'She paid me cash in advance. There's nothing in there she could nick or damage. And if she gave me any trouble, I was quite capable of handling her.'

'Can you describe her?'

'Five foot eight or nine, about twenty-six, slim, long red hair – a real looker.'

The red-headed tart again, Slider thought. This was better. 'Could you help us put together a photofit of her?'

Gorgeous shrugged. 'It wouldn't do you much good. She wore very heavy makeup – clever stuff, like theatrical makeup. Without it, she'd look quite different. And the red hair was probably a wig. Have you ever seen a tom off duty? Well, then, you know all about the world of illusion.'

'Was she a tom?'

'Not quite.' George hesitated. 'Not a regular one, but there was something about her. She was putting out, but it didn't come from the heart – or the loins, if you like. The way she looked at you – she had the cold eye. Like a parrot, know what I mean? I suppose if she was doing research, she must have been a student of some kind, which is much the same thing.'

Slider smiled at this jaundiced view of youth. 'What sort of accent did she have?'

Gorgeous shrugged. 'Standard south-east.' He drew thoughtfully on his cheroot. 'She was good class, not a poor white. Well fed. A big, strong girl, like a basketball player. I watched her carry her suitcase up the stairs and, she handled it like it was nothing.'

61

Slider sighed inwardly. No two things George had said about her added up so far. 'How did she find out about your flat?' he asked next.

'I didn't ask,' Gorgeous said indifferently. 'Business is business. Anyway, everyone round here knows about it. She could have asked in a shop or a pub.'

'Do you advertise it anywhere?'

'I used to, in the newsagent at the end of the road, but I don't bother any more. Like I said, everyone knows about it, and I don't let it out all the time.'

'When exactly did she first approach you?'

'It was a Monday at the beginning of March.' He glanced at the calendar on the wall. 'When would that be? The fifth, I think. Yeah, Monday the fifth. She said she wanted the flat for three weeks from the following Monday, up to this Monday just gone. Paid me cash in advance.'

'Did you see her about much? What did she do all day?'

George shook his head. 'She wasn't there all the time. I'd see her coming and going for a few days, and then she'd disappear for a few days. Then she'd be back. Like that.'

'Did any other men visit her at your flat?'

'What d'you mean, any other men?'

'Apart from him.' Slider gave the photograph of Neal a little push.

Gorgeous George sighed and looked deeply at him. 'Don't do that to me, Bill. Not to me. No little traps. I never saw that man go up to her flat.'

Slider looked back. 'There's no grief for you in this, George. I just want to know.'

'I never saw anyone go up there, with her or without her. That's the truth.' Slider said nothing. 'What does it take to convince you? Look, I rented the rooms to her, and after that the place was hers for three weeks. It's got a separate entrance, up the old iron fire escape round the back, so she could come and go as she pleased, and so could anyone she wanted to invite home. I never saw this bloke go in there, or any other bloke, and for the matter of that, I never saw *her* to speak to but the twice, once when she moved in, to collect the key, and once when she moved out, to give it back.'

62

'When exactly was that? When did you last see her?'

'On Sunday morning. She rang the bell of my flat, about half elevenish, and said that she'd changed her plans. She wouldn't be staying on until Monday after all, she was leaving right away, and she gave me back the key and off she went.'

'She went? Are you sure?'

'Yeah, I watched her go. She had her suitcase with her. She crossed the road and went down Ravenscourt Road as if she was going to the station. I went straight up to the flat to have a look round, make sure it was all right, and it was clean as a whistle, polished and everything. She'd gone all right. And that was the last I saw of her.'

Slider contemplated the new information with faint dismay. If she left on Sunday morning, that put her out of the frame, didn't it? And what, then, was Neal doing in the area on Sunday night? Unless she had already set up the meeting with Neal, which the murderer was to keep in her stead – and that had always been a possibility.

Gorgeous had been watching him. 'What's this tart done, anyway?' he asked.

Slider came back. 'Nothing, as far as we know. We just want to ask her a few questions.'

Gorgeous George grinned. 'She doesn't seem all that eager to talk to you, or anyone else for that matter, to judge by the way she's covered her tracks.'

'What sort of a woman was she?' Slider asked abruptly. 'Did you like her? You've known a lot of women in your time, George. Just person to person, on your instinct, what did you think of her?'

George drew again on the cheroot, and blew a cloud up to the ceiling, watching it with narrowed eyes. 'It's hard to say. She was a good-looking skirt, and showing it off, except in a kind of way she just wasn't there at all.'

He thought a moment. 'You know how female crabs grow a new shell every couple of years? They just climb out of the old one, and the new soft one underneath hardens up. And when you go diving on the reef, you see what you think is a crab, but when you pick it up, it's just

63

an empty shell, perfect in every way, except there's no eyes in the eye stalks. That's how you tell. You look at it, but it doesn't look back.' He tapped an inch of ash delicately into the ashtray, where it lay like the pale ghost of its parent cigar. 'That's how she was. Maybe it was all that makeup. It kinda depersonalises a woman.'

'I wouldn't have thought you'd want too much personality,' Slider said, from his knowledge of George's sexual appetite.

'I like women,' George said. 'I don't let 'em bother me, but I like 'em. But this one—' He shrugged. 'Well, when I'm on the job and giving my all to a woman, I prefer her to be there.'

CHAPTER FIVE

Kicking the Puppy

IT WAS VERY LATE WHEN Slider finally started off on the drive to the Catatonian outpost of Ruislip, where, until Joanna, he had spent the little left over bit of his life that was not work. Atherton's dinner had had to be cancelled, of course, and he had snatched time only for a telephone conversation with Joanna, but she had taken it very well.

'It's all right, I need to practise anyway,' she said. 'We're doing Scheherezade on Friday. It's not called Sheer Hazard for nothing, you know. Shall I see you tomorrow?'

'I hope so,' he said, and then felt mean about it. 'Yes, of course. I'll make time, somehow.'

'All right,' she said pacifically. 'You sound tired.'

'I am,' he said, and left it at that.

And that had been what seemed like hours ago, and now he was very, very tired. His mind nudged at the various situations he was supposed to be getting to grips with, without biting into any of them. The drive home along the Western Avenue was usually good thinking time, when a lot of sorting and clearing went on in his back brain; but tonight he was too tired to do more than fret and mourn.

Home. Strange that he should ever have called it home, and yet he still did when he wasn't thinking; when Joanna wasn't about. There was no pleasure there, no companionship and very little comfort, and as far as he could remember there never had been. He hadn't particularly wanted to move out there, but Irene had liked the house and the neighbourhood, and in fairness he had felt it

65

should be her choice that prevailed, since she would be there a great deal more than him.

Of course, they might have moved onwards and upwards to better things if he had fulfilled Irene's ambition and got himself promoted with proper regularity. The glamorous M40 corridor lay within tempting reach; the social cachet of the detached house was not an empty dream for the man who Got On as he should. The children might have gone to a private school; Irene could have made friends with people who drove Range Rovers and Volvo estates; and Slider might once more have lived in a house with chimneys, and windows that stopped a respectable distance from the floor.

But when promotion to Chief Inspector came at last, it was as a kind of booby-prize, which a man would have had to have had no pride at all to accept. And besides, the rank itself was uninviting – a desk job, an administrative cul-de-sac between the working ranks of DI and Superintendent.

He sighed as he thought about it. It was another reason not to want to go home: since he'd told Irene he'd turned the promotion down, the atmosphere had been so inhospitable it made the surface of Saturn look like the Butlin's camp at Skeggy by comparison.

The moment he'd done it, he'd realised from the intensity of his relief how much he'd always dreaded promotion. It was strange that he hadn't suspected it before. He must have been more affected by Irene's ambition than he'd thought.

It was not unprecedented in the Met. There were cases in his own experience of DIs voluntarily going down to DS, in order to get back on the streets and away from the paperwork – and so he had told Irene, defensively. She, of course, had thought he'd gone mad.

'After all these years!' she raged, tearfully. 'To throw it away, all of it, with both hands, everything we've worked for!'

'I don't want to spend the rest of my life in a meeting,' he said. 'I'm not good at meetings.'

'And you didn't even have the decency to consult me!'

Well, yes, that was bad, but of course he had not consulted her – and she knew it – because he'd known she wouldn't agree with him. She'd been delighted when he was finally offered the promotion. It had touched him to see how happy she was about it, how she'd had no doubts that he deserved it. She had brushed aside his own conviction that he had been promoted merely to shut him up after he had made so much trouble over the Austen case.

'Nonsense,' she said robustly. 'Nobody promotes people for that reason. You're the best, and they know it. Now we'll really start to go places!'

But the places she wanted to go were not the places he wanted, and they never had been. It was the great tragedy of life that it was hardly ever possible to know that kind of thing about each other when you married in your twenties, as most people did. And when you finally discover that you're just not suited to each other, what do you do? In Slider's case he had compromised, lived Irene's life at home and his own life at work, and struggled not to let the dichotomy wear away his soul.

But of course it did: the friction slowly deadened you. Joy went, and curiosity, then anger, and lastly even despair. That was the way he'd have gone, too, if it hadn't been that at the moment of his one last struggle with disillusionment he had met Joanna.

He had thought he'd seen all the kinds of humanity there were, but Joanna surprised the socks off him. It was comparable in effect to that time in 1967 when they'd first cleaned the generations of soot off St Paul's Cathedral. He'd been a probationary PC at the time, and St Paul's was on his beat. He had never previously considered that it was not, in fact, built of black stone. When he'd seen it clean for the first time, set forth in all its fairytale, honey-coloured splendour, it had seemed literally like magic. He'd been suddenly filled with an excited sense of *possibility*.

So Joanna had affected him, with her undisguised face

and frank enjoyment of him. He had grabbed at her with the last of his survival instinct. She was an unexpected and undeserved last chance to live his own life, the way he wanted to live it.

Ah, but that still left Irene, didn't it? And the children; and the house with its mortgage and maintenance; and then there was insurance, pension top-up, bank loan repayments ... When the euphoria of being whacked unexpectedly on the head by True Love at the age of fortysomething subsided slightly, there remained the whole ill-fitting but extremely tightly-knitted garment of his married life to unpick, and he just didn't know where to start.

How did other men do it? When he thought simply about the practical difficulties of moving himself and his belongings out, to say nothing of the cost of it all, he wondered that anyone in the history of matrimony had ever left anyone else. The disruption, the exhausting scenes, the tears, the silent reproaches – he could imagine it all, and all too easily.

And then there was love to consider: his for Irene – uncomfortable and unwelcome as it was, it still existed. You can't look after and worry about and placate and care for someone for all those years and not become attached to them. And hers for him – and oh God, that was harder still to bear. Because for all her disappointment and her contempt for his ineffectuality, she did love him, and he knew with a sort of tearing sensation of self-hatred that he was her whole world. Love like that, however little you asked for it in the first place, was hard to betray.

He thought about Mrs Neal, forgiving her erring husband, waiting for him to come back; being there, like the dog with its nose pressed to the door, always waiting. He didn't want to do that to Irene; she had not deserved it. And he didn't want her to be in the position of being able to do it to him. She'd forgive him to death.

All the same, he wanted Joanna, needed the wholeness of life with her, and for that he had to leave Irene. He didn't baulk at the logic. It was simply the doing of it which so far had defeated him. There were those who were constitutionally unable to kick puppies. Ah, but supposing you were given the choice between kicking the puppy, and your own death? You'd do it then, wouldn't you?

Except, of course, that for survival reasons, the human animal was rigged not to be able to believe in its own death. Perhaps, he thought wistfully, he just wasn't desperate enough yet.

Jacqui Turner opened the door wearing practically nothing but an anxious expression.

Slider showed his brief. 'I'm sorry to disturb you so early, but I wanted to catch you before you left for work.'

'It's all right,' she said vaguely. 'I wasn't going in anyway. I've been having the week off.' She looked dazed, and her eyes were puffy – either through crying, or lack of sleep, or both, Slider thought.

He followed her into the hall. She had a ground-floor flat in what had been a handsome, three-storey Victorian family house, almost overlooking Ealing Common. The conversion had plainly been done in the worst period of the seventies. A series of despicable doors and cardboard partition walls gave access at last to two thirds of a large and splendid room, with a marble fireplace and French windows into the garden. The ceiling mouldings running round three of the walls collided with the fourth, a false wall which partitioned off the remainder of the room. Through the open doorway Slider glimpsed curtained gloom and a tumbled bed.

'I hope I didn't wake you up,' he said contritely. A valiant effort kept his eyes away from the hem of her shortie nightie.

'No, it's all right,' she said, turning to face him, which was worse. 'Would you like a cup of coffee or something? Or tea? I was just going to make some.'

'No, thanks all the same. It's just a brief visit. I won't keep you a moment.'

She seemed suddenly to realise he was a man as well as a

detective inspector. 'I'll go and put something on, then,' she muttered, and disappeared through the door in the carton wall.

Slider looked around the room. It was determinedly untidy, considering how large it was and how little there was in it in the way of furniture. Clothes were strewn everywhere, magazines and crumpled tissues, and there was much evidence of eating and drinking. Miss Turner seemed to have been exorcising her grief in the time-honoured fashion with chocolate biscuits, tinned rice pudding, milky drinks, Kit-Kats, whisky, crisps, satsumas, Kentucky Fried Chicken, Coca Cola, popcorn and pickled gherkins. A closely-written five-year diary lay open on the sofa, along with a scattering of letters: from Neal, presumably, and evidence if so of his carelessness.

On the mantelpiece amongst the miscellanea were two framed photographs. One was of Neal, rather blurred as if it had been blown up from a slightly unsuccessful snapshot, with the river and trees in the background – probably at Strand on the Green, Slider thought. The expression on his face was surprised and not entirely pleased. Early in the relationship, probably: she had snatched the picture in order to have some permanent record of him, the one thing at that stage he wouldn't want.

The other photo was of Neal with his arm round Miss Turner's waist on the front at Brighton, with a resigned and faintly embarrassed smile. It was plainly taken by a seaside photographer, who was probably glad of the work, since the empty parking spaces and the deserted state of the street behind them showed it was out of season.

And there were two videos in hire-shop covers lying on top of the television. He drifted over to look at the titles. *The Way We Were* and *Brief Encounter*. It was all so very, very sad, he thought.

Miss Turner came back in, wearing a very unglamorous towelling bathrobe, her hair still tangled and her face uncared for. She had obviously taken a sabbatical for the moment from the search for everlasting love.

70

'Do sit down,' she said wearily. 'I suppose you want to ask me some more questions.' She glanced at the sofa, and her face trembled. 'I'll clear those away,' she said abruptly, crouching down and trying to shuffle the letters together.

'No, it's all right, don't bother,' Slider said. 'There's no need—'

She looked up and he met her eyes unwillingly. He didn't want to have to look in at this door, too.

'It's all I've got of him,' she said. 'Just a few letters, and only one of them's a proper one, the others are just notes.' She gulped and made the final, humiliating confession. 'To do with work, actually. There's one that says – that says—' Tears filled and spilled over from her eyes with amazing facility. She thrust the piece of paper at Slider and groped in the towelling pocket for a handkerchief.

Jacquie, the note said – had he not known, then, how she preferred to spell herself, or was it a protest on his part? – *can you look me out the Valdena correspondence please, asap. DN.*

Yes, he got the picture. Slider waited in silence while she mopped up the latest overspill, and then as she gathered the rest of the papers together, gently laid the precious note on the top. She took the whole pile up and held them against her chest. It was a universal, unthinking gesture, essentially female, he thought. Give a man a burden, and he'll first look about for something to make a barrow out of, but a woman just picks it up and trudges.

She looked at him again and read his sympathy. 'Pathetic, isn't it?' she said, but without self-consciousness at last. 'When I think of all the hours we spent together, what we did together, and I've got nothing to show for it. Just a few bits of paper. I told your friend, the other one, that he wanted to marry me, but I knew deep down he didn't really. I was just fooling myself. He'd never have left her. It was just a bit of fun for him. He only said that, about marrying me, because I made him. Just to keep me quiet.'

Slider's mind jumped before he could stop it to Joanna. What would she have to remember him by, if he were to

71

die tomorrow? He'd never had occasion to write to her – their communications were all by telephone. She was not interested in photography, and the only presents he had ever brought to her were consumable – bottles of wine, cheese and pâté from the deli at Turnham Green, occasionally flowers if he had happened to pass a seller on his way round. If he were to be snatched away suddenly, he'd have left no trace behind in her home or her life.

But the cases were not comparable, he told himself savagely. He yanked his mind back determinedly, wanting to be out of here. The place stank of grief and deceived womanhood, and they were the last things he needed to be exposed to at the moment.

'There's really no need for you to disturb yourself,' he said desperately. 'I just wanted to ask you if you could let me have a recent photograph of yourself.'

'Yes, I suppose so,' she said, and then surprise caught up with her. 'What do you want it for?'

'It's just to eliminate you from certain lines of enquiry,' he said. 'It's nothing to worry about. I'll let you have it back in a day or two.'

'Yes, all right,' she said. 'I'm sure I can find you one.' She drifted back into the bedroom, and some moments later came back with an eight-by-twelve studio print, which she proffered tentatively. 'This was taken last year, but I don't think I've changed much.'

It was a black and white glossy of Miss Turner in a smart suit with attenuated skirt against a background of a tree in spring blossom and two municipal tubs of daffodils. On the back was an ink stamp *Brighton Evening Argus* with a telephone number and the copyright negative number.

Slider looked the question.

'It was in the paper, on the women's page – spring fashions. You know, what women in Brighton are wearing, sort of thing. I liked it, so I bought some copies. You can do that,' she assured him gravely.

He nodded.

'I used to live there,' she added. 'That's where I met Dick, in fact.'

72

'Oh? I thought you met him at work.'

'No, I took the job at Omniflamme so we could be near each other. He happened to mention that the girl before, Lorraine, was leaving, so I phoned up the Accounts Director and asked for the job. He was so impressed by my initiative he gave me an interview, and, well, I got it. I was already doing the same sort of work, you see, for DSS – Dolphin Security Systems. I met Dick when I was on the DSS stand at SafeCon – you know, the trade fair. They hold it in Brighton every year.'

'Did he know you were applying for the job at Omniflamme?'

'No, I kept it a secret till I got it, to surprise him.'

I'll bet it surprised him, Slider thought. What was the old adage about never fouling your own nest? And she'd be a far tighter curb on his roving than a well-trained wife who never asked questions. How, he wondered, had Neal been proposing to sort out that little tangle in his life?

'Was he pleased about it?'

'Of course he was,' she said quickly, 'only we had to keep our relationship secret until he'd got everything sorted out with his wife and we could be officially engaged.' She caught herself up. 'There I go again, you see. But that's what he pretended, and I let myself believe him. I suppose now,' she added hopelessly, 'I ought to go back to Brighton. There's nothing to keep me here any more.'

'When you saw him on Friday evening,' Slider asked, 'how did he seem? Was he just as usual, or did he seem worried or preoccupied at all? Was he cheerful?'

'He was always cheerful,' she said, and she seemed to sag a little at the recollection. 'That was one of the things people loved about him. Of course, he'd had a lot on his mind recently, but he never let it get him down. Only on Friday he was a little bit – well—' She hesitated.

'Yes?' Slider encouraged. 'Anything you can tell us, anything at all, might help us to find out what happened to him.'

'Well,' she said again, reluctantly, 'we did have a bit of a row in Crispin's, about – well, when we were going to get married. I was impatient, you see. I wanted him to get on with it, get things sorted out.' She gulped. 'So we had a bit of a tiff. But we made it up when we got back here. He never carried things on, you know – not sulky, like some men, wanting to punish you for stepping out of line.' Slider nodded encouragingly. 'He'd been being so nice to me, and then when he told me he couldn't see me on Saturday, I felt sort of – well, I didn't feel I should—' She paused again.

'Did you perhaps feel that you couldn't be angry over that, because of the quarrel you'd had earlier?'

'Yes,' she said eagerly, turning her face to him. 'That was just what it was. I felt bad about nagging him about his wife, and so when he said that, about Saturday, I thought, well, just keep quiet, Jacqui. Enough's enough.'

He could never know for certain, of course, but Slider would not have been surprised if Neal had deliberately stage-managed the earlier quarrel. A man in his position must learn unusual social skills to survive.

'Are you sure he didn't tell you anything about the person he was going to visit, except that it was an old friend? He didn't mention where he knew him from, for instance – school, work, golf club, whatever?'

She shook her head slowly. 'No. No, nothing at all. He was being secretive, laughing to himself, you know. Sort of teasing me. Except—' She stopped abruptly, looking thoughtful.

'Yes?' he encouraged.

'Well, it sounds silly, but – when I asked him who he was going to meet, I thought he said *mouthwash*.'

'Mouthwash?'

'I said it was silly,' she backpedalled.

'No, no, please. Nothing is too small to mention. Tell me exactly what you said and what he said.'

'I said something like, "Who do you have to see tomorrow that's so important?" and he said, "Mouthwash". Well, that's what it sounded like. And I said, "What did you say?" thinking he was, like, swearing at me, you know?'

'You thought it was like saying "Rubbish" or "Nonsense"?'

'Yes, like that! So I said "What did you say to me?" And he said, "It's no-one you know. Just an old friend I haven't seen for years." And wouldn't tell me anything more about it.'

Mrs Neal opened the door to Slider, dressed in black, sensible shoes and no makeup. Her face was old with misery, and Slider was forced to conclude that there must have been something essentially lovable about Neal, for two women to mourn him so sincerely.

'Your friend's already here, Sergeant Atherton,' she said by way of greeting.

'Yes, I saw his car outside,' said Slider.

'Looking through Dick's things.'

'Yes. It's very kind of you to allow us the run of your house like this,' Slider said.

'If it helps, I don't mind. Anything that helps,' she said bleakly. The harder part would come later, Slider thought, when all the excitement was over and they were no longer around to provide a counter-irritant: then she would have to come to terms with the sheer emptiness where her husband had been. He knew of his sympathy, if not of his own experience, that being without someone who's going to be back sometime is quite different from being without someone who'll never be coming back.

'There are just a couple of things I'd like to ask you, ma'am, if you wouldn't mind,' he said, following her into the plump pink sitting-room. She sat ungracefully on the brocade sofa and looked at him patiently out of her suffering. Like Jacqui Turner, she felt no more need to be attractive. The world was now simply a place full of people who weren't Dick.

'Firstly, if you'd have a look at this photo – is that the woman you saw getting out of your husband's car?'

She took the picture flinchingly, and then looked puzzled. 'No, that's not her. Who is it?'

'You've never seen this person before?'

'No, not that I remember.' Slider took the photo back. 'Who is she?' she asked again.

75

'Someone we hoped to eliminate from our enquiries,' he said, and went on quickly, 'Does the word *mouthwash* mean anything to you? Did it have a special meaning for your husband, for instance? Perhaps a story, an experience, an old joke connected with it?'

'Mouthwash?' She looked bewildered. 'No, not that I know of. I mean, other than what you wash your mouth out with, I've never heard of it.'

'Have you ever heard him use the word in an unusual connection? Or seen it written down anywhere?'

'No, never. What's this all about?'

He avoided that one, too. 'Mrs Neal, has your husband seemed in his usual spirits lately?'

'I suppose so,' she said doubtfully.

'Did he seem as though he had anything particular on his mind?'

'I don't think so,' she said, but again without great conviction. 'Not more than usual. He always thought a lot about his job. He was very conscientious.'

'On Sunday,' Slider pursued, 'I think you said he was at home all day?'

'Yes, until about seven, when he left for Bradford. At least, he was supposed to be going to Bradford.'

'And that was his usual practice when he was going away on a trip? To leave the night before?'

'Yes, if it was any distance, so he could be fresh for his first appointment in the morning.'

'Did he do anything at all unusual on the Sunday? Anything he didn't usually do?'

'No.' She looked bewildered again. 'He read the papers, had his lunch, made a few phone calls, packed his case. Nothing at all, really. And then he went.' Her mouth quivered.

'Do you know who he telephoned?'

'No. He always made his phone calls from his study. You can't hear anything with the door shut.'

'How did you know he made calls, then?'

'Because the phone in the hall goes ping when you pick up either of the extensions, or put them down. And when

76

you dial out, it kind of tinkles.'

Slider nodded. 'How many calls did he make?'

'Two or three. I wasn't really counting.'

'And he didn't tell you who he was ringing?'

'No. I didn't ask. I never interfered in his business.'

'You assumed they were business calls?' She shrugged. 'Did anyone ring him?'

'I don't think so. Wait, yes, the phone did ring once, in the morning. I was in the kitchen doing the potatoes. Dick answered it, and then went into his study to take it, so it must have been for him.'

'And he didn't tell you who that was, either?'

'No.' She looked miserable. 'If it had been a friend, anyone we both knew, he'd have told me, so it must have been business, mustn't it?'

How easy she had made it for him, Slider thought. Was that indifference, weakness, pride, or self-defence, he wondered? Or perhaps it was all part of the conflict: Neal tried to make her curious about his movements, and she refused to be curious. We all have ways of punishing each other, if only we work at it.

'So he was his usual cheerful self all day, was he?'

'Yes, I suppose so. Well—' She paused a moment. 'I wouldn't say he was exactly cheerful. But he wasn't the opposite either. He was just ordinary.'

'Thoughtful?' Slider suggested.

'Yes, perhaps. I suppose so. He spent quite a long time in his study after lunch, so I expect he was going over his papers and things for the trip. He had one or two of his biggest clients in Bradford and Leeds, so he'd want to be sure he was properly prepared. He had to give technical advice, you see, which people relied on. His job was important – it wasn't just a matter of selling things.'

'And when he left, at seven o'clock, did he say or do anything unusual?'

Her eyes filled with tears, and she shook her head. 'He just – he kissed my cheek and – and said "Cheerio darling," just as if – as if—'

She wasn't going to get any more out at present, he

77

could see. He nodded sympathetically. 'Yes, I understand. Thank you.' He waited while she dabbed her eyes and blew her nose, and then stood up. 'I'd like to have a word with Sergeant Atherton now, if I may?'

'Yes. He's in the study.' She stood up too, and sniffed bravely. 'I'll show you.'

'Oh no, that's all right, please don't bother. Along here is it?'

'Yes, round the corner, and it's the last door on the right. It used to be the back part of the old garage, but Dick had it made into a study when we had the new double garage built.'

'Have you tidied it at all since Sunday?'

'I haven't been in it. I never went in his study. A man has to have somewhere to be private.'

Bloody Nora, Slider thought – quite mildly, considering.

The study was hardly more than a cubbyhole, about eight feet by eight, with a desk under the window, a filing cabinet beside the door, and shelves round the other two walls. Atherton more or less filled what space remained with his long legs and large, elegantly-shod feet. He seemed to have the entire contents of desk and filing cabinet spread out on every available surface.

'Hullo, Guv. I thought I heard your voice.'

'Jacqui Turner is not the red-headed tart,' Slider told him. 'I just tried Mrs Neal with a photograph and she says she's never seen her before.'

He related the substance of his interview with Miss Turner. Atherton whistled soundlessly.

'Be sure your sins will find you out. I begin to feel almost sorry for Tricky Dicky. It must have been a hell of a shock when his Brighton bird turned up out of context. Cornered in his own place of work, forced into promising marriage – and I wonder how many others there were? Nature, as they say, doesn't work in isolated examples.'

'Have you found anything?'

'I'm working on it. I think friend Neal may have been in financial trouble as well.'

'As well?'

'As well as woman trouble, I mean. There's a clutch of unpaid bills here, and a mortgage arrears notice. He's been running the total up on his credit cards, and his bank account's gone into overdraft. It seems to be of recent origin. Up until about six months ago, he seems to have been pretty sensible about money – bills all paid on time, regular transfers out of his current account into a savings account. Then suddenly all the money disappears. The last quarterly statement I've found is over two months old, so he must be due a new one at any moment.'

Slider nodded. 'We'll get hold of it.'

'I think his cancelled cheques might stand looking at, as well. He's been parting with considerable amounts of folding, to judge by all the cash withdrawals, but that's not where it's all gone by a long chalk.'

'Blackmail?'

'It's possible, isn't it? But his income's dropped as well. His salary's paid direct to the bank, and the totals have been going down for the last six months. It can't be his basic, so it must be his commission. It looks as though he hasn't been selling much.'

'We can check that with his firm,' Slider said.

'Jacqui Turner said she was worried he'd been skiving off, not keeping his appointments,' Atherton said. 'He may have had something very serious on his mind that was putting him off his stroke. Or maybe it was the whole syndrome of drink and women building up to critical point.'

'Right. We'll look into every aspect of his financial setup. Of course, if he was being blackmailed, it gives us a suspect at last, which is something we've been woefully short of so far.'

Atherton looked round the tiny room and sighed. 'We won't be short of something to pass the time, that's for sure. This bloke was a squirrel. I don't think he could have thrown anything away in years.'

'I'll have a word with Mrs Neal, and you can bundle it all up and take it back to the factory. Get the others to help you go through it.'

'It's funny, though, that Mrs Neal didn't seem to know about the money situation,' Atherton mused.

'I imagine Neal dealt with all that side of things. It isn't uncommon for women of her generation to rely entirely on their husbands for everything to do with finance. He'd give her the housekeeping money, and she'd ask no questions. She said she never wanted for anything and that he was generous with presents and so on. I dare say it suited them both that way.'

Atherton sighed. 'She made it easy for him. I'll tell you another thing, Guv – he wasn't a secretive man. I've found a couple of phone bills here, and he had itemised calls.'

'I suppose he'd claim some of them on expenses,' Slider said.

'Maybe so, but I've seen Jacqui Turner's number on the list a few times. Not only did he call her from here, with the risk of his wife picking up the extension, but he kept the bill where she could find it, with the chance she might decide to check up on who the numbers belonged to.'

Slider looked into the tangle sadly. 'Maybe he wanted her to find out. Maybe he hoped to provoke her into divorcing him. That would have been one way out of his troubles, if Jacqui Turner was pressing him to marry her.'

'Out of the frying pan into the fire,' Atherton said. 'And likewise, better the devil you know.'

'How true,' said Slider. He held out his hand. 'Give me the list of numbers. I'll have them checked out. And get BT to give us the rest of the numbers, up to date – I'd like to know who he called on Sunday. I'd like to know who called him, too,' he added, 'but that's another matter.'

CHAPTER SIX

Haddocks' Eyes

'THAT'S WHAT I LIKE TO see,' Atherton said, strolling into the CID room with an armful of paper bags. Every head was bent, every desk covered in bits of Neal's accumulation of paper. 'The whole Department hunting for haddocks' eyes.'

'Eh?' said Anderson, looking up from the stack of cancelled cheques before him.

'For our beloved leader to work into waistcoat buttons,' Atherton explained, dumping the bags in the nearest out tray and sorting through them. 'What else do any of us do in the silent night? Except for Phil the Pill, of course, who reads his PACE handbook and polishes up his tongue. Where is he, anyway?'

'Bog,' said Norma economically.

'And you, Norma, you police siren: you who comb visions from your hair upon the midnight rocks of illusion.' He bent over her seductively. 'Was yours the corned beef and pickle or the liver sausage and tomato?'

She pulled the bag from his hand and pushed him away in the same movement. 'What were you eating last night? Your breath is straightening my perm.'

He straightened. 'Don't get the hump. Here's your lunchpack, Notre Dame.' She snorted derisively without looking up. He peered into another bag. 'Whose was the roast beef? Oh, that's mine.'

'That greasy-looking bag must be my hot sausage roll,' said Anderson.

81

'Don't talk about Norma like that,' Atherton reproved, moving out of range. 'And two cheese salad rolls for Polish – now she wouldn't push me away. She's a woman with taste.'

'I wouldn't know,' Mackay said, 'I've never tasted her.'

'Tasted who?' Hunt asked, coming back into the room.

'Can't think of her name, but she's been on the tip of my tongue a few times,' Mackay answered.

'Don't be disgusting,' Atherton said. 'Where is my lovely Polish plonk, anyway? I've got something I want to give her.'

'You're not the only one,' Anderson said with a secret smile. 'She went in to see the Guv'nor, and hasn't been heard of since.'

'Stop panting,' Atherton said. '(a) he wouldn't, and (b) she wouldn't. Maybe I ought to rescue her, though. He has a mind above food. She might starve entirely away.'

On cue, the door opened and Slider came in with Polish behind him. Atherton gazed avidly at her spiky head and neat little ears. She made him want to sink his teeth into her neck and keep nibbling until he got to her toes; but then he hadn't had his lunch yet.

'Ah, good, you're back,' Slider said, gathering Atherton with his gaze. 'I think we ought to have a chat, lay out what we've got so far. There are some—' He took in the sandwich bags. 'You can go on with your lunches while we talk.'

Polish beat Atherton to it. 'Can I get you something, sir? It won't take a minute.'

'I'll catch up later.' He carefully cleared the end of a desk and perched on it. 'Okay, let's have a look at what we know about Neal.'

'He was Jack the Lad,' Norma offered. 'Well known around that part of the ground. Tony and I got a number of nods to his mugshot – pubs mainly, and betting shops.'

Anderson nodded. 'Fond of the gee-gees.'

'Lucky?' Slider asked.

Anderson grinned. 'Who is? He was free with his money, though. And popular. People seemed to like him.'

'Well they would, wouldn't they?' Norma said, faintly indignant. 'Fleas are bound to love their dog.' She looked at Slider. 'He was known as a womaniser, too.'

'Prostitutes?'

'More of a ladies' man. He was good-looking, as we know. Nice manners, free spending, that sort of thing.'

Mackay spoke. 'I had a word with some of the local tarts, sir, but they didn't bite. I don't think he had the notion of paying for it. Well, he never had to, did he?'

'Why that area, in particular?' Slider asked, in Socratic mode.

'He worked for Betcon in Glenthorne Road at one time,' Beevers said. 'Security guard. That was before he married, of course, and he was living the merry bachelor life, drinking, clubs and so on.' There was the faintest of envy apparent in Beevers voice, the regret of a man with a new baby in the house and a wife still off-limits. 'I spoke to a Doug Gifford who worked with him at Betcon, and he said Neal was quite a wild character – he called him a, quote, mad bastard, unquote. And a hard drinker – though a lot of security guards are, of course. Neal had a flat in Dalling Road, and Gifford said he was always taking women back there.'

'So there was nothing strange about his being in that area,' Slider said. 'It was home ground.'

'And he preferred it to his new beat,' Atherton said. 'We know he told his wife he went to the golf club every Saturday, to have lunch with friends and play a few rounds in the afternoon. Except of course that the Secretary says he's only been there half a dozen times in the past year, and hasn't been out on the greens since last summer.'

Atherton remembered what Beevers had said when he came back from taking statements at the golf club: 'You should have seen the smiles when I asked how often he'd been in. One of the members at the bar told me Neal's what they call a "periodic member" – only turns up when his tart's got her period. Gawd, it's made easy for some blokes, isn't it? His wife never even used to phone up and check on him.'

83

But Atherton didn't convey it to Slider in quite those words, having regard for his guv'nor's own new foray into adultery. 'Neal used the golf club as his excuse to get away, sometimes to see Jacqui Turner – and perhaps other women we don't know about yet – and sometimes to go back to his happy hunting ground for a spree.'

Slider nodded thoughtfully. 'So the redhead at Gorgeous George's may just be—'

'A red herring?' Atherton offered.

'There may be nothing fishy about her at all,' Slider said. 'He might simply have met her on one of his jaunts, quite coincidentally.'

'But then what was *she* doing there?' Norma asked.

'What she said, perhaps,' Slider suggested. 'It isn't beyond the realms of possibility that she was a student, or in town temporarily to do some research, met Neal by chance and simply joined him for a good time.'

'Then why did she leave so suddenly?' Norma pursued.

'Just *before* Neal was killed,' Beevers pointed out. 'We don't know she's even involved.'

'At the moment she seems to be a bit of a dead end, until we can find her and talk to her. No luck tracing her from her name?'

'No sir,' said Norma. 'She's not in our records.'

'All right, keep trying. But leaving her aside for the moment, let's look at Neal's latest situation. He'd got himself into money-trouble. Bills unpaid, big overdraft, running up credit everywhere.'

'I spoke to his bank manager,' Atherton said, 'and it seems about a month ago he made enquiries about a second mortgage on his house. The bank seemed to find that quite amusing. They said that since he'd already run up an unauthorised overdraft about equal to a second mortgage, they'd sit this one out thank you very much.'

'So he was looking for extra money – why?' Slider said.

'Gambling debts?' Anderson suggested. 'He'd been losing fairly heavily on the ponies.'

'And his income had fallen,' Atherton said. 'These things can be cumulative.'

Slider smiled. 'It was a semi-rhetorical question,' he said. 'Jablowski's come up with something.'

'I think Neal was up to something in Brighton,' Polish said. 'I was checking through the phone numbers on his itemised bills, and I found a lot of numbers with the Brighton code. Well, we knew he went down there regularly on business, and a lot of the numbers were businesses and hotels. But he also made a lot of long calls – fifteen, twenty minutes sometimes – to a number which turned out to be registered to a C. Young, with an address in Carlton Hill.'

'Nice,' Atherton said appreciatively. 'That's the old part of town – Regency houses.'

'Expensive?' Slider asked.

'Depends. If you bought a whole house it would be. But a lot of it is run down, and the houses are cut up into flats and bedsitters.'

'I did some checking via the electoral register,' Polish went on, 'and C. Young turns out to be a Miss Catriona Young – and it is a flat in a house, by the way, Jim.'

'So, Neal had yet another little bit of heaven,' Atherton said. 'Well we didn't think he lived a monk's life.'

'Ah, but you missed the exciting bit,' Norma said with a grin. 'While you were out and Polish was chasing up numbers, Tony found a whole lot of cancelled cheques made out to C. Young—'

'For quite large amounts,' Anderson concluded. 'And at almost regular weekly intervals.'

'You might have waited till I got back,' Atherton complained.

'So it could be blackmail,' Norma began.

'It sounds more like maintenance,' Atherton finished.

She shrugged. 'Much the same thing when the bloke's a married man.'

Atherton looked disbelieving. 'Have you seen Mrs Neal?'

'All right,' Slider intervened, 'we've obviously got to follow up the Brighton business. Anything else occur to anyone?'

'Well, Guv,' Mackay said, and Slider turned to him encouragingly. 'It seems to me the only real villain remotely in the frame is Gorgeous George – even if he's got no actual form, he goes about with some very naughty boys. What if he was into Neal for something? We've got Neal sighted in Gorgeous's drum very near the scene and the time.'

Slider considered. 'It would be nice and tidy that way, I agree, but if Gorgeous George wanted to give Neal a smacking he'd just do it one dark night up an alley. I can't see him working out this devious plan.'

'Everyone says he has got a very funny sense of humour,' Mackay said hopefully.

'And he likes women,' Hunt said. 'He can get them to do anything for him. He could have set this redhead up as bait.'

'But why would he go to such lengths to compromise himself by using his own premises? That's not the way he's kept his record clean all these years.'

Mackay folded his fingers together precisely. 'No, Guv. But we don't know what Gorgeous is on the fringes of. I mean, what we do know about his business ventures can only be the tip of the iceberg. And by the looks of it, Neal was down some very big numbers. Suppose we give Gorgeous a tug—?'

'We'd need something more than supposition,' said Slider. 'We've binned people up on a wing and a prayer before now, but a prayer alone is not enough. No harm in keeping your eyes and ears open in that direction, though. Anyone else got any ideas?'

'Yes, Guv,' said Beevers smartly. 'It occurs to me that we know Neal was a club man in his bachelor days, and once a club man, always a club man in my experience. We know he didn't use the golf club – and in any case, it doesn't look as though that was his scene. So I think we ought to be looking around his old ground to find out what club he *was* using.'

'Okay. I'll leave that one to you,' Slider said, and Beevers smiled with gratification – or at least, his moustache changed shape. You couldn't see his mouth underneath it. 'In the mean time, we still don't know who the old friend was he went to see on Saturday.'

'Unfortunately, The Wellington's always busy on a Saturday lunchtime,' Atherton said. 'One of the barmen thinks he saw Neal sitting talking to a man, but that's as far as it goes. The other bar staff don't remember him at all.'

'Very Little Else said he was sitting in the window seat,' Norma said, 'Which means he'd have been facing the bar. If the person he was talking to was sitting opposite him, the barman could only have seen the back of his head anyway. A face you might notice, if it happened to fit into a gap in the crowd, but would you really notice the back of an anonymous head?'

It was a fair point. 'Probably not,' said Slider. 'Still, there's no harm in keeping on asking. You might find a customer who was sitting near Neal and his friend.'

'Couldn't it have been Gorgeous George he met?' Mackay suggested.

'Couldn't it have been the mystery redhead?' Polish countered. 'If we assume that he spent the afternoon with her, maybe he had lunch with her too.'

'Else said he came out of the pub alone,' Atherton pointed out.

'He might not want to be seen with her in public,' said Polish. 'She might have followed him – or gone on ahead.'

'If Very Little Else can be relied on at all,' Beevers said sourly. 'She's as mad as a bandage, everybody knows that.'

'The fact is, we just don't know who he was with,' said Slider. 'If we start from the assumption that he wasn't entirely lying when he told Jacqui Turner he was meeting an old friend, we'll have to begin by eliminating all of his old friends we can lay hands on.'

'Male and female?' Atherton said. 'That could take the rest of our lives.'

'To move on to Sunday,' Slider said quellingly, 'he was at home all day – no mysteries there, except that he received a phone call, which we may or may not ever learn about; and he made several phone calls out—'

'I'm still waiting to hear from BT, sir,' Polish said. 'They're going to send me the up-to-date list of his itemised calls. Though of course if they were short, local calls, they won't appear anyway.'

Slider nodded. 'We can only hope. To continue – Neal packed his suitcase and left home at around seven that evening, saying he was going to Bradford where he had appointments the next day.'

'Did he, in fact, have appointments in Bradford?' Norma asked.

'Oh yes, they were genuine enough,' Slider said. 'Whether he meant to keep them or not we don't know, of course. If leaving the night before was a cover-up for some other activity, he could still have got to Bradford in time by leaving early the next morning. Or he may have intended to phone in sick the next day, or to have given some other excuse – say the car had broken down or something. At all events, there are five hours unaccounted for. He left home at seven, and turned up at the motel just before midnight, and we don't know where he was in between.'

'We know he spent some of the time drinking,' Atherton said, 'and since he had beer in his stomach, it's likely he was in a pub somewhere.'

'We must keep checking that,' Slider said. 'Every pub – and club—' with a glance at Beevers, 'in the vicinity. Someone must have seen him.'

There was a brief silence as they all contemplated the task, and the massive invisibility of the average person in the average pub.

'And then there was the brandy,' Slider went on. 'The motel clerk, Pascoe, told us Neal had been drinking, but wasn't drunk when he arrived. Cameron tells us that from the quantity of brandy in his stomach, he must have been as drunk as a wheelbarrow. So we can assume he drank it after he arrived at the motel.'

'Jacqui Turner said Neal didn't usually drink brandy—' said Atherton.

'Which his wife confirms,' said Slider. 'He was properly a whisky man.'

88

'So does that mean the brandy was forced on him?' Anderson asked.

Slider shook his head. 'I doubt it. When a man drinks alone, or at home, or in a public house, he chooses his preference. But if he's in a private place with someone else, and the other person provides the drink, if he's a drinking man he'll just drink what's there. And we know that Neal was a drinking man.'

'It's another indication that there was someone else with him at the motel,' said Atherton. 'Whom, for the sake of argument, we might as well call the murderer.'

'But don't we have to assume it was a woman?' Polish said. 'I mean, surely a man wouldn't go to a motel room with another man, unless he was bent?'

'Maybe he was bent,' said Anderson. 'Or maybe they wanted to watch a blue movie—'

'No video in those rooms,' said Norma.

'They might have gone to talk business,' Slider said. 'Or laugh about old times. Or just go on drinking – the pubs were shut, after all. Pascoe says Neal was merry, so we have to assume that he wasn't there under duress. He invited whoever it was into his motel room, so presumably it was someone he knew – either an old friend, or someone he struck up an acquaintance with during the evening. And there'd be no difficulty for the murderer in getting his dear old buddy Dick Neal to invite him back to his motel room to knock off a bottle of the good stuff together.'

'There's a hell of a lot we don't know,' Atherton complained, 'when you think Neal wasn't really a secretive man. Still, it's early days yet.'

Slider thought of Dickson's warning. It wasn't even definitely down as a murder yet. 'Early days may be all we have on this one,' he said. 'We've got to get some results, and soon.'

Dickson had levered himself out of his chair, and was standing by the window. It was more than usually difficult to see out of. Someone – his wife, perhaps – had once

89

given him a tradescantia for his windowsill. It had flourished to begin with, resting its long tendrils against the window and growing towards the ceiling; but then it had been allowed to die of drought in the searing glasshouse heat, leaving the brown husks of its leaves stuck to the panes, where they blended with the natural dirt to make an impenetrable fog between Dickson and the outside world.

He glanced over his shoulder briefly as Slider appeared. 'Ah, Bill, come in.' He turned his head back to the window. He had his hands jammed in his trouser pockets, making his hips look wider than ever, and was jingling his change in a Latin American rhythm. That, plus the fact that he couldn't possibly have seen anything out of the window unless he had X-ray vision, gave Slider the impression that he was pretending insouciance.

'You wanted to see me, sir?' he said quietly. Vertical, Dickson seemed to fill the tiny room even more thoroughly than when penned in his chair. Slider thought they would only need to add a fairly small policewoman to put up a respectable challenge to the students-in-a-phone-box record.

Dickson played his trouser maracas. 'How's your case proceeding?'

'With all the smoothness of a bull rhinoceros being eased through a Chinese laundry press' would have been the honest answer. Slider rejected it, however, in favour of 'We've got some promising lines of investigation to follow up, sir.'

Dickson turned and surveyed him long and hard. He almost seemed to be debating whether to continue. The uncertainty was more surprising than worrying to Slider, whose conscience was clean: he met the gaze patiently, and with faint enquiry.

At last Dickson sighed, extricated his hands with some difficulty, put them on his desk, and leaned on them. 'You're a good man, Bill,' he said, frighteningly. 'I wish you'd taken that promotion.'

'You know why I didn't,' Slider said.

'*I* do. And, off the record, I don't blame you. But it's not regulation behaviour. Makes you look like a subversive. A bloody pinko conchie collaborator leftie long-hair agent provocateur, to coin some phrases. *Not sound.*'

'Oh.' There didn't seem to be much more to say to that.

'Not to be promoted isn't a sin. To refuse to be promoted – that's different.' He sat down, with an air of giving up an unequal struggle. 'There's a new spirit abroad, Bill. I don't have to tell you that. *Accelerated promotion* – need I say more?'

It was a scheme by which graduates could move more quickly up the ranks – aimed, quite laudably, at attracting able, educated men into the service, but always controversial, and deeply resented by the old-style coppers who believed everyone should learn the trade by serving before the mast. Slider, as befitted a man born under the blight of Libra, was in two minds about it. The service needed thinking men; but nothing could replace the experience gained on the streets.

'Someone doesn't like you, Bill. And on a completely different subject, I've had Detective Chief Superintendent Head on the blower.'

'I see, sir.'

'He wants to know why we're still treating the Neal case as murder. Says Neal was in bad financial trouble, multiple woman trouble, maybe being blackmailed, and was a known drinker. To his mind that adds up to misadventure or suicide – he's not particular within a point or two. We haven't got a suspect of any sort, or even the smell of a motive, and the only witness we've got is an old bag lady who's as mad as a tricycle.'

Slider gazed deep into the poached and impenetrable eyes. Multiple woman trouble? Blackmail? But they had only found that out today, and formal report hadn't yet been made to Mr Head. 'How does he know all the detail, sir?'

'He wants it crashed, Bill,' said Dickson imperviously. Slider said nothing, holding his gaze steadily. 'Not everybody on your firm is as unambitious as you,' Dickson yielded at last. 'And holding onto the ankles of the man who's about to be shot from the cannon may be the best way of getting to the top of the tent, if you take my drift.'

Hunt, thought Slider. It's got to be. Bloody Phil Hunt. Never trust a man who wears cutaway leather driving gloves in his car, he told himself bitterly. He must have found some excuse to call Head, and then allowed himself to be pumped.

'What are you going to do, sir?' Slider asked.

Dickson moved restlessly. 'Ordinarily I'd tell anyone who tried to interfere with my team to get stuffed,' he said. 'But – and this is confidential—'

Slider nodded. More and more terrifying.

'You've heard of the expression Required to Resign?'

Christ, not the old bull as well, Slider thought. A world without Dickson was hard to imagine.

'Sir?'

Dickson made a sound of contempt. 'Some people should read their history. "The Old Guard dies, but never surrenders." You know who said that?'

'No sir.'

'Nor do I. All the same, these are tender times. Not the moment for heroics. This is when you sit it out, and await developments. Take a day at a time. So I want something on this Neal case, Bill, and I want it today. A suspect, a motive, a good witness, a decent amount of circumstantial – anything, so long as it's convincing. The ball's in the air, and I want no dropped catches, you comprendy?'

'Yes sir.'

'And for fucksake sort out your firm. This is not a John Le Carré novel.'

'Yes sir.'

'That's all.'

Slider turned to go, but felt the restlessness behind him, even though Dickson didn't move so much as a finger. With his hand on the doorknob he looked back at the ash-strewn, firebreathing mountain behind the desk. There was a great deal he'd have liked to say, about loyalty for one thing, and his own hatred of power-politics, and the importance of the Job as against all considerations of career and status.

He sensed that there were things Dickson wanted to communicate; but even in his present approachable mood, he was not a person to whom you volunteered things on a personal theme. And if the skids really were under him, anything that even smacked of sympathy would surely bring about a violent eruption.

So Slider didn't say anything; but Dickson met his eyes, and for a moment his seemed almost human. He drummed his thick fingers on his desk top.

'Bill?'

'Sir?'

'You should think again about accepting that promotion.' Slider opened his mouth to protest, and Dickson cut him off with a lift of the hand. 'I know what you feel about it, but it's only another half-step from DCI to Superintendent.'

Slider said patiently, 'I don't think I want to be a superintendent either, sir.'

Dickson smiled mirthlessly. 'Then you're more stupid than you look. The higher you are in this game, the harder it is to make you fall. If they'd been after you as long as they've been after me, believe me you'd be walking Fido round some bloody factory perimeter by now, with the *Daily Mail* in one pocket and a packet of cheese sandwiches in the other.'

'Warning, sir? Is someone after me?'

'You're the type that some people will always want to take a pop at. Christ, you must know that by now. Take the bloody promotion.'

'I'll think about it, sir,' Slider said, holding his gaze stubbornly, and it was Dickson who finally looked away.

'Go on, bugger off,' Dickson said, waving a dismissing hand; but he smiled as he said it.

CHAPTER 7

Brighton Belle

'I TOLD YOU I'D SEE you today,' Slider said as they headed South.

'An afternoon at the seaside,' Joanna said admiringly. 'I don't know how you manage it.'

'And not just any seaside, but your actual Brighton,' he pointed out.

'Yes,' she said doubtfully. 'I'm not too sure about the connotations, but I accept the invitation. And what shall I do while you work?'

'You could lie on the beach, have a swim—'

'At this time of year?'

'I could leave you with the local CID – I know how much you like policemen.'

'Well, I do as it happens. They're very like musicians.'

'I pass over the slur. Or you could wander round The Lanes—'

'Oh yes! You know what a mug I am for antique shops. Who is it you're going to see?'

'Another of Neal's secret harem, so it appears.'

'The man had stamina,' Joanna said, impressed. 'I wonder when he found time to work.'

'And afterwards, we can go for a meal somewhere. Would you like to go somewhere in Brighton? Or stop at a pub on the way home?'

'What's the local beer? Oh, Harveys, isn't it? Pub then. I haven't had a decent pint all week.'

'Spoken like a true policeman.'

'From what you've told me, there aren't too many of us left.'

Slider smiled in self-mockery. 'All policemen have always said that. It's the old "nostalgia isn't what it used to be" syndrome.'

'But?'

'But nothing.' She looked at him. 'Oh well,' he yielded, 'I've been having a chat with Dickson. There's an element that's out to get him.'

'Get rid of him?'

Slider shrugged. 'They'd try, but I doubt it would come to that. More likely a sideways move, into something non-operational – records or the training school or whatever. Slow death, for someone like him.'

'But why do they want him out?' Joanna asked. 'I thought he was a good copper. You seem to think so, anyway.'

'He is. I do. But he doesn't fit in with the new image. He's untidy. He does things his own way. He doesn't automatically respect those in authority over him. He doesn't mind his tongue.'

'Yes, but what will they get him out *for*? I mean, what can they accuse him of?'

'Drink's always a good one. You know that it's a disciplinary offence for a member of the Department ever to be drunk, on or off duty?'

'No, I didn't know. But you've told me before Dickson's never the worse for it.'

'True. They'd find it hard to prove he was actually drunk. But given the amount he drinks, he'd be hard put to it to prove he wasn't. Or there's poor results. Lack of discipline below him. Saying the wrong things to the media. There's always a way, if they're determined and you haven't got the right connections.'

She thought about it. 'Does that mean you're in danger, too?'

He didn't answer directly. 'I hate politics,' he said eventually. 'I don't think they'll get the better of Dickson, but the fact that they're even trying makes me sick.'

'Yes,' she said. 'There's a lot of that going on in the music world, too – the whizz-kids straight out of music college, trying to get rid of the older players. They think technique is all there is to music, and experience counts for nothing. And they think they've a God-given right to have a job – someone else's if necessary.'

He glanced sideways at her, smiling. 'Listen to us,' he said. ' "Youngsters today—!" Of course old fogeys like us'd be bound to think that experience is more important than ability.'

'I wish you wouldn't always see the other side. It's disconcerting,' she complained. She laid a hand on his knee. 'And in any case, I've always said it's not what you've got, it's what you do with it.'

'I'll try and bear that in mind,' he said.

Miss Catriona Young turned out to have the basement flat, but she had done her best not to live down to it. There were stark white walls and polished wood floors, the sort of Swedish-style bare blonde furniture that was never meant to be sat on, and a great deal of brass pierced-work which went with the smell of joss-sticks in the air and the beaded cushions lined up along the sofa, defying relaxation.

Miss Young was one of those tall, white-fleshed young women who favour long skirts and flat sandals, perhaps in an attempt not to look any taller. Her blouse was of the sort of fine Indian cotton you never have to iron, and over it she wore a short sleeveless jacket – which Slider would have called, rather shamefacedly, a bolero – made of embroidered black velvet with those tiny round mirrors sewn into the cloth. Her tough, gingery-fawn hair crinkled in parallel waves and hung down behind to her waist, held back by two brown hairslides, one over each ear. She had sandy eyelashes and fine freckles, and her face was full of character. Slider didn't know what effect she had had on Neal, but she scared the hell out of him.

She also had a baby, of the surprised-looking sort, large

and pale, which was sitting on the floor in the middle of the sitting-room, playing with its toes, which were unusually long and looked slightly crooked, though he couldn't quite see why. As he watched the baby raised a foot effortlessly to its mouth and sucked on it, staring at Slider with detached interest, like an early luncher at a Parisian street café watching the world go by.

'I've only just got in,' said Miss Young briskly. 'Can you wait while I put him down? There's some juice in the fridge if you like. I haven't got anything stronger.'

She whipped the baby off the floor, and it soared upwards with the equanimity of one who, having had such a mother from birth, could find nothing much else disconcerting. Left alone, Slider wandered over to the bookshelves, on the principle that you could learn a lot very quickly about a person from the books they kept by them.

The shelves were low down, near the floor, and ran for an impressive distance along one wall. Bending double, he looked at the titles. A lot of foreign novels – Dostoyevsky, Flaubert, Gide – and what looked like a full set of Dickens, along with George Eliot, Thomas Hardy, and the novels of Charlotte Brontë that weren't *Jane Eyre*. Punishing reading, he thought: the mental equivalent at the end of a long day of 'Get on the floor and give me fifty'.

There were also a large number of non-fiction titles, about economics, statistics, basic law, and computers. Slider wondered why it was that books about computers were always made the wrong shape and size for bookshelves – contempt for the printed word, perhaps? Then came a green forest of the tall, slim spines of the Virago imprint, then Fay Weldon and Mary Wesley, and then serried ranks of detective fiction: P.D. James, Patricia Highsmith, Ruth Rendell – the posh ones – along with Dorothy L. Sayers, Margery Allingham, and the Penguin reissues of the classic thirties collection in those distinctive green-and-white jackets.

And finally, on the bottom shelf, tucked away in the corner and almost hidden by the fold of the drawn-back curtains, fifteen volumes of the Pan van Thal collections of horror stories, so well-read that their spines were creased almost white. Slider straightened up, feeling nervous. Who in the world keeps their books in alphabetical order? The bookshelf, so they say, was the window on the soul. Perhaps he shouldn't have come here alone.

'Sorry to have kept you waiting,' she said, making him jump. She had come back in on silent, sandalled feet, and stood in the middle of the room looking at him.

'I was just looking at your books,' he said, startled into foolishness, and then, feeling he couldn't leave it at that, 'You're fond of detective stories.'

'Yes. I find them relaxing – my equivalent of watching television. I'm sure they aren't anything like real life, however,' she added out of politeness to his calling. 'Please sit down. Can I get you some juice?'

For some reason, 'juice' without any qualifier always struck him as vaguely indecent. 'No thank you,' Slider said. He lowered himself gingerly into a wood and canvas construction which looked like the illustration in an old scouting manual of some kind of extempore bathing equipment. The canvas part was of a shade between grey and beige so featureless as to defy even depression. What exotic name would today's interior decorators give to that shade, he wondered? Spring Bandage, perhaps: or Hint of Webbing. Professional tip: for a really stylish effect, try picking out cornice, picture-rail and skirting-board in contrasting Truss Pink.

Miss Young sat down opposite him, folding her hands together in her lap. There was nothing reassuring in the pose: her hands seemed all knuckles, and she kept her feet together and drawn back, as if ready to leap into action at any moment. She was as alert and potentially dangerous as a spider with one foot on the web, testing for vibrations.

'So what did you want to talk to me about?' she asked.

'It's about Richard Neal,' Slider began. Her face seemed to go very still – a determined lack of reaction? he wondered. 'I understand you know him.'

He could almost hear the whirring and clicking as she calculated the optimum reply. Then she said, 'Yes.'

'Have you known him for long?'

'About three years.'

'In what capacity?'

She hesitated, and then said, as if it were not necessarily an answer to the question, 'I met him at university when I was doing a post-graduate course.'

'Sussex University?'

'Yes. That's where I work now. I lecture in Political Economy.'

'And Mr Neal went to Sussex University?'

She seemed to find the question disingenuous. 'He wasn't a student, which I'm sure you must know. Look, what do you want to know for?'

She was too intelligent to be fed a line. He looked at her steadily. 'I will tell you that in a moment, but I'd like to ask you a few basic questions first, if you wouldn't mind. How did you come to meet Mr Neal?'

'He was advising the university on new fire safety systems. I bumped into him on campus a few times, and we got friendly – it's as simple as that.'

'But you have been rather more than friends, haven't you?'

She almost smiled. 'The way you people put things! Well, on the assumption that you aren't just being prurient, yes, Dick and I are lovers, if that's what you want to know. I've no reason to hide it.'

'You did know he was married?'

She turned her head away slightly. 'That's his business, not mine. I never enquire into his life when he's not with me.'

A cosy arrangement, thought Slider. This man seemed to have been surrounded by complacent women, none of whom wanted to give him trouble. How lucky could a man be?

'It seems,' he continued carefully, 'that Mr Neal has been in the habit of paying you sums of money on a regular basis.'

99

'Oh, is that what this is all about?' She looked at him sharply, and snorted. 'Good God, do you think I've been blackmailing him? You're very wide of the mark. Do I look like a blackmailer?'

'Not at all.' She looked as though she would be capable of anything she set her mind to, in fact, but he could hardly say that.

'I didn't ask him for money – it was his idea. If you ask him, he'll tell you. He sends it because he wants to. And it's for Jonathon, not me.'

'Jonathon?'

She gestured with her head towards the bedroom. 'Jonathon is our son – Dick's and mine.'

Thicker and thicker, Slider thought. The wife who couldn't, the London mistress who'd like to, and the Brighton mistress who had. And this one was one hell of a tough cookie. She'd give Neal trouble all right, though it would probably not be of the expected sort.

She had been reading Slider's face the while, and now said with a firmness he would not have liked to have to refuse, 'You'd better tell me what all this is about. Why are you asking questions about Dick and me?'

'I'm afraid I have some bad news for you,' he said in the time-honoured formula, and paused for a moment for the implication to sink in. 'I'm sorry to have to tell you that Mr Neal was killed last Monday.'

She drew a short breath, and her eyes searched his face busily. 'What do you mean, killed? You mean murdered?'

'I'm afraid so.'

'How?' she said urgently. 'How did they do it?'

'He was suffocated with a plastic bag.'

'Oh good God!' It was a genuine cry of pity, sprung out of her by an unwelcome instant of clear imagination. He felt obliged to try to ease it for her.

'He was very drunk at the time. I don't think he would really have known what was going on, if that helps at all.'

'I don't know,' she said seriously. 'I don't know if it does.' She shivered, a curious reaction, but one he'd seen before. 'I've never had to think about something like this before. I

100

can't take it in. He's dead? Dick's dead?'

Slider nodded. 'It takes a while to sink in, I know.'

'Yes. Of course, you must have had to tell hundreds of people things like that,' she said. That was the academic intelligence still at work, he thought, still running around the farmyard, unaware that its head was off. 'How do they react? Do they cry and scream? I don't know what I should be doing.'

'It takes different people different ways,' he said. 'But most people are quiet at first, with the shock.'

'The shock, yes,' she said. 'Oh God, poor Dick!' He actually saw the next thought impinge on her. 'And what about Jonathon? Now he hasn't a father.' Her eyes were suddenly wet. Interesting, he thought, that she would cry for the child's loss, which the child could not feel, rather than her own. 'But who would do such a thing? Do you know who did it?'

'No, not yet. That's why I've come to see you – to find out as much as possible about Mr Neal's life, in the hope that it will throw some light on the business.'

'Yes, of course. Well, I'll help you if I can. But I don't really know anything about it.' She looked and sounded dazed now.

'There's no knowing what may help,' Slider said coaxingly. 'Tell me, if you will, about your relationship with Mr Neal.'

'What do you want to know?'

'Start at the beginning,' he said. 'Tell me as you would tell a friend, about you and Dick.'

'Yes,' she said, staring at the wall over his shoulder. 'Me and Dick. Well, it was one of those cases of instant attraction. We just fell for each other the moment we met. The first two weeks were like a passionate honeymoon – he was staying down in Brighton to do the campus consultancy, and after the second day he left his hotel room and moved into my digs. I wasn't here, then – I had rooms in a house on Falmer Road. Almost every instant he wasn't working we were together, and a lot of the time we were in bed. It was a very physical attraction between us,'

101

she added, looking at him to see if he was shocked by her frankness.

He nodded. 'Go on.'

'I cared for him too, of course. I wouldn't have had Jonathon otherwise. We were always good friends.'

'But?'

She looked at him.

'It sounded as if you were going to add a "but",' Slider said.

She lifted her shoulders. 'He was—' she hesitated. 'I don't know quite how to put it. At first, we both just wanted what we had. He came to Brighton pretty regularly on business, and when he did, he stayed here, and we had a wonderful time together. But as time went on, he started to want more out of the relationship. Something more continuous, more—' she hesitated again. 'Intrusive.'

It seemed a curious choice of word. 'Did he want to marry you?' Slider asked.

She didn't seem to like it plain and simple. 'I suppose so. I suppose that's what you'd call it. He wanted to be with me all the time, but I had my own life. I'd finished my post-grad course and started teaching, and I had different interests from him, different friends and so on, and Dick didn't fit in with that. I loved seeing him when he was here, but—'

'I understand.'

'Do you?' she said sharply.

Slider nodded, but didn't elaborate. Dick Neal the great cocksman, the hard-drinking, swashbuckling rep, served a need for her, but he was not the sort of man a woman like her could think of marrying. He probably didn't go down too well with her academic friends, and may have made his resentment of her intellectual life plain. Slider could imagine only too well her taking Neal to a university drinks-and-shop-talk party, and Neal, feeling left out and imagining everyone was sneering at him, getting drunk and being outrageous to get his own back. It took a strong man to cope with a woman who was his intellectual superior.

'I think he loved me more than I loved him. And then

there was his wife.' She looked at him with the faint defiance of the recent religious convert, someone about to impart something they knew was claptrap, but that they badly wanted to believe in. 'I wasn't about to take him away from her. Women are a sisterhood. We have to stick together, not betray each other by playing the game the men's way.'

'Hadn't you already done that?' Slider asked mildly.

'Of course not. The bit of him I had, she wouldn't have got anyway. But what she had – marriage, him coming home to her, the certainty – that's what she wanted, and I wouldn't take it from her.'

Well, there was a certain amount of truth in that, Slider thought, albeit reluctantly, for she pronounced it with the readiness of dogma, which of course always got up the recipient's nose. 'And what about the baby? Whose idea was that?'

She shrugged. 'Both, really. Dick actually mentioned it first, but I'd already been thinking I'd like a child. With my job it was perfectly easy to fit it in, with the long vacation and everything, and it suited me that Dick was tied up with someone else. And on his side – well, his wife couldn't have children, so unless he divorced her, this was his only solution. Of course, I had to get him to understand that I wouldn't give up my independence. Our relationship was to stay the same, with or without a child.'

'Did he accept that?'

'Not at first. And even after he agreed, he still went back on it, first when he knew I was definitely pregnant, and then again when Jonathon was born. He wanted to move in with us, and be a proper father, as he put it, but I wouldn't have that. We had a bargain, and he had to stick to it. I was perfectly willing to acknowledge him as the father, and to allow him to visit whenever he wanted, but I wasn't going to be taken over, or to give him legal rights over Jonathon.'

My God, thought Slider, the biter bit. After being will o' the wisp to God knew how many women, Neal suddenly found one who wouldn't let him tie himself down when he actually wanted to.

'I think that's why he started to send the money,' she

continued. 'To feel that he had some kind of hold on us. He couldn't understand, you see, that the simple fact of his physical relationship to Jonathon should be enough. Jonathon has half his genes, but he kept whingeing because his name wasn't on the birth certificate, and I wouldn't let him come and live with me.'

'Did you quarrel about it?'

'Sometimes. He had a quick temper.'

'Was he violent? Did he threaten you?'

'God, no! Well, only over the phone, when he was drunk. He drank too much – but I suppose you know that. And then he'd get maudlin and sentimental. I hated that most of all. Stupid, drunken, weepy phone calls at one and two in the morning, waking me up, disturbing the baby—' She made a sound of disgust, and then her face froze, as she remembered. 'And now he's dead,' she said blankly. 'Oh my God, I didn't believe him. I thought it was just another of his tricks, to get my sympathy.' She shut up abruptly, thinking hard.

'*What* was one of his tricks?' Slider asked.

The blank look continued, the sort of internally-preoccupied look of someone at a dinner party who has got a raspberry pip stuck between their teeth and is trying to work it loose with their tongue without anyone's noticing.

'Miss Young, what didn't you believe?'

She focused on him. 'He phoned me on Saturday. It was about three in the afternoon – closing time, you see – so I assumed he was drunk. He sounded peculiar—'

'In what way, peculiar?'

'Well, I don't know. As if he was drunk, I suppose. Laughing in an idiotic way, when there wasn't anything to laugh at, saying stupid things.'

'What things?'

'Well, he started off saying that someone was trying to kill him.'

Slider's attention sharpened. 'Yes?'

'He said it, and then laughed as if he didn't mean it, or didn't want me to think he meant it. I told him not to be stupid, assuming—' she looked at him appealingly.

'That he was drunk, yes. Well, you would, wouldn't you?'

She took it as a criticism. 'He'd said stupid things before when he was drunk. Threatening suicide, for instance.'

'Yes, I understand. Did he say who it was that wanted to kill him?'

She shook her head. 'He said he'd been having lunch with an old friend, and *he'd* said someone was out to kill him, that's all. And then he started to get maudlin, whining that I wouldn't care if he was dead, and Jonathon would never know his face, and – well, you can imagine.'

'Yes,' Slider said absently. 'Did he say who the friend was, that he lunched with?' Shake of the head. 'Not a name? Or where he knew him from? Nothing about him at all? Or why anyone would want to kill him?'

'No,' she said. She raised her eyes to him guiltily. 'I wish I'd asked him now. If I'd known there was anything in it, I'd have got it all out of him. But I was annoyed, and I thought he was being stupid, and – how was I to know?'

Guilt, regret, wish-I'd-been-nicer-to-him – it was a bugger, especially when mixed with the irritation one naturally felt towards a person who loved you more than you loved them.

'It wasn't your fault,' Slider said. 'But if you have any idea at all about who might have had a grudge against him, I'd be grateful to hear it. You probably knew him better than anyone, and you seem to me to be an observant and intelligent person.' No harm in a bit of flannel. 'Did he have any enemies? Was he involved in anything, or with anyone, that might lead him into danger?'

'No,' she said slowly, 'but thinking about it, there was something about him. I'd noticed it before. A sort of – melancholy. As if he'd gone through something at some time in his life which had made him—' She hesitated. 'How can I put it? Desperate?' She frowned, thinking. 'You know the American soldiers who came back from Vietnam, who'd seen such terrible things they couldn't adjust to normal life? A bit like that. I think something really bad had happened to him, so that afterwards he could never really come to grips with life.'

'He seemed to want to come to grips with you and Jonathon.'

'With Jonathon, maybe. I think perhaps he hoped the baby would make things all right for him again. But I've often thought that the way he drank, and gambled, and ran after women – it wasn't just me, you know, by any means – was a sign of a deep unhappiness in him.'

'It often is,' Slider agreed cautiously. 'But what has that to do with this threat on his life?'

'Well, I don't know, of course,' she said with faint irritation. 'But if he had some secret bad thing in his past life, they may be connected. In fact,' she added with a burst of academic logic, 'I should think they'd pretty well have to be, wouldn't they? I mean, ordinary people don't get murdered in mysterious circumstances, do they?'

'How do you know the circumstances were mysterious?' he asked, secretly amused.

She eyed him acutely. 'I may read a lot of detective novels, but I do know that in real life the vast majority of murders are carried out by the victim's nearest and dearest, usually the husband or wife. Isn't that so?'

'Yes,' he said, broadly.

'And if it was Betty Neal that killed him, you'd know.' She shook her head suddenly. 'Listen to me talking! I just can't take it in, you know, that it's *Dick* we're talking about. Ordinary peopole don't get murdered, not people one knows. It can't be true. He'll ring me up in a minute to tell me he's coming down tomorrow and can I meet him for lunch.'

A few questions later, Slider stood to go. 'If you think of anything, anything at all, however trivial it seems,' he began, giving her his card.

'Yes, I'll call you,' she finished for him.

'Especially if you have any idea who the friend he met on Saturday might be.'

'I'll try to think. But I'm sure he didn't say who it was.'

Slider eyed her curiously. 'Do you think he believed it – the threat?'

'Yes,' she said. 'Looking back, yes, I think he did. That

nervous laughter – I thought it was drink, but now—' She shook her head.

'Was that the last time you spoke to him?'

'No, he phoned me on Sunday, to tell me he was sending me a cheque for Jonathon.'

'How did he sound?'

'Oh, just ordinary. A bit tired, perhaps. Not upset. We chatted a bit, but it wasn't a long call. He sounded rather preoccupied.'

'Did the cheque arrive?'

'Yes, on Tuesday. It was larger than usual.' She sighed. 'I paid it in on my way to work. I suppose it won't go through, though. They'll have frozen his bank account, won't they?'

'Yes,' said Slider, 'I expect so.' They moved towards the door. 'Is there someone you can telephone, a friend or relative who can come and be with you? You probably shouldn't be alone.'

'I'll be all right,' she said almost absently. 'I've lots of friends. It's nice of you to worry, though,' she added with faint surprise. The caring face of the Met, he thought. Well, we are wonderful, of course – and compared with the toughs of Sussex Constabulary, we're furry white bunny rabbits.

'By the way,' he said, remembering at the last moment, 'does the word *mouthwash* mean anything to you?'

'You mean, other than—? No. Why?'

'You never heard Mr Neal use it?'

'No. Nothing like that.'

'Oh well, it doesn't matter,' Slider said.

The sunlit world outside beckoned him. He'd always hated basements. Catriona Young stood framed by the darkness within, overgrown and pale and fleshy like the grass you find when you lift the groundsheet after a fortnight's camping holiday. He thought of the large, pale baby, and wondered what sort of life it would have, growing up there, and with her for a mother. But then life was always a lottery, whatever you started with. The world's a wheel o' fortune, as O'Flaherty often said.

107

Joanna was leaning on the railings, staring at the sea. The sun was almost horizontal, and her eyes were screwed up against the dazzle.

'Hullo! How was the Brighton Belle?'

'Surprising.'

'How?'

Slider picked one thing from the many. 'She has a baby.'

'Crikey,' said Joanna after some silence. She turned her back on the sea, hitched herself up onto the top rail, tucked her feet behind the lower one for stability, and gave him her whole attention.

He placed his hands one either side of her and longed to bury himself in her up to his ears. She was so warm and furry and comfortable, like a favourite stuffed toy. She looked as though she'd never been near a basement in her life. He just wanted to grab handfuls of her and shove them in every available pocket in case of famine later.

Instead he told her about Catriona Young, and she listened with that childlike capacity of hers to concentrate absolutely on the thing before her.

'She sounds utterly creepy. I begin to feel almost sorry for Tricky Dicky,' she said at the end.

'Only begin to? He seems to me to have been a sad, pathetic creature.'

'Yes, but pathetic creatures so often cost other people dear.'

'I think in the case of Catriona Young, she was using him more than he was using her. She wanted a baby without the complications of marriage, and poor old Dick Neal was the sucker she picked on.'

'What's she called Catriona for anyway?' Joanna said with a belated burst of indignation. 'Is she Scottish, or Irish?'

'She didn't seem to be.'

'Well then! Stupid woman.'

'It probably wasn't her choice,' he said, spreading reason on her slice of rough wholemeal irrationality.

'I can see you didn't like her. Are you lining her up for suspect?'

'My not liking her doesn't make her a murderer. She's a lecturer in economics—'

'Same thing, then,' Joanna nodded reasonably. She jumped down from the rail and shoved a hand through his arm. 'Let's walk, I'm getting cold. What makes her a suspect?'

'Nothing really. I don't know. Only that some of her reactions didn't quite ring true. I don't think she was quite surprised enough that he was dead, for one thing.'

Joanna pressed his arm. 'If she's intelligent, as you say she is, she'd probably guessed before you told her.'

'Yes. And I suppose it must be difficult to behave naturally if you believe someone's analysing your every gesture.'

'Like Basil Fawlty and the psychiatrists. Do you think she was right that Neal had a dire secret in his past?'

'If he did, his wife doesn't seem to know about it.'

'Perhaps it was before he met her.'

'They were married fifteen years. That's going back a hell of a long way.'

'Pasts often do,' she pointed out.

'Still, wouldn't he have told her about it? The wife of his bosom?'

'Mrs Neal doesn't sound as if she ever was the wife of his bosom – of his convenience, more like. Besides, if he was donning the motley to hide a broken heart, he wouldn't tell anyone, least of all the person closest to him. And the sort of loud talking, loud laughing, hard drinking, one-of-the-boys types are usually covering up a deep chasm inside. Don't you think it sounds as if there was something rather desperate about the way he savaged the pleasures of life?'

'That's pretty well what Catriona Young said,' Slider said.

'I expect we read the same sauce bottles. Have you finished here now?'

'Yes, I think so.'

109

'Then let's get the car and head off, and find a country pub. We'll have a lovely pint of Harveys, and something nice and simple and English to eat, and then we'll go home and make wild passionate love on the hearthrug. How does that sound?'

'How did you get to be such an abandoned hussy?' he asked sternly.

'I practised. Nothing important was ever achieved without practice.'

'Is being abandoned important?'

'It'll save your life,' she advised him seriously.

CHAPTER EIGHT

Rather Grimm

YOU CERTAINLY GOT TO TRAVEL in this job, Atherton thought as he cruised along the A40 interstate freeway back towards Hanger Lane. Yesterday, Park Royal – today, Perivale! A convertible Porsche which hadn't noticed that the motorway had run out shot past him doing about a hundred and twenty. It had a notice in the rear window which said *My other car is also a Porsche.* Atherton had a brief spasm of longing for a uniform and a flashing blue light. Strange how motoring brought out the beast in everyone.

Perivale. What a magical name. The Vale of the Peris. He imagined Persian houris drifting gracefully through a smiling green valley in the heart of the English countryside. Then he looked at the arterial road hinterland around him and thought, perhaps not. There were other words beginning with those four letters. Perineum, for instance; peristalsis. Yes, that was getting closer. And perilous. Perhaps that was the closest, at least as far as Richard Neal had been concerned. Why couldn't the horrible little man have conducted his amours in Paris or Picardy? To be dingy in a dingy place was unfair on those who came after you.

It was Norma who had found it, as she toiled through another drawerful of Nealorabilia. 'Jim? Come and have a look at this.'

A billydoo, it was, from someone signing herself 'Pet' on mauve paper with a little decoration of violets in the top right-hand corner. Looking over Norma's shoulder, Atherton read it aloud.

'*Dearest Dickie, I waited until after ten, but you never showed up. I hope your all right* – sic.'

'Quite,' said Norma.

'Oh, that too,' said Atherton, '*I suppose something happening to stop you coming, well these things happen, as long as you still feel the same about me. I still feel the same about you. If you want to see me again, give me a ring at home but if Dave answers just say wrong number or something. Don't get chatting because it makes me jealous when he can talk to you and I can't. But not Monday, that's when I go to the hairdressers, must keep myself looking beautiful for you, ha ha! Yours ever, Pet.* Yeuch!'

'Friend Neal sure knew how to pick 'em.'

'Presumably she had other compensatory qualities,' Atherton said. 'But why did he keep this dangerous missive? It could hardly have been sentiment.'

Norma produced the envelope and turned it over. Written at an angle across the back was a telephone and extension number and *B. Wiseman, 2.30 Monday 12th.*

'I've tried the number, and it's a department of the civil service in Holborn,' said Norma. 'Wiseman is the establishments officer. The glamorous Pet sent this to Neal at work – see the address? – and presumably he took a phone call around the same time and wrote down the appointment on the first thing that came to hand.'

'Yes, that sounds suitably haphazard,' said Atherton. 'The man was suicidally careless.'

'I thought you might want to follow it up,' Norma said. 'If Pet of the Purple Prose was a current complication, she might know something about his movements and/or his friends.'

'It could be recent. There was a Monday the twelfth last month,' Atherton noted. 'Unfortunately, the lady didn't write her address at the top of the page, not even on the outside of the envelope in the Post Office Approved manner.'

Norma gave him a withering look. 'Don't be a stiff. If he knew Dave well enough for her to worry he might get chatting, he probably knew them as a couple, and if he did, there's at least a sporting chance that Mrs N knew them as well.'

'True, oh queen. I'll give it a whack.'

Mrs Neal's reaction was unexpectedly violent. 'That slut! I don't want to talk about her! Trying to turn me against my own husband. And trying to make trouble between Dick and Dave.'

'How did she do that?'

'She forced herself on him like a common – well, the word's too good for her! He was always a soft-hearted man, too soft. He didn't like hurting anyone's feelings, and she knew it. She made it very difficult for him, too, with him and Dave being friends. But there was nothing in it as far as Dick was concerned – I knew that. She was just a troublemaker. I could see it at a glance.'

'You met her, did you?' Atherton asked when he could get a word in.

'She came round to the house,' Mrs Neal admitted, half angry, half sulky. 'Painted hag, all in mauve, cheap jewellery, and hair out of a bottle if I know anything about it. She came banging on the door one evening, shouting and sobbing – had the neighbours at their windows right up and down the street. Threatening to kill herself. Dick had to go out there and quieten her down, or we'd have had the police round. He put her in his car and drove her home, and that was the end of that.'

'Your husband had been having an affair with her?'

'He had not!' she said indignantly. 'That was just what she said, trying to get attention. I could guess how it happened. She was attracted to him – most women were – and threw herself at him, and when he turned her down, she got mad and tried to get her own back by making trouble for him. I told her I knew my husband a little better than to think he'd do something like that. I thought she was mentally unbalanced actually. I told Dick he ought to warn Dave about her, but he didn't want to upset him, because he said Dave thought the world of her. Anyway, he seemed to have put her off all right, because we never heard another thing out of her.'

'So Dave was a friend of your husband's? Did they see a lot of each other?'

'I don't know. I don't think so. They used to meet for drinks and things, and they played golf together up at the club sometimes.' Oh? thought Atherton. 'They worked together years ago, in insurance. Dave's a rep at Newbury's now.'

'You've never mentioned him before,' Atherton said patiently. 'When we asked you about your husband's friends—'

'He had so many,' she said impatiently. 'Mostly they were just like Dave – people he'd worked with, and met for drinks now and then. I can't remember them all. I told you, everyone liked him.' Her voice wavered, and recovered. 'I don't think he saw much of Dave after that woman made her little scene. He didn't mention him at home. I suppose he'd have felt embarrassed about it.'

'And when was it, exactly, that Mrs Collins came round to your house?'

'Ages ago. I don't remember. Well, let me think a minute. I suppose it would be about six months ago. Some time in October, or November. No October. I'm almost sure.'

Atherton found the house, an end-of-terrace in Jubilee Road, its small front garden concreted over to make a hard standing, and an overweight Cyprian cat sitting on the windowsill of the front bay. Atherton parked, and stepped out into the afternoon street. The spring air was sharp with the smell of car exhaust and dog shit, the traffic on the Western Avenue crooned in the background, and overhead a jumbo jet headed for Heathrow, with another already in sight, two minutes behind. This, then, was Perivale. He started towards the front door, and the Cyprian cat gave him an affronted look, leapt off the windowsill and fled under the privet with a flash of striped trousers.

The window frames were painted mauve and the door was glossy dark purple. The walls were clad in imitation York stone, and the door bell chimed three and a half bars of *There's No Place Like Home*. This place has everything, Atherton thought, except a brass knocker in the shape of a Cornish piskie. After a short pause Mrs Collins opened the door. She brightened when she saw him. She was plump in an inviting sort of way, her body coaxed into a clinging mauve jersey dress and her feet into ambitiously high heels. She had a rather lumpy, soaked face, too much makeup, short hennaed curls, and gold hoop earrings which caught the light as she reached up automatically to touch her hair.

'Hullo, love,' she said in a friendly manner. She had large teeth, which pushed her lips from underneath into fashionable fullness. 'If it's double glazing, I'm afraid you're out of luck – we've already got it on order. We're having the whole house done.'

I knew it, Atherton thought. He was delighted, however, at this ready identification of him as a salesman. He must congratulate his tailor. 'Mrs Collins? Mrs "Pet" Collins?'

She dimpled. 'Silly name, isn't it? My mother named me after Petula Clark. She was quite a star when I was a born.'

Ungenerous to Miss Clark, Atherton thought. He flashed his brief and her smile wavered and sank to be replaced by wariness.

'I understand you and your husband were friends of Richard Neal?' he said pleasantly. 'May I come in for a moment? I'd like to ask you a few questions.'

She was unexpectedly quick on the uptake. 'What d'you mean, "were"? What's happened? Has there been an accident?' She fell back a step as if he'd hit her, and her mouth fell open shapelessly. 'Omigod, he's dead, isn't he? Dave's killed him! I knew it, I knew it would happen! Oh Jesus, I warned him!'

And before Atherton could speak, she flung back her head and howled like a bereaved she-wolf.

*

It was a long time before he could calm her down enough to talk to him, and then she didn't make much sense. At the table in the kitchen (mauve paintwork and textured vinyl wallpaper with a closely-repeated pattern of violets) she sobbed until her false eyelashes soaked off, while Atherton made her a cup of tea and tried to sort fact from the fiction in her overwrought outpourings.

It seemed that Dick Neal and Dave Collins were closer friends than Mrs Neal supposed. Collins was older than Neal, something of a father-figure to him; he had been in some way instrumental in getting Neal the Omniflamme job, or at least had pointed him in that direction. Atherton gathered Collins thought Neal had reason to be grateful to him, and perhaps didn't show it enough. Mrs C was equivocal on the point.

Pet was Collins's second wife. The first Mrs Collins emerged briefly from the tirade as 'that bitch', whose occupancy of the former marital home in Harrow, along with the two children of the marriage, had led to her successor's having to make do with 'this rat-box' instead of the semi she desired and properly deserved.

Atherton gathered Pet's disappointment with Collins sprang from his failure to provide for her both financially and sexually, and that she had fallen pretty heavily for Neal when she first met him – though that was not quite the way she presented it. In her version Neal had made all the running, and her beleaguered virtue had succumbed reluctantly to strenuous pleading one day on the marital sofa when he had called round to see Dave and Dave was not in.

Perhaps Mrs Neal's outrage at the suggestion that anything had been going on between Dick and Pet was not entirely misplaced. Reading between the lines, Atherton guessed that Neal had slipped Mrs Collins a spare length once in the heat of the moment, and afterwards, horrified at his own weakness and perfidy, had tried to convince her that it was a one-off aberration. Pet had then thrown a

116

mega-wobbly, had gone round to his house to give him a sample of the kind of scene she was prepared to make if he pulled the plug on her, and had forced him to go on servicing her by threatening to tell her husband all about it.

As her makeup was rubbed and washed off by her grief, Atherton could see that it had been concealing a fading but extensive bruise on the side of her face. That bumpy look of hers was probably the long-term effect of being knocked about. It looked as though the amiable Dave Collins might not be averse to the odd smack in the puss when his lovely mate got on his tits.

The division between men who hit women, and men who didn't, was absolute, but if Neal was Collins's friend, he must surely have known what Collins was capable of. Atherton wondered a little, in that case, that he could have believed Mrs C would spill the beans. Surely it would have been worse for her than for him if she had? On the other hand, all the evidence was that Neal was dedicated to the quiet life and the avoidance of strife, even to the point of giving his private parts the sort of punishment few men dared even to dream about.

It was clear, however, that the affair certainly did not end back in October. Neal had been banging his purple partner as lately as a week ago; and the letter Norma had found had indeed been sent last month, to keep old Dick up to the mark after a failure to deliver.

It was also clear that despite Mrs Collins's fear that her husband would find out and beat Neal up, she'd had no intention of giving up the relationship. Was that the measure of her grave stupidity, or her passionate devotion to Neal's active member? Or had she just believed that her luck would hold up for ever?

The answering-machine was flashing when they got back to Joanna's flat.

'Bet it's for you,' she said resignedly, and it was: a request to ring Atherton at the station. 'I'll go and make

117

some coffee,' Joanna said. 'Or would you like another drink?'

'Let's make a pact about drinking,' Slider said, dialling.

'Okay.'

'Let's never stop.'

'Right,' she said, departing.

Atherton answered. 'Ah, you're back. Any luck?'

'Yes and no. What are you still doing there?'

'Stacking up some overtime. Polish has gone home, and I've got no-one to play with. There've been some developments here. Since you're at Joanna's, why don't I come straight around, and we can have a mutual debriefing session.'

'I'll have to check with Joanna . . . Jo? Atherton wants to come over and take your knickers off.'

'Fine by me,' she called back from the kitchen.

Half an hour later they were sitting around the fire with thick cheese sandwiches and glasses of malt whisky. Joanna was kneeling in the hearth holding a sheet of newspaper over the fireplace to hurry up the flames.

Atherton sat on the shabby old chesterfield and pondered the surrealist shape of the sandwich on his plate. 'You're the only person in the world I know apart from me who doesn't have sliced bread,' he said to Joanna.

'I was in a hurry,' she protested. 'You can't cut bread straight if you rush it.'

'Oh, I wasn't complaining. I'm all for novelty. And I must say it's a novel experience to be eating anything without Oedipus patting my hand to see what it is—'

'He's the paw you have always with you,' Joanna said.

'—or trying to draw attention to himself by tiptoeing through the china on the mantelpiece with that wilful smile on his face, like a cross between Olga Korbut and a Visigoth.'

'But you know perfectly well he can walk the whole way along without knocking anything off,' she said. 'I've seen him do it.'

'Yes, but only if he wants to. He knows I know what he can do. It's a subtle form of blackmail.'

118

'I suppose that's why you call him Oedipus?'

'Uh?'

'Because he wrecks.'

'Talking of blackmail,' Atherton said firmly, turning to the patient Slider, 'how about casting this Catriona Young in the role of suspect?'

'She wasn't blackmailing Neal. The money was his idea – his way of keeping a hold on her and the baby,' said Slider.

'So she says,' Atherton pointed out. 'But we've only got her word for it. And no jury would ever believe it. Far more likely that she wanted him to marry her, and he refused.'

'I see, all women long to be married, is that it?' Joanna enquired ironically over her shoulder. 'God, you men are so arrogant!'

'Even if she was blackmailing him,' Slider intervened, 'that doesn't give her a reason to kill him. Rather the opposite.'

'If what she says was true,' Joanna said, folding up the paper now that the fire was leaping, 'that she wanted the baby without the man, and he was trying to muscle in on the arrangement, she might well hate him.' She moved over and sat down at Slider's feet, leaning an elbow on his knee to aid thought. 'A man like that would have been a real threat to her tranquillity – and the more so since he had a perfectly legitimate reason to come visiting. She'd probably feel she oughtn't to cut the child off from its father.'

'Yes, I see,' Atherton said, picking up the thread happily. 'He wasn't in her class. He was her bit of rough, and that was very nice thank you, but she didn't want him hanging around the campus embarrassing her in front of her friends. Or lurking about the house with a chip on his shoulder every time she wanted to do something a bit more mentally challenging than going down the pub for a pint.'

'It wasn't a problem that was going to go away,' Joanna said. 'It could only get worse, as long as Neal lived.'

'So she just took him out,' Atherton concluded. 'God, you women are so ruthless!'

'Stop clowning,' said Joanna. 'We're only talking about logical possibilities. The question is, is she that ruthless? She frightened you, didn't she, Bill?'

'Did she?' Atherton asked with interest.

'She struck me as a powerful and determined woman,' Slider said doubtfully. 'There was something about her that made me nervous.'

'But then you like your women old-fashioned,' Atherton said. 'More to the point, has she got an alibi?'

'She was at home alone all Sunday afternoon and evening. No witnesses.'

'She also has a small baby,' Joanna pointed out. 'What would she do with that when she went out a-murdering?'

'She could put it to sleep on the back seat of the car,' Atherton said easily.

'Suppose it woke up?'

'She could have given it something to make it sleep.'

'Oh come on!' Joanna protested. 'Drugging the baby while she murdered its father?'

Atherton smiled at her. 'These are only logical possibilities we're talking about. But she is tempting as the suspect in one particular way – she's a woman.'

'So are Mrs Neal and Jacqui Turner.'

'Yes, but Catriona Young is intelligent – would you say even ingenious, Bill? – and reads a lot of detective fiction,' said Atherton. 'I've always fancied a woman for the murderer. The cover-up was so absurdly elaborate and cruel. No man would ever think up something like that.'

'Quote Kipling now,' Joanna warned, 'and you're a dead man.'

'That's all very well,' said Slider, passing, 'but what about this story that he phoned her on Saturday afternoon and told her that someone wanted to kill him?'

Atherton shrugged. 'There you are, you see – ridiculously melodramatic! Trying to set up a false trail. A mysterious warning, an unknown assailant, a deep secret in his past. All you need is the country-house weekend and the sealed room, and you've got the whole Cluedo set.'

'The bit about having lunch with an old friend ties in with what Jacqui Turner said,' Slider pointed out.

'There's no reason why that shouldn't have been true.

Or why she shouldn't have known about it. She may have just decided to use it to make her own story more convincing.'

'So where did he phone her from? He wasn't at home on Saturday afternoon, and there's no telephone in Gorgeous's small flat.'

'From the pub, before he left, perhaps,' Atherton said.

Joanna put in, 'But you've only got the bag lady's word for it that he went to that flat. He could have been anywhere really, couldn't he?'

'Ah, well, now we come to this afternoon's developments,' Atherton said. 'We got the rest of the itemised calls in from BT. Unfortunately, none of the Sunday ones show up. They only list anything over ten units, and you get a lot of time for ten units on a Sunday, even long distance. He could have made any number of shortish calls, and we'd be none the wiser. But he did make one operator-assisted call on Sunday, at 11.17, which of course is listed. And the number belongs to the public call-box outside Gorgeous George's car lot.'

'Helen Woodman,' said Slider happily.

'Who?' said Joanna.

'The red-headed tart. That was the name she gave Gorgeous George.'

'Exactly. Gorgeous George said she suddenly changed her mind about staying and handed him back the key, on Sunday morning at about half past eleven. Suppose Neal was calling her – at a prearranged time, I suppose – to agree a meet? The tart, having set him up for the murderer, has done her bit, and legs it to establish her alibi elsewhere—'

'I thought you said you fancied a woman for the murderer,' Joanna objected.

'So I did,' Atherton said benignly. 'Well, why shouldn't Woodman have been a friend of Catriona Young? These man-haters like to stick together, don't they? They were probably lesbians—'

'Why couldn't they be one and the same?' Joanna provoked back. 'How many tall, strong, red-haired women do you want in your story?'

121

'It's a nice idea,' Atherton said, 'but the baby's a bit of a handicap there. And what about her job? She couldn't be absent from that for three weeks, could she?'

'Gorgeous George said she wasn't there all the time. And university lecturers have lots of time when they're not actually teaching. Some of them only do a few tutorials a week, and the rest of the time they could be absolutely anywhere.'

'This is all just fairy stories,' Slider said, bringing them firmly down to earth. 'We haven't got a scrap of evidence against anyone.'

'True,' Atherton allowed. 'But at least Catriona Young has a possible motive and no apparent alibi. We could at least have a look at her, couldn't we? Map her movements for the last three weeks, find out if she leaves the baby with anyone, if anyone phoned her on Sunday, and so on.'

'Yes, all right. I'll send Polish down there to exercise her tact.'

'Oh no, not Polish! I'm still working on her. How am I ever going to get her into bed if you keep sending her out of Town?'

'Polish or no-one,' Slider said firmly. 'Make your mind up.'

'Oh all right. Catriona Young isn't a suspect, if you insist,' said Atherton. 'I've got something better for you, anyway. How would you like a man-eating woman with a violent and potentially jealous husband?'

'Depends how attractive she is,' Slider said judiciously.

'She has a passion for mauve and purple – possibly to match her bruises – and appalling punctuation,' said Atherton, and told them about the Collins complication.

At the end of it, Slider said, 'Now I really am sorry for Tricky Dicky. Good God, the man was in every sort of trouble!'

'Right! He had Jacqui Turner taking a job at his office and expecting him to marry her; Catriona Young with his firstborn son, refusing to marry him; his long-suffering wife forgiving him every time he came home; and the purple python with a stranglehold on his pod, threatening to tell his best friend all about it if he didn't perform like a man. If only he'd humped for charity,' Atherton said, 'he could've made Bob Geldof look like Attila the Hun.'

'He does, a bit,' said Joanna.

'It's no wonder his commission had dwindled to nothing,' Slider concluded. 'The poor man could hardly have had time to go to work.'

'Oh, that's typical,' Joanna said. 'Pity the man, of course. What about all the women he was deceiving?'

'The only woman he was deceiving was Turner – the others knew about him.'

'And he wasn't really deceiving her,' Atherton put in. 'She was deceiving herself. She knew he was married, after all.'

There was a short, appalled silence as each of them hoped neither of the others would make the connection; and Atherton hurried on, 'And you've missed out one: presumably he was having to fit in the red-headed tart as well. He must have longed for death at times – it was the only way he'd get any sleep.'

Joanna struggled only for a moment, and then laughed. 'You are an 'orrible bastard, Jim Atherton!'

'I aim to please. But look here, Guv, this is much more promising, isn't it?'

'I thought you wanted a woman for the murderer?' Joanna interrupted.

'That was just a joke. I can't really see a woman killing poor old Neal, especially in such a revolting way. Screw the poor bugger to death, yes, but setting him up like that in that motel room – that was the work of a nasty twisted mind, and I'd be loath to think any woman could be so beastly.'

Joanna leaned across and patted him. 'You're a nice old-fashioned thing underneath, aren't you? And quite ashamed of your snips and snails and puppy-dog tails, like all men. You all carry such a load of guilt about with you, it's heartbreaking.'

'In the case of Neal, he had plenty to feel guilty about,' Atherton said, sidestepping the analysis. 'Especially with

Petula Collins, his friend's wife – maybe his best friend's wife. I think we ought to look into it, don't you, Guv? I mean, dear old sexual jealousy is a nice, comprehensive motive; and Mrs C says that Collins and Neal used to drink together at the Shamrock Club in Fulham Palace Road, which is not a hundred miles from the motel.'

'Hmm. Beevers was right, then, about the club syndrome. But this isn't a nice, comprehensible murder, don't forget,' said Slider. 'Neal wasn't shot, or knifed, or bludgeoned to death in the heat of an argument. And why would a jealous husband do the roping and wiring? That doesn't fit in.'

Atherton would not be cheated of his prey. 'No, it makes sense. Look, Mrs C hinted that Collins was a bit short-staffed in the men's department. She also apparently nagged him about not providing her with the wordly goods, nagged him until he walloped her in fact – she had the remains of a black eye when I spoke to her. Then there's his mate, Dick Neal, who not only lived in a gorgeous detached bungalow in Pinner, and whose wife is dripping in baubles and bangles, but who is known as the leading pork purveyor of the western world. When Collins discovers that said friend has had it in for him, as the saying goes, his rage might well be mighty. And what better revenge, having murdered said conjugal bandit, than to set him up for posterity as the lowliest and most pathetic sort of sexual inadequate?'

He drew breath, rubbing the back of his left hand with the fingers of his right as he viewed his own story with growing enthusiasm. 'In fact, it's the only answer that does make sense. If it wasn't some form of exquisite revenge, then what *was* all that sexual strangulation set-up for? Because as a scent-thrower, it was a wash-out.'

Slider contemplated the scenario. 'Then who was the red-headed tart?'

Atherton shrugged generously. 'Just another bird he was jumping.'

'And the man he met on Saturday? Who said someone wanted to kill him?'

'Just another drinking-mate. We know he was well-known on that ground. Why should the Saturday meet be anything to do with anything? And it's only Miss Young of the Agatha Christie fixation who says he was given a death-threat. Mrs Neal says he was perfectly normal on Sunday—'

'I don't think she's a very noticing person. Or she may be deliberately un-noticing.'

Atherton waved a hand. 'In any case, we know he had a phone call on Sunday, which he took in his study so that his wife shouldn't overhear. Say that was Collins: "You've been screwing my wife. Do you want me to come over there and make a scene in front of Betty, or will you meet me and have it out man to man?" Neal says, okay, I'll see you later in the Shamrock, or wherever, hoping to talk his way out of it and still drive up north to make his appointments the next day. They meet, have a few drinks, Collins lets Neal think he's charmed him out of his righteous anger. They get pretty spiffed together, like old buddies. Then Time is called. Collins says, "Shame to spoil a good evening. I've got a bottle of good stuff in the car. What say we go somewhere and polish it off, and talk about old times." But where can they go? Not to Collins's house, with the wife-in-contention waiting up, probably wearing suspenders and black stockings and those knickers designed for three-legged ladies. Not to Neal's house – Mrs N would want to know why he hadn't gone to Bradford. And in any case, Neal is too bagged to drive all the way up there tonight. So they head for the motel, where Neal can sleep it off afterwards – or so he thinks. "You go in and book the room, old man," says Collins, "while I get the stuff out of the car." And that way, Pascoe only gets to see Neal.'

'And what about Neal's car?' Slider asked, fascinated.

'They leave it where it's parked, because he's too drunk to drive, and go in Collins's. Collins drops Neal at the door, and parks somewhere out in the street. Afterwards, he takes Neal's keys and goes back to bring Neal's car a bit nearer to the scene. It might look a bit odd if it was found miles away. He parks it in Rylett Road, and chucks the keys away down a drain somewhere on his way home.'

'I have to hand it to you,' Slider said when Atherton stopped. 'When it comes to weaving fiction, you're up there with the greats. Eat your heart out, Hans Andersen.'

'It all holds together,' Atherton said indignantly.

'It does,' Slider said. 'It's beautiful – but we haven't investigated Collins yet. We've only got to discover that on the night in question he was guest speaker at the annual dinner of the Ancient Order of Buffaloes, and your coach is a pumpkin.'

'His wife said he went out for a drink on Sunday night, she doesn't know where,' Atherton said triumphantly. 'She doesn't know what time he came back. And on Monday he went away on a business trip and she hasn't seen him since. She was pretty narked about it, because it was her birthday on Monday, and he didn't give her a present. Doesn't that sound as though he had something on his mind?'

'Men are always forgetting birthdays,' Joanna pointed out. 'It's a secondary sex-characteristic.'

'And we still don't know where he was on Sunday night,' Slider said patiently. 'He might have fifty witnesses to say he was in The Dog and Duck or The Froth and Elbow.'

'All right,' Atherton said with sweet reasonableness, 'if we discover he's got an alibi for the time, well and good. All I'm saying is that it's worth looking into.'

'It wasn't all you said, by a long chalk,' Slider said. 'But you can have a look at Collins. It's the best lead we've had yet.'

'It makes more sense to me than suspecting any of the women,' Joanna said.

Slider reached out and pulled a lump of her hair through his fingers. 'Of course it does. And it has the virtue that it will engage Head's attention, maybe long enough for us to find out what really did happen.'

She glanced at him, disappointed. 'You don't like the Collins theory?'

'It's not a theory, until we have some facts. And even as a

potential theory, it has its drawbacks.' He sighed. 'I wish I had Head's capacity for self-deception, then I'd be able to believe Neal committed suicide, and all would be well. If it weren't for that one piece of wire . . .' He stroked Joanna's head absently. 'He certainly had enough reason to want to get out. His life was in a sodawful mess.'

Joanna kept very still, trying to listen through his hands to what he was thinking. He was a man with a conscience, and she was hoping hard he wouldn't start to draw conclusions about his own situation from what he had discovered about Neal's. She didn't want to be given up, for however noble a reason. For his sake as well as hers, she would have to make sure that in the constant battle between his animal instincts for pleasure and self-preservation, and his better self, his better self didn't get enough of an upper hand to make them all suffer.

CHAPTER NINE

The Snake Is Living Yet

THE SHAMROCK CLUB BY DAYLIGHT was a dismal place, with a false and improbable air, like any piece of theatre scenery viewed from the wrong side. There was a depressing smell of cheap carpet about it, old cigarette smoke, stale beer, and dead illusions.

It was a simple enough proposition: a wide, shallow basement room, with a bar running along the long side, opposite the stairs down from the street. There were toilets off to one side, next to the fire exit, and tables and chairs cramming all the rest of the available space, leaving only a pathway, one waiter wide, tracking from the bar past every table and back to the bar, in a sort of ergonomically-efficient one-way system. It was impossible to go even to the bog without passing the bar both ways.

There was no stage, nor even a sound system, for this was a serious club, dedicated to drinking and talking, without any frivolous notions of entertainment. It was a man's club. There was no rule that said you couldn't bring a woman in, but it would be a strange woman who'd want to come with you a second time. There was a ladies' loo next to the gents, but it didn't have *ladies* on the door – a subtle discouragement that would be enough for any but the most brazen female.

Behind the bar was the usual long mirror, reflecting the backs of the usual optics and the bottles stacked along the glass shelves. There was an unusually large collection of different whiskies, including twenty-three Irish, some of which weren't known by name to any revenue collector on earth. There was also a surprisingly wide range of cigarettes and cigars on sale, and – sop to the younger generation and frowned upon by the older regulars, by whom women had never been regarded as a source of pleasure – a display rack of condoms, tucked away at the end beside the rows of personal pewter beer-mugs.

Along the pelmet above the mirror was a string of coloured lights, sole gesture to festivity. The bulbs were green and red and blue, but so coated in nicotine from thousand upon thousand cigarettes that the colours were virtually indistinguishable from each other. And stuck to the ceiling over the door of the gents was a brown and ghostly piece of Sellotape, with a fragment of silver lametta still adhering to it, where the experimental Christmas decorations of 1985 had been taken down, never, owing to general apathy to the notion, to be restored.

Such daylight as there was came down from above through the glass pavement bricks, and down the stairs from the street door, which had been left propped open while cleaning and delivering went on. The former task was being performed by a tiny old lady in a green nylon overall, who was being towed back and forth across the stub-and-spillage-coloured carpet by an outsize industrial-strength Hoover. The chairs had been set up onto the tables with their legs in the air, but still it was taking all her concentration to avoid hitting anything, and she didn't even notice Atherton cross her path on his way in.

A man's spirits ought to have plunged at the first step into this dismal boozerama, but Atherton, whom nothing ever depressed, was wearing his David Attenborough look, which meant that even the most loathsome invertebrate he might come across down here would have the loveliness of discovery for him. To think people actually chose to come down here, he told himself in anthropological wonder – and in their leisure hours!

'Help you, guv'nor?' A figure had popped up from behind the bar, a tall, muscular Irishman with a bright complexion, gingery, fluffy hair, and ears standing so nearly at right angles to his head that for a moment Atherton thought they were a joke pair.

He recovered himself quickly. 'Shepherd's Bush CID. Detective Sergeant Atherton.' He presented his card. The barman took and scrutinised it, as hardly anyone ever did. He looked at Atherton intently as he handed it back.

'Doesn't look much like you,' he commiserated. 'Shepherd's Bush, eh? D'you know Sergeant O'Flaherty?'

'Yes, I know him.'

'He used to come here a lot. Said we had the best pint east of Dingle.'

'Pint?'

'The Guinness,' he elucidated simply. 'Haven't seen him for a while. Tell him hello from me when you see him. Say Joey Doyle says there's one in the tap for him, any time.'

'I'll see he gets the message.' Atherton took out the photograph of Neal. 'Have a look at this, will you? I believe you know this man.'

Doyle flung the teatowel in his hand over his shoulder and took the photograph. 'Ah sure, yes, Dickie Neal,' he said at once. 'Is that right he was killed in the fire on Monday?'

'I'm afraid so,' Atherton said.

He nodded. 'They've all been talking about it. Poor feller. What did you want to know about him?'

'He was a regular here, was he?'

'He'd been coming in for years, but not on regular nights. It was just now and then.'

'When did you see him last?'

'Sunday night, it would be.' Atherton felt an inward glow. At last they were on the trail! Doyle grinned suddenly. 'Caused a bit of a stir, didn't he, coming in with a woman — the like of which had to be seen to be believed! Well, Dickie was always one for the ladies, but this one was a real cracker — and young enough to be his daughter, the owl beggar!'

'What did she look like?' Atherton asked.

'Tall girl, about twenty-five, gorgeous. Long red hair and long white legs a man could get himself tangled up in.'

There was a touch of poetry about Doyle, Atherton noted. 'And was he?'

'Tangled?' Doyle asked intelligently. '*He* was, that's for sure.'

'Not her?'

'Well, he was a lot older than her. He was a nice man, but—' An eloquent shrug. 'I don't say she was playing hard to get, but she wasn't giving it away, either. Dickie was all over her. Like the divorced man that only gets to take his little daughter out once a month. She was just sitting tight, waiting to see if there was an ice-cream in it for her.'

A graphic picture. They could do with more substance, though. 'Do you remember what time they came in?'

Doyle thought. 'Not to swear to the minute. Between eight and half past, I should think. It was still early, anyway. They came and sat at the bar to begin with, but when it started to get crowded later on they went off to bag a table before they all got taken.'

'Were you serving at the bar all evening?'

'Till about nine, then Alice came on. Then I went on the tables.'

'Did you notice what time Neal left, and who was with him?'

Doyle looked at Atherton thoughtfully. 'Is it the row you want to know about, with Dave Collins? There was nothing much to it – just a bit of a barney between friends. When Alice told them to take it outside it was pretty well all over anyway. I don't believe it would ever have come to blows, if that's what you're wondering. Not them two.'

Atherton practically quivered with triumph. 'They were friends, you say?'

'What, Dave and Dickie? Since dot. Sure they used to argue all the time, but it never meant anything.'

'But wasn't Collins a violent man?'

'Violent? Not that I know of. He had a temper, but it was more shouting and roaring, kind of style. He and Dickie were always at it. And Dickie would never have risen to it, only he wanted to show up well in front of the girl. Normally he just let Dave get on with it.'

131

'Did you hear anything of what the quarrel was about?'

Doyle raised his eyebrows. 'Everyone in the whole club heard what it was about. That's why Alice put a stop to it, in the end – people were listening instead of drinking.'

'About women, was it?' Atherton asked casually.

'Money,' said Doyle, little knowing that with that one word he had shattered a man's dreams. 'Dickie owed Dave some money, and he'd promised to pay him back that weekend, only it seems he'd lost quite a bit at Newbury, and couldn't cough up. It wouldn't have mattered, only it was Dave's missus's birthday the Monday, and he wanted to buy her something special, so he needed the cash. So he got mad. Well, Dickie didn't like being embarrassed in front of the girl – she got up the moment it started and went off to the loo and stayed there – so he got mad back. They went at it hammer and tongs for a bit, until they realised the whole bar was listening to every word, and then they started to look a bit embarrassed. Then Alice tells them to take it outside. They went out all right – glad to hide their faces, I should think – but they weren't gone more than a minute or two. Then Dickie come back in and fetched the girl, and that's the last I saw of him.'

'Neal came back in on his own?'

'Yes. He just came back down and fetched her away. She'd come back from hiding by then, d'ye see.'

'So you didn't see Collins again?'

He shook his head. 'He hasn't been in since.'

'And what time did all this happen?'

'It'd be half-tennish, something like that.'

A bit early for their purposes, Atherton thought. Still, men with a pint or two on them could stand on the street talking nonsense for an hour together, in his experience.

'You say Collins wanted the money to buy his wife a present,' he asked.

'So he said. Thought the world of her. And he was always strapped for cash, where Dickie generally sported considerable amounts. So it was a bit ironic, really, Dickie saying he couldn't pay.'

Atherton thought for a moment. 'Had you seen the girl

before, the girl Dick Neal was with?'

Doyle thought a moment before answering. 'I'm not sure, now. He never brought her in here before, but I had the feeling when they came in that I'd seen her somewhere, only I couldn't put me finger on it. No, I don't know. I don't think so.'

'If you should happen to remember, you will let me know? We'd like to have a word with her, but we haven't been able to find out so far who she is.'

'Sure, if anything occurs to me,' Doyle said. He looked at Atherton keenly. 'Is there something funny about the fire? It was an accident, wasn't it?'

'Has anybody been suggesting it wasn't?'

'No, only that it was pretty ironic, given that Dickie was a fire alarm salesman. There've been some woeful jokes going up and down the bar, I can tell you. Along the lines of "Come home to a living fire".' He shook his head. 'Some people have a narful sense of humour.'

'But Neal was liked, wasn't he?'

Doyle hesitated a telling second. 'He was liked well enough. He was one of the lads, told a lot of jokes, you know the way his sort are. He was free with his money, always bought his round and more.'

'But?'

Doyle wrinkled his nose. 'I dunno. I never got the feeling he was anyone's best buddy, d'you know what I mean? It was all front and no back – if he'd've been in trouble, they'd've looked the other way, and vice versa. Well, most people don't care, do they, as long as someone else buys the drinks? And then, he was always with a different woman. There's a lot of fellers, particularly the married ones, don't trust a man who gets on with women like that.'

'He died because he never knew these simple little rules and few,' Atherton observed.

'Come again?'

'Oh, nothing. I was just thinking, if you want sober analysis of the human condition, you should always ask a professional barman.'

'You said it, boy,' said Doyle.

When Detective Chief Superintendent Richard 'God' Head turned up at the department meeting, they all knew they were in trouble. He walked in ahead of Dickson, tall, Grecianly fair, immaculately suited, with a high enough gloss on the toecaps of his shoes to have dazzled an oncoming motorist. He strode with measured tread the length of the room, parting the throng ahead of him like Moses on a particularly good day, and Dickson surged after, massive, stony-faced and ash-strewn: a perambulating Pennine Chain smoker.

At the far end Head turned to face them, unbuttoning his jacket with an air of being about to get down to it really seriously, chaps. Slider noted gladly that their Adonis-like leader had a slight but satisfyingly incongruous paunch.

'Right,' he said, 'now we've got a lot to get through and not much time, so let's get on with it. I'm not here, I'm just a fly on the wall, so I shall leave it to Detective Superintendent Dickson to conduct this meeting in his usual way. Just ignore me, everybody. George?'

Slider winced at Head's bonhomous smile. No-one called Dickson 'George' and lived. Wisps of steam drifted out of the old mountain's ears, and the floor seemed to shift slightly underfoot.

He began. 'In the matter of the death and presumed murder of Richard Neal—'

'Yes, now are we still presuming it's murder?' Head trampled in. 'It seems to me that we've no evidence whatsoever that it wasn't just an accident. Or suicide.'

'There are a number of small points that are inconsistent, sir,' Dickson said with furious patience. 'The post mortem report suggests the hands were tied behind the back, which would be—'

'May have been,' Head interrupted. 'Only may have been.'

'And the wreckage of the room has been searched, but deceased's car keys have not been found—'

'He could have dropped them somewhere on the way to

the motel. Come on, George, you'll have to do better than that. Look, Neal was in dire financial straits, he had women chasing him right left and centre, his job was going down the toilet, the whole thing was going to blow up in his face at any minute. Isn't it much more likely that he'd simply reached the end of his tether?'

Someone, probably Anderson, snorted audibly at the choice of metaphor.

'If he went to the motel to hang himself, sir, why did he seem so cheerful to the desk clerk? And what about the wire around the genitals?'

'You can't expect a suicide to act rationally,' Head said blithely. 'And there's no knowing what sort of perversions he was used to practising. The fire team found pieces of leather straps and the remains of strop magazines in the room, which suggests he'd gone there for his own strange purposes. After all,' he flashed a titillating smile about the room, 'what else does a man go to a motel for? It ain't to get a good night's sleep, boys.'

Only Hunt laughed, and finding himself alone in his adoration, stopped abruptly.

'Now you've been on this over a week, and you haven't got the sniff of a suspect,' Head went on, 'whereas you've all the evidence you need for suicide. Unless you can show me some good reason not to, I'm going to close it down. We can't keep this sort of show running on public money for ever, you know.'

Dickson rolled flaming eyes towards Slider. 'Bill – let's hear what you got this morning.'

Slider laid out the business of the quarrel in the Shamrock Club, together with the complication of Mrs Collins's sexual appetite. 'We haven't been able to interview Collins yet, to find out what happened afterwards. We've spoken to Mrs Collins, but she doesn't know what time her husband got in that night, because she took a sleeping pill, and slept right through until half past nine the next morning, when she woke alone in the house.'

'Why haven't you interviewed Collins?' Head asked restively.

135

'He's somewhere west of Exeter at the moment, sir. We're still trying to find him. He's a commercial traveller.'

Head's head went up, and he sighted on Slider down his nose. 'It doesn't sound as if you've got anything to go on there. Your witness says the quarrel was about money, not about the wife.'

'Sir, we—'

'No, I'm sorry,' Head said. He turned to Dickson. 'My mind's made up. Unless anything better comes in today, I'm crashing this one, George. I'm sure you've got far more useful things for your men to be doing. Our clear-up rate isn't so good it can't stand improvement. So now if we can move on to other things—'

He swept the troops with his eye. 'There've been quite a few complaints from members of the public that break-in reports are not being followed up quickly enough. Now I'm sure you all realise that this is the very area where the public has most opportunity to get a good look at us and how we work . . .'

Slider avoided looking at Dickson, as one might look away from a nasty road accident. The fly on the wall, he thought ferociously, had a hell of a lot to say for itself.

Atherton arrived chez Château Rat in the middle of what was obviously a row. There was a car on the hard standing – a Ford Orion in the colour known to the trade as Gan Green, with a sticker in the back window which said *If you can read this you're TOO BLOODY CLOSE* – which told him that the master was home even before he got near enough to the purple door to hear the raised voices inside. The door chimes cut the quarrel short, and a moment later the door was opened abruptly by a furious scowl.

'David Collins?' Atherton said pleasantly, flashing his brief. The scowl disappeared, leaving behind it only a wary expression on the very tired face of a man in his mid-fifties. He was a five-niner with enough body to have gone round a six-footer comfortably, and Atherton guessed from the meat across his shoulders that he had

136

once gone in for weight training – a grave mistake when the greatest weight you were ever going to handle in real life was a pint pot. *A pint of cold water weighs a pound-and-a-quarter*, a junior school memory chanted from the back of his mind. Plus the weight of the glass, and it added up to a lot of muscle going rapidly to seed.

There was also the sneaky, soft, middle and lower spread of the long-distance car-driver, and the fullness of jowl of the beer drinker and travelling eater. A man away from the disciplines of home had no reason not to eat chips which was anywhere near as strong as his reasons for doing so.

That apart, Collins was not a bad-looking man, with strong features, a good mouth, and curly grey hair. Atherton guessed that until recently he had looked much less than his age. Now, however, he looked exhausted, and there was something about his eyes and the lines around his mouth that suggested recent shock or pain.

'That's me,' he said, in a voice without inflexion. 'What do you want?'

'I'd like to speak to you for a few minutes, sir, if that's all right?'

The hand gripping the door forbiddingly high up tightened a little, but Collins did not move to allow him in. 'What about?' he said in the same flat voice. Behind him in the passage Mrs Collins appeared with a handkerchief to her face, saw Atherton, and ducked back whence she had come. Collins must have seen the reflection of it in Atherton's eyes, for a look of faint annoyance flickered through his face, and he said, 'Was it you came round here yesterday, bothering my wife?'

'Yes. But it was really you I wanted to see,' Atherton said blandly. 'Could I come in, do you think? Unless you really want to talk to me on the doorstep?'

For a moment a number of possibilities seemed to be being debated inside Dave Collins's grey head, not all of which would have entailed Atherton's getting to draw his pension one day. Atherton felt the slight quickening of his pulses, caught that faint prickly whiff of adrenalin on the

137

air, which always reminded him of the first time as a child he had seen the lion-tamer's act at the circus. You *knew*, really, that the lions wouldn't eat the tamer; and yet there was always the distant, intriguing possibility . . .

'Come in,' said Collins at last, stepping backwards. He retreated a few steps up the passage and opened the door to the room at the front of the house, standing just beyond it so that there was no alternative route for Atherton. 'In here.' It was the sitting-room, and had the same stiffness and cold smell of unuse it would have had in Victorian times. Atherton entered obediently, and Collins turned his head over his shoulder to yell simply, 'Pet! Make some tea!' Then he shut the door behind him, closing himself and Atherton in the cage together.

'Well?' Collins said unhelpfully.

'I want to talk to you about your friend Dick Neal, Mr Collins,' said Atherton. 'I suppose you must have heard about his death by now?'

Collins took the time to gesture Atherton to sit, and sat down himself on the chair opposite. 'Yes,' he said at last. 'Pet told me. Died in a hotel fire, didn't he?'

'Mr Collins, you may have been one of the last people to see Dick Neal alive. It would be very helpful if you'd tell me exactly what happened on Sunday evening.' Collins made a non-committal shrugging movement, and Atherton went on, 'I understand you met in the Shamrock Club. Was that by arrangement?'

An extra degree of weariness seemed to enter Collins's face. 'You've been down there asking questions, have you?' he said. 'Well then, you know all about it, don't you?'

'I know you and Mr Neal had a quarrel—'

'Oh God!' It was an appeal both weary and angry. Collins laid his hands on his knees and leaned forward, searching Atherton's face. 'You're not going to try and make something out of that, are you? Look, I'll tell you the absolute truth, and I hope to God you believe me, because you don't look stupid. Dick and me were pals. I was probably his oldest friend – maybe his only real friend, because he didn't have the knack of keeping them, I'll tell

138

you that for nothing! And yes, we did have a bit of a barney down the club, but it wasn't serious. We often used to argue. It didn't mean anything.'

'Yes, someone else has said that,' Atherton said soothingly. A brief but enormous relief flickered through Collins's face, which Atherton noted with interest. 'Just tell me exactly what happened on Sunday.'

'All right.' He seemed to have decided to take the plunge. His words became more fluent, and the deadness went out of his voice as he talked. 'Dick was supposed to meet me Sunday night at The Wellington to give me back some money he owed me—'

'How much?'

'Hundred quid. He borrowed if off me nearly three weeks before, but every time I asked for it back he made some excuse. Well, a century may not be a lot to you, but it was to me, and Dick knew it. That's what I mean by not keeping his friends. He wasn't a bad bloke, just careless. He earned twice or three times what I did, *and* he didn't have a bitch of an ex-wife and two kids sucking his blood, but he kept me waiting for that cash week after week.'

'So you arranged this meeting with him – how?'

'I telephoned him at his office Friday morning, asked him when I was going to see the money. Then it was more excuses – he couldn't meet me Friday because of work, he couldn't meet me Saturday because he was seeing some old friend he hadn't seen for yonks, he couldn't meet me Sunday because he was going away up north. Handing out all the usual old toffee. I wasn't having it. I told him he had to meet me Sunday night, latest, because I had to have the money for Monday for a particular reason.'

'Your wife's birthday,' Atherton suggested.

Collins looked surprised, and then a spot of colour flamed in his cheeks. 'Right. You know all about it, I see. Yes, I wanted to buy my wife a present. Anything wrong with that?'

'Nothing at all,' Atherton said soothingly, wondering at the reaction. 'Please go on.'

Collins looked at him suspiciously for a moment, and

139

then continued. 'Well, I arranged to meet him in The Wellington at half past seven, but he never showed. I rang his house, but his wife answered, so I put the phone down. I knew he'd gone, because if he was in he never let her touch the phone. So then I started looking for him. I knew the places he drank. And when I finally ran him down in the Shamrock, having a whale of a time with some tart on his arm, it turns out he'd forgotten all about our arrangement.'

His face darkened with anger at the memory. 'Not so much as an apology. "Come and have a drink, join the party," he says. "Eat drink and be merry, for tomorrow we die," he says. So I said, not on my hundred quid you don't, or you'll die tonight, never mind tomorrow.'

He heard himself, stopped short, and then eyed Atherton defiantly.

'All right, I said that, but it's just a figure of speech. I didn't mean anything by it. When I heard what happened to him – I could have bitten my tongue out. But I'm telling you, because I suppose some other bugger will if I don't.'

'It's all right. Go on,' Atherton said. 'Just tell me what happened, in your own words.'

Collins stared a moment, then shrugged. 'Then he says he hasn't got it, just like that. So that's how it started. We had a row, and I called him some things I'd been thinking up over the past three weeks. To see him sitting there with his arm round that tart, spending money on her like water, while Charlie Muggins here sat around in The Wellington waiting for him, nursing a pint because that's all I had the cash for! And then when he said he couldn't pay me back—!'

'You could have killed him,' Atherton finished for him.

Collins drooped. 'Oh Christ,' he said. 'All right, I've got a temper, I don't deny it, but I wouldn't hurt a fly. And Dick Neal was my friend. He was a selfish, thoughtless bastard, but he was still my friend. I'd never have laid a finger on him.'

Atherton nodded non-committally. 'What happened afterwards? You were told to leave the bar, weren't you?'

140

'Yeah, we were chucked out. But it was all over by then anyway. We'd been shouting at each other, and then we suddenly realised what idiots we were making of ourselves, and started to calm down. By the time we got up into the street, we were more or less back to normal. So I said, why not come back to my place for a drink or two—'

'What time would that be?'

'I don't know, about ten, half past ten. I didn't look at my watch.'

'Go on.'

'Well, Dick said okay, and he'd go and fetch Helen – this bird. I'd forgotten about her – she pissed off to the loo when we started the shouting match – so I said something like, "Oh, can't you get rid of her?" I wanted a quiet drink, you see, just the two of us. But he put on this silly smile and said no he couldn't get rid of her, and said some other stupid stuff, and to cap—'

'What stupid stuff? What did he say exactly?'

Collins seemed to be embarrassed by it. 'He said, well, he said "I'll never leave her as long as I live". And this was some piece of skirt he'd only picked up five minutes ago! Then he calmly proposed bringing her back to my place. Said she'd be company for Pet. Well, I just lost my temper with him then. I wasn't having him talk about my wife like that. I – I called him a few names, and stormed off. And that's the last I saw of him.'

'You're sure you didn't take a swing at him as well?'

'I told you, I wouldn't hurt a fly. It was just that he made me mad, talking about Pet like that when—'

'When what?'

'Nothing,' Collins said sullenly.

'But you took a swing at your wife when you got home that evening, didn't you? She had the remains of a pretty nice black eye when I called yesterday. Isn't the reason you got mad at Neal that you knew he was having an affair with your wife?'

Collins came to his feet so quickly that Atherton was rapidly revising his previous assessment from weight training to boxing, when the door opened and Pet Collins

141

came in with a tray of teacups. Perfect timing, he thought with relief – or had she been listening at the door? She looked apprehensively from one to the other, and the cups chattered in the saucers as she stood in the doorway. She had renewed her makeup while the kettle was boiling, but her eyes were red and swollen, as was the end of her nose.

Atherton got up, too, and took the tray from her. 'Thank you, Mrs Collins,' he said. 'That's very kind of you.'

'Do you want biscuits?' she asked, trying for a normal tone of voice and getting it half right.

'Not for me, thanks,' Atherton said, blandly social.

'All right, Pet, wait in the kitchen,' Collins said sharply with a jerk of his head, and she went with automatic obedience. Atherton kept hold of the tea tray, on the principle that no man could hit a chap thus encumbered, and after a moment Collins sat down again, and slumped back in his chair wearily. 'Bloody tea and biscuits,' he said. 'Like a bloody church social.'

Atherton put down the tray on the coffee table and sat too, took a cup, and sipped, watching Collins carefully. After deep thought, he seemed to rouse himself. He looked tired and strained, with the pallor of someone who has been forced to stay awake for much too long on the trot.

'If you know about Dick and Pet, you probably know all you need to know about what sort of a man he was,' he said. 'We were mates; I'd have done anything for him, and he knew it, but still he couldn't resist the chance to bang my wife. I think sometimes he had a bit missing up here.' He tapped his temple significantly. 'He was mad for women. Couldn't keep away from them. It was like a disease with him. If it moved, he'd have it. He didn't seem to care about the risk, or who got hurt.'

'Did he know you knew?'

Collins shook his head with weary disgust. 'There was no point. It wouldn't have stopped him. It would just have meant I'd've had to have a scene with him, and I didn't want that. Anyway, I don't doubt it was as much Pet as him, in this case. She's – well, I won't go into that. But Dick

– since I first met him, he seemed to have this thing about women. It was almost like he couldn't help himself. And it didn't even seem to make him happy.'

Atherton remembered what Catriona Young had said to Slider, about Dick Neal's possible secret past. 'Was there some tragedy in his past life that might have made him that way?'

Collins brooded. 'What, like some woman did the dirt on him, you mean? It's an idea. I don't know. He never spoke about his private life. I met him – what – sixteen years ago, just after he married Betty, and we worked together in the same firm for eight years. But he never talked about his past or his childhood or anything like that.' He mused. 'He was a funny man in some ways. Secretive. He didn't like inviting anyone back to his house, either. In all the years I've known him I've only been there three or four times, and that was only like to pick him up to go on somewhere else. You'd almost think he was ashamed of something. I felt sorry for Betty, poor cow. He practically kept her in purdah.'

Atherton felt they had gone down an unhelpful cul-de-sac. He sipped some more tea and said, 'Can we go back to Sunday night? I'd like you to tell me what you did when you left Neal.'

Collins sighed, and then seemed to want to get it over with. 'I walked around a bit, in a temper, and then I decided I needed to get drunk. So I started on a bit of a club-crawl.'

'Really? I thought you didn't have any money? You say you could only afford one pint in The Wellington.'

'Dick gave me some. When we were out in the street, and we'd calmed down a bit, he said he didn't have the hundred, but he could let me have a score to be going on with. So I took it.'

'I see. And where did you go?'

He looked awkward. 'I don't really remember. I wandered around a bit. I was pretty pissed by the time I got home.'

'What time did you get home?'

143

'About midnight, I suppose. Pet will tell you.'

Atherton smiled lethally. 'She told me yesterday she didn't know when you came in. She took a sleeping pill, and when she woke in the morning you'd been and gone, taking your bag with you.'

Collins reddened. 'She was lying. She was awake all right.'

'Why would she lie?'

'I don't know.' He looked uneasy, as well he might. 'Maybe because she was pissed off with me for not buying her a present for her stupid birthday, the silly cow. I don't know. You know women. They'll say anything.'

'You had a quarrel with her about money when you got in, didn't you? Is that when you hit her?'

'I didn't hit her,' he said, his anger breaking suddenly. 'She must have fallen over or walked into something. She always was clumsy.'

'But you did have a quarrel?'

'She went on at me for blowing the twenty Dick gave me. I told her I'd spend it how I liked, seeing it was my money, and – oh Christ, you know how these things go!'

Not from first hand, thank God, Atherton thought. Another excellent reason not to get married. 'Did you quarrel about her and Dick?'

'I've told you, I never told her I knew about that. What was the point?'

'That was very forgiving of you.'

'If it had been anyone except Dick—' He shut his mouth and stared broodingly at the floor. Atherton felt an unwelcome twinge of sympathy. Probably he hadn't mentioned it because he was afraid of having his inadequacy thrown back in his face. What a hell of a life the man had been leading. All the same . . .

'All right, so you had a quarrel, and then what?'

'I went to bed. And the next morning I packed my bag and went to Exeter. On business. I've been in the west country all week.' He watched Atherton's face warily. 'You can check it all with Pet. And with my firm, and my customers.'

'You had business down there the whole week?'

He hesitated. 'No, only Tuesday and Wednesday. But I was pissed off with everything here. I didn't want to come back right away.'

'Not even when you heard your best friend was dead?'

Again the flaming spots of embarrassment and anger. 'I didn't know until last night, when I phoned Pet, and she told me. So I came home. But there was nothing I could have done, was there?'

Atherton kept his voice neutral. 'Gone round to see Neal's widow, perhaps.'

'I wouldn't have done that anyway. I told you, Dick never liked anyone going round his house or talking to his wife.' He made a futile gesture of the hand. 'I can tell you where I was the rest of the week, if you really want to know.'

'Thank you,' said Atherton. 'And I'll have another word with your wife before I go.'

Collins shrugged. 'If you must.'

'But right now, I'd like you to start remembering where you had those drinks after you left Dick Neal, so that we can find out if anyone saw you.'

'What d'you mean?' Collins stared. 'You mean, I've got to give you an alibi? But I didn't kill him!' His voice rose. 'Dick Neal was my friend, even if—'

'Even if he owed you money and was screwing your wife into the bargain?'

'Oh Christ.' The face crumpled, and for a moment Atherton thought he was going to cry. 'Listen, you stupid bastard,' he said, with an almost childlike hitch in his voice, 'I liked him. I wouldn't hurt him for the world. I *liked* him!' The words were emphatic, but the tone was almost bewildered. Atherton felt that if he had not been a man talking to a man about a man, he might have said *loved* instead of *liked*.

'Guv?' Atherton sounded excited.

'What have you got?'

'Anderson and I have checked with the staff of every club

Collins named. No-one remembers him going in that night. The wife is sticking to the New Revised version, that he came home at midnight, but her eyes are all over the place – she'll say whatever will stop him thumping her. And he had no appointments before Tuesday, in Barnstaple, so there was no reason for him to get out of Town on the Monday.' There was a doubtful silence. 'What d'you think?' Atherton prompted the airwaves. 'Brilliant motive, violent quarrel only hours before the murder, no alibi, and he does a runner early the next morning. What more can a man want?'

Slider spoke at last. 'All right. Nick him.'

Atherton breathed a sigh of triumph. 'Thanks, Guv.'

'Do it at home, so you can search his drum. Find out from his wife what clothes he was wearing that night, and bag 'em up. We'll have his car in, as well, do the thing properly.'

'Right.'

'D'you want back up? Is he likely to be violent?'

'I'll offer to let him make my day,' Atherton said cheerfully. 'I can't stand a man who hits women.'

'All right, St George. Just be careful.'

'I didn't know you cared, sir.'

'I don't want a suspect covered in bruises, that's all.'

CHAPTER TEN

Candlewax and Brandy

ATHERTON PUT HIS HEAD ROUND the door of Slider's room, and found Dickson in there as well.

'It's all right, come in,' Slider said. 'How's it going?'

'He's sticking to his story,' Atherton said. He looked ruffled, Slider noted – a bad sign with Atherton.

'Still not asked for a lawyer?' Dickson put in.

'No sir.'

Dickson exchanged a look with Slider. That was not good news. As it said in the Bible, the guilty man singeth for his brief, but the righteous man is bold as a lion.

'He's quite willing to talk,' Atherton said. 'He says he got home about midnight, pretty drunk, and went to bed. He got up at about seven, packed his bag, left the house about quarter past. Drove down the Western Avenue to the M25, then round to the M3 and onto the A303. We've got some corroborative evidence on the journey – he filled up at the BP station at Hillingdon Circus at half past seven. The night clerk remembers him: unshaven, looking as though he'd slept in his clothes, smelling of drink. That time of the morning its mostly commuters, sir, so he did rather stand out from the crowd. And he stopped to eat at the Little Chef at Bransbury on the A303 at around half past eight. They remember him there as well, and it's all right as far as time goes.'

'That's all very well, but we don't much care what he got up to on Monday morning, do we?' Dickson said. 'We know he must have gone back to his house before he went down to the West Country, because he had to collect his bag. He could have been killing Neal at two o'clock and still have gone home, to leave at seven-fifteen.'

'Yes sir,' said Atherton uncomfortably.

'What about the neighbours?' Slider asked. 'Any of them remember the car coming home?'

'No sir. The next-door neighbour says he left for work at half past six on the Monday morning, and he thinks Collins's car was on the hard standing then, but that doesn't help us much, either.'

'I'm glad you realise that, son,' Dickson said flintily.

'We've got everybody out still checking the bars,' Slider said. 'We've had a couple of possible sightings, but not close enough to the time to rule him out. And we've not managed to place his car near the motel for the crucial two hours, even with the witty rear-screen sticker. The trouble is, people just don't look at parked cars.'

'Tell your grandma,' Dickson growled.

'I thought the fact that he'd done a runner would tell against him,' Atherton said hopefully.

'What does he say about that?'

'He says everything just got on top of him, and he had to get away. He still denies having a row with his wife, or hitting her, but admits he was short of cash, and he makes no bones about knowing about her and Neal.'

'I think she's your best bet as a weak link, Bill,' Dickson said.

Slider nodded. 'She must already feel resentful towards Collins. Have another crack at her,' he said to Atherton. 'Let her know he denies hitting her – that ought to fuel her fires.'

'Yes Guv. I'll remind her that while he's inside, he's not in a position to hit her again. And of course, if she really was in love with Neal, she ought to shop her old man if she really believes he killed him.'

'All right,' Slider said. 'Keep everybody on it. Remember we've got to put it up before the Magistrates by tomorrow morning.'

'Yes sir. Neal desperandum, eh?' Atherton went out.

'What about the forensic report, Bill?' Dickson asked.

'Not in yet, sir. I'd better roust 'em – not that I've much hope. It's too long between. And even if we can find evidence that Neal was in Collins's car, well, so what?'

'Precisely.' Dickson got creakingly to his feet. 'In the old days we could've given it a run with about a sixty per cent chance of getting him sent down. But not now. The CPS won't buy it without a money-back guarantee plus ten-year free service warranty. I tell you, Bill, it's a bloody mug's game being a copper, now. They tie one arm behind your back and then ask you to clap your hands.'

Slider nodded dutifully.

Dickson reached the door and turned back. 'You don't think Collins is our man, do you?'

Slider looked up warily. 'No, sir.'

Dickson exposed what was widely regarded as the most threatening porcelain in the Job. 'Then you'd better bloody well find out who is, hadn't you?' he suggested pleasantly.

When Slider passed through the front shop, O'Flaherty was there, back from his three days off. He was dealing with a woman who had come in to show her driving licence and had taken the opportunity to point out with some vigour that if the police spent less time harassing law-abiding citizens in their motor cars they'd have more time to catch criminals, and in particular the ones who had stolen the decorative urn from her front garden over *three weeks* ago and appeared to be being allowed to get away with it scot-free.

O'Flaherty had only encountered this line of reasoning about thirty-two thousand times before, but he dealt with it with such fluid ease that in the time it took Slider to get from one side of the counter to the other, he had got her apologising for taking up his valuable time and promising to be more careful about zebra crossings in future.

'Thank you very much, ma'am.' He gave her his Simple Son of the Soil beaming smile. 'Much obliged to you. Oh,

149

Bill, a word with you please! Good day to you, ma'am. Mind the step, now. That's right.'

Slider turned back with O'Flaherty's meaty hand on his forearm, the thick fingers permanently curved at exactly the circumference of a Guinness glass. A stout fellow, O'Flaherty.

'Nice footwork, Fergus,' he said, nodding at the retreating back beyond the shop door. 'I didn't know if you were going to book her or ask her to dance.'

'Ah, sure God,' O'Flaherty said modesty, 'didn't I train at the Arthur Murray School of Policing? Listen, can I get you interested in this play the Commander's putting on?'

'Wetherspoon's charity performance? Not likely,' Slider said hastily.

The working copper's life had recently been further burdened by the Plus Programme, some bright lad's idea for transforming the leathery old Police Force into the slimline, glossy new Police Service: giving it a 'corporate image' and making it more user-friendly. It was just like their Area Commander to take the whole thing to extremes.

They had always raised large sums of money annually for charity, but they'd done it quietly, and with dignity. Now Wetherspoon wanted them literally to make a song and dance about it: a Joint Services performance of 'The Sound of Music'. Good publicity, he'd said. Show Joe Public our caring face. It was all about Communication, the new police buzz-word. And it would all end in tears, Slider predicted.

'I thought you wanted me for something important,' he complained.

''Twasn't one of his better ideas.' O'Flaherty's face registered profound gloom. 'Mind you, some of the firemen are dead keen. The Hammersmith lot are mad about th'amateur theatricals.'

'Must come from living their whole lives in a state of high drama.'

'It's all right for them, the public loves 'em anyway,' Fergus mourned. 'But for us – sure, a nice dinner-dance is

150

one thing, or a raffle, or a bit a tombola for the owl ones. But we've got to be careful on our own ground. I'm not for Chrissake getting into tights anywhere where me face is known.'

'I don't think it's your face they'd be looking at,' Slider said heartlessly. Fergus was buttocked like a Shire horse. 'But cheer up – if it's a success, Wetherspoon might decide to take it on the road.'

Fergus brightened. 'Is that what you'd call a tour de Force? Ah no, I'm leaving the RADA business to the young lads. I'll stick to selling tickets. Can I put you down for two?'

Slider shuddered. 'Tell you what, I'll pay not to come.'

'That's what Anderson said, and Norma Stits,' he sighed. 'There's no joy outa the whole lot of yez up there.'

'The Department always sticks together.'

'You're like bananas,' Fergus growled. 'Yellow, bent—'

'—and go round in bunches, yes, I know. Have you finished now? Can I go?'

Fergus eyes him thoughtfully. 'How's this case a yours going, Billy sweetheart? I heard God Head got his little chopper out and then he put it back again.'

'It may yet reappear. It's up and down like the Assyrian Empire, is Head's chopper.'

'Sure God, but haven't you a nice little suspect binned up in there?' O'Flaherty enquired in amazement. 'What in God's name are we feedin' the bastard for?'

'I'm not convinced he's the man. He ought to have put his hand up by now, but he hasn't even asked for his brief.'

'Dem's the worst sort,' O'Flaherty observed. 'What've you got on him then?'

'Good motive, no alibi, and sod-all else. When I tell you the most telling piece of evidence against him is that he's a brandy drinker, you'll see the strength of our case.'

'A man who'll drink that stuff, insteada God's own pint – an' maybe just a spot o' Jimson's at weddins an' funerals an' th'like—' Fergus agreed sagely. 'What's brandy got to do with it, anyway?'

'The victim was a whisky drinker, but was found with a

151

bellyful of brandy.' Slider sighed. 'I'm not sure we're going to get there on this one. I wouldn't mind really – I mean, we've always plenty of other things to be getting on with – but it was a particularly nasty piece of work—'

Fergus wasn't listening. 'Wait a minute, wait a minute, there's something in the back of me mind—' His face grew congested with thought. 'Brandy is it? Brandy. Now what does that—?'

Slider waited for a moment or two, and then glanced at his watch. 'Come on, Fergus. Constipation is the thief of time, you know.'

O'Flaherty would have snapped his fingers if they hadn't been so thick. 'That's it! I knew there was something. Listen, don't you remember the Harefield Barn Murder, when was it, three–four years ago? The geezer that was found hanging from the rafters and the straw set on fire.'

'Harefield's not our ground,' Slider said blankly.

'Don't you ever read the papers?' O'Flaherty said witheringly. 'An' you a Ruislip man! They thought it was suicide at first, but the post mortem turned up he was already dead when he was strung up. They never did get anyone for it, as far as I know.'

'What's that got to do with brandy?'

'It was brandy that was used to start the fire. And he'd had a bellyful, like your man, but the johnny's wife swore Bible he never touched spirits. Strictly an ale man. That's what put me in mind. If there's not a lead for yez there, my arse is an apricot.'

'It's worth looking into,' Slider agreed cautiously.

'A carse it is. Would I sell you a pup?' O'Flaherty smiled beguilingly. 'Cliff Lampard over at Uxbridge will tell you all about it. He's a darlin' man – and a Guinness man, what's more, so you can trust him wit your life.'

'It may come to that. Oh, that reminds me, Joe Doyle sends you his regards. Via Atherton, from the Shamrock Club,' Slider elaborated, seeing the name drew a blank on Fergus's face.

'The Shamrock? I haven't been in there in centuries.

Sure God, the man's a chancer. Wait a minute, though – that'd be a grand place to sell a few tickets, now! If they're not breaking some law down there, the Pope's a Jew.'

'If you've got to resort to blackmail to sell tickets for this show, it must be bad.'

'It is not!' Fergus said indignantly. 'It's cultural and educational. And the sight of Leading Firewoman Tamworth dressed up as a nun is enough to make a good Catholic boy apostasise, just to be allowed the lustful thoughts.'

'Pass.'

'Ah, now, didn't I just give you valuable information, darlin'?' he wheedled. 'Is that not worth two tickets to you? Sure, you could take your totty, make an impression, show her a good time.'

'You must take me for an idiot,' said Slider.

'That sounds like a fair swap,' Fergus agreed.

The CID room at Uxbridge was wide and sunlit, and like every good CID room, deserted of personnel. Slider was met by DS Martin Brice, who led him into Inspector Lampard's office and apologised for his absence.

'He's asked me to go through the file with you and answer any questions. I was Office Manager on the case, sir, so I'm pretty well up on it. And he said please to feel free to use his room.'

'Right, thanks,' said Slider. 'I'll want to read everything in detail, but perhaps you wouldn't mind giving me the outline of the story to start with.'

Brice settled himself, and obliged.

'The victim's name was David Arthur Webb. He was a double-glazing salesman, but he hadn't been doing too well at it. The firm he'd been working for had laid him off about eighteen months before, and he'd had to take a job on commission only, for one of those fly-by-night, cowboy firms. Money had got tight, and things were bad at home – mortgage arrears, HP debts, and so on – and he and his wife had been quarrelling a lot.'

'Over money?'

'Bit of everything really, sir. Money was at the bottom of it, I suspect, but he was drinking too much as well, and she thought he was seeing another woman.'

Slider nodded slightly. There were parallels already with Neal.

'And was he?' he asked Brice.

'I don't think we ever really established whether he was or not. But she believed it, which was good enough for her. Anyway, the climax came when he got done for drink-driving and lost his licence, which meant he couldn't do his job any more. You know what the area around Harefield's like, sir – practically open countryside. You have to have a car to get about.'

'Yes. I'm always surprised anything so rural can exist so near London.'

'Well, sir, one night he told his wife he was going out for a drink and he didn't come back. Late that night a motorist driving up Breakspear Road North saw a flickering light in a barn beside the road, thought it looked like a fire, and went to investigate. He found Webb hanging from a cross-beam, and a pile of straw nearby already blazing. Luckily he was able to put it out – beat the flames out with Webb's leather jacket as a matter of fact.'

'How was Webb dressed?'

'Fully dressed, sir, except for his jacket and shoes.' Brice looked enquiringly, and seeing the answer had satisfied, went on. 'Anyway, he managed to put the fire out, and rushed off to the nearest house to raise the alarm.'

'He didn't interfere with anything?'

'No sir, except the fire, of course. We were lucky,' he smiled. 'The intelligent witness.'

'A rare bird. So when you got there, you thought it was a suicide?'

'Yes, sir. Webb was hanging there with a rope round his neck and all the signs of strangulation.'

'How high was he strung?'

'Not dangling, sir. His toes were actually scraping the ground, though the doc said that was due to his neck and

154

the rope stretching. He'd have been just clear of the ground before that. But there was a straw bale just behind him, looked as though it could have been kicked out of the way. We assumed he'd stood on that, sir.'

'And what about the fire?'

'That puzzled us at first. It was about two feet in front of him, a pile of loose straw, and a trail of straw leading to the main stack, as if it was meant to make the whole place go up. But straw doesn't catch all that easily, as you know, sir, unless it's very dry, and all the loose straw we found was pretty damp. We assumed he'd got the first heap going and then nipped back and hanged himself, though we couldn't quite see why he'd want to do that; but we only found one used match, which we didn't think would have been enough.'

'Unless he was very lucky.'

Brice shook his head. 'He'd've needed to be more than lucky, sir. We found one used match, and nothing to strike it on.'

'No match box?'

'No, sir. And no lighter, either, though there was a pack of cigarettes.'

'Ah. You think the murderer put the box in his pocket automatically, without thinking?'

Brice smiled. 'That's what the Guv'nor decided in the end. Nobody can think of everything, that's what he says.'

'And how *was* the fire started?'

'The forensic team worked it out that the straw was doused with brandy, and a candle stood up in it and lit. When it burned down far enough, it would have set the straw off.'

'A candle,' Slider said. A smile flitted across his face. Candlewax and brandy. Beautiful! Despair and die, Head.

'They found quite a lot of wax in the ashes,' Brice said, 'and there was an empty brandy-bottle near where his coat had been lying. Of course, we were still thinking that Webb had done it himself, and it looked like quite a clever plan to destroy his own body and conceal the suicide – perhaps so that his wife could claim the insurance, sir. That was the way

155

we were thinking.'

Slider nodded.

'But when the post mortem report came through, it turned out that the rope had been put round his neck after death. He had been strangled, but with electrical flex, not rope. The ligature marks were quite plain, but the flex wasn't there, so that proved, of course, that someone had taken it off after death, and then rigged the scene to look like suicide.'

'But why would they do that, if they intended to burn the barn down anyway?'

'We couldn't work that one out, sir – unless it was an extra precaution, in case the fire didn't destroy all the evidence. Which it didn't, of course.'

Slider shook his head. 'Ridiculously elaborate.'

'Well, that's what I've always felt,' Brice said. 'But all we've got is questions, no answers.' He shrugged. 'Perhaps it was just a pyromaniac.'

'You've never made an arrest, I understand?' said Slider.

'No sir. Not even a suspect.'

'What about the wife?'

'The Guv'nor did consider her, of course, sir. She was the only person with a motive, and it usually is the nearest and dearest. But she's a little slip of a thing, about five feet two and slightly built. She'd never have managed to hoist him up like that, especially deadweight.'

'Did she have an alibi?'

'She was at home with the kids, sir, watching telly. There was no outside corroboration, but the Guv'nor decided she wasn't the type to go out and leave the kids alone in the house – they were only toddlers. And she remembered the television programmes well enough. Actually, we never really suspected her, it was just that there wasn't anyone else.'

'Yes, I see,' said Slider. 'A nice little problem.'

Brice cocked his head a little. 'May I ask sir – have you got something on it?'

'We've had an incident on our ground which has

156

similarities about it,' Slider said. 'But like you, we haven't really got a suspect.'

Brice nodded sympathetically. 'Whoever he is, he covers his tracks well.'

Slider phoned Joanna late, and she answered at once.

'Are you still up?'

'You know what it's like after a concert – I won't come down for ages yet.'

He smiled. 'I didn't mean that. Can I come round?'

'What, not working all night?'

'You can't interview people in the middle of the night, and the troops are doing the boring bits. I can have a few hours with you.'

'Are you hungry?'

'Starving,' he discovered.

'Wonderful. So am I. Hurry round, then.'

By the time he got there, she had assembled a supper of pâté sandwiches, crisps, and a bottle of cold white Beaujolais on a tray, which she carried into the bedroom. She sat cross-legged on the bed while he leaned, Roman-style, on one elbow, and they ate while he talked.

'So you think you're onto something at last?' she said.

'I'm not sure. We don't know if Webb and Neal knew each other, but they were both killed in similar unusual circumstances. And even if Neal could have killed himself, Webb certainly didn't.

'Maybe Neal killed Webb, and then committed suicide.'

'Don't even think it,' he shuddered.

'But what about Collins?'

'We'll probably have to let him go tomorrow. We've nothing really concrete against him, except for motive. Though his wife's gone back to her first story, that she doesn't know what time he came in, which buggers his alibi. She now says she took a sleeper around eleven when she realised he was spending all evening on the piss. That way, if he hit her when he got back drunk, she wouldn't feel it.'

'Oh brave new world,' Joanna said.

'But she woke up accidentally at seven o'clock the next morning – when he got up, according to his story – and they had a brief but violent row about his spending money for her birthday present on drink. He thumped her, took the housekeeping money out of her purse, packed his bag, and left.'

'And do you believe that version?'

'It has the ring of truth about it, as far as her side goes. Of course, it means we don't know whether Collins really did get back innocent at midnight and go to sleep, or whether he got in in the early hours of the morning, having killed Neal, just to collect his bag. Collins can't prove it one way, and we can't prove it the other. Not much of a case.'

'It sounds all right by me. A man who would hit a woman is capable of anything.'

'You sound like Atherton.'

'I love Atherton.'

'Murdered Mistress's Love-Nest Confession. But you can't hang a man just for having no alibi.'

'You're not allowed to hang them any more.'

'Damn. Why didn't somebody tell me?'

'Anyway, isn't it always the most obvious suspect who turns out to be the right one?'

'Not always, just usually.' Slider sipped his wine. 'Besides, the Collins solution leaves out the Webb killing.'

'Maybe that's just a coincidence.'

'I don't believe it. The methods and the background are too similar. I think whoever killed Webb killed Neal. We've got to find someone who knew them both, and that means starting all over again and putting in a lot of plain, hard work.'

'If they were both womanisers, maybe they were both having the same woman. What about the mystery redhead?' She leaned over to refill the glasses, and her robe fell open a little, distracting him. He felt a pleasant warmth start up below his belt that had nothing to do with the wine.

158

'I wish to God we knew who she is,' he said.

'Well, I expect Dickson must be glad about this new development. At least now Head can hardly claim Neal was a suicide, can he?'

'You never know with top brass. Logic isn't their strong point.' Slider drained his glass and put it down. 'It's very odd to see Dickson being such a pussy-cat over Head, though. He's always been such a roaring lion. He never cared what anyone thought, he just did his own thing and to hell with the regiment.'

'You like him, don't you?' she said, licking butter off her fingers.

Slider smiled suddenly. 'I'll tell you a story about him that illustrates the measure of the man. It happened when he was a DS, so of course I can't swear to the truthfulness of it, but it comes to me on good authority.'

'A thing isn't necessary a lie, even if it didn't necessarily happen,' she said.

'Well, you know that the top detective in the whole of the Met is the Assistant Deputy Commissioner?'

'I'll take your word for it.'

'Good. Now the ADC used to be a man called Maguffy, a ferocious disciplinarian, and totally out to lunch. Everyone went in fear and trembling of him. They used to call him Madarse Maguffy. His favourite trick was to mount little surprise raids on CID rooms to catch people out, and then throw the book at them.'

'Nice.'

'So one Monday, late morning, slack period, he turned up in Dickson's CID room. There was one DC, dozing at the crime desk, and Dickson with his feet on the desk, glass of whisky in one hand, and *The Sunday Times* in the other.'

'I thought you said it was Monday?'

'He was a slow reader. Don't interrupt.'

'Sorry.'

'Well, the DC jumps to his feet, so terrified he can't so much as squeak, and by the time Dickson finally looks up, Madarse has gone deep purple, his eyes are bulging, and steam's coming out of his ears. Dickson doesn't move a muscle. Nothing left to do, you see, but brazen it out. He says casually, "Yes, can I help you?" like a lady shop assistant, and Madarse, totally beside himself, screams, "Do you know who I am?" Dickson can't resist. He looks calmly across at the the DC and says, "Colin, there's a stupid sod here doesn't know who he is. Can you help him?" '

When they'd made love, Joanna fell instantly asleep with her nose pressed into the pillow and her short hair sticking up every whichway, like a bronze cactus dahlia. Slider lay back, his body deliciously tired and his mind slowed down to walking speed at last. It connected things up and took them apart again, at random but not frantically, like a child playing with a lego set. He couldn't see his way through the maze of the case yet, but at least now he was sure he had a case. He could fight his corner with confidence against Head's scepticism.

All the same, they badly needed a result on this one. He thought of Dickson – a good copper, yet there was some bastard busily sawing half-way through his chair legs, for no better reason than mindless ambition. And what about his own chair legs? Maybe he should take the promotion after all. But there were others who had stayed put at the sharp end, for love of the job, and not been blamed for it. Look at Atherton, for instance – brain the size of a planet, and still only a DS. But everyone knew Atherton was harmless. Now there was an odd perception from a tired brain! He had managed to surprise himself. He tried to imagine Atherton as a Detective Inspector, and succeeded quite easily. He was perfectly capable of doing the job, of course – it was just that he'd hate it. A DS had the best of all worlds: independence of decision plus almost complete unaccountability.

For himself – Slider knew, without necessarily liking it, that he was born for responsibility, that if he hadn't been given it, he'd have found his own mine and dug some out. That's the kind of dull dog he was. He was a good copper

160

not because he was brilliant, but because he was painstaking. Good old reliable Bill. Why on earth did Joanna fancy him, as there was no delicious doubt she did? She must just be strange that way.

But he was a good copper, and he didn't want to take promotion if it meant moving from operations to administration. Still, there was no ignoring that the extra money would come in handy, and it would make Irene happy. Irene! Yes, he was conveniently forgetting he was supposed to be leaving Irene – and if he did, by God he'd need the extra money! A divorce would cost you thousands, first and last. Why was life so complicated? he wondered resentfully, like so many men before him.

He looked down at Joanna, and felt how large and simple the joy was of being with her. When you let a stable-kept horse out into a field, there was a first moment of grateful surprise in its eyes at the open expanse of grass in front of it. Joanna was his wide-open space – as unexpected as pleasurable. With her he didn't feel like a dull dog, or, not to mix his metaphors, a harness-galled dray horse. She unhitched his cart, and he discovered a surprising turn of speed in himself.

He looked down at her heavy, bronze hair, the tip of her naked ear revealed, the line of her jaw, the laughter lines at her eye-corner, and the curious rough mark on her neck from the pressure of the fiddle. One hand rested beside her sleeping head, a strong hand with long, beautiful fingers. Looking at them made a shiver run down his back. She had a talent he couldn't begin to understand. She was separate from him, a discrete and beautiful thing, to be admired as you admired, say, a wild animal, knowing you could never possess it.

You could never possess another person anyway. All you ever owned in life were your responsibilities, he thought, coming full circle. They were yours all right. They had all the reassurance of discomfort; like piles or aching feet, they could be no-one else's.

She stirred and turned over, opened her eyes and looked up at him, as suddenly awake as she had fallen asleep.

161

'What?' she said.

'I was thinking.'

'I can see that. What about?'

'Us. The situation.'

She sat up, yawning, and stretched. 'You do pick the time, don't you? Well, what conclusions have you come to?'

'No new ones. I was just thinking how much I love you.'

'Well then,' she said pointedly.

'Yes, I know.' He sighed. 'It's just doing it. I don't want to hurt anyone. I have to wait for the right moment.'

She seemed to find that amusing. 'Oh, and what would the right moment look like? Is there a perfect sort of occasion for telling someone you're leaving them?'

'Don't. I don't know how to do it. I wish she'd just find out, and throw me out. Or go over the side herself, get herself a toyboy.'

'Of course you do. That would be so much easier. But it isn't going to be easy. You have to make your mind up to that.'

'It's all right for you,' he said, stung to resentment. 'You don't have to do anything.'

'You think that's easy?' She shoved her hand backwards through her hair, a residual movement of anger, like the lashing of a cat's tail. 'How long has this been going on, now? And who's been bearing the brunt of it? At the moment, you're making me pay for your indecision.'

'Yes,' he said.

'Bill, for God's sake don't do that!'

'Do what?'

'Make me feel unkind. Make me feel I'm rubbing your nose in it. I hate this situation!'

'I know.'

'But do you? The whole point is that there's nothing I can do about anything! It's all in your hands, and I hate to be helpless, and if I keep nagging you about it, it makes me look like a shrew. I can't win. I know it will be hard for you to leave Irene and the children, but if you want me, you have to do something about it, that's all.'

'Yes, I know that. I'm sorry to put you through it. It's just—'

She rounded on him. 'It's got to be soon. It can't go on like this, don't you see? Because it will sour everything. It's not fair on any of us.'

'I know. But I can't do anything while I've got this case on,' he said – automatic defence, but true as well.

'Yes, I know. But when this case is over, one way or the other it's got to be resolved. Either you've to take the plunge, or—'

'Or?'

'Or we'll have to split up,' she said reluctantly. She looked up and met his eyes, and he saw without at all wanting to a whole range of her thoughts: how she disliked the very idea of an ultimatum, resented being forced into the position of giving one, hated to be made to sound like the ungenerous party. He also saw that at the bottom, she feared that when it actually came to it he might not choose her after all. Don't, he wanted to cry. Don't make me feel that it's possible to hurt you that much. 'I love you,' he said helplessly, and it sounded horribly like an apology.

She put herself into his arms and rested her face against his neck. 'This is the moment when I'd really like to be able to cry at will,' she said. 'It might convince you how weak and helpless I really am.'

He had never seen her cry. He didn't believe he ever would see her cry. But he would have liked to be able to tell her so that she'd believe it, that he knew that that did not make her strong.

CHAPTER ELEVEN

A Fish by Any Other Name . . .

ATHERTON GATHERED HIS PAPERS TOGETHER. 'That's it then,' he said. 'Collins is a blow-out. He's not going to put his hand up for it, and we can't prove anything. So what do we do?'

'Let him go,' Slider said simply.

Atherton sighed, scratched the back of his head, drummed his fingers once on the edge of the desk in frustration. 'It really burns my toast! It was him all right, but I just can't pin it to him.'

'Not so the Muppets'd give it houseroom. But don't worry, he's not going anywhere,' Slider said. 'We can always arrest him again. We've got time left on the clock.'

'Yes, I know. I was just so fond of this file. And everything seems to peter out, doesn't it? Maybe it was accidental death after all. Maybe Neal really was just an ordinary old pervert.'

'What, with all the women in his life?'

'Smokescreen. Methinks he doth protest too much.'

'You know it doesn't work that way. Pin your faith on the Webb connection. If we find that Collins knew Webb – which isn't impossible, they were both reps – we can do a whole new number on him.'

'I suppose so,' Atherton said, without great enthusiasm. 'What's happening on that, anyway?'

'I'm going over to see Mrs Webb myself this morning. When you've finished processing Collins, you'd better read the file, familiarise yourself with it.'

'I hope there's a map,' Atherton complained. 'Pinner was bad enough, but Harefield is real carrot-country. Next time I want a nice civilised murder in the Theatre District, with trails leading to the Loire Valley in time for the grape harvest.'

'I'll speak to the author,' Slider promised.

'Meanwhile, I hope you're taking a track-laying vehicle, Guv?'

'Hail or snow, the mail always gets through.'

Slider came away from Mrs Webb's house more cheerful, though no less baffled.

'I knew from the beginning it wasn't suicide,' she said, sitting on the sagging and hideous sofa in the tiny Victorian workman's cottage she still inhabited with the three children. 'Davie would never have done a thing like that. He was a cheerful man, a good man. He'd never have done that to me and the kids.'

'I understand he was in financial trouble?' Slider said.

She looked at him sharply. 'You're thinking of the insurance? Yes, it paid for the house and everything. Davie was a great believer in insurance. But that's another reason he'd never have killed himself – suicide invalidates the policy. I'm surprised you don't know that, being a policeman.'

He decided to tackle the hostility straight away. 'Mrs Webb, I've read the file. There's no question that it was suicide. That's not what I meant. I'm simply trying to get the picture.'

'I told them all this at the time, your friends,' she said resentfully, looking away. Everything in the room was unrelentingly ugly, and there was the rank smell of too many children in too small a space, a smell Slider associated with poverty. The animal kingdom was full of violent death, but there was nothing like the human race for inflicting long, slow suffering on its members. 'If you've read the file, what do you have to come stirring it all up again for?'

'There's always the chance that you'll remember something else – or even that I'll ask a different question. I know it must be painful for you to think about it, but another man's been killed, and the circumstances are similar to those surrounding your husband's death. I really would appreciate your help.'

She sighed, and looked at him, and the lines of her face softened. She must have been very pretty once, he thought. And she was indeed a mere snip of a thing, too slight by far to have strangled a grown man and rigged up a hanging, even had there been anything to suggest she might have wanted to.

'Well, go on then, ask,' she said resignedly.

'Your husband had been drinking a lot around that time. Was that unusual?'

'He was always fond of his pint. He was a drinker, but he wasn't a drunkard. He could handle it,' she said defensively.

'A social drinker?'

'I suppose so. He liked a pint or two with the lads. He was always that way, even before I met him. I used to go with him to begin with, but I never really liked pubs. In any case, it was his mates he wanted to talk to. He was happier there without me. So I stopped going.'

'So he wasn't drinking more than usual?'

She shrugged. 'Maybe a bit. He was worried about his job. But it wasn't a problem. The police tried to make out he was some kind of alcoholic, especially after the accident, when he lost his licence. It wasn't like that. He was a good man, and he was worried about me and the kids, that's all.'

'It says in the file that you suspected him of seeing another woman. Is that true?'

She sighed. 'They pick you up on things, and then you can't ever convince them it isn't important.'

'So there was nothing in it?'

'Look, any man will flirt a bit, if a pretty young woman makes up to him,' she said, looking him straight in the eyes. 'It doesn't mean he'd take it any further than that.'

'Tell me about it,' Slider suggested.

166

'There's nothing to tell. I met a neighbour in the street, who happens to serve on the food bar at The Breakspear lunchtimes – or she did then, anyway – and she asked me who the girl was Davie came in with. That's all.' Slider waited, and she went on reluctantly, 'Apparently he took a girl in there one lunchtime, and because she was young and pretty, naturally everyone assumed he was having an affair. Which he wasn't.' She displayed a grim humour. 'How could he afford to have an affair, when he was out of work?'

'I don't mean to sound as if I'm picking you up on this,' Slider said carefully, 'but you said at the time that he was "carrying on all over the place" with this young woman.'

'I was angry, all right? I mean, he was dead, wasn't he? The police come and catch you for a statement when you're out of your head with shock, you don't know what you're saying and you don't care either, and then afterwards they stick to it and go on and on at you like a broken record—'

'Yes, I understand. So he only saw this girl once, to your knowledge?'

'Once, twice, what's the difference? A few times. They were seen together a few times. It didn't mean there was anything going on. People can be friends, can't they?'

'And you didn't know who she was?'

'No. She was probably just someone from work.' She digested for a moment, and then in a calmer voice said, 'When I asked him about it, he denied it all. That's what upset me. I mean, I know Connie, she wouldn't have made it up about him coming in with the girl. If he'd said, oh yes, she's so-and-so, a friend of a friend, or whatever, it would've been all right. But he didn't trust me enough to tell me the truth. I suppose he thought I'd think the worst. That's what really got to me.'

'Yes, I understand,' Slider said.

She looked up sharply. 'Do you? It's a wonder if you do. All men are the same – think they can lie their way out of anything. If they'd only tell you the truth, it wouldn't be half so bad. But you can never convince them of that.'

He was glad to change the uncomfortable subject. 'Do you know of anyone who might have had a reason to kill

167

your husband?' She shook her head. 'Did he have any enemies?'

'Davie? No,' she said simply.

'He was short of money, wasn't he? Did he owe money anywhere? Had he borrowed from anyone?'

'Not that I know of. No-one ever came and asked for it, anyway, except the hire purchase and the mortgage and stuff.' The grim humour again: 'You don't think the Woolwich sent a hit man round after him, do you?'

'Was your husband friendly with a David Collins? He's a salesman too, with a firm called Newbury Desserts. This is a photograph of him.'

She shook her head. 'I've never seen him before. Of course, he may have met all sorts of people on the road that I didn't know about, but I never heard him mention that name.'

He showed her the photograph of Neal without much hope, and she shook her head at that, too.

'No, I've never seen him before either.'

'His name's Richard Neal — Dick Neal. Did your husband ever mention him?'

'I don't think so. Not that I remember.'

And so he was back where he started. As the last stone not to be left unturned, he asked, 'Does the word *mouthwash* mean anything to you?'

'What d'you mean?'

'Did your husband ever use it in an unusual context? Could it be a codeword for something else, for instance?'

'I never heard him use it, but it sounds like one of those silly nicknames, doesn't it?'

'Nicknames?'

'Firemen all give each other silly nicknames, don't they? It's traditional.'

'Yes, so I understand,' Slider said, still faintly puzzled. 'Was your husband a fireman, then?'

'Oh yes, years ago, before I met him. He was just a part-timer, on retained service, when we first got married, but he gave that up as well when the kids came along. Well, he'd taken the job with Clearview by then, anyway, and of

168

course he couldn't be on call when he was on the road selling windows. I think he missed his mates and everything, but I wasn't sorry when he gave it up. I don't think any woman likes her husband taking those sort of risks. And of course the money was nothing.'

'I suppose not,' said Slider.

He couldn't see where it was leading, but there seemed to be a definite fire motif in all this. Fire, and the mystery tart, and jack-the-lad reps in money-trouble. Was it a lead? Was it a clue? Something was fishy, at any rate, and a fish by any other name would still never come up smelling of roses.

Norma came rushing in, looking excited and triumphant.

'Got it, Guv!' she said. 'This is it, the connection we've been looking for!'

'All right, sit down – and don't disappoint me now. You wouldn't like to see a strong man weep, would you?'

'No, no, you'll love this,' Norma promised. She sat down and crossed her long, long legs, well above the knee. Slider fixed his eyes on her clipboard and concentrated on breathing evenly. 'I've been checking up on what Mrs Webb gave us about her husband. He was a full-time fireman at the Shaftesbury Avenue fire station, but that was closed down in 1974 during one of their economy drives. Then Webb became a part-time fireman at Harefield, which of course was his local station. Retained personnel have to live and work near the station, so they can be bleeped when they're needed. In fact, all firemen are expected to live near their station, except for those serving in Central London, where it wouldn't be possible, of course.'

'Of course,' Slider said.

'Oh, well, you know that, obviously,' Norma said, catching herself up. 'And obviously you know that firemen usually have some other trade under their belts, because they have so much time off – four days on and four days off on full-time working.'

169

'What was Webb's trade?'

'Carpenter. I suppose that's why he went into double-glazing – the window connection. Anyway, Webb combined carpentry with part-time fire service for four years. He married in 1976, and took the full-time job with Clearview in 1978, and gave up the fire service at the same time, as we know. The children were born in 1978, 1981 and 1983. In 1986 Clearview went bust, and Webb took a commission-only job with Zodiac. And in 1987 he was murdered.'

Anatomy of a life, Slider thought. How little it all boils down to.

'Right, so what's the connection with Neal?'

'I've just got the list through of the personnel at Shaftesbury Avenue station immediately before it closed down. Richard Neal was a fireman, on the same watch as David Webb!'

Oh joy!

'So they knew each other,' Slider said happily.

'Yes, and intimately at that, I should think. From what I hear, there's a very strong bond within a watch. They live and work together for intense periods. The wonder of it was that Webb never mentioned Neal's name to his wife. I'd have thought he'd have forever been telling stories of the good old days. You know what men are like, sir!'

'Well, a bit,' Slider said modestly. 'But since it was all over two years before he married her, perhaps it just never happened to come up. And she may not have liked to hear about it.'

'Jealousy, you mean? Yes, I can understand that. There's another thing I was thinking: this business about nicknames. There was a man on the same watch as Neal and Webb whose name was Barry Lister. I know it's a bit of a long shot, but supposing he's "Mouthwash"? You know, Lister – Listerine?'

'It's possible,' Slider conceded. 'All those names will have to be checked, but you can start with Lister, by all means. Get everyone working on it right away. We want to know where they all are, what they've been doing, who kept in touch with whom – especially Webb and Neal – who's had recent contact with Neal, and any other possible connections there may be between them. Not forgetting whether any of them knew our old friend Collins.'

'It's not going to be easy to track them all down, after sixteen years. People move around such a lot, inconsiderate bastards.'

'Try the short cuts. Check the names against the subscribers to the telephone numbers on Neal's itemised bills, to start with. Polish has them all indexed. And have someone run the names past Mrs Neal, see if she's heard of any of them, and Mrs Webb ditto.'

'Right.'

'And try the London telephone directory. It's an obvious source, but it's funny how often people forget it.'

'Yes, sir.'

'And you can tell Mackay to put all those names into the computer, see if we've got records on any of them.'

'Right.' She stood up, smiling at him. 'Overtime all round, Guv?'

'It's going to be a busy night,' he said. Dickson was going to love explaining this to the keeper of the privy purse. 'Is the Super still in, d'you know?'

'I just saw him come out of the lav.'

'Right. I'd better catch him before he goes home.'

He decided to clear the decks while he was at it by phoning Irene. 'I'm going to be very late tonight. In fact it may be an all-nighter. We've got a new lead to follow up, and Head's about to pull the pin on us, so we have to move fast.'

Irene hardly listened. She had news of her own, which she was breathlessly eager to tell him. 'I've had a phone call from Marilyn Cripps!' she said with unconcealed triumph.

Slider tried very hard to be interested. 'Oh? What did she want?'

'Well, you know her boy's at Eton? Well, they're doing a special gala variety show for charity at Easter – singing and dancing and little sketches and so on, but all in good taste, not like the Palladium or anything. They're getting one or two other local schools to join in, and one of the royals is going to be there – I think it's the Duchess of Kent. Or did she say Princess Alexandra? Well, anyway, one of them is definitely going to be there, and there'll be a supper afterwards, and all the organisers will be presented to her, whichever one it is.'

'Yes, but what's this got to do with you?' Slider asked when she paused for breath. 'I suppose she wants to put us down for tickets—'

'No, no, you don't understand!' Irene said rapturously. 'Marilyn Cripps has asked me to help! She's asked me to make some of the costumes. She says they've got to be really professional-looking, and that's why she thought of me.'

'She wants you to make costumes for a school play, and you're pleased about it?'

'It's not a school play,' she said indignantly. 'It's a Gala, and it's at *Eton College*. Don't you understand? It means I'll be invited to the reception as well, and I'll get to meet the Duchess of Kent!'

'Or Princess Alexandra – whichever it is,' Slider said, and then wished he hadn't.

'I thought you'd be pleased for me,' she said, hurt.

'I am,' he said hastily. 'I'm delighted. It's wonderful.'

It gave him a pain like indigestion to think what a dismal thing had the power to thrill her. Marilyn Cripps was one of the world's greatest organisers, a gigantic woman like a rogue elephant – not physically large, but unstoppable. Not the least of her talents was being able to pick the very people who would do the hardest work for the least reward, and think themselves privileged to be asked. Irene had been involved in making costumes for Kate's school's play once, and he knew how much time and effort was involved – tedious, neck-aching work bent over the dining-room table in poor light night after night. But for something at Eton College, Irene would work until her fingers came off and her eyes stopped out, and the Cripps woman knew it.

'Will I be expected to turn up for this do?' he asked

tentatively. He knew how ballsachingly ghastly it would be. He had nothing against putting on a monkey suit for the Duchess of Kent (or Princess Alexandra) but he was afraid only having his jaws surgically wired would prevent him from saying something unforgiveably fruity to Mrs Cripps.

'Oh no,' Irene said promptly, and with faint and pardonable triumph. 'They can't have too many people to the supper, especially with a member of the royal family there. It will just be the guests of honour and the main organisers with their husbands or wives, and the rest of the helpers will be asked on their own. But you probably wouldn't have been able to come anyway, would you, so it doesn't matter.'

'No, of course not.' He made an effort on her behalf. 'Well, I really am pleased for you, darling. I hope you'll be—' He nearly said very happy. 'I hope you'll enjoy it very much.'

'It's going to take up all my time for the next few weeks,' she said happily, 'so don't expect me to be around to cook your meals whenever you come home. And there'll be meetings and fittings and things at Marilyn's house or up at the College,' – how gladly that word tripped off her tongue – 'maybe several times a week. We'll have to have a babysitter when I'm out: it's not fair on Matthew to leave him in charge so often. I hope we can afford it.'

He heard the faint irony in the question, and responded with an irony of his own. 'When it comes to your happiness, of course we can afford it.'

Irene didn't notice. She was busy looking forward to the rosy future which had suddenly replaced the dreary grey vista of heretofore. 'To think of her asking *me*! She must think more of me than I realised. When it's over, perhaps I'll invite her and some of the others over to our house for something. A bridge evening with supper would be nice. I've got a book somewhere with some marvellous recipes for finger-food! Our lounge is so small, though, I'd have to move the suite out to the—'

'I've got to go now, darling,' he said hastily. 'The other phone's ringing—'

'Oh, yes,' she said vaguely, and actually put the phone down on him in sheer absence of mind. He could almost see the young bridal look her face would be wearing as she planned the social life she had always dreamed of. Bridge, garden parties, cocktail parties . . . the Crippses usually made up a party for Ascot, too . . . and they went to Glyndebourne *several times* most summers . . .

He hoped Irene wasn't going to be let down too hard when her usefulness was over. For the moment, however, much as he hated Mrs Cripps for exploiting Irene, he had to admit she had made her happier than he had been able to in years.

And, of course, he was guiltily glad that with Irene fully preoccupied outside the home, it would be easier for him to see Joanna for the next few weeks.

'Who on earth would want to murder a fireman?' Joanna said. 'I mean, of all people in the world, you'd think they'd be the last to have enemies.'

Slider smiled into the darkness. They were in bed, Joanna was in his arms, with her face on his chest and the top of her head tucked under his chin, and he was so blissfully comfortable he almost couldn't be bothered to correct her wild delusions.

'You know that there's a saying in the Job, whenever a probationary PC complains about the attitude of the public: *if you wanted to be popular, you should have joined the fire brigade.*'

'Quite right. I mean, what they do is so absolutely heroic and unselfish, isn't it? They risk their lives for other people's good, and you can't even suspect them of ulterior motives, like policemen or soldiers who might just possibly be doing it for the power.'

'You have got it bad, haven't you? But Neal wasn't a fireman, he was a fire alarm salesman. He hadn't been a fireman for sixteen years.'

'Sixteen years. A big part of his life. And his life was real to him, not just a set of statistics, a list of facts on an index card,' she said thoughtfully. 'He ate and slept and thought and felt; the most important person in the world to himself. The epicentre of a whole universe of experience.'

Slider grunted agreement.

'It's easy to forget him in all the excitement, isn't it? That was something that worried me when you were investigating Anne-Marie's murder, that I'd become interested in the problem of it, without remembering there was a person attached.'

He grunted again. It was amazing, when you thought how knobbly and uncompromising the human body was compared with, say, a cat's, how Joanna's contours fitted against his so easily and perfectly.

'But I suppose you'd have to do that, wouldn't you, out of self-defence? You couldn't really allow yourself to care personally about every victim?'

And then again, when you thought how different her contours were from his – yet you couldn't have got a cigarette paper between them at the moment, always supposing you were abandoned enough to want to try.

'Have you got any real picture of Neal in your mind? I mean, is he a person to you?' Joanna pursued. 'You were saying the other day that you felt sorry for him, but it sounded as though it was partly a joke.'

Slider roused himself. She was in one of her interrogative moods, and there was only one way to silence her. The romantic touch – charm, flattery, seduction – make her purr, make her feel like a queen. Time for the sophisticated approach.

'C'mere, woman,' he said.

Ten minutes later she murmured in a much more relaxed voice, 'I love being in bed with you.'

'Pity the nights are so short,' he said. 'It'll be an early start for me tomorrow. But at least we can have breakfast together. And the A40 traffic can get along without me for once.'

'You'd better go on sleeping here while I'm away,' she said. 'Get Irene into the habit.'

175

'What d'you mean, while you're away?'

'You haven't forgotten I'm going to Germany for four days?'

He'd forgotten.

'Mini-tour,' she reminded him. 'What we call the Cholera Special. Three towns in four days – Cologne, Düsseldorf and Frankfurt.'

'I didn't know that was yet, I thought it was weeks away,' he said. 'Hell's bells!'

'And damnation,' she added. 'Berlioz, *La Damnation de Faust*. If it wasn't a tour, it'd be a pleasure: music so beautiful it's an erotic experience just playing it, and a luscious tenor singing in French – *in French!* I could listen all day.'

'Never mind all that. You're going away! Why did it have to be now, just when I can be with you?'

He went cold as soon as the words were out of his mouth, but, prince of a woman, she didn't point out the obvious this time, as she might have. 'Think about me,' she said, 'stuck in boring old Germany without you. I hate these short-haul tours – they're exhausting, too much travelling for too little playing. And it's yummy music, but with the world's most hated conductor. If we do well, it's in spite of him, not because of him.'

'How can he be that bad? He's world famous,' Slider argued. 'Surely no-one would hire him a second time if he were incompetent?'

'How little you know!' He felt her writhe a little with frustration. 'He's a box-office draw. The public don't know any better. They want a show, and since all they see is his back, there's got to be some spectacular swooping about, or they'd think he wasn't doing anything. The really good conductors, from our point of view, are nothing to look at, so they hardly ever get famous.' She sighed. 'It's hard not to hate the public sometimes. You have to keep reminding yourself that they're who we're doing it all for.'

He smiled unwillingly. 'That's exactly how we feel.'

'I know.' She pressed herself against him. 'I told you, musicians and coppers are very alike,' she said.

His hand lingered on the curve of her buttock, and her breasts were nudging his chest like two friendly angora rabbits. 'I can think of lots of differences,' he said.

'Tell me about them,' she invited.

CHAPTER TWELVE

Strangling in a String

WHEN DICKSON BREEZED INTO THE department meeting, Slider stiffened with surprise: his suit was innocent of ash, and he smelled of aftershave. True, it was only Brut or Old Mice, one of those that very old aunts or very young children give you for Christmas because they can't think of anything else to get, and you put the bottle in the back of the medicine cabinet because you're too fond of them actually to throw it away. Still, it was definitely aftershave and not whisky; and his nostril hair was freshly trimmed.

'Morning!' He flashed his Shanks Armitage smile around the bemused troops, and unbuttoned his jacket. Some of his body took the chance to make a dash for it, and got as far as his shirt buttons before being stopped. 'Right, Bill, carry on. Let's hear what you've got.'

'As you know, we've been trying to trace the men who were on the same watch as Neal when the Shaftesbury Avenue station was closed in 1974,' Slider said. 'We knew it wasn't going to be easy after a gap of sixteen years, and especially since the men were pretty well scattered to begin with. We started by checking with the Neal paperwork, his itemised calls list, and with Mrs Neal. That was our first surprise: Mrs Neal had no idea her husband had ever been a fireman.'

Dickson stirred a little. 'Wait a minute – that burn on the back of Neal's hand. Didn't she say he got that when a friend of his died in a fire?'

'That's right, sir,' Atherton answered. It had been in the

178

report of his first interview with Mrs Neal. What a memory the old man had! 'Apparently, that's literally all he told her. "A friend of mine was killed in a fire once."'

'He never talked about the past, and she never asked about it,' Slider said. 'Not a woman of great curiosity.'

'I suppose it suited him that way,' Dickson grunted. 'Suited 'em both, probably. Go on.'

'With no help from the Neal end, we thought we'd have to do it the hard way, from the Shaftesbury Avenue end, move by move. But one of the names on the list was unusual – Benjamin Hulfa – and there was only one Hulfa in the London Telephone Directory. We took a shot at it, and it turned out to be Ben Hulfa's widow.'

'Widow?' Dickson glanced behind him for a desk, parked his rump on the edge of it, and folded his arms across his chest, like an old-fashioned housewife by a garden fence.

'Swilley went round to interview her,' Slider said, and cued Norma with a glance.

'Hulfa died last year, sir. He was an insurance investigator, but he'd been off work for almost ten weeks with depression, taking various drugs prescribed by his doctor. Mrs Hulfa was a BT telephonist, doing shift work. She came home one night after the late shift and found all three services outside her house. There'd been a fire, and her husband was dead.'

'Killed in the fire?'

'Apparently not, sir. He'd taken a mixture of sleepers and brandy, sitting on the sofa in the living room. He was a heavy smoker, and it was assumed that he'd dropped a lighted cigarette as he grew drowsy, and set light to the upholstery. A passer-by saw the curtains on fire and called the fire brigade. Hulfa was already dead when they got to him, but from respiratory collapse from the drugs rather than smoke inhalation. There was some talk of suicide, but it was eventually brought in as accidental death.'

'Well?' Dickson asked, reading her tone of voice. 'What's wrong with that?'

'Only that the post mortem found there was no carbon

at all in the lungs or in the nostrils,' Norma said. 'It seemed to me, sir, that if he dropped the cigarette as he grew drowsy, you'd expect him to have breathed in at least some of the smoke before he died. Death from respiratory collapse isn't instantaneous.'

Dickson gave no encouragement to supposition. 'You don't know how rapid the collapse was, or how slow the fire was to start.'

'No sir,' Norma said, meaning the opposite.

Slider took the ball back. 'At all events, that made three dead out of the eight we were interested in. I thought it was worth running the rest of the names through the Cumberland House computer, to see if there were death certificates for any more of them. The results, now they've finally come through, are very interesting.' He gestured behind him towards the whiteboard. 'Of the eight men of Red Watch, six are dead: five of them violently, and only one from natural causes.'

'Seventy-five per cent,' said Dickson. 'In sixteen years? It's on the high side of average. Well, let's have it. Take us through 'em, Bill.'

'In date order of their deaths: first, James Elton Sears of Castlebar Road, Ealing, full-time fireman, died November 1985, age thirty-one. He had his head stoved in by a person or persons unknown as he walked home from the pub one night. No robbery from the person. No witnesses. No arrest was ever made.

'David Arthur Webb from Harefield, double glazing salesman, murdered April 1987, aged thirty-six. We know about him, of course. Again, not even a suspect.

'Gary Handsworth, of Aldersbrook Road, Wanstead, chimney sweep, died in August 1988, aged thirty-three. He apparently crashed his car into a tree when he was the worse for drink, and the car caught fire. He had head injuries and a broken neck, either of which could have caused his death. There were no witnesses. It was brought in as accidental death.

'Benjamin Hulfa, of St George's Avenue, Tufnell Park, insurance investigator, died January 1990, aged forty-four, of an overdose. Accidental death, or was it suicide?

'Then we come to our own Richard Neal from Pinner, security systems salesman, died March 1991, aged fifty, in mysterious circumstances.

'The sixth member of Red Watch to die was Barry John Lister of Dorking, Surrey, retired builder, aged sixty-six. It turns out that he was "Mouthwash", as Swilley guessed, and she near as dammit got to speak to him. She finally managed to track him down – he'd moved around a lot – only to discover that he died on Thursday last, of a heart attack.'

'A real heart attack?' Dickson asked.

'It looks that way. He died at home, with his wife present, in his own sitting room, watching *The Bill* on television.'

Dickson nodded. 'That'd do it.'

'He had a known heart condition, and his own doctor gave the certificate without any hesitation, so it looks all right. That only leaves two survivors from 1974: John Francis Simpson, age thirty-six, self-employed builder and decorator, with an address in St Albans, and Paul Godwin, age forty-one, who's still a fireman, and lives in Newcastle.'

'It certainly looks like a pattern,' Dickson conceded, 'and it's not one out of *Woman's Weekly*.'

Slider rubbed his hair up the wrong way in frowning thought. 'Leaving aside Lister, there's a little over a year separating each of the deaths. All could possibly have been murders, and Webb's certainly was. All but Sears, the earliest death, involve a fire. Two of the bodies, Neal and Handsworth, were badly burned, but none of the deaths was caused by fire. The two earliest deaths, Sears and Handsworth, involved head injuries. The later three, Webb, Hulfa and Neal, died of suffocation, though the method by which it was induced was different in each case. The same three also had a background of personal problems – money troubles, depression.' He rubbed his hair back the other way. 'I'm not sure where that gets us.'

'Strange, isn't it,' Atherton mused, 'that only two of them stayed in the fire service after Shaftesbury Avenue closed?'

'I don't know,' Slider said. 'Nobody stays a fireman for ever.'

'It does seem like rather a large drop-out rate, though.'

Dickson seemed to find this line unhelpful. 'What about Lister?' he said. 'He's the odd man out, isn't he? What do you make of him?'

'It looks as though he may have been onto something. Mrs Hulfa told us that Lister was in fact known as "Mouthwash" when he was in Red Watch. Jacqui Turner said that when she asked Neal who he was going to see on the Saturday, he said "Mouthwash", though she didn't realise it was a name, of course. I think we can assume that Lister was the mystery man Neal met in The Wellington.'

'Well that's one burning question answered, at least,' Dickson said ironically.

'Neal told Jacqui Turner he hadn't seen the old friend for years, so the meeting wasn't a matter of course. And Catriona Young said that Neal told her he had met an old friend on the Saturday who had warned him that someone was out to kill him. So it looks as though Lister may have decided for himself that all these deaths were more than coincidence. Presumably he presented Neal with at least some of the same information about his old colleagues that we have here. Exactly what he told Neal – whether he knew more than we do – of course we don't know. And we don't know how Neal took it, whether he believed it or not. He doesn't seem to have said anything to Mrs Neal – but then he doesn't ever seem to have talked to her much.'

'What does Lister's wife say? Presumably if he thought he had a good chance of being rubbed as well, he'd have told her about it,' Dickson said.

'We haven't had a chance to interview her yet, sir. That's next on our list.'

'Right, let's get to it, then. Someone tactful had better go and interview Mrs Lister, seeing she's so recently bereaved. This is not the moment to get complaints laid against us, even frivolous ones.'

'Norma, you take it,' Slider said. 'You've got a nice, kind face.'

'There's the two survivors, too,' Atherton said. 'Simpson and Godwin. If Lister warned Neal, he may have tried to warn them as well.'

'That's priority,' Dickson said. 'They're also presumably on the hit-list. We want to get to them before the murderer – if any – does. You'd better go and see Simpson yourself, Bill, and send Beevers up to Newcastle.' He intercepted the disappointed glances of the others and said with spare humour, 'He's a Methodist. He can be trusted in a strange town full of pubs.'

'The rest of you divide up the other deaths between you,' Slider said, suppressing a smile. 'Pull the records, go over everything with a toothcomb. If there's anyone to interview, go and interview them again. These men last worked together in 1974, but the deaths don't start until 1986. What happened in between? What happened in 1986 to start it all off? Was there any other connection between the men, apart from working together? All right, let's go.'

Muted conversation broke out as the troops got up from their various relaxed positions and moved away. Dickson, taking his departure, rubbed his hands. 'We'll beat that bastard yet!' he said to no-one in particular.

It was perfectly possible, of course, to assume he meant the murderer by that; but given the aftershave and clothes-brush phenomena, Slider felt inclined to make a different identification.

The little Victorian terraced house within bonging distance of St Albans' Cathedral yielded up Mrs Simpson, a pretty, harassed, freckle-faced woman. Her hair was tied up into a knot with a piece of string, from which it was escaping, and slipping into her eyes. She was wearing muddy rubber gloves, and there were streaks on her forehead and cheek where she had pushed the hair away without thinking.

'I'm doing a bit of gardening,' she explained hastily, seeing the direction of Slider's eyes. 'Jack's up in the attic, doing something to the electrics. Is it trouble? He hasn't been doing anything he shouldn't, has he?' A smile accompanied the words, and her eyes were limpid with an enviable lack of apprehension.

'No, nothing like that. I'd like to have a word with him, that's all,' said Slider. From beyond her, through the tiny house, came the captive roar of a washing machine in the kitchen, and the high, penetrating voices of two young male children playing in the garden.

'I'll go and get him, then,' she said. 'Come through to the kitchen, will you? Only if I don't keep my eye on the boys, they forget and trample on the borders.'

The kitchen was full of sunshine, and beyond the window the dayglo yellow of a forsythia whipped back and forth in the sharp breeze. The washing-machine's scream reached a peak of agony, and subsided into gurgles and whimpers as it passed from fast spin into second rinse. Outside a boy's voice pronounced deliberately: 'This is the goal, between here and here, all right? And I'm Peter Shilton.'

Slider went over to the back door and looked out. It was a tiny garden, with a square of lawn surrounded by crowded but neat borders, bright with genuflecting daffodils. The grim, square tower of the Cathedral rose behind the lacework of trees in the background. The sky was a pale, April blue, and large, leaky-looking clouds were bowling fast across it. England, my England, he thought.

Two boys of about eight and six occupied the lawn. At the far end the elder boy clutched the football to his chest as he gazed down the pitch, waiting for Gascoigne to shake off his marker and make himself a space. The chanting of the England supporters and the hooting and whistling of the Italian crowds were faint and far off in his ears. He was the greatest goalkeeper the world had ever known: nothing could shake his professional concentration.

Slider recognised the intensity of imagination which transformed the everyday with such elastic ease at that age. It was soon lost. Children grew up quickly – too quickly for a man who was hardly ever home. He remembered teaching Matthew to play cricket one

184

summer on the beach at Hastings. Matthew had been a bit younger than this boy, of course, but there had been the same intense concentration in the face, the same light of shared manhood in the eyes. That time had passed and gone. Even were Slider at home and at leisure, Matthew was now of an age to prefer the company of his peers and to find parents an embarrassment. It was desolating to Slider to think that he would probably never again feel his son's arms around him in a spontaneous hug.

Both boys had noticed him now, and were looking at him with their mother's clear, guiltless eyes; but Mrs Simpson had come back into the kitchen, and Slider turned away from the door towards her.

'Here he is,' she said. A male figure loomed in the narrow passage behind her, too big for the tiny house which had been built for a less well-nourished generation. 'Jack, this is Inspector – I'm sorry, I've forgotten your name already. How awful of me!'

'Detective Inspector Slider, Shepherd's Bush CID,' Slider said. Simpson came into the kitchen, a tall, loose-knit man wearing corduroy trousers and a well-ventilated navy jumper, through whose holes a check shirt provided relief and contrast. He had a good, open, healthy face, clear eyes, and tough springy hair that seemed to grow upwards, like heather, towards the light.

'How d'you do,' he said formally, shaking hands. His hand was large, very hard and very dry, with a workman's grime under the nails and a fresh scrape cross the knuckles. 'Shepherd's Bush? You're a long way from home.'

Before Slider could answer, the boys had come running into the kitchen, clamouring gladly for their father.

'Daddy, have you finished?'

'Come and play football.'

'Daddy, you know you said you'd show me about electric plugs and everything? Well, Jason says his Dad—'

Simpson fielded them expertly, turned them around with the swift efficiency of a BA ground team handling two 737s, and sent them back into the garden with orders to stay put until called for.

'Sorry about that,' he said, returning his attention to Slider. 'I usually take them out somewhere on a Saturday afternoon, but I had a little bit of a job to do today that couldn't wait – dodgy wiring.'

'You're an electrician?' Slider asked.

'Jack can turn his hand to anything. Would you like a cup of tea, Inspector?' Mrs Simpson asked.

'Well, if it's no trouble—'

'I'd like one, anyway, love,' Simpson said.

'Right then, I'll put the kettle on.'

'Now then, Inspector, what can I do for you? won't you sit down? Or would you prefer to go somewhere else to talk?' Simpson offered a chair at the kitchen table.

'This is fine by me,' Slider said, sitting where he could see out into the garden. The sunshine was too good to waste. The table was covered with a plastic tablecloth, and the smell of it, warmed by the sun, suddenly reminded him of the American cloth on the kitchen table at home, when he was a boy. Smells, more than sights or sounds, had the power instantly to carry you back. Kitchen, sunshine, green check American cloth, woman making tea – the rush of water into the kettle, the hiss and whap of the gas being lit – they were immutably parts of his childhood. All that was missing was the itch of a healing scab on the knee. Slider doubted whether, in those days of short pants, it would have been possible to find a single boy anywhere in Britain between the ages of five and thirteen without a scrape at some stage of healing on at least one kneecap.

'Right.' Simpson sat opposite him, laying his big, strong hands on the table and leaning back in the chair. All his gestures were large and open, the very antithesis of concealment. 'So what have I been up to?'

'I'd like to talk to you about a former colleague of yours, from the days when you were in the fire brigade.'

A cloud crossed the clear blue eyes. 'Oh Lord, it's not that silly business of Barry Lister's is it?'

'Ah, so Mr Lister did contact you?' Slider said.

Simpson gave a little exasperated snort. 'Poor old Mouthwash! I think he must be going a bit daft. I told him if he really believed all that rubbish to go to the police with it, but I didn't think he'd really do it. I'm sorry if you've been bothered with it.'

'I wonder if you'd mind telling me exactly what Mr Lister told you,' Slider said, flipping open his notebook. 'How did he approach you?'

'Well, he rang me up first of all – when would that be, Annie?' he asked over his shoulder.

'Oh, let me see, now – about a fortnight ago, wasn't it?' she answered from the worktop where she was assembling the tea-things. 'He came to see you on a Tuesday—'

'No, it was the Wednesday, don't you remember? Clashed with the football on the telly.'

'Oh yes, that's right.' She smiled at Slider. 'They're all mad about football, my men-folk. Yes, he came round on the Wednesday, so it would have been the Monday he phoned Jack. That's Monday week past.'

'Right,' said Simpson. 'Well, he phoned me up on the Monday night, completely out of the blue – I hadn't so much as thought of him in years. We used to be on the same watch when I was a fireman – well, I suppose you know that?'

'At Shaftesbury Avenue station.'

'Yes, that's right. I was there four years, until they shut it down. Then I went to Pratt Street, because I lived in Camden Town in those days, but I was only there about eighteen months. My Dad wanted me to go into his business – he's a builder and decorator – and that's what I've been doing ever since.'

'He's got his own business now, though,' Mrs Simpson said quickly, anxious there should be no mistake. 'He's self-employed.'

'I couldn't have done it without Dad,' Simpson said, turning his head. 'He taught me everything I know.'

'Your Dad had his money's worth out of you,' Mrs Simpson retorted. 'He'd have kept you fetching and carrying for him until you were old and grey if he'd had his way.'

'I had to learn the trade, didn't I?' Simpson said

187

indignantly. 'It was better than the City and Guilds, what I got from Dad.'

It was evidently an old friction. He noticed, not for the first time, how couples with an unresolved conflict liked to air it in front of a detached third party – the philosophy, he supposed, behind the Marriage Guidance Council.

'Had you had any contact with Mr Lister since you left Shaftesbury Avenue?' he asked.

Simpson turned back, embarrassed. 'No, not really. Well, he was a lot older than me, so it's not as if we'd've seen each other outside work anyway. I think he retired, actually, when Shaftesbury closed down – health problems of some sort,' he added vaguely.

'So you were surprised when he telephoned you?'

'A bit, yes. But then I thought he was probably lonely, poor old boy, so when he said could he drop in and see us, I said yes.' He slid a sideways look at his wife. 'Got it in the neck from Annie for that, as well.'

'Not for asking him,' she protested quickly. 'Only because you didn't find out if he was coming to tea or not.' She appealed to Slider. 'Not that I begrudged, I've never begrudged, but I like to know. It made it awkward not knowing if we ought to have it early and get it out of the way, or wait it for him.'

'Did he tell you when he phoned why he wanted to see you.' Slider asked Simpson.

'No. He just said he'd like to call in and have a bit of a chinwag about old times.'

'Yes, I see. So he turned up on Wednesday night—?'

'That's right. We'd had our tea, so Mouthwash and I had a couple of glasses of beer, and at first it was just general chat about what had he been doing and what had I been doing and so on – the usual sort of thing. Then he asked me if I'd heard from any of the others from Red Watch since the close-down. So I said no, not for years. Well, I went for a pint with Cookie and Moss a couple of times at first – that's Jim Sears and Gary Handsworth. They were what you'd call my best mates at the time. But we gradually drifted apart – you know how it is. After all, it was sixteen years ago. I haven't heard from any of them for years – or thought about them, either.'

He paused, and Mrs Simpson drifted closer, as if she sensed he was in danger. Simpson looked straight across the table at Slider, and his clear eyes were suddenly troubled.

'And then Barry comes out with it, all of a sudden. He says he thinks someone is trying to kill everyone on Red Watch.'

Mrs Simpson laid a hand on her husband's shoulder, and he put his own over it without looking round.

'You must have been very surprised,' Slider helped him along.

'I was shocked. I thought poor old Mouthwash had flipped his lid. I mean, he's pretty old, and he wasn't looking too chipper—'

'Downright ill, I would have said,' Mrs Simpson said. 'He wasn't a good colour.' Her head snapped round sharply and she said, 'Jackie, Tom, go and play. Your Dad's told you once.' The boys, who had drifted up to the open door, drifted away again, disappointed. 'I don't want them to hear any of this,' she said when they were out of earshot. 'It's not healthy.'

'Did Mr Lister explain why he made this astonishing claim?' Slider asked.

Simpson nodded. 'Oh yes, but I didn't believe a word of it. I mean, it was just a load of rubbish. He said four of us had been murdered already, and that unless something was done, we'd all be bumped off one by one.' His hand tightened around his wife's, and she interrupted.

'I stopped him. I wasn't having it. It was making Jack upset. I told him, I said it was just an old man's sick fancy, and that he should go and see a doctor. Well, of course, he was already seeing a doctor, but that isn't what I meant.'

'What did he say to that?'

'Oh, he said it wasn't imagination, it was all true, and that my Jack ought to take action before it was too late,' she went on, her eyes bright and hard. 'I said if he didn't stop I'd throw him out myself.'

189

'Now, Annie, don't get upset.' Simpson smiled weakly at Slider. 'You wouldn't think to look at her, but she can be a fierce little thing when she's roused.'

'Did Mr Lister tell you who he thought was responsible?'

Simpson looked apologetic. 'Well, no. I didn't let him give me any details.' He rolled his eyes significantly towards his wife. 'Annie was getting upset, and it was just a load of – a lot of rubbish anyway. So I told him I didn't want to know, and that if he really thought there was anything in it, he should go and see the police. And that was it, really.'

'He didn't say any more?'

'Not about that. He sat quiet for a bit, and then he asked could he have a drink of water to take a pill. He wasn't looking too clever. I think he might have had a bad turn. Anyway, he took a pill, and then he talked about the football for a bit, and then he went, and I haven't heard from him since. So he really did take it to the police, then?'

'No, he didn't,' Slider said. 'I don't know whether he would have done so or not: as it came about, he missed his chance. He died last Thursday evening.'

Simpson's eyes only widened slightly, but Mrs Simpson gave a loud and surprising cry. 'Oh my Lord!'

'It was a heart attack. He died at home, in front of the television.'

The Simpsons exchanged a swift glance – relief? Reassurance?

'The poor old blighter,' Simpson said. 'Well I never. So he really was sick?'

'In his body,' Slider said. 'Not necessarily in his head. I'm sorry to say that it seems as though there may have been some substance in what he came to warn you about. At the time of his visit to you, four of your former colleagues had met violent deaths. Two of them at least were murdered. And there's been another murder since then. Last Sunday—'

'I don't want to hear it!' Mrs Simpson suddenly cried out. 'That's enough about death and murder! I won't hear another word!'

190

'Be quiet, Annie,' Simpson said, not loudly, but firmly, and she shut her mouth sharply, pulling her hand back from his and holding it with the other one at the base of her throat. Simpson looked steadily into Slider's face, waiting to hear the worst. 'Who – which of them are dead?'

'Sears, Handsworth, Webb and Hulfa. And Richard Neal was murdered last Sunday night,' Slider said.

Simpson said nothing at all, but his skin seemed to pull tighter over his bones.

'I have reason to believe that Mr Lister tried to warn Neal, as well. Mr Neal told someone that an old friend he hadn't seen for years had warned him that someone was trying to kill him.'

Simpson breathed heavily through his nose. The constriction of his face muscles made it look as though he were starting to grin. 'Poor old bugger. No-one believed him, and he was telling the truth all the time. Poor old bugger.'

'Jack!' Mrs Simpson protested.

'So Cookie's dead too, eh? And Mouthwash. And that leaves only me.' He really was grinning now, but his eyes were frightened.

'And Paul Godwin,' Slider added.

'Paul doesn't count. He was only with us a few weeks, just before the end, to replace Larry. He wasn't really part of it. All the rest are dead now. How does it go, that old rhyme? And then there was one!' He laughed, and the sound of it seemed to shock him as much as his wife, for he stopped immediately, and put his hands to his face in a curious gesture, as if to see what it was doing. Slider looked past him to Mrs Simpson.

'How about that cup of tea? I think we could all do with one.'

'He really was shocked, then?' Atherton asked.

'It was two cups before he could go on. There was certainly strong emotion at work there.'

'Which could be explained by a number of things. So then he told you about the last days of Pompeii, did he?'

191

'They were all one big, happy family, it seems – one for all and all for one—'

'Twice over, since there were eight of 'em.'

'Within the group, of course, there were minor alliances. Simpson and Sears were best buddies. Richard Neal's closest friend was Gilbert Forrester.'

'Forrester? He wasn't on our list.'

'I'm coming to it. Neal apparently practically lived in Forrester's house, and he, Forrester and Mrs Forrester were inseparables. Went out together, went on holiday together, everything. Neal wasn't married then, of course, and already had a reputation for chasing women, but Forrester didn't seem to have any fears about it.'

'Was Simpson suggesting—?'

'No, rather the opposite. He seemed to think it was a miracle Neal wasn't; but he was quite young at the time, and probably not very interested in the doings of his elders. Anyway, to the story: about a month before the Shaftesbury Avenue station closed down, Red Watch was called out to a fire. It was a Saturday night, traffic was terrible, and by the time they got there, the fire had taken a good hold. It was one of those flats in Ridgemount Gardens, you know?'

'Near the University?'

'Yes. And apparently there was an old woman still inside. Neal and Forrester went in to get her out. Neal came out with the old girl over his shoulder, got her down safely, and then realised Forrester hadn't followed him out. Before they could stop him, he went back in, although conditions had deteriorated by then. Sears followed him.' Slider paused. 'The trouble is that it's double hearsay. Simpson wasn't on duty that night – he was off sick – so he was telling me what Sears told him.'

'And there's now no-one to confirm or deny the story,' Atherton observed. 'Neat.'

'It seems that part of the ceiling had come down, and Forrester had got tangled up in the electrical flex which had come down with it. Sears found Neal trying to release him, but the flex was round his neck and he was apparently already dead – accidental hanging. Then the rest of the ceiling came down, and the floor looked about to go too, and Sears dragged Neal out. That was when Neal got that burn on the back of his hand, by the way – the one that left the scar we identified him by.'

Atherton nodded.

'Anyway, it wasn't until the fire was out that they managed to recover Forrester's body. It was pretty charred, but the post mortem showed that he died by hanging, which vindicated Sears and Neal for saving themselves, and the inquest cleared them of any blame. All the same, Forrester's death seemed to take the heart out of Red Watch. The station closed down soon afterwards, but Simpson says they probably would all have left the service if it hadn't, or at least have transferred away from each other.'

'Who blamed who, and for what?'

'They all felt guilty, according to Simpson, for not realising sooner that Forrester hadn't come out. Seconds can make all the difference in a situation like that. And they felt bad about not getting the body out before it got burnt.'

'Group guilt?'

'There was an unpleasant little incident to help them along – Mrs Forrester came round to the station a few days later. She made quite a scene, called them all murderers, accused them of negligence and I don't know what – generally threw grand hysterics centre stage.'

'Embarrassing.'

'Exactly. So it isn't too surprising that afterwards – after the station closed – they didn't keep in touch with each other. In fact, only Sears continued as a full-time fireman. All the others left the service, so it was presumably a pretty traumatic experience.'

'And we know that Neal didn't talk about it at all, to anyone. Not even his wife. But who was Paul Godwin?'

'He was transferred onto their watch for the last month, to replace Forrester. So he wasn't really a part of it.'

'And he hasn't been murdered. Suggestive, isn't it?'

'Nor Simpson, who wasn't on duty that night.'

'So he says. It would bear checking, don't you think?'

Slider smiled. 'You fancy him for the murderer?'

'He's the only survivor. Neal and Lister snuff it immediately after Lister tells Simpson his suspicions, and, presumably, tells him that he's also warned Neal. You say he's a big, strong man, with strong hands, and as an ex-fireman he'd be accustomed to handling bodies. Rigging up Webb as a hanging wouldn't present him with any problems. He's an electrician, with plenty of electrical flex on hand. He knows about fires, so he'd presumably have an idea of how much evidence would be concealed by the appropriate blaze. And you've only his word for it that he didn't keep in touch with his former mates. As one of them, he'd be in an ideal position to do so, if he wanted to.'

'Very nice. And what's his motive?'

Atherton shrugged. 'We'll think of something. I can't do everything at once. Maybe Forrester's death was really his fault, and he was getting rid of everyone who could point the finger at him.'

'It looks as though Catriona Young was right, at any rate,' Slider said thoughtfully. 'Neal did have a great tragedy in his life.'

'Has Simpson got an alibi?' Atherton asked, pursuing his own line.

'Not one we can check. He says he was at home, which is what you'd expect on a Sunday night, and his wife confirms—'

'Which is what you'd expect of a loyal wife.'

'There is another tempting suspect, of course,' Slider said. 'The hysterical wife. Mrs Forrester. A revenge killing.'

'Of the whole watch?'

'Why not? Group responsibility. Or blind grief. You didn't mind it being the whole lot when it was Simpson, and that was without a motive at all.'

'True. But listen,' Atherton said, doing a right-about-face, 'we don't really know that the deaths were linked at all. Sixteen years is a long time, and apart from Webb, we

194

can't even be sure they were murdered. Sears mugged, Handsworth killed in a car crash, Hulfa OD'd, Neal just possibly accidental death while pursuing sexual gratification—'

'Yes, I'd thought of that, too,' said Slider. 'And the simplest solution is often the right one.'

'In that case, maybe Webb was murdered by a person or persons unknown, and Collins really did kill Neal after all.'

'Oh thanks!'

'But then the Webb and Neal cases do have similarities,' Atherton went on perversely. 'Maybe they were connected, and all the other deaths were just coincidence.'

'Thanks again.' Slider eyed him sidelong. 'No offers on Catriona Young? The Boston Strangler? Edward VII?'

Atherton looked dignified. 'Give me time. I'll get around to them.'

CHAPTER THIRTEEN

The Dear Dead Days of Long Ago

MRS LISTER, DESPITE HER RECENT bereavement, was perfectly willing to talk. She was a strong woman in her sixties, whose thick-skinned, coarse-pored face had blurred into hermaphroditic ugliness, while her voice had deepened and hoarsened like a man's, as if Nature had realised that in old age there was no more need for sexual differentiation.

She welcomed Norma, disconcertingly, like an equal, dismissed the neighbour who was hovering about her, and put the kettle on. Norma had long since learned that tea was always on the go in the house of the dead.

'That's better,' Mrs Lister said when they were alone together. 'They do treat you like a child, don't they, when someone's died? Fussing round, practically tying your shoelaces for you. Oh, Mavis means well, but I'm glad you came, dear, to give me an excuse to get rid of her. She's been driving me barmy all morning.'

The tea was made, the tray was laid, the cigarettes were lit, and in the tiny parlour, with the heavy lorries thundering past through Dorking High Street only a few feet away beyond the window and the narrow pavement, the story unfolded.

'Yes, Dad told me about his theory that everyone was being murdered. I just let him get on with it – silly old fool,' she said, not without affection. 'You know what men are like, dear. Once they retire, they feel left out of things. They need something to occupy them, make them feel important again. I told him there wasn't a scrap of proof, but it didn't make any difference. Milk and sugar, dear?'

'Milk please, no sugar. Thanks. Do you think he really believed it, though?'

'Well, now, funny you should ask that. Have a biscuit, love – help yourself. There's Bourbons under the Rich Tea. Well, I'd have said no, because after all, if he believed it, he'd have been worried for his own skin, wouldn't he? Which he wasn't really. It was more like, well, a puzzle, sort of, like a crossword puzzle, something he was trying to work out. Until after he'd been to see Dick Neal, anyway. When he came back from London on Saturday evening, he was a bit funny.'

'How d'you mean, funny?'

'Quiet, thoughtful, you know. I thought he'd overdone it, and made himself tired. He had this heart condition, dear, and he wasn't supposed to overdo. Of course, it may well've been that. But on the other hand, he might have got worried all of a sudden. Dick may have said something to him, I don't know, to make him think.'

'Did he tell you who he thought was the murderer?'

'No. I don't think he'd thought that far himself – unless Dick Neal gave him some ideas. That might be what made him so quiet the last few days.'

'So when did he first get the idea there was something going on?'

'It was after Ben died, Ben Hulfa. When he heard about that, he said to me, "Winnie," he said, "there's not many of us left off the old Red Watch. You'd almost think someone had it in for us." And after that he started thinking about it, and putting two and two together and making ten. I got fed up with it in the end. I told him he shouldn't dwell on that kind of thing – unhealthy, I called it – but I don't think it stopped him.' She sighed. 'He just kept it to himself after that.'

'And what suddenly made him decide to warn Mr Neal and Mr Simpson?'

'Your guess is as good as mine, love. I don't know. I don't suppose he did, either. This last year, since he

197

retired, he's been getting very strange. I didn't want him to give up his work, but he got the bee in his bonnet, and that was that. I said to him, I said, I know you've got a heart condition, but you can't let it rule your life. What are you going to do with yourself, sitting about the house all day? Getting under my feet and driving me mad. I said better you go on doing a bit, part-time at least, just to give you an interest, keep you occupied. He was a builder and decorator, dear, and there's always little odd jobs that people want doing. Begging for it, really, because there's no trusting these fly-by-night firms. People want someone they can trust to do the job properly. But no. Dad wouldn't have it. He said sixty-five was enough for any man, and that was that. There's no shifting them once they've made their mind up. And then when Ben Hulfa died he started thinking about who was left, and, well, one thing led to another, and he came up with this silly idea. I reckon it's that that killed him in the end.'

'How d'you mean?'

'Well, it was Thursday he heard Dick Neal was dead. He came back in and he said, "Dick Neal's been murdered, Winnie," just like that. So I said, what d'you mean, murdered? And he said Dick'd been killed in a hotel fire. "But I bet you anything it was murder," he said. I told him not to be silly, and he never said anything more about it. The telly was on, you see, and I was watching. I thought he was, too, but when the adverts came on I said, "D'you want a cup of tea, Dad?" and he never answered. And I looked across at him, and he was dead.'

Her eyes filled suddenly with tears. She picked up her cup and bent her head over it to hide them, and her lips trembled as she sipped. When she put the cup down, she was in control again, but there was a lost and lonely look about her.

Here was the end of forty years of taking care of the silly old fool, Norma thought: the rough endearments, the shirts ironed and the cups of tea brought. The chair opposite was empty. Winnie would watch telly alone from now on.

And the last word Barry John Lister ever spoke, it suddenly occurred to Norma, was *murder*. How very odd!

'What did you mean when you said he came back in?' she asked. 'Came back in from where?'

'From the kitchen, where the phone is. That's how he knew Dick was dead.'

'Oh, he had a phone call, did he? Do you know who it was from?'

'Marsha. Marsha Forrester. That's what he said when he came back. "That was Marsha," he said. "Dick Neal's been murdered," he said.'

'And who,' Norma asked, 'is Marsha Forrester?'

Two cups of tea later, Norma had had the whole story of Gilbert Forrester's death, plus sundry details of his home life, and his friendship with Richard Neal.

'I always thought it was a bit queer, the way Dick hung around their house all the time,' Mrs Lister told her. 'To see the three of them together, well, you'd've had a hard job knowing who was married to who.'

'Do you think Neal was having an affair with Mrs Forrester?' Norma hazarded.

Mrs Lister didn't answer directly, but her lips pursed as though someone had pulled a drawstring round her mouth. 'I never liked her. There was something hard about her. Well, to my mind a married woman had no business going out and doing a job anyway, leaving her husband to fend for himself, to say nothing of her daughter. Of course, with the shifts, he was home quite a lot looking after the kiddie himself, but that's no excuse. There was always something mannish about that Marsha,' she brooded. 'The three of them were more like three men going out together. And the language! Well, I suppose any woman who'd do a man's job would have to be unwomanly, wouldn't she?'

Norma passed this tactless question by. 'What job did she do?'

'She worked in a hospital – not a nurse, which wouldn't

have been so bad. She was a – I can't think of the word. One of those people that cuts up dead bodies.'

'A pathologist?'

'That's right. Makes me shudder to think of it. And her a qualified doctor! You'd think she'd want to do something better with her life. Not that she'd any business being a doctor in the first place, when she had a husband and child of her own. But there – people are all different, I suppose.' And she looked sharply at Norma, to see if she disagreed. 'Gil thought the sun shone out of her eyes, at all events. Are you married, dear?'

'Not yet. I'm still hoping to meet Mr Right,' Norma said unblushingly. 'So had your husband kept in touch with Mrs Forrester since the station closed?'

'Well, he was the union representative at the time of the accident, so of course he had to see that Marsha was all right. There was the death benefit from the widows and orphans fund, and the pension and everything. But I think he felt sorry for her anyway, so he kept a sort of eye on her for the first few months. He didn't have all that much to do with her once he left the service – just a Christmas card every year, and a phone call now and then.'

'Did he keep in touch with any of the others?'

'No, not that I knew of. I dare say Marsha might have told him the news now and then when he phoned, but you'd have to ask her that.'

'Did you think it was strange that the men didn't keep in touch with each other afterwards? I mean, they were a very tightly-knit unit, weren't they?'

'What, all one happy family, you mean? You don't want to believe all you hear about that. You know what men are like when they get together. It was like that with the National Service – all boys together, horseplay and getting drunk every night and singing, but once they were demobbed, off they went to their homes and never gave each other a second thought.'

'But it seems that Richard Neal didn't even tell his wife he had ever been a fireman. He never spoke about it at all, to anyone. Don't you think that was strange?'

'He was strange,' Mrs Lister said emphatically. 'The way he ran after women, I think there was something wrong with him. It's a pity you can't have men like that doctored. He even made a pass at me once, you know, at the Christmas dance.'

Now that *is* strange, Norma thought, but with a noble effort managed not to say it.

Joanna phoned to say goodbye.

'I wish you weren't going,' Slider said plaintively.

'I wish you were coming with me,' she returned.

'Still, I expect you'll have a lovely time,' he said, trying to be gracious about it. 'They'll probably give you wonderful parties and receptions and things, and you won't miss me at all.'

'Stop fishing. Besides, you know receptions are always ghastly.'

'I know you always say they are, but maybe German ones will be different.'

'They won't. They're all the same: a glass of cheap white wine, and an hour being ballsachingly nice to the sponsors, which is awful, and their wives, which is worse.'

'Why worse?'

'Oh – I find it depressing that we've got to the last decade of the twentieth century and still define women according to the man they're attached to. And worse still, that women allow it.' She chuckled suddenly. 'It reminds me – did I ever tell you about Gary Potts?'

'That's a made-up name if ever I heard one. Who's Gary Potts?'

'He used to be our principal trumpet. He's left now, gone to Australia, and the world's a duller place without him, I can tell you! He was a real gorblimey Cockney, about five feet tall and four feet wide, utterly shameless, with a wicked sense of humour – and the best trumpet player in the known universe to boot. I loved him.'

'I thought you loved Atherton.'

'Oh yes, I forgot.'

'What brought this Potts to mind, anyway?'

'Well, we had to go to one of these receptions one evening at the Festival Hall – the Waterloo Room, or some such nirvana. The usual speed is for the orchestra to hang around the bar looking sheepish, eating all the free canapés and totally ignoring the punters, which is not the purpose at all. So on this occasion the orchestra manager came and rousted us all out and made us go off and do the pretty. He grabbed hold of Gary and pointed him in the direction of this fabulous-looking old dame with a blue rinse and a fur coat and said, "She looks as if she's rolling in it. Go and be nice to her."

'So old Gary goes up to her, and, typical style, gives her a huge grin and says, "Allo darlin', oo are you?" The old girl looks a bit surprised, but she dimples gamely and says "Oh, I'm not anyone important, really, but my husband's in oil." And Gary stares at her with his mouth well open and says, "What is 'e then, a fuckin' sardine?" ' Joanna sighed happily at the memory. 'God, I miss him! Dem were de days, Joxer, dem were de days.'

'A pathologist?'

'Yes Guv, at University College Hospital in 1974,' said Norma. 'She and her husband had been living in Hampstead Garden Suburb—'

'Nice.'

'Yes, and handy for both their jobs. But about six months after he died, she moved to a similar post in Hammersmith Hospital, and she and the child moved to a house in Brook Green.'

'Interesting,' Slider said. 'Neal had been living in Golders Green—'

'About half a mile from Hampstead Garden Suburb—'

'And when the Shaftesbury Avenue station closed, he moved to Hammersmith, got a job at Betcon and a flat in Dalling Road—'

'About half a mile from Brook Green,' Norma concluded. 'Coincidence?'

202

'I hope we shall find out,' said Slider.

'But a pathologist, Guv – could be very helpful if you wanted to kill a whole string of people.' She started to tick off the points on her fingers. 'In the first place, you'd be cold-blooded enough about bodies. In the second place, you'd know enough about post mortem effects to rig your murders to look like accidents or suicides—'

'You'd also know that the ligature mark of electrical flex on Webb's neck would prove that he'd been murdered,' Slider pointed out.

'But the murderer obviously expected the body to be burned in the fire,' Norma said.

'Even so, she couldn't have been sure the ligature mark would be sufficiently burned as to be unrecognisable. And changing the flex for rope was an unnecessary act, if the idea was to fake suicide. Webb could just as easily have strangled himself with flex as hanged himself with rope, and a pathologist would know that.'

'Maybe she got careless. But you must admit she's got a very good motive,' Norma hurried on. 'Classic revenge. Her mind turned by the terrible tragedy, she blames the whole watch for his death, and sets about murdering them one by one—'

'Very MGM. I can see Bette Davis in the part,' Slider agreed. 'All the same, if you're thinking she moved to Hammersmith to keep tabs on Neal, the more easily to rub him out, tell me why didn't she get to him for another sixteen years?'

'Saving the best till last, perhaps. If she considered him the most guilty—'

'But he wasn't the last. There was Barry Lister – and two left alive.'

'But the two left alive weren't on duty on the night of the fire,' Norma said triumphantly, 'and poor old Mouthwash'd had a heart condition for years. She may well have thought she wouldn't need to do him at all, that nature would do it for her. As was the case in the end. We don't know that he wouldn't have been next on the list, if he hadn't popped his clogs of his own accord.'

'She may have moved to Hammersmith simply to be near Neal, her former best buddy and putative lover,' Slider pointed out. 'Nothing more suspicious than that.'

'Yes sir,' Norma said, giving him a sample of her West Coast smile, which had been known to disarm the most thick-skinned villain and reduce him to stammering self-consciousness. 'But on the other hand—'

'Yes,' Slider said. 'The hysterical outburst at the fire station helps the thing along. All the same, why wait eleven years to begin the murders? That rather takes the edge off the idea of the white-hot fury of revenge.'

'But revenge is a dish best eaten cold.'

'Who said that?'

'I did.'

'Ah,' Slider said. 'Well, I'd better go and see Mrs Forrester, find out what sort of a cook she is.'

The house Marsha Forrester lived in, three floors and a semi-basement, had been built for one moderately wealthy family, and now, through the turning of the wheel, was divided into four flats for only slightly less wealthy people. Mrs Forrester had the drawing-room floor: high ceilings, mouldings, and a handsome fireplace. She had a collection of early English landscape watercolours that Slider would almost have contemplated crime for, and a seven-foot grand piano which seemed to have been designed for the sole purpose of displaying the Chinese bowl full of pot-pourri which admired its own reflection in the polished surface of the lid.

'I knew I shouldn't have tried to have a day off,' she said, returning from answering the telephone, which had rung just as she was showing Slider in. 'So much for my *dolce far niente.*'

'Sorry,' said Slider.

'Never mind, you can't help it. A glass of sherry?'

Sherry was a drink he'd never seen the point of. The sweet, he'd found, tasted like cough syrup, and the dry like old tin cans; but on the other hand, the bottle she was hovering over didn't have either of the words *Harveys* or *British* on it, so he thought he might be in for a new experience.

'Thank you,' he said.

She brought the glass over to him, and then sat down on the chesterfield with her own, tucking one leg up under her. She was half a dozen years or so older than him, Slider thought, but looked very, very good for it. She was wearing jeans and a chambray shirt, and her short grey-sandy hair, cut in what used to be called a page-boy bob, was shoved back out of the way behind a cloth-covered Alice band. Clothes and style would not have looked out of place on an eighteen-year-old, but Marsha Forrester could carry it off. She must, he assumed, be wearing makeup, but it was applied so as to look as though she was not wearing any, and about her there hung a faint and evocative fragrance which he tracked down through memory at last as Balmain's *Vent Vert*. If she went to all this trouble on her day off, he thought, what would she have looked like *en fête*?

He sipped the sherry cautiously. It was almost colourless, and tasted of grapes, with a slight hint of burnt sugar. He looked up and found her watching his surprise, and smiled, and said 'Delicious.'

She smiled too. 'Good. So, then, what's all this about? I suppose it's to do with poor Dick Neal, is it?'

'Why should you think that?'

'So cautious, Inspector? Well, I can't think of any other reason you'd be coming to visit me. Was there something untoward about his death? Am I suspected of something?' Despite her light and teasing tone, there was a watchful look about her, Slider thought. Before he could answer she went on, 'You'd better tell me straight away, when is the alibi required for?'

'If you know about his death, you ought to know that,' he said, equally lightly.

'Yes, but I've a terrible memory. I know it was some time at the weekend, but I can't remember if it was Saturday or Sunday. Oh well, no matter, I'll tell you what I was doing both days. On the Saturday morning I was at the hospital. I had lunch with an old friend, did some shopping in the afternoon, came back here for a bath, and then went out to the opera with a gentleman, and supper afterwards at Bertorelli's. On the Sunday I got up late, and left about twelve to go down to the country. Some publishing people who have a place in Gloucestershire. I'm hoping for great things from them – a little book I've written that I'd like to see in print.'

She sipped her sherry and made a face. 'They turned out to be rather hard work, or she did, at least. He was sweet, but very nouveau, and they had the most ghastly friends in who simply talked about ski-ing *all the time*. They turned out to be vegetarians, so the food was grisly, too, but he had a grown-up son by his first wife, who, thank God, had a sense of humour or I might have left embarrassingly early. As it was, I drove back at a respectably late hour, and went straight to bed with a book.'

She looked across at him with a faintly challenging smile. 'Does that let me off the hook? Aren't you going to take it down? I should hate to have to say it all again.'

'I haven't come to take a statement from you,' he smiled. 'At the moment I just want to find out some background information.'

'About me?' she asked. Was there the faintest edge to her voice?

'About Richard Neal. We've had a difficult time getting any sort of picture of him. He seems to have been a very secretive man.'

'If it's pictures of him you want,' she said, getting up.

'I didn't mean that literally,' Slider said.

'I know you didn't,' she answered, crossing the room to the bureau. 'But if you want the story about Dick and me – which I assume is what you've come for – you're going to have to let me tell it in my own way. With illustrations.'

She brought back a cardboard box – it had 'Basildon Bond' on the lid in curly script, and the corners were battered with age – and sat down with it on her knee. She lifted the lid, and began to sort through the photographs inside.

'This is one of the earliest pictures I've got of Dick and me,' she said.

He took it. It was an old black-and-white print, taken, he would guess from the style, in the late fifties or early sixties. A country lane – pale road, rough grass verge, tall hedge and dark trees beyond in full summer leaf; a young man and a young woman standing astride their stationary bicycles, hands on the handlebars, smiling for the camera. The front wheel of his bike had swung in to touch the front wheel of hers, like carriage horses touching noses.

'He was eighteen and I was seventeen,' said Mrs Forrester. 'Weren't we beautiful?'

They were both wearing shorts and shirts with the sleeves rolled up, ankle socks and lace-up shoes. Neal had thick curly hair, cut very short at the sides – was it that which made his ears seem to stand out, or did everyone have sticking-out ears in those days? With his straight nose and engaging grin, he looked like every girl's dream boyfriend. He even had good-looking knees, Slider noted.

Marsha Forrester – or whatever her name had been then – looked ravishingly pretty, even in black and white. Her hair was in much the same style as it was now, except she had a fringe then, and it was held back with hair-slides instead of a band. She was smiling too. They looked like clean-limbed, happy young people – advertising archetypes – and the sun was shining down on them, as it always did in that far-off, innocent land.

Slider felt a cold shiver go down his spine. Old photographs like this made him feel melancholy. The world had moved on so far and so fast from that carless, crimeless, tellyless, always summer place he'd grown up in. The Richard Neal in this photograph had – and thank God! – no idea what a horrible, pitiful, grievous end he would come to; but the fact that he was there smiling out of the photograph made Slider feel that the young man still existed somewhere, and that the bad end was still to come, without his being able to do anything to prevent it.

It was like those dreams where you tried to shout out a warning, and could only whisper.

'You'd known him a long time, then,' he said at last.

'Dick used to say we went to different schools together,' she smiled, taking the photograph back. 'His grammar school and mine were almost next door to each other, and we lived in adjacent streets. We started going out together when I was sixteen – my mother wouldn't have let me have a boyfriend before that. It seems impossible to imagine nowadays, doesn't it? But Dick had been waiting outside the school gates for me and walking me home since I was fourteen.'

While she spoke, she handed him other photographs: variations on a sunlit theme, Dick and Marsha doing innocent, healthy, Famous Five things together. Bicycles and rickety tents and country lanes featured prominently in their activities. And here they were at last actually holding hands with a mountain in the background.

'When we were in the sixth form our schools did a joint school journey to Switzerland. Pretty revolutionary stuff in those days. Of course, we were put up in different hotels, the boys and the girls, but all the same . . .'

'Yes,' said Slider.

'When we got back, I told my mother that Dick had kissed me. She tried so hard not to be shocked, poor dear.' She took back the Swiss mountain. 'We were the ideal couple in those days. Everybody thought we'd get married eventually.'

'Why didn't you?'

'I don't know really,' she said vaguely, hunting through the box. 'Maybe just because everyone expected us to. You know how contrary young people can be. Then when I left school I went to University College to train as a doctor, and Dick and I didn't see so much of each other for a while. Our experiences were very different – he had to do his National Service, of course.'

'Where did he serve?'

'Oh, right here in England. At Eastbourne, in fact – a cushy number, as they used to say. We used to have frightfully naughty weekends in Brighton. I was still living at home at that time, so I had to pretend I was going to visit a girlfriend. And to book into a hotel we had to pretend to be married – a Woolworth's wedding ring, and signing in as Mr and Mrs Neal, so funny when you think back!'

She handed him a black-and-white snap of her and Neal on the front at Brighton. He had his arm round her waist, and they both looked faintly apprehensive through their smiles. Brighton, Slider thought. Jacqui Turner, seafront photographers – how the wheel turns.

'You were obviously a trail-blazer,' he said.

'Oh, I think studying medicine gives you a sense of proportion. You can't worry too much about purely local and contemporary taboos when you're dealing with the eternal verities of life and death.'

He handed back the picture. 'So you went on seeing each other for the whole two years?'

'Yes. It was a really happy time, when I think back on it. Perhaps the best time.' She was silent a moment, with a smile hovering near the surface. Then it went in. 'When he was demobbed he joined the fire brigade. His parents were terribly upset – they wanted him to pick up where he left off and go to university. They thought he was letting himself down, and I must say I was surprised myself. He had a good brain, and it seemed dreadful to me that he should waste it doing a job like that. We quarrelled about it when he told me. It was almost the end of us.'

Echoes of Catriona Young, Slider thought – the intellectual girlfriend who thought she was too good for the likes of him. It was almost as if Neal was acting out his own life story.

'Why do you think he did it?' he asked.

'He said he'd always wanted to be a fireman, ever since he was a little boy. You know, one of those eternal passions like wanting to be an engine driver. I don't know if that was true – he'd never mentioned it to me before. But on the other hand, he seemed perfectly happy afterwards being a fireman, so maybe it was. He told his parents he didn't want to go to university and be another three years behind everyone else, which made sense, but they never really accepted it. It caused a breach between them, which was never properly healed. They died without forgiving him – Dick minded that very much. He was a very sensitive person underneath it all.'

Yes, he could believe that, Slider thought. Only a man obsessed with his own emotions could spread so much devastation around him. 'And you, meanwhile, were still studying to be a doctor?'

'Five long years,' she said with a faint smile. 'It was a hard struggle, too. My father died, and all his estate was tied up in a trust, so my mother had very little to live on, and I had less. Still, one manages.' She shrugged. 'They say adversity builds character.'

'Why did you decide to specialise in pathology? That was an unusual choice, wasn't it?'

'The perversity factor again: just because it was an unusual choice. I liked shocking people, and *were* they shocked at the idea of a young lady cutting up dead bodies! But there were also practical reasons – it was the least well subscribed specialisation, which meant there was no competition for places, and none later for jobs. I can't say I've ever regretted it,' she added thoughtfully. 'When I think of my contemporaries who went on to be GPs, being coughed over by ghastly, washed-out, depressed women, and dragged out of bed at all hours . . .'

'Surgeons have a pretty decent life, though, don't they?'

'Yes, and I did use to think I'd like to be a surgeon. That would have been almost as shocking, too. But to be a surgeon you first have to go through being a houseman, and they never get to bed at all. No, I made the comfortable choice, I think.'

'And did you go on seeing Dick Neal?'

'Oh yes. We were always friends. And of course he introduced me to Gil – my husband – so I have him to thank for that.'

'How did he take it, when you got married?'

She hesitated. 'He didn't like it, of course. I think he still thought we would get married one day. For a while he was furious with both of us. But Gil asked him to be best man, and managed to talk him round. Gil was a great diplomat. And Dick really loved him. I don't think he could have borne to lose both of us. So he had to accept it.'

'Your husband knew that you and Dick had been – fond of each other?'

'Gil knew everything,' she said firmly, and looked at him, and then away again in a curious access of embarrassment. Now what, he wondered, did that relate to? 'The three of us were always close, from the first day we all met. It was a very equal relationship. No-one was left out. All for one and one for all, as Gil used to say.'

Slider flinched away from Dumas-yet-again and tried a banana shot. 'Why *did* you marry him instead of Dick?' he asked, as though she had already admitted there was something odd about it.

She had taken out another photograph, and stared at it unseeingly as she answered. 'Because I knew he would make a more suitable husband than Dick.' She drew a faint, shaky sigh, and then looked across at Slider. 'There, that's said. Not much of a reason, is it? But it seemed a good one at the time. Gil was a steady, reliable man, the sort who'd make a good husband and a good father, who'd save, and get on, and provide for one. I was sick of being a poor student by then,' she went on in a muted burst of passion. 'Scrimping and scraping and making do, never having anything nice to wear, or going out anywhere. I couldn't bear that kind of life. Gil was kind and generous, and he cared for me as a husband should. Dick was a spendthrift. Oh, he was good fun to be with, but you'd never have known from one day to the next whether the bailiffs would be knocking at your door.'

'Yes, I understand,' said Slider.

She looked up. 'Do you?'

'Yes. But did Dick?'

'You'd hardly expect him to, would you,' she said. 'Especially as—'

'Yes?'

211

She obviously changed her mind. 'When I was twenty-five the Trust ended and I came into Dad's money,' she said, and it made enough sense to have been a sequitur, but Slider felt certain it was not what she had been going to say. 'It wasn't a huge fortune, but it was enough to be comfortable on. So I could have married anyone, you see – even Dick. But by then it was too late. In the mean time, there was Eleanor.'

She handed him the photographer she had been holding. There in the middle was Marsha Forrester, looking like Millicent Martin by now, only prettier, in an A-line coat that showed her knees and little hat perched above her curved hair, holding a baby whose dress and shawl trailed almost to its mother's knees. On one side of her stood Neal in a suit, button-down collar and narrow tie, his hair brushed straight back but still unruly: handsome, debonair, faintly raffish,

On the other side was a taller man, broad-shouldered, fair, with straight, light hair, already thinning, and a pleasant, kind, unemphatic sort of face. The kind of man any child would want as a father. The men were wearing identical proud smiles and carnation buttonholes; Marsha looked faintly apprehensive, as if she was afraid she was going to drop the baby. Behind them was a large-stoned wall and the corner of a church window; and the sun was shining down on them still, dropping short shadows on the grass at their feet.

'My hostage to fortune,' Mrs Forrester said. 'After that, I couldn't have left Gil, even if I'd inherited fifty fortunes.'

'She's your only child?'

'Yes. I think Gil would have liked more, but it just never happened. So she was extra special to him. She was Daddy's Little Angel.'

There seemed to be a faint irony in the last words. Had she been jealous of the child's adoration of her father? Or was she apologising for the pukey nature of the words?

Still, it must have been nice for Forrester to feel he had beaten his rival at something. Slider was not entirely convinced by this Three Musketeers baloney: it would be a very strange man who would welcome his wife's ex-lover into the fold without even a hidden reservation. Slider stared at the photo. Whoever had taken it was less than expert: he had not centred the group properly, with the result that Dick and Marsha held the middle of the frame, and Gil Forrester was almost off the edge of the picture. It made him look, poor man, like a hanger-on at his own daughter's christening.

CHAPTER FOURTEEN

O'Mafia

THE SHERRY GLASSES HAD BEEN refilled. Mrs Forrester was talking freely now. It was an effect Slider had seen before, a sort of self-perpetuating hypnosis. By talking to him she had produced the atmosphere in which she felt it was safe for her to talk, and the longer she went on, the safer she would feel. All he had to do was not to alarm her, or break the mood.

The box of photographs had been put away. Those she had shown him had been more variations on the same theme: the three of them being happy together in fields, at fairgrounds, on beaches, before notable buildings, always in the sunshine, domestic or foreign. Marsha, Dick and Gil, where before it had been Marsha and Dick; and later Marsha, Dick, Gil and Eleanor.

A remarkably pretty, dark-haired little girl grew up through the pictures: pick-a-back on Gil, perched on Dick's shoulder, swinging between the two with a hand held by each; seven years old sitting between them on a wall with her short legs dangling and a smile with gaps in it; nine years old astride a pony with two unnecessary guiding hands on the bridle; eleven years old and solemn with new self-consciousness at the top of the Eiffel Tower.

Slider was glad when there were no more photographs. They made him feel desperately sad. Which was perhaps just as well, when they came to discuss the subject of Gil's death.

'Why did you go round to the station afterwards?' he

214

asked. 'Did you really feel the others were to blame?'

'In the philosophical sense, they were,' she said. 'That was where Gil's one-for-all-and-all-for-one really applied. But if you mean, did I think there was any negligence on anyone's part – no. I certainly don't now. Whether I really did then I can't honestly remember. It's a long time ago, and I was in a state of shock. I wasn't really responsible for my actions.'

'Do you remember anything of what you felt at the time?'

She thought about it. 'Anger mostly, I think. I was angry with Gil for being so stupid, so careless, as to get himself killed. Is that shocking?'

'Understandable,' he said.

'I was always that way with Ellie, too. If she hurt herself, fell down and cut her knee or whatever, my first reaction was furious anger with her. But it was only because I cared about her. I couldn't bear her to be hurt, to feel pain or fear, and that's just the way it came out in me. Can you understand that?'

He nodded. Her focus sharpened.

'Are you married?' she asked suddenly.

'Yes,' he said.

'Children?'

'A boy and a girl,' he said. She needed something back from him, reaction to having given so much out. He had seen that before, too.

'You're lucky,' she said. 'They are, too. I hope they realise that.'

He smiled by way of answer, and said, 'How did Eleanor cope with her father's death?'

'Very well, really. She was very upset at first, of course, but she recovered much more quickly than I expected. She had a week off school after the funeral, and I would have been happy to keep her at home longer – in fact, I did think of taking her away for a holiday somewhere. But she said she wanted to go back to school, so I let her. She was starring in the school play, and said she didn't want to miss the rehearsals. I suppose she needed something to keep her occupied,' she added, answering her own unasked question. 'She was probably right. I know I felt better once I went back to work. Stopped me thinking all the time.'

'You changed your job about that time, didn't you?'

'I wanted to get away. Everything reminded me of Gil and what had happened. I wanted a complete change. So I applied for a new post, and when it came through, I sold the house and we moved here. Eleanor changed schools at the same time, and I think that did her good, though she wouldn't admit it at the time. She said she hated the new school, but she did very well there.'

'Which school was it?'

'Burlington Danes, in Wood Lane.'

'Ah yes.'

'She got four A levels – chemistry, physics, biology and maths,' she said proudly. 'Three "A"s and a "B", and in those days grades still meant something.'

'Bright girl.'

'She always was. Gil would have been proud of her. She was always a daddy's girl, but after he died, and we moved here – well, it seemed to bring us closer together. She used to drive in with me every day – I'd drop her off at the corner of Du Cane Road – and that time together in the morning we talked more than at any other time in our lives. There's something about being in a car.'

'Yes. It gets the mind working, doesn't it?' Slider said. 'What did you talk about?'

'Oh, I don't remember. Everything. My work, her progress at school, things in general. It was very precious,' she added sadly.

'Did you keep in touch with any of the others on Red Watch after you moved?'

'Only poor Cookie – that was Jim Sears. Well, he kept in touch with me rather than vice versa. I think he felt particularly bad about what happened. He used to haunt the place at first, trying to make amends. Actually he was very useful, putting up shelves and things. It was nice for me to have a man about the place while I was settling in. But after a while I got tired of finding him under my feet,

216

and hinted him away, and he gradually stopped coming. And of course that tedious Barry Lister phoned me up every now and then. He's the sort who's always last to leave a party, never knows when it's time to go.'

'None of the others?'

She shook her head indifferently. 'They scattered to the four winds when the station closed.'

'But Dick Neal was only just round the corner from you, wasn't he? Living and working in Hammersmith.'

It came perilously close to being the question that would stop her talking. 'What are you suggesting?' she asked coldly. 'That I moved here because of him? Because you're very wide of the mark, I assure you.'

'I didn't mean to suggest anything in particular,' he said soothingly. 'I just wondered whether your closeness survived the tragedy. I mean, once you were over your period of mourning, you'd be free to marry again, wouldn't you?'

The formality of his wording seemed to please her. 'Yes, and of course that occurred to him,' she said with a faint smile.

'Not to you?'

'I'd had my chance to marry him when he was younger and nicer. I'd turned him down then. There was no reason why I should change my mind.'

'But he did ask you?'

'Many times, very emphatically. Starting when Gil was barely cold in his grave, I might add.' An unfortunate choice of words, Slider thought. 'You see, you had it the wrong way round – it was Dick who followed me here, not vice versa. He bore a terrible burden of guilt for Gil's death – not that anyone else blamed him, but he blamed himself – and I think he thought the only way he could make up for it was to take care of me and Eleanor.'

'But you didn't want that.'

She evaded the question. 'It would have been a difficult time to remarry. Ellie was at an awkward age, and she wouldn't have welcomed any step-father, least of all Dick. For about a year he kept asking, and I kept saying no, and

217

then he tried to make me jealous by going out with other women. And when that didn't work, he married one of them, and simply dropped out of my life. I never saw or heard of him again, and from what I gathered from Barry's tedious little bulletins, neither did anyone else.'

'Don't you think that was odd?'

'Not particularly. Gil was his great friend. He never much cared for any of the others.'

'But you had been his friend far longer. Isn't it odd that he dropped you, too? And so completely?'

'He took Gil's death very hard. Of the three of us, I think it affected him far the worst. He was a broken man afterwards. That's another reason I couldn't have married him.'

A slight hardness had crept into her voice, which Slider stored for later analysis. Poor old Dick had been found wanting again, had he? By then, of course, Mrs Forrester would have been a successful consultant, and probably pretty well-off into the bargain, while Dick Neal was merely an ex-fireman who had taken a job as a security guard. Yes, it would have been something of a mis-match from her point of view. Miscegenation on a grand scale. Had she tired of her faithful swain at last, and hinted him away too?

'So once Dick married, you had no contact with any of his former colleagues, except for the phone calls from Barry Lister?'

'And poor Cookie, of course – but that wasn't for my sweet sake. Eleanor was his object.' She grew grim. 'I wasn't too keen on the idea of becoming his mother-in-law, I can tell you.'

'Jim Sears was courting your daughter?'

She smiled. 'You have a lovely old-fashioned vocabulary, Inspector. *Mourning* and *courting*. I imagine you'll expect your future son-in-law to call you "sir" when he first comes visiting.'

'Of course,' Slider smiled back. 'But when did Jim Sears "first come visiting"? He must have been quite a bit older than your daughter?'

218

'Seven years. Not such a great difference, I suppose, but he'd already had a failed marriage. He wasn't what I wanted for my only daughter. I had no idea, actually, that she looked on him as anything but an honorary uncle. He used to come round and fix things for me, as I said, when we first moved here, but I discouraged him gently and that all stopped after a month or two. Then we didn't hear anything more from him for years.'

Slider nodded. 'So how did he come back on the scene?'

'Well, Eleanor went and did VSO after her A Levels. Four years on a kibbutz in Israel.' From the tone of her voice, it might have been four years in Holloway. 'A terrible waste of all that education. And then when she came back, she said she wanted to join the fire brigade and follow in her father's footsteps. I was furious – it was like Dick all over again. With her brains and looks she could have done anything she liked. But in the end I just had to let her get on with it. I hoped she'd find out eventually that it wasn't for her. But then the first person she met when she joined her station had to go and be Cookie.'

'He was at Ealing station, wasn't he?'

'That's right. How did you know?'

'His address was in Ealing, so I assumed he worked at the nearest station. Was your daughter still living here?'

'No.' Very brief – terse, in fact. He waited in silence, and she expanded with apparent reluctance. 'We'd had a terrible row over this fire brigade business, and she'd gone off and got herself a flat. Oh, we made it up after a while, and I suppose it was time for her to have a place of her own anyway. She got a little flat in Northfields and joined the Ealing station – and there was Cookie. Before I'd drawn my breath, almost, they were going out together, and talking about getting married.'

'You didn't approve of that, I take it?'

'It wasn't for me to approve or disapprove. She was twenty-three years old, she could make up her own mind,' she said stiffly.

'Twenty-three is very young,' Slider said. 'A lot of mistakes are made at that age.'

219

She yielded to the inner pressure. 'I tried to tell her she was throwing her life away, but she wouldn't listen! He had no prospects, no education, and he'd had one failed marriage already. The next thing you know she'd have been one of those downtrodden housewives hanging around the doctor's waiting-room with half a dozen snivelling brats in tow.' She heard her voice rising and checked it with an obvious effort. 'But she'd made up her mind, and I didn't want to alienate her any further. So I said nothing more.' She sighed. 'And how glad I was in the end that I hadn't. She needed all my support, poor child, when he was killed in that dreadful way.'

'Yes, I read about it. He was mugged, wasn't he?'

'On his way home from the pub. I didn't want them to marry, but I wouldn't have wished that on him.'

Praised with faint damns. 'Your daughter wasn't actually with him that night, was she?'

'No, thank God! It was bad enough as it was.'

'Yes, it must have been enough to make her want to change her job.'

'I hoped she would, but all she did was to change stations. She moved to Hammersmith, and there she is still. I hoped, too, that she might come back and live at home again, but she said it wouldn't work. Perhaps she was right. She has her own place in Riverside Gardens, and we see each other now and then. Not often enough for my liking, but she has her own life, and I have mine.'

'But you're on friendly terms again?'

'Oh yes. We keep in touch.' That answer seemed to leave something to be desired in the matter of frankness. It sounded as thought there was some resentment between them still. Mrs Forrester probably wouldn't be able to help letting her daughter know she was a disappointment to her; which the daughter would probably know well enough anyway, from comparing her own career with that of her high-powered, successful mother.

'I understand you telephoned Mr Lister to tell him about Dick Neal's death? How did you come to hear about it? Wasn't it usually he who phoned you?'

'I read about it in the *Hammersmith Gazette*,' she said
promptly. 'I phoned Barry to see if he had any more
information, but he hadn't heard about it at all. Obviously
his grapevine wasn't working in Dick's case. But then Dick
had cut himself off from everyone since he got married.'

'You didn't have any contact with Dick at all in all those
years?'

'I've said so.'

'What about Jim Sears' funeral? Didn't you go to that?'

'No. I don't care for funerals. But Dick didn't go either.
Why should he? They'd worked together ten years before,
that's all. Do you keep in touch with all your
ex-colleagues?'

'No, of course not. But in this case – he'd been so fond of
Eleanor; he watched her grow up. He must have been like
an uncle to her. And Sears was her fiancé. You'd think
he'd want to be there.'

'I don't suppose he knew about it. Dick hadn't seen
Eleanor since she was twelve years old,' she said harshly.
'He'd never so much as sent her a birthday card since then.
I doubt whether he'd have recognised her if he passed her
in the street.'

'Did Barry Lister tell you about any of your husband's
other colleagues dying?'

'No. Why should he? I think you overestimate his
contact with me – and my interest in the matter. I got a
Christmas card every year from Barry and the occasional
phone call, but I assure you all the contact between us was
entirely at his instigation and for his benefit. He was a
retired man with nothing to do, and missing his job. My
days as a fireman's wife are far, far behind me – and I
assure you I don't miss them at all.'

'What about Dick? Do you miss him?'

She looked at him for a long moment. 'Is that a shot in
the dark, or a shrewd guess? No, I don't miss him – but I
miss what we were together. I never regretted marrying
Gil instead of him. He'd have made a hopeless husband,
and my life would have been grim. But—' She hesitated. 'I
think a woman always feels a special fondness for her first

love, especially when he's also her first lover. We were young and happy together. When I read about his death, I felt – a great loss.'

The loss of innocence, Slider thought. In every life there was a moment when the gates of the garden shut behind you, and you realised that from now on, the pleasure you had always taken for granted would have to be worked for. Joanna had put it once – a quotation from somewhere, he thought, but he didn't know where – 'Before, one thing wrong and the day was spoilt; afterwards, one thing right and the day is made.'

That was the message in the snapshots, of course. In the photographic past, every day was sunny, every face was smiling. She should have married Neal in the very beginning, before they got thrown out of Eden. But the road to Hell is paved with missed chances, and no good deed ever goes unpunished. Nostalgia isn't what it used to be, he concluded with a sigh.

'Interesting,' said Atherton. 'Very, very interesting. And what did you make of her overall?'

'I'm not sure,' Slider said, staring into his tea. The canteen had started using those teabags on strings, which meant that you always had it lying in the saucer, a disgusting little corpus delicti spoiling your pleasure and making the bottom of the cup drippy. 'I thought she was a very sad woman, with an empty life. She loved Dick Neal but decided he wasn't good enough for her, and made them both unhappy.'

'But if he wasn't good enough for her because he was only a fireman, why on earth did she marry Forrester?'

'That's what I can't understand. The only thing I can think of is that she did it to spite him – married his best friend to make him jealous and serve him right.'

'Serve him right for what?'

Slider shrugged. 'For letting her down, perhaps. She went to University and made something of herself, while he dropped out – at least in her terms – and made himself ineligible. She was still quite young, remember – only about twenty-one when she married – and passion can be as irrational as that, particularly when it's intense.'

'Do you think they were lovers while she was married?'

'I've no idea. But it hardly matters, does it? Whether they actually did it physically or not, they were still lovers in every other sense. You could see it in the photographs – the belonging between them. Forrester must have been one hell of a patient man.'

'So if all the passion was still alive, why didn't she marry him when Forrester was dead?'

'I suppose the same problem still existed – he wasn't good enough for her. She was even further above him by then. Her career was advancing, and she had private income from her father's will.' Slider frowned. 'I can imagine a scenario where he proposed, and she said, "Yes, all right, as long as you make something of yourself. I'm not marrying a security guard." '

Atherton joined in enthusiastically. 'His pride would rear its head. He'd say, "I like me as I am. You'll have to like it or lump it." '

'She calls him lazy and lacking in ambition—'

'He calls her a frightful snob – they quarrel – tears all round and stormings out with slammed doors.'

Slider sighed. 'Hurt feelings can be the very devil. Probably they'd both want to make it up, but wouldn't know how to start.'

'Why did she change jobs?'

'She lied about that, at any rate,' Slider said. 'She said Neal followed her to Hammersmith, but we know from the dates that's not true. He started with Betcon two months after Shaftesbury Avenue closed, and gave his address then as Dalling Road. She didn't move to Hammersmith until four months later.'

'So she followed him?'

'Maybe. It may even have been a coincidence. But it's also possible that she genuinely remembers it the other way round.'

'Hurt pride again.' Atherton drained his cup. 'At all

events, it doesn't detract from her motive. She's furious that he doesn't care enough about her to fulfil her conditions of marriage. Instead of improving himself to be worthy of marrying her, he prefers to remain a bum, and even marries an inferior woman just to spite her. If that's what he did,' he added, 'they were a lovely couple all right, and deserved each other.'

'Thwarted passion,' Slider said. 'It's dangerous. But that only gives her a motive for killing Neal, not all the others.'

'Oh, I don't know. She didn't want her darling daughter to marry a nasty fireman, and since the daughter was stubborn, the only answer was to put him out. And the others—'

'Just a bad habit?' Slider enquired ironically.

'Give me a chance, I'm thinking. No, it makes sense all right, when you think what she'd been through, the conflict at every turn, the emotional suffering. It all built up over the years into an obsession. Neal let her down by becoming a fireman. Her husband let her down getting himself killed by being a fireman, and thus making a mockery of her sacrifices. Her daughter betrays her brilliant intellect by becoming one and wanting to marry one. Mrs F hates them all, more and more as her empty life unrolls before her. Most of all she hates her own particular ones, her husband's "mates" whose society Dick preferred to hers – the final insult – and who let her husband die. She wants them all dead.'

'So long after the event?'

'It had been building up. But Sears had only just come back on the scene, wanting to marry her daughter. That's obviously what triggered it off. The stimulus acute enough to make her kill. She killed him, and after that the rest would be easy. She started on an elaborate plan to off them all, leaving, as Norma put it, the best till last.'

'The murders get more and more elaborate as they go on,' Slider mused. 'Starting with a simple bash on the head, and ending with Neal's ridiculously elaborate set-up.'

'And there's the sexual jealousy motif we needed to

make sense of *that* particular scenario. She not only killed him, she emasculated him.'

'If they were a series at all.'

Atherton sighed. 'You are caution personified.'

'Just trying to second-guess our lord and master. And of course we still have to prove it.'

'Her alibi's only for Sunday evening. She could still have been at the motel killing Neal at two in the morning. What we've got to do is find out where she was when Webb and Sears were killed, but that won't be easy, after all this time. Another cup of tea?' Atherton stood up, and Slider pushed his chair back too.

'No thanks. I'm going to go home. I need to think a bit, get all this straight in my head.'

Of course, Atherton thought, Joanna was away. Well, he would just tidy up a few things, and then see if he could persuade Polish to let him take her out for a meal. There was that marvellous Jewish family restaurant in Finchley Road, where they did a chicken soup with dumplings you could spend a week trapped in a lift with and not tire of its company. Polish needed feeding up – at least, that was his excuse. And afterwards, back to his artesian cottage for coffee and cognac and sexy Russian music.

Tonight could be a memorable evening, he thought. And he'd do his best not to think of his guv'nor driving back to the grey wilderness of Ruislip and Irene's bony arms – the fruits of hasty marriage. Slider was a walking object lesson to Atherton. He only wished he didn't like him so much, so that he could appreciate the fact with unmixed feelings.

On his way out, Slider came upon O'Flaherty, overflowing the chargeroom door and talking to Nicholls, who was custody skipper.

'Ah, Billy!' The Man o' the Bogs turned and caught him. Last night's Guinness hung around him like a miasma, sublimating out of his pores, perfuming even his serge-induced sweat. 'I've got a curious little piece of information for yez. I was just telling Nutty about it.'

Slider paused unwillingly. With all the new information his head was perilously full and close to slopping over already. 'Is it about the case?'

'Trust me,' Fergus invited. 'Would I waste your time?'

Slider caught Nicholls' eye across the wide, upholstered shoulder, and Nutty shrugged non-committally. 'What is it, then?'

'I went down the Shamrock Club last night, to see if I could sell some tickets,' Fergus began in a once-upon-a-time manner, 'and guess who I saw in there?'

'Hedy Lamarr? Richard Nixon? The Dalai Lama?'

'None other than our owl friend, Gorgeous George Verwoerd. Now I thought to meself, that's a strange place to find a geezer like him, with not a drop of Irish blood in him—'

'I thought everyone had a drop of Irish blood,' Nutty put in. 'How did your people miss him out?'

Fergus ignored him. 'So I asked Joey Doyle, an' he said that Gorgeous was well known in there. *And*, what's more, he's seen him there several times talking to Richard Neal.'

'Gorgeous told me he didn't know Neal,' said Slider.

O'Flaherty nodded. 'Wait'll I tell ya, now. Joey was fairly poppin' with it all, which was why I reckon he sent that message of love to me—'

'If he had something to say, he could have said it to me,' Slider said. 'Or any member of the Department, for that matter.'

'Ah, now, don't be hard on me, Billy. I knew he wouldn't a come across for you. Joey an' me go way back. I knew his ma back in the owl country, and I did him a bit of a favour when he was younger. He'd had his germans in the till of the bar where he was working – oh, he wasn't a bad lad: he'd got in a spot of bother, and he was going to put it back, only he got found out before he had the chance. Well, I knew the guv'nor and I got him to take the money and drop the charges, for his ma's sake. Anyway, the long and the shart of it is that Joey's always got his eye out to do me one back.'

'Yes, I see,' Slider sighed. 'I don't know why we bother

226

coming in to work. We should let you lot handle the detective work.'

'It's a tempting offer, Bill,' Nicholls mused seriously.

'Would yez stop interruptin',' Fergus said to him sternly. 'Go and clank your keys somewhere. Listen, Billy, you remember the Neary boys?'

'The O'Mafia? Who could forget them? The nearest Shepherd's Bush ever got to Chicago. They made our lives hideous while it lasted. Don't tell me they're back?'

'Micky and Hughie are still inside, praise be t'God and HMP, and Johnner and Brendan went back to Dublin, as you know. But the youngest, Colum, came outa the Scrubs about six months ago.'

'He must have been keeping low – I haven't heard anything about him,' said Slider.

'Well he has. Sure, I only heard yesterday what Joey Doyle told me. You remember Colly Neary only got twelve months, because he didn't seem to be so involved as his big brothers?'

'Yes, I remember. I was never convinced by that fresh-faced look of his.'

'You were right,' said Nicholls.

'Well, but you know how it is in Irish families,' Fergus said apologetically. 'Colly's the baby, and Micky and Hughie always swore he was only on th' fringes of it. But Joey Doyle says that since Colly got out, he's been fronting for his brothers inside, making to build the whole empire up again for when they get out – protection, lotteries, money-lending, the whole shebang.'

'Oh good! Life was getting so samey,' said Slider.

'Just wait. You haven't heard the best bit yet,' Nicholls warned.

'Now we know Gorgeous George was involved with the Neary boys last time, though we could never prove it,' Fergus ploughed on. 'Add to that, he's now in pretty heavy with Colly Neary, and it starts to look very interesting that friend Neal was chattin' away with your man nineteen to the dozen – and that Joey Doyle saw him on one occasion stowing a serious amount o' wedge, which he reckoned

227

Gorgeous had just slipped him. Now then!'

Slider stared, working it through. 'Doyle thinks Neal was working for the Neary boys, with Gorgeous George as contact man?' he said disbelievingly.

'No chance,' Nicholls said promptly. 'The Nearys may be all sorts of bastard, but they're not suicidally stupid. They'd never work with a rank amateur.'

'I never said they would,' O'Flaherty said, goaded. 'Joey reckoned Neal'd been borrowing not wisely but too well. Twouldn't be from Gorgeous – he wouldn't lend a drowning man a sip o' water – so he must only a been the go-between. Now if the O'Mafia was into Neal for the change, and he'd not come up with it—'

'His finances had been getting more and more desperate,' Slider said. 'If he'd borrowed from the Nearys, and he got to the point where they believed he couldn't pay, or wouldn't pay—'

'They'd have no choice but to take him out,' Nicholls finished.

Slider frowned. 'But in that particular way? You know how he was left, don't you?'

O'Flaherty shrugged. 'That might justa been a joke. If it was Gorgeous George did the contract, now, he's a very funny feller.'

'It's a lot of ifs,' Slider said doubtfully.

'All right, but listen – wasn't your man Webb, the Harefield Barn victim, deep in debt? And didn't the Neary boys own a pub in Newyear's Green – not half a mile across the fields to the barn where Webb was murdered?'

'Yes, that's right,' Slider said. He looked at Fergus wearily. 'You know what you've done, don't you? You'd just added to the confusion, and given us another thousand things to check up on.'

'He's a one-man job creation scheme,' Nicholls said.

'If you buy two tickets to Wetherspoon's Spectacular, I'll forget I ever told you any of that,' Fergus offered. 'Nutty's in it,' he added temptingly. 'He's playin' the Mother Superior.'

'My *Climb Every Mountain* is going to bring the house

228

down,' Nutty said.

'Probably literally,' Fergus added.

Slider shuddered. 'No thanks. Not even for a quiet life will I sit through D Relief dressed as nuns singing *How do you solve a problem like Maria?* in two-and-half part harmony.'

'You're a miserable bastard, so y'are,' O'Flaherty said, heaving himself off the door jamb. 'And after I give up me precious time to come and tell y'all this. Well, I must get back to me desk.' He eyed Slider compassionately. 'It'd give you a leg-up with God Head, at least. He loves gangs and hideouts and dawn raids and th'like. Reminds him of his uniform days. He was never so happy as when bustin' down a door with his size elevens.'

'I know. I just don't want it to turn out to be Gorgeous George, that's all. I can't help liking him.'

'You've a hell of a funny taste, boy,' Fergus observed, as Slider took his departure.

So now he had two hares running, Slider thought as he drove home, and running in different directions at that. But there was no doubt gangland would seem more tempting to Head than the world of thwarted passion.

It would have to be looked into. If Gorgeous George had indeed given money to Neal, then Neal had been in big trouble. The fact of the Nearys' pub being near the Harefield Barn might turn out to be sheer coincidence; but if the two murders were connected, which seemed overwhelmingly likely, and Gorgeous was in the vicinity both times, Nearys or not it was going to be hard to keep him out of the frame.

Then there was Marsha Forrester. He had a bad feeling about her: a strong, passionate, intelligent woman – well able intellectually to plan the murders and emotionally to want to commit them. Her being a pathologist meant she'd be able to cope with them physically, and live with the memories. And her contact with Barry Lister meant she'd be able to keep tabs on her victims until their turn came round. It also made sense of the fact that he hadn't been killed – she'd have needed him for information.

She was perfect for the frame, but it would be hard work proving it. And he wished he hadn't seen all those photographs. The emptiness of her life, and the strong force that had driven her through the centre of it, and created her own loneliness, affected him deeply. He had to remind himself of Dick Neal's ruined life, his hunger that couldn't be filled, and his beastly, pitiful death, not to have too much sympathy with her.

His thoughts churned as the Western Avenue rolled by. A red GTV went past him, and his mind twitched towards it automatically, as a sleeping dog will thump its tail if you call its name. They were all Joanna-cars to him now. God, he missed her! Why couldn't he be going back to her, instead of to Ruislip? No-one there wanted him. He was extraneous, just a nuisance, like the men who came back after the war and found the woman and children had got on very well without them. Would they miss him if he went? What was he doing, sustaining the unnecessary edifice of his marriage? The sooner he made the break, the better for everyone. Get the agony over with.

If only Joanna hadn't gone away, he might have done it now, tonight. He was in the right frame of mind for it. But he couldn't do it if he couldn't go to her afterwards. The thought strayed past that he could do it anyway and then go and stay at Atherton's, or even a hotel for the night; that it would actually be better, philosophically speaking, to do it when Joanna was away. He let the thought go, rejecting it untested. If only she hadn't gone away, and he wasn't in the middle of a serious case . . .

He found his children sitting side by side on the sofa watching a game-show hosted – he noted almost with disbelief – by Bruce Forsyth, and eating Hula Hoops. Their hands moved dreamily back and forth from packet to mouth, and their jaws champed slowly and in perfect rhythm with each other upon the shaped pieces of expanded potato starch. They reminded him of a couple of sea anemones on the Great Barrier Reef, stirred only by the

230

eternal tides of the Pacific Ocean.

'Hullo,' he said. 'Where's Mummy?'

It was a while before his words sank the necessary fathoms to reach them in their sunless submarine caverns.

'In the dining-room,' Matthew managed to articulate at last, without breaking his feeding rhythm. 'Doing, you know——' There was a long pause before the last word floated up and burst on the surface. 'Costumes.'

'Thanks,' Slider said with unperceived irony.

Alfred the Sacred River ran past them unheeded, and Bruce Forsyth, measureless to man and miraculously not looking a day older than he was, conducted the audience in the response to his old, familiar catchphrase. *Nice!* the audience bellowed. At any moment, Slider thought weakly, the Television Toppers would snake on with their single giant horizontal leg, and he would know his mind had finally gone. He beat a hasty retreat to the dining-room.

'Hullo,' he said at the door. 'How's it going?'

Irene was bent over her sewing-machine, which was set up on the dining-table. All around were heaps of material, boxes of buttons and trimmings, magazine cuttings, library books on costume, and lists of instructions from Marilyn Cripps – he recognised the layout and dot-matrix printing of her rinky-dinky little PC. That would be the next thing Irene would want, he thought. He would have to restrain himself when she asked from making a joke along the lines of her having had a PC years ago, when they first married, and not using it then.

She looked up at the sound of his voice, and he saw with surprise that she looked flushed and eager, suddenly much younger and almost pretty in her preoccupation.

'Oh, don't bother me now,' she said happily, 'I've got far too much to do.'

'I wasn't going to bother you,' he said.

'Well I can't think about cooking at a time like this. You'll have to fend for yourself. The children have had theirs. There's some cold meat in the fridge. Or there's an individual pizza in the freezer you can put in the microwave. I can't stop in the middle of this lot.'

231

'Don't worry, I'll get myself something,' he said. Next time he married Irene, he was going to make sure they lived next door to a fish-and-chip shop. 'What are you doing there?'

'The costumes for the Gala,' she said with a disproportionately huge indignation that he recognised from Kate – or did Kate get it from Irene? 'I should have thought you'd remember *that* at least, even if you don't care about anything I do.'

'I know it's the costumes for the Gala,' he said patiently. 'I meant which particular one are you working on at the moment?'

She had the grace to blush. 'It's going to be a sort of crinoline affair, Charles Dickens type thing. It's a scene from *Bleak House*, I think.'

'Didn't they do that on the telly a while ago?' he offered intelligently. Taking An Interest, Mum used to call it. She'd been so good at it – asking the right questions of dull relatives and casual acquaintances so that they could expand on the one subject they were expert in.

A vagrant memory strayed across his brain of Mum engaging Irene's father in best-parlour conversation about his job as a pensions clerk. God, what a thing to give head-room to! He hadn't thought of Mr Carter in years.

Mum's trick had worked with Irene though: she looked pleased. 'Yes, that's right, with Diana Rigg as Lady Whatsername,' she said. 'Of course it's a lot of work, with all those flounces and tucks, and puffed sleeves, and all the lace will have to be sewn on by hand if it's going to sit right. Just this one dress is going to take me days,' she added with deep content.

Slider felt a sadness under his ribs like mild indigestion. She asked so little of life, and even that little had been denied her until now. And now that she had it, it aroused a deep and unwelcome pity in him.

'Of course,' she went on proudly, 'Marilyn said I needn't take so much trouble, because the costumes would only be seen from a distance, but I said to her, it's no trouble to me to do a thing right. It would actually be harder work for me to skimp it, I said. I'm funny like that. If I do a thing at all, it's got to be perfect.'

This was a remarkable new view of her character that he had never heard expounded before. He didn't know how to respond to it, but that was all right, because she didn't want him to respond, only listen and admire.

'And in any case, I said to her, there's no knowing whether the Royal Party will want to come backstage afterwards, and have some of the cast presented in their costumes, and then, well, you wouldn't want anything to've been skimped, would you? I said. I mean, I'd be mortified if a member of the Royal Family was to see my work close up and find it wanting. But she said to me, Irene, if *you* do it, I know it'll be perfect.'

'Quite, right,' Slider said, seeing a tempting pause laid before him. 'You're a fine needlewoman, everyone knows that.'

She smiled, and her cheeks were pink. She practically had dimples, he noted. 'Well it's true, I am,' she said, as though someone had argued. 'Everyone always used to say how nicely I turned the children out, when I used to make their little dresses and shorts and things.'

Did they? Slider wondered, searching through this unfamiliar terrain for some landmark he recognised. Who was everyone? As far as he knew, she had never had any social contact with other mothers, and he couldn't think of anyone else who would ever have commented on the children's clothing. It occurred to him that his wife was engaged in rewriting her life to suit her new acquaintances. Why did it make him want to cut his throat and get life over with?

'Well, I'm very glad you're being appreciated at last,' he said. She was in such a good mood, it was probably a good time to break the news that he would be not be home tomorrow. 'By the way, I'm afraid I've got to work tomorrow,' he began apologetically, but she had already gone back to her whirring, and he was addressing the top of her head.

'Oh, I haven't time to worry about that,' she said airily.

'I've got to go over to Marilyn's for a meeting at lunchtime, and I expect it will last all afternoon. She's doing a buffet for all of us, and she said we can bring the children if we like. They've got a *huge* garden, so all the children can play together while we get on with things. I'm so pleased,' she burbled, 'that Matthew will have a chance to get to know little Edward Cripps. He's such a nice boy, and just the sort of friend I've always wanted for Matthew. I never did like that Simon he's always hanging about with.'

Edward Cripps went to Eton, Slider reflected, while Simon had adenoids, red hair, and a mother who went to work. No contest, Simon. Bad luck, son. He backed out delicately, like a cat that's just spotted the travelling-basket being got out of the cupboard, and Irene didn't even notice him go. It was a good thing that getting to Eton was not just a matter of money, he thought as he headed for the kitchen and the delights of frozen pizza, or that'd be the next thing he would discover he had failed her in.

CHAPTER FIFTEEN

Best Eaten Cold

HAVING DISCOVERED BY AN EARLY call that she was on her day off, Slider went the next morning to visit Eleanor Forrester in her flat in Riverside Gardens. It was a late Victorian block in handsome red brick and white stone of what used to be called service flats. Such blocks were usually called Something Mansions; the flats were dark and stately inside, and cost, in his experience, a tidy rent.

Riverside Gardens, for a wonder, actually was alongside the river, just by Hammersmith Bridge, and Miss Forrester had a top flat with a wonderful view across the Thames to the school playing fields which, by some unexpectedly intelligent planning, had preserved the waterfront from development. She couldn't afford this on a firewoman's wages, he thought as he followed her into the sitting-room. Presumably she had inherited something from her grandparents.

In contrast with the bright, river-reflected light outside the room was extra dark, and he had difficulty for a moment in making it out. When his eyes adjusted, he saw that the walls were papered with a Victorian-style wallpaper of a darkish fawn patterned with small brown flowers. The picture-rail, dado, skirting board, door and window-frames were all painted dark brown, and there was a small fireplace with a dark wooden surround.

The carpet had an old-fashioned pattern in chocolate, coffee and cream shades, there were three buttoned leather club chairs, and under the window a gate-legged table flanked by two Windsor chairs. Add to that that the table and the mantelpiece were covered with ginger plush cloths with bobble fringes, and the whole effect was charming, very much in keeping with the style of the building, and terribly depressing. How could she bear to live here? It would be like living on a theatre set.

She had been watching him looking. 'Do you like it?' she asked.

'You've taken a lot of trouble to get it right,' he said. 'I was wondering where you got the wallpaper. It looks original.'

'It almost is,' she said. 'It was underneath when I scraped off the top layers. It was damaged, though, by the scraping, so I sent a sample to a firm that specialises in reproduction papers – the National Trust use them all the time – and they made it up for me.'

Clever how they reproduced the dinginess, he thought. Or did she order that specially? 'It must have been terribly expensive,' he said.

'It was,' she said indifferently, and then, as if she had divined the reason for his curiosity, 'Grandad left me quite a lot of money, and I've nothing else to spend it on. Everything's original, except the wallpaper.'

He turned now from the room to examine her. She was taller than her mother, almost as tall as him – which was no great feat, of course – and had a great deal of her mother's prettiness. The hair was short and dark brown and rather clumsily cut, as thought she'd had a go at it herself, with a fringe that had grown too long and was almost touching her eyes. She gave the impression of looking out from under it warily, like a cat under a hedge.

Her face was innocent of makeup, and perhaps for that reason looked rather pale. It also made him think of Joanna – again, no difficult feat – and predisposed him to like her. She was wearing a baggy maroon cotton sweatshirt and black Turkish cotton trousers, and her feet were bare. She had long toes, and he noticed that the fourth toe of her right foot was slightly crooked – the joint stuck up a little above the level of the rest, rather like somebody with a teacup crooking their little finger.

236

'What can I get you?' she asked. 'Some tea? Do you like mint tea? I was just going to make some for myself.'

'I've never tried it,' he said cautiously, and she took that for acceptance.

'All right. I won't be a second – the kettle's already boiled.'

Outside on the grey-brown river a pair of lighters went past, going down on the slack, and a red double-decker bus cruised majestically across the bridge above them. On the far bank, the plane trees were showing tender new leaf of improbable green, with dabs of yellow beneath them where some public-spirited person had planted daffodils. London's unchanging beauties, he thought. If the double glazing weren't so effective, he was sure he'd hear sparrows chipping away in the guttering just above the window.

Better to look out than to look in, he thought. Why did this room make him feel so sad? Was it simply what he knew about the young woman who lived here? Or the very fact that she did live here, like this, all alone, rebel without a cause? Gil 'Larry' Forrester's daughter; Jim 'Cookie' Sears' fiancée. Both gone and left her.

'Here we are.'

She came back in so quietly on her bare feet that he flinched at her sudden voice, and turned feeling foolish. She put the tray down on the plush-covered table under the window. 'Shall we sit here? Then you can watch the river. I saw you were fascinated.'

'Where Alph the Sacred River ran,' he heard himself say.

'Through caverns measureless to man, down to a sunless sea,' she finished for him. 'Were you made to recite poetry when you were little, too?'

'Only at school,' Slider said, sitting down across the table from her. '*The Wreck of the Hesperus* and so on.'

'Daddy made me, at home. He said it was good for the diction and the delivery. I'm glad now that he did, but I hated it at the time, because of course I never understood a word I was saying. *Eyeless in Gaza, at the mill with slaves,*' she pronounced suddenly.

'What's that?'

'Milton. Samson Agonistes. Wonderful stuff for

237

proclaiming, very gloomy and profound. *The sun to me is dark, and silent as the moon, when she deserts the night, hid in her vacant something cave . . . To live a life half dead, a living death!* It rolls around the tongue, doesn't it?'

'Very jolly,' Slider said.

She smiled. 'Have some tea.' she poured it into the two pretty, fluted cups, and it was greenish-brown and rank-looking and smelled like hot river-water. 'Mother said you'd been to see her. She telephoned yesterday after you'd left.'

'Yes,' said Slider neutrally. Had some kind of warning been conveyed? The eyes opposite were watching him very carefully from under the thatch.

'I don't quite know what help you think I can be. I know less about it even than Mother. You haven't tried your tea.'

Slider picked up the cup and brought it towards his lips. The smell was brackish and uninviting, and he found himself reluctant to touch it. It made him think, not for the first time, how social custom would make it pretty easy to poison someone, if they'd been brought up properly. He put the cup down untasted. 'Too hot still,' he said.

She didn't try her own, only watched him, a faint smile on her lips that didn't touch her eyes. 'Well then, what did you want to know?'

'I'm making enquiries in connection with the death of Richard Neal.' He didn't want her to force him into being formal and allowing her to shelter behind that. He smiled and said casually, 'What did you call him when you were a little girl?'

'Uncle Dickie,' she responded automatically, and then an unexpected blush stained her cheeks, and as quickly receded, like the blush of rage that passes through an octopus when you lift its rock away.

Slider followed up quickly, before she could have time to get back under the stone. 'He was always around the house, wasn't he? Did he use to listen to you reciting, too?'

'No, that was just between Daddy and me,' she said. 'I never did it in front of anyone else. Daddy used to say it

238

was silly, and I'd never get to be an actress that way, but to me it was a special thing, just for him.'

'Did you want to be an actress?'

'Not really. It's just a thing you say when you're little, like wanting to be a film star.'

'Or wanting to be a fireman, like your father?' A swift series of associations came to him, and he continued smoothly, 'Of course, at Hammersmith station you can combine the two, can't you?'

'I could, if they'd put on a proper play, instead of *The Sound of Music*.'

'Oh, aren't you going to be in it?' he sounded disappointed.

'I am not.'

'That's a pity. I'm sure you have a lot of talent.'

'I got rave reviews as Lady Hamilton in *Dearest Emma* last year,' she said quickly. Her mouth curved down. 'Then they spoiled it by following it with *Privates on Parade*.'

Slider had seen the film version. He thought it must be rather a good play. Now was not the time to say so, though. Instead he said, 'What sort of things did you do with Uncle Dickie, if it wasn't reciting?'

She looked at him. 'You don't have to call him that. I stopped doing it years ago.'

He tried frankness. 'Sorry. It's very difficult to know what to call people you don't know, when you talk about them to someone who does.'

'I suppose so,' she said unhelpfully.

'What do you call him now?'

'He's dead,' she said stonily. 'I don't call him anything.'

Oh boy! 'All right, how would you refer to him if you spoke about him now?'

She couldn't get out of that one. 'Dick, I suppose. Look, do we have to talk about him?'

'That's what I'm here for. What would you like us to talk about? The World Cup? The University Boat Race?'

She opened her mouth and shut it again, surprised by his rudeness. Then she said in a quieter voice, 'I'm sorry. I suppose you have to do your job. It's just that—'

239

'Yes? Just what?'

'It's just that I don't like to think about it. He's dead, and nothing that happened can be altered. I just want to forget now.'

'Forget what?'

She looked away for a moment, and then back, gathering herself. 'You know, don't you, that he and my mother were lovers?'

'Before she married your father.'

She looked at him levelly. 'And afterwards.'

'What makes you think that?'

'I don't think, I know,' she said patiently.

'But you were only a child at the time. You were too young to fully understand the relationship between three adult—'

'Children aren't deaf and blind, you know. They know a lot more about what's going on than people give them credit for.'

'Yes,' he said. 'I know that—'

'You don't know what Mother was like then. She was very beautiful for one thing.'

'She's very beautiful now,' Slider said.

She looked faintly surprised, as if that had never occurred to her. How young she was, he thought, for her age. Probably the tragedies in her life had retarded her emotional growth. There was something very inward-looking and stunted about this gloomy flat.

'Well, she was beautiful then, and she loved to be admired. Everyone had to be fawning on her all the time, or she wasn't happy. Unfortunately, men were quite willing to fawn. The whole of Red Watch was in love with her, you know. At the socials all the men were falling over themselves to light her cigarette and pull out her chair.'

'Do you hate your mother for that?'

'I don't hate her,' she said at once. Slider waited. She went on, 'We've had rows in the past, lots of them. We think differently about a lot of things. But I don't hate her. I feel sorry for her, really. Some women are just like that. She can't help the way she's made.' She paused, and then said in a very different voice, light and cautious, as though feeling a way along a previously untrodden path, 'You know that he killed my father, don't you?'

'Dick Neal killed your father?' This was a new track. Slider looked his incredulity.

'I know what I'm saying. You don't need to sound as if you're humouring me.'

'I'm sorry. But you can't really know. You were only eight years old at the time. You weren't even present at the fire when your father died.'

'The person who told me was there,' she said.

'Who would that be?'

'Jim Sears.' She looked at him enquiringly. 'Do you know anything about him?'

'Your mother told me how you and he were going to be married, but he died. I'm very sorry.'

She ignored the sympathy. 'How much do you know about the fire? You know Cookie was there?'

'I've read the report,' Slider said. 'Your father and Dick Neal went in to rescue an old lady. Dick brought her out, then realised your father hadn't followed. He went back to get him, and Jim Sears followed. They found your father tangled up in some wiring, and already dead, and had to leave him and get out to save their own lives.'

'Yes, that was the way the report told it. It sounds all right, doesn't it? But that's not the way it happened. Cookie told me the truth, years later, when we were engaged.'

'So what was the truth?' he asked.

She looked at him doubtfully. 'If I tell you, will you believe me?'

'Have I any reason not to?'

She hesitated a moment, and then took the question as rhetorical. 'All right. Well, then, Cookie told me that it was true about Dick and Daddy going in to get the old lady out, and Dick coming out alone. Barry Lister was Leading Fireman. He realised Daddy was in trouble and shouted to Cookie and Gary Handsworth to go in for him. But Dick jumped up and said he was going back for Daddy, and he

241

was off before they could stop him. He shouldn't have gone in a second time, you see. That wasn't the way it was done.'

Slider nodded.

'Cookie went after him. Barry stopped Gary from following. Of course, everybody knew about Dick and Daddy being special friends, so nobody thought it was strange that he went back in, only not procedure.'

'Yes, I understand.'

'Cookie was a bit behind Dick. When he got inside, he found Daddy as it said in the report, hanging dead, with the wires around his neck. And Dick was there, but he wasn't doing anything, just standing looking at him. Cookie said, "Help me get him free," and pushed past him to get to Daddy, but Dick said, "It's no use. We're too late." Cookie grabbed hold of Daddy, to try to get him down, and then Dick grabbed him and pulled him away. But in that moment Cookie saw that Daddy wasn't just tangled in the wire – the wires had been twisted together round his neck at the back, so that he couldn't have got himself free. Dick dragged Cookie away and shouted "We've got to get out," and then the ceiling fell and the floor started to go, so they left Daddy there and got out.'

It sounded like a wild story. After a moment or two Slider said, 'He could have been mistaken, you know, about the wire. The place must have been full of smoke and dust, and it was a very emotionally charged moment.'

'That was the first thing I thought when he told me. But Dick more or less confessed to Cookie afterwards, when they were in the ambulance together on the way to hospital. Dick's hands had been badly burned, you see, and Cookie was suffering from smoke inhalation. Cookie said Dick gave a funny sort of smile and said, "No-one would believe you, you know. It'd be your word against mine, and it's me they'd believe." And Cookie knew that was true, so he never said anything to anyone. I suppose,' she added thoughtfully, 'he must have hoped over the years that he had been mistaken. Or that Dick was talking about something else.'

'Perhaps he was,' Slider said. 'If that's all he said, there's really nothing specific to go on. He might just have meant that they should have tried to get your father's body out, that they saved their own skins too readily, or something.'

She seemed to tire of the discussion. 'Maybe,' she said indifferently.

'Why do you think Cookie told you that story?'

'Because he wanted to marry me. He said he felt he couldn't ask me if I didn't know the truth. He felt guilty about it – that he hadn't saved Daddy, or got him out, and that he'd let Dick get away with it.'

'Did he tell your mother?'

The question seemed to surprise her. 'I don't know. I've never thought – she's never mentioned it to me.'

Well, after all, would she? 'But Jim Sears was quite close to her at one time, wasn't he? Didn't he use to come round to the house a lot, when you first moved to Hammersmith?'

'Yes. I suppose he might have said something to her. And that would mean she—'

'Yes?' he encouraged.

Her eyes slid away. 'Nothing. No, he couldn't have told her, or she'd have told me long before Cookie did.'

Slider doubted the logic of that, but said, 'Supposing that it was true, why would Dick want to murder your father anyway?'

'Because he was in love with Mother,' she said. 'He and Mother were lovers, and Dick wanted to marry her, but Mother wouldn't ask for a divorce because of the disgrace. So the only alternative was to get Daddy out of the way.'

'Do you really believe that?' Slider asked.

She didn't answer directly. 'Cookie believed it,' she said flatly. 'Anyway, what other reason could there be?'

'But your mother and Dick didn't get married afterwards.'

'That was Mother. She refused him, because he wasn't good enough for her.' She stared at her cooling tea. She hadn't drunk any of it and nor, he was happy to say, had Slider. 'Poor Cookie. I wonder now whether – do you think it's possible that it was Dick Neal who murdered him? They never did find out who did it.'

'Why would Dick Neal want to murder him?'

'To shut him up. Cookie had just got engaged to me. Maybe Dick was scared that he'd tell me – which he did, of course – and I'd make trouble for him.'

'In that case, who do you think murdered Dick?' Slider asked, playing along.

She raised her eyebrows. 'It was an act of God, wasn't it? Isn't that what you call an accident?'

'It wasn't quite that simple,' said Slider. 'Someone a little less omnipotent had a hand in it.'

Her eyes widened. 'You mean – he was murdered, too?'

'It looks that way.'

She thought for a long moment, her eyes blank. 'I suppose I should have guessed. I mean, if it was an accident, you wouldn't be here asking questions, would you?'

'Probably not.'

She focused on him suddenly. 'You don't think my mother killed him, do you?'

That was an interesting jump of logic. 'Why should I think that?'

'Oh, I don't know. It's just that you've been talking to her, and now you come here checking up on her with me. It made me think you might – but it was a silly thing to say, of course. Forget it, please.'

Slider tried a different line. 'When was the last time you saw Dick?' he said abruptly.

'At Daddy's funeral, I suppose,' she said indifferently.

'Oh, surely not. He wouldn't just cut off relations so abruptly. He must have come to see you and your mother after that?'

'I don't remember. Maybe he did.' She shrugged. 'It was all so long ago.'

'What about when you moved to Hammersmith? Didn't he come to the house there?'

'No. Not when I was around, anyway. Mother used to go to his place to see him.'

244

'And when you were engaged to Cookie? Didn't you see Dick then?'

She looked surprised. 'Why should I? He and Cookie had nothing to do with each other.'

'Do you remember what you were doing on Sunday and Monday, the 25th and 26th of March?'

'That's easy,' she smiled. 'I was on duty. Does that let me off?'

He smiled back. 'I should think it's just about a perfect alibi.'

He drove away with his head more stuffed than ever. Was there any truth in it, he wondered? Was it possible that Neal had killed Forrester, that it had not just been a tragic accident? He supposed there was no way to find out for sure, with both Sears and Neal dead. Eleanor had certain things right about the background – about Marsha and Dick being lovers, for instance; about it's being Marsha who ended the relationship, and her thinking Dick wasn't good enough for her. But she had said Marsha had visited Dick when they lived in Hammersmith, and that didn't accord with what Marsha said. Slider couldn't imagine Marsha popping over to the flat in Dalling Road for a quickie. He was inclined to think Eleanor had got that part wrong.

But if Dick Neal really did kill Forrester – seizing an opportunity, very much in the heat of the moment, pardon the pun – how bitterly must he have regretted it afterwards? For there was no doubt – those photographs as mute witness – that there was a deep friendship between the men. If his passion for Marsha overcame him sufficiently to murder his best friend, and then afterwards he found it was all for nothing, because she wouldn't have him, it was more than enough reason for his life to go to pieces. Pity for Neal reasserted itself. What a hell of a life the man had led, and the fact that it was all his own fault could have been no comfort.

If Neal did kill Forrester, did Marsha know? Did she

think they must all have known, all of Red Watch, and killed them for their complicity – starting with Cookie, who was there and next most guilty, and saving Dick Neal until last? Or was the whole thing a misunderstanding of Eleanor's? She had been so very young at the time of the fire, and probably still emotionally troubled at the time of her courtship by Sears – very likely to get hold of the wrong end of the stick.

But in any case, how was he going to prove anything, one way or the other? The more he discovered about this case, the less progress he seemed to make. It was taking all the running he could do just to stand still, as Atherton said sometimes.

Meanwhile, of course, the troops were out scouring the ground for news of the O'Mafia, which their Beloved Leader would very much like to find at the bottom of everything, with solid evidence attached, and Gorgeous George trussed up and gift-wrapped with pink ribbon round his testimonials. Slider sighed. He was getting that internal sensation of pressure under the skull which came from absorbing too many unconnected facts which led nowhere, rivulets of water running away into sand. And there was a tune wandering around in there, too, using up valuable space and driving him mad. He laid hold of its tail as it went past and hauled it out to see what it was.

How do you solve a problem like Maria? The Sound of Bloody Music. Combined Services Gala Charity Performance, with the dead-keen-on-Amdram Hammersmith Fire brigade. Round in circles, he thought. The facts don't run away into sand, they disappear up their own logic.

Anderson bounced into Slider's office.

'You sent for me, Guv?'

'Yes, sit down. Where's Hunt?'

'On the blower. I left a message for him.' Anderson sat.

'All right. You can start without him. How did you get on?' Slider asked.

'We found out that Colum Neary and Gorgeous have

been hanging out together at the Philimore in North End Road.'

'Freddie O'Sullivan,' said Slider flatly. 'That's all I needed.'

'S'right Guv. They've been seen with their heads together. We also heard that the three of 'em'd been to some place out in the country to see about renting a house.'

'A place in the country? That sounds familiar. Go on.'

'Well, Phil and I went and rousted Firearms Freddie, and he was as nervous as a turkey in December. We leaned on him a bit, and he let slip some old horse apples about meeting the Nearys purely for social purposes – *Nearys* plural, you notice. So, since we know Mickie and Hughie are still banged up, it must have been Johnner or Brendan he was talking about, or both, back from the Republic and raring to go.'

'It's possible,' Slider said.

'Unless there's some more cousins we don't know about yet.'

'God forbid.'

'So what d'you make of it, Guv? We reckoned it must be something pretty big: Firearms Freddie for shooters, Gorgeous George for wheels, and the little house on the prairie for a base—'

'Who's we?'

'Phil and me. We think it looks like a big armed robbery.'

'The house doesn't come to much. They've got to have somewhere to live, and we know they've always preferred the wide open spaces.'

'Still—' Anderson said hopefully.

'Yes,' Slider agreed. 'It looks as though they're certainly planning something, and whatever it is, I don't like it already. Did you get anything on Neal while you were carousing in the Philimore?' Anderson looked blank for a moment and Slider raised a patient eyebrow. 'You did remember that was the point of the exercise, I hope?'

'Yes, Guv. I mean no, we didn't manage to tie Neal in with Neary. But we've got him seen with Gorgeous George at the Shamrock all right.'

'Thanks. We knew that already.'

'And if we put salt on Freddie's tail, he's bound to crack sooner or later. He can't stand being leaned on. His nerves've never been the same since that firebomb went off in his lock-up and set his hair alight.'

'I don't think Detective Chief Superintendent Head will authorise any more overtime,' Slider said, 'even for the pleasure of rousting Firearms Freddie.'

'Well, I don't know, Guv. He's very keen to get something on the Nearys, and Phil's asking him—'

'What?'

Anderson looked studiously unembarrassed. 'That's who he's phoning – didn't I mention? Mr Head asked him to let him know as soon as he got back.'

'And you let him?' Slider put his hands on the desk with soft menace. 'Get Hunt in here now.'

'Yes sir,' Anderson said. 'I think he—'

'Now. And don't you leave the building until I've spoken to you again.'

Hunt faced him across his desk woodenly.

'What the hell are you playing at?' Slider asked.

'Sir?'

'Don't you "sir" me, you two-faced, conniving little shit,' he said pleasantly. 'When you get back off an assignment, you report to me, not to the DCS. How long have you been in the Job?'

'Sir, Mr Head asked me to let him know what went down—'

'I always knew you were stupid, Hunt, but I never knew your name derived from rhyming slang.'

That one was over Hunt's head. 'I was just obeying orders from a senior officer, sir,' he said stubbornly.

'You were what?' Slider said dangerously.

Hunt's eyes shifted a little. 'I – er – I thought it was a special mission, sir.'

'Who d'you think you are, George Bloody Smiley? Special mission! I know what you're after, and if you think that's the way to get it, you're even more stupid than you look, which I would have thought was actually impossible. Just listen to me, peanut-brain. I'm going to be around a lot longer than Detective Chief Superintendent Head, and when he's finally got his shiny new buttons, and he's just a cloud of dust on the distant horizon, you'll still have me to answer to.' Hunt stared at his feet, but the tips of his ears were red. 'Did you really think he was going to take you with him on his way to the stars? You pathetic pillock. Nobody's got room on their firm for a backstabber. Not Mr Head, not anyone.'

'Well, what am I supposed to do, if he asks me?' Hunt said sulkily.

'You come to me, and let me sort it out. I shouldn't have to tell you that. Now you can make your report to me, as you should have done in the first place. And if you ever pull a stunt like that again, I promise you I'm going to make your life such a misery you'll wish you were pushing paper at Interpol. I'll stick you on every time you so much as blow your nose. Do you understand?'

'Sir,' Hunt said again. He seemed abashed, at least; but being Hunt, he was probably still not entirely convinced he wasn't being mightily put upon.

Dickson listened in impassive silence, but at the end a slow smile flushed through his face, finishing up in a full Thomas Crapper of gleaming white porcelain.

'Now we've got him,' he said – he almost chortled.

'That's what I thought,' Slider said happily. 'Thank God for Hunt, and I never thought I'd hear myself say that.'

Dickson eyed him with what in anyone else Slider would have been sure was shyness. 'Thanks for coming to me with it.'

'They taught us in the army never to waste ammunition, sir.'

'You were never in the army.'

'No sir.'

Dickson stared at him, perplexed. 'You're a funny bloke,

Bill. I never quite get the hang of you.'

'Thank you,' Slider said modestly.

Dickson reached into his desk drawer and pulled out a bottle of Bells. 'Glasses in the top drawer of the filing cabinet,' he said. Slider fetched them, and Dickson poured two healthy-looking well-tanned drinks. He handed one to Slider. 'I didn't mean that as a compliment, you know,' he went on, lifting his own glass and contemplating the contents. 'People don't like what they can't understand – particularly in the Job. Well, I don't have to tell you that, do I? If people don't understand you, they assume you're laughing at them, and that won't make you popular.'

' "Be popular" has never been number one on my list of things to do today,' Slider said indifferently.

'There you go again, you see. I'm telling you this for your own good Bill: you're a damn good copper, one of the best I've ever worked with, but unless you change your attitude, start polishing what needs to be polished and licking what needs to be licked, you'll be a DI for the rest of your life.'

Slider smiled. 'Thank you very much, sir.'

'I give up.' Dickson shook his head sadly, gestured with his glass, and drained its contents. The strain of so much personal exposure was telling on him, and when he put the glass down his face was its usual terrifying mask of conviviality.

'About this case: Mr Head, with the aid of our little department mole, has got very excited about the Nearys. Colum's obviously up to something, probably on his brothers' behalf, and he's keeping some very unhealthy company. Now Mr Head wants to redirect our resources to breaking up the O'Mafia before it gets going again. That's far more important than Neal's murder – if indeed a murder it be, quoth he.'

'But I thought—'

'Well don't. Breaking up a gang bent on armed robbery scores fifteen points with Special Branch. Catching a local murderer can't compete with that.'

'No sir.'

'It'll make the troops happy,' Dickson observed judiciously. 'Lots of overtime, surveillance details, hanging around pubs and clubs, which is where they like best to be.'

'Yes sir.'

Dickson drew breath and shed the complaisant mien. 'But I decide how my own men are deployed, not the DCS. He's spending tomorrow with his beloved wife, poor bitch, and his three charming children, so that gives us twenty-four hours unmolested. You've still got some lines to follow up, haven't you?'

'Yes sir.'

'Good. Stay on the case, use everyone you've got, get me something I can use to buy us more time. I don't like leaving jobs half done. Keep plugging away at it, Bill. Something's got to give, and an old copper's instinct tells me it's going to happen soon.'

CHAPTER SIXTEEN

Half Some Sturdy Strumpet

'I TOLD DICKSON I STILL had lines to follow up, but I'm damned if I know what they are,' Slider said.

'There's Gorgeous George,' said Atherton. 'He's got to be involved somehow.'

'Yes, and the bastard did lie to me. We must have another chat with him, point out the error of his ways. I think I'll save that pleasant little task for myself.'

'You deserve a treat,' Atherton agreed.

'Meanwhile there's the Forrester side to pursue, and I don't see how to proceed.'

'There are still Mrs Hulfa, Mrs Sears number one, Gary Handsworth's mother, and the beguiling Mrs Mouthwash who were around at the time. One of them might have heard something about Forrester's death not being an accident. And at least we can get some idea if it was commonly held that Neal and Mrs F were consorting.'

'But that's all sixteen years ago. We still have to prove she was there on the night of Neal's murder. She has no alibi for the time of death, and the logic of it holds up, but that's not enough even to give her a tug and search her flat.'

'Oh well, you know what you always say to me,' Atherton said cheerfully. 'Go through the motions, Guv. Go through the motions. You never know what will turn up.'

'Thank you, Mr Micawber. All right, put the team onto it, check everything that can be checked on the other deaths. And find out where Mrs Forrester was when Sears was murdered. She must have been interviewed at the time. If we can connect her with the Sears murder, that'll be a start.'

'Right, Guv. Of course, she might have hired a hit man to off him, had you thought of that?' Atherton grinned.

'Oh, go away,' Slider said wearily.

He drove slowly, hoping the magical properties of forward motion would turn over the heap of leaves in his brain and uncover something that wriggled. He had the sensation that something was missing, or had been forgotten, but that, of course, might be perfectly normal paranoia. Mrs Forrester was a very intelligent and, he had no doubt, determined woman, but there was no such thing as the perfect murder. There must be some way of proving she had been there.

Perhaps this long trip into the past had clouded the issue. There were too many people to think about. Perhaps he should go back to first principles, look at the Neal case as it had first appeared to him, before all the personalities and emotions got in the way. He turned down Conningham Road to cut through to Goldhawk Road and avoid the traffic, and thought, the Red-Headed Tart: he still hadn't sorted her out. Perhaps, after all, she was the key to everything. If he could only find her, she might supply all the missing pieces.

And almost at the same instant – or perhaps it was what had made him think of her at all – he saw Very Little Else, sitting on a garden wall on the corner of Scott's Road, scrabbling through her latest carrier. Luckily there was a gap in the end-to-end parked cars along the kerb just ahead. He pulled into it, and got out to walk back and talk to her.

'Hullo, Else. How's it going?'

She looked up at him warily for a moment, and then recognition spread over her features. 'Oh, 'allo Mr Slider.' She went back to her scrabbling. 'Got a biscuit in 'ere, if I can only find it.'

'You picked a nice sunny spot to sit down,' he said, parking himself beside her, though not too close, and upwind.

'Yeah, I got my special places,' she said, relinquishing the search. 'You gotter know where you can an' where you can't, see? No good if they come and turn you off, is it?'

'That's right. What about Gorgeous George's? Is that one of your places?'

'What, his garridge? No, that's no good. Too much shadder. Corner of the park's better. I can see his place from there all right, though. Told you, didn't I?' she chuckled.

'Told me what, Else?'

'Told you he knew all about it, didn't I? That feller what got killed in the fire.'

'Yes, I remember. And Gorgeous George was a bit naughty. He said he didn't know the man.'

'Lyin' sod. He knew 'em both – him and the girl.'

'Well, the girl was renting his flat, we knew that.'

'He knew her from before that. He's known her years and years,' Else said scornfully.

'Are you sure?'

'Course I am. Why else'd he let her have his flat? He don't let no strangers stop there.' She lost interest in the subject abruptly, and resumed her burrowing in the murky recesses of the bag.

'But how do you know?' No answer. 'Else, how do you know he knew the girl before?'

She looked up. 'Got a biscuit on you, Mr Slider? I had a whole packet in 'ere. Dunno where they've gone.'

'Never mind biscuits, what about the girl?'

'What girl? They was Lincolns an' all. None of your cheap rubbish. Y'know what I really like? Custard creams. I ain't 'ad a custard cream in years.'

He got up, and felt in his pocket for change. 'Here you are, Else. Go and buy yourself a packet.'

'Gawd blesher, Mr Slider,' she said, cupping her hands. 'You're a gent. Better'n that Mr Raisbrooke. Whass gone of 'im now, anyway? I ain't seen 'im for months.'

254

She was such a frustrating mixture of sense and forgettery, he thought as he climbed back into his car, there was no relying on her. But on the principle that the broken clock is right more often than the slow one . . .

Gorgeous George showed no resentment at being interrupted a second time. It was all part of the perpetual psychological warfare he waged that he sat relaxed and smiling, leaning back in his chair and playing gently with his gold cigarette lighter, almost as a man fondles a dog's ears.

'I hope you won't be keeping me too long. I've got an important meeting to get to by two-thirty.'

'They'll run all right without you,' Slider said firmly. 'I'd just like to have a little talk to you about Richard Neal – and please don't put on that enquiring look, like a friendly guide dog looking for a blind man. You know who Richard Neal is. I'm surprised at you, George, telling me lies.'

'Lies?'

'You said you didn't know him when I showed you his photo.'

'As I remember, I told you'd I never seen him going into the flat,' he said smoothly. 'That was perfectly true.'

'A very selective truth.'

Gorgeous lit a cigarillo unconcernedly. 'I've got nothing to hide. If you ask me the right questions, you'll get the right answers.'

Slider leaned forward and laid a fist down on the table. 'This is not a game, George, and I'm not here for the pleasure of your company. You were seen handing Neal a large sum of money in the Shamrock club, and having conversations with him on more than one occasion. Now I suggest to you that you're in serious trouble, and it's time you started being a bit more frank with me.'

He smiled. 'Is that a warning, man to man? How can I be in trouble, arranging a few bets for a bloke? Successful bets at that.'

'Come on, George, you can do better than that.'

'Can I? This man you're so interested in was a gambler, didn't you know that? A bad one, like all amateurs – too fond of mug doubles and the fancy stuff, and ready to take anyone's tip, if the odds were long enough. He was in bad money trouble and thought he could gamble his way out of it. He knew my reputation, and asked me if I'd choose some horses for him, and put the bets on.'

Slider stared in rank disbelief. 'This is a new you I hardly recognise. A tender, caring creature, ready to go to any lengths to help his fellow man. What happened, George? Why the sudden benevolence? Did you find Jesus, or what?'

Gorgeous smiled lazily, his eyes gleaming like those of a cheetah that's just spotted a wildebeest with its mind on other things. 'It wasn't benevolence, it was business. I did it on a commission basis. Do you think I'm stupid?'

'Not at all. I have the highest respect for your animal instincts – self preservation and the like. But animals don't do each other favours. It was a lot of trouble to go to for a complete stranger.'

Gorgeous shrugged. 'It was no trouble. I was betting on the horses for myself anyway. The commission paid my expenses for the day nicely, with a bit to spare. Never say no to a spot of bunce, Bill, no matter how small. Contempt of money is the root of all evil.'

'I've heard that. So the money you were seen giving to Neal was his winnings.'

'Exactly.'

'Lucky.'

'Not luck – science.'

'I suppose you wouldn't happen to remember the names of those galloping horses, by any chance?'

'I've got them all on file, of course. With the dates and the odds, if you'd care to check them.'

'I'd be delighted to,' Slider said. 'But it was all a bit risky from Neal's point of view, I should have thought. The horses might just as easily have gone down. I wonder he didn't want a more reliable source of extra income, if he was in trouble. You wouldn't by any chance have put him in touch with someone who lends money at a high, not to say punishing, rate of interest, would you?'

'Do I look like a bank clerk?'

'You don't look like a bookie's runner. No, I was thinking more along the lines of some of your entrepreneurial friends. I was wondering if you made Mr Neal known to the Neary brothers.'

George shook his head sadly, and showed his white, carnivorous teeth in a pitying smile. 'I don't know who you're getting your information from, but you ought to be sending him for immediate outplacement counselling. Everyone knows the Nearys are inside – where you, I might mention, helped to put them.'

'Not Colum,' Slider said gently. 'Colly Neary's out – sent on ahead, to get everything ready for the happy day when the Neary family is reunited on the outside. The old firm, back in business at the usual stand. In business lending money, for instance, on the Shylock principle, to those unfortunates who can't persuade Barclays they're a good risk.'

Gorgeous tapped the long ash from his cigarillo with complete unconcern. 'I'm surprised at you, going fishing during working hours. All I know about the Nearys is what I read in the papers, like everyone else. You're throwing out spinners and hoping I'll do your job for you. Not on. Sorry.'

Slider leaned forward. 'Look, George, I'd just as soon write you out of this one, because, God help me, I like you. But you keep coming into the frame, and when a head pops up, it's only human nature to shoot at it. I know you were involved with the Nearys before, and the word on the street is that you've been asked for another dance. And you've been seen in company with Colum Neary, so don't give me that innocent crap. Now you and Neal were locked into some large sums of money together, and Neal's turned up dead. If you'd like to show me how I can add all those twos together and come up with less than four, I'll be happy to go along with it.'

Gorgeous George looked up and smiled, but his eyes had the long, remote stare of the veldt, as unrevealing as mirrors. 'Neal approached me in the Shamrock club. I put some money on some horses for him, and they won, and I took a cut for myself. That's all there was to our relationship. As for Colly Neary – I sell second-hand cars.'

'To a man who's driver for a gang of bank robbers, protectionists and racketeers?'

'Erstwhile,' said Gorgeous. 'Colly didn't go over the wall, remember. He's paid his debt to society. And as long as my cars aren't stolen, I can sell them to anyone who wants to buy them. Unless the law's changed since I set up in business.'

'How would you like to tell me exactly where you were on the Sunday night and Monday morning that the Master Baker Motel caught fire?'

'Happy to oblige. As it happens, I went up to Chester on Sunday afternoon to stay with some friends – the Wilmslows, very nice respectable people. They had a few people in to dinner on Sunday night, and I stayed over until Monday for the race meeting.' The smile was gentle and tormenting. 'I have the perfect alibi, you see. Rotten luck for you, though.'

Slider was not surprised. He was dealing with a professional, and he knew the alibiferous Wilmslows would check out, and that the horses would have run, and won, as per the list he would be given. And the sums supposedly won for Neal would be small enough not to be remembered by the bookies at the courses. The question was, why did Gorgeous feel he needed to exercise his professionalism over this matter, unless there was something dodgy about it?

'I'm a thorough man,' Gorgeous George said, reading his mind. 'You're on the wrong track,' he added softly. 'The wrong track altogether.'

'All right. Let's talk about something else, shall we? Let's talk about Helen Woodman.'

For the first time something flickered in the golden eyes. 'Helen Woodman?'

'Oh, don't say you've forgotten her, George? A lovely-looking young woman like her, who rents your flat from you for three weeks, and disappears without a trace on the day Richard Neal does his now famous Burger King impersonation? She'd be heartbroken to think you didn't remember her – particularly after such a long and fruitful acquaintance.'

'You call three weeks long?'

'Ah, you do remember her then? But it was more that three weeks, wasn't it? You knew her before she came asking to rent your flat. Otherwise you wouldn't have rented it to her at all.'

The Wilhelm stuck to Gorgeous's lower lip. He removed it carefully, wet the centre of his lip with the tip of his tongue, took a long draw, and then put the cigarillo down on the edge of the ashtray as he blew the smoke slowly out towards the ceiling-fan.

'Your two minutes is up, George,' Slider said pleasantly. 'You're going to have to answer, or you're out of the contest, and you lose your deposit.'

The head was lowered, the eyes levelled, the shoulders squared, the hands placed side by side on the desk top. The body language was that of a man preparing against all the odds to tell the truth and be damned; which, Slider thought, probably meant he was about to be presented with the finest pork pie since Messrs Saxby's Gold Medal winner took the 1928 Northamptonshire Cooked Meats Exhibition by storm.

'Look,' said Gorgeous – sure sign of impending prevarication – 'I want to be shot of this. I want to tell you the truth, but I'm not sure you'll believe me.'

'Why shouldn't I? You've told me so many lies already, you must be nearly out of stock.'

Gorgeous sighed. 'Don't take it like that, Bill. This Helen Woodman business – it looks worse than it is, which is why I want to be rid of it, because it's going to bugger up my legitimate business. And no-one is going to believe it's got nothing to do with anything, which it hasn't. You're my best chance.'

'Thanks. You think I'm more gullible than the rest, do you?'

'Not at all. It's just that you've got more imagination than the average copper. You're not dead from the neck up, like the rest of 'em. I have great respect for you, Bill: I wouldn't offer you a plastic daffodil.'

'How do you feel about profiteroles?'

'Come again?'

'Skip it,' said Slider. 'All right, I'll buy it. Tell me about Helen Woodman.

'I did know her from before. You're right about that. But it was a casual and completely innocent acquaintance. She was a barmaid in a pub I used to go to sometimes a few years back.'

'How many years back?'

'1987. The early part of 1987.'

'What was the name of the pub?'

'The Cock.'

'Appropriate. Where?'

There was a hesitation this time. 'Newyear's Green,' Gorgeous said at last, reluctantly.

Slider felt a low hum of triumph in his cortex. The Cock at Newyear's Green was the pub formerly owned and run by the Neary brothers, where they had planned and out of which they had mounted their operations – the operations no-one had ever managed to tie George in with. And Webb had been murdered in a barn not half a mile away from there in April 1987.

'Oh George,' he said softly. 'Ain't life a bitch?'

Gorgeous met his eyes defensively, a wonderful new experience for Slider. 'That's exactly why I didn't want to tell you. You're going to make all sorts of deductions and they'll all be wrong. Helen Woodman was a barmaid at the pub, and that's all I know about her, or knew about her then. I noticed her because she was a looker. You know how I am about women. But I never had any other dealings with her, except for the drinks she served me in that pub, and that's the truth, if I was to die for it this day.'

'You didn't take a crack at her then?'

260

'Not then or later. I didn't fancy her. I've told you that already.'

'Presumably, then, she was known to the Nearys,' Slider mused. Gorgeous looked away, and didn't answer that one. Well, it would have been hard for him to do so without incriminating himself. 'Where did she go when we nicked the Nearys and the pub closed down?' he asked instead.

'She left before that, of her own accord. She was only there a couple of weeks.' George looked at him again. 'I don't know where she went. I swear to you I never saw her from that day to the time she came into my office here and asked to rent my flat.'

'It explains how she knew it was for rent, I suppose,' Slider said kindly. 'And what did she say she wanted it for?'

'I've told you that, too. She said she was doing some research and needed a base for three weeks.'

'And you didn't ask her what research?' Shake of the head. 'Why didn't you just tell her to fuck off, George?' Slider asked silkily. 'If I was in your position, I'd be inclined to think she was a lot of trouble in size nine shoes. You didn't fancy her. What did you want her about the place for?'

George sighed like a dying man. 'I didn't know what she was up to – or who'd sent her,' he said.

'Ah, I see,' Slider said. 'You thought she'd been sent by the Neary brothers, and that refusal to co-operate might upset them.' He didn't answer that. Slider shook his head. 'It's not like you to allow someone to incriminate you. It was very careless.'

'I wish to God I had told her to get lost. But it's too late now. All I can tell you is the truth – that I knew nothing of what she was doing while she was here. I made sure it was that way. I was careful never to see her coming or going, and when she left I made sure there was nothing left in the flat that anyone could light on.'

'And you don't know where she went? Where she came from? Where she lives? Anything about her?'

'No. I swear it.'

Slider shook his head. 'Curiouser and curiouser.'

'You believe me, don't you?' Gorgeous said, as close to anxiously as it was possible for a man who'd eaten more wild animals than he'd shot hot dinners.

'Well, oddly enough,' Slider said, 'I do. It's the final touch of obscurity I was looking for, to make this case completely opaque.' He stood up, and George's eyes rose with him. 'Thanks,' he said. 'And, by the way, this is a warning, man to man – keep away from all Nearys, great and small, and Firearms Freddie. And I should give the Shamrock club a wide berth too. Smoking Irishmen are bad for your health, you know.'

He walked to the door, and turned only to say, 'And don't ever lie to me again, George. Truth is beauty, remember that. I'd like you to keep yours if possible.'

Helen Woodman was the Nearys' barmaid. What the hell was he to make of that? He drove without seeing one yard of the road he covered, his mind revolving like a hamster in a wheel. Dick Neal was poking the Nearys' barmaid. She rented Gorgeous George's flat for three weeks, gave it up on the day Neal died. But before Neal died, that was the sticky point. Packed her case and left; but met Neal in the evening and went with him to the Shamrock club. Ran away to the loo when he had his quarrel with Collins, reappeared when it was over.

Was she with him at the motel? Or did he ditch her before he went there? Did she see the murderer? Did she set Neal up for the murderer? She was the Nearys' barmaid – maybe Colly Neary rubbed him out. Maybe Neal's murder was for debt after all, or some other associated trouble, and the rest of the firemen's deaths were just coincidence.

Was she at The Cock at Newyear's Green the night Webb died? Did she know Webb? Did he drink at The Cock? Was he in debt to the Nearys? If that was the reason for Webb's death, was the connection with Neal

coincidental, or had Webb put Neal onto them? God damn
it, either the deaths were connected or they weren't. And if
Webb and Neal were both Neary deaths, what about the
rest of Red Watch? Chance, pure chance – Head would
like it that way. Sears was mugged, the other two were
accidents. And Mrs Forrester was as innocent as a newborn
lamb.

A newborn lamb. A newborn lamb? The whirling leaves
inside his head slowed, began to fall gently downwards,
drifting, landing softly, making a pattern, not leaves after
all, but the pieces of a jigsaw puzzle. A newborn lamb. My
God, it had been staring him in the face. Why hadn't he
seen it before?

He took the first available right turn off Goldhawk
Road, heading back towards Hammersmith, King Street,
and the offices of the *Hammersmith Gazette*. He wished
Joanna were here, so that he could talk the thing out with
her. Or Atherton. Things sounded better or worse – more
themselves, at all events – if you said them aloud.

A newborn lamb. There had been little pieces all over
the place, things people had said, dropped separately into
his consciousness, then covered over by dead leaves so that
they couldn't be seen all together, side by side. A big
strong girl, like a baseball player. Made nothing of
carrying her case up the stairs. Best eaten cold. A nice,
civilised murder in theatreland. Following in father's
footsteps – what was that song? I'm following the dear old
Dad.

The red-headed tart held the key, he'd known that all
along, really. Clever makeup, like theatrical makeup. A
cold eye. And Marsha Forrester was a pathologist. Some of
the firemen are dead keen – O'Flaherty's voice. Rave
reviews. Four days on and four days off. Reciting poetry –
good for the delivery. The surprised, pale baby in the
basement. I'm following in father's footsteps, I'm
following the dear old Dad . . .

But there was one more thing he needed to know. Just
one more thing. Well, he knew it already, really, but it had
to be confirmed, made sure, made final. Hammer the last

nail into the lid. He put in a call to the factory on the radio. It was Norma who answered him – thank God for Norma, the best policeman in the Department.

'Righto, Guv. I'm pretty sure we've got that already indexed, but if not I'll find out. And I'll get onto the other thing.'

'Good girl. I'll come back to you for it. I don't know where I'll be for the next hour or two. But hold yourself in readiness.'

'Yes sir.' A pause. 'Are you all right, Guv?'

At any other time, from anyone else, it would have been an impertinent question, but he supposed the strain must be showing in his voice.

'Yes, I'm all right. We're nearly there, Norma. Nearly there.'

CHAPTER SEVENTEEN

Not Even a Bus

'DO YOU KNOW THE EXACT date?' said the girl in the photographic department.

'No, only that it was last year.'

'Oh well,' she said with a little helpful laugh, 'we'll find it all right.'

'You'll still have the negative?'

'Oh yes. We keep them for three years, just in case. And important ones even longer.'

'Then I shall want a print made to take with me.'

'Right now?'

'Yes, right now. As quickly as possible.'

'Whatever you say.' She looked doubtful. 'I don't suppose I charge you for that, do I?'

I bought some copies – you can do that, a voice said in his head. He pushed it away impatiently. The girl came back with two volumes of bound backnumbers and dumped them onto the slope.

'It'll be quicker if you do one while I do the other,' she said apologetically.

'Of course,' Slider said.

It was she who found it, ten tense minutes later. 'Here we are,' she said. 'Nearly the last page, wouldn't you know it? Is this the one?'

Slider bent over to look, and his eyes grew moist. *Hammersmith Fire Brigade Amateur Dramatic Society in their superb performance of 'Dearest Emma'.* A black-and-white photograph, of course, and in the centre of the smirking cast, the lovely leading lady in what appeared to be a long white nightgown, low cut to show a surprisingly magnificent cleavage. She had long, loosely curling hair – a wig of course. Red? Perhaps.

'That's the one.' He cleared his throat. 'Can you blow up the centre part? Just this figure here.'

'Yes, okay. No prob.'

Mrs Webb's friend Connie was a well-preserved, well-corseted bottle blonde, with the firm upper arm of the lifelong barmaid, and a sharp but not unhumorous eye. She stepped aside willingly enough when Slider asked her, but when he got out his ID she looked over her shoulder nervously and said, 'Put that away. Do you want me to get the sack?'

'Not at all,' Slider said politely. 'I just want a word with you about David Webb. Do you remember—'

'David Webb? Rita's husband? That hanged himself in the barn up the road? But that was years ago,' she said indignantly. 'What've you come wasting my time over that for?'

Slider looked round. The bar was quiet, there was no-one waiting to be served. 'This won't take a minute,' he said. 'Then I'll be gone. You remember you told the police at the time that you'd seen Webb come into this bar with a young woman?'

'Yes, and I wish I never had! What did they go and do but blab it to poor Rita, the cretins, practically broke her heart. She worshipped that man. But there's no point expecting coppers to have any tact, I suppose.' She sighed, and her hard bosom lifted accusingly, pointed at Slider, and sank again.

'I promise you I won't mention this to Rita – word of honour. But tell me, was it really just the once you saw her with him?'

'Only once in here, but I saw him with her other places. I make it a rule never to drink where I work, you see, so i get around in my time off. He was carrying on with her something rotten all over the place, and the wonder of it is

266

Rita never found out sooner, because she's not blind and deaf. But I suppose she didn't want to know, and that's the long and short of it. He was barmy about this girl, for all she was young enough to be his daughter, dirty bastard. But that's men for you.'

'You didn't know who she was? Where she lived or anything?'

'No. I only saw her with him.'

'Did you ever visit The Cock at Newyear's Green?'

'What? That place? Not likely! What d'you take me for?' The bosom heaved again.

'A very shrewd and observant lady,' Slider said politely, and it sank to rest. 'I'd like you just to have a look at this photograph. Take your time, and tell me if you think it could be the same woman.'

She looked, tilting the photograph to get a better light on it, and nodded. 'That's her all right. What's she in her nightie for? Is she in a loony bin? She should be, the way she was carrying on.'

'You're sure?'

Caution came over her belatedly. 'As sure as you can be from a photo. It looks like her, and that's all I can say.'

'Thanks,' said Slider. 'That's good enough for now.'

Joey Doyle looked nervous at the second intrusion, but covered it with cheerful banter. 'What is it, are you trying to ruin me trade?'

'If I wanted to do that, I wouldn't have come here before opening time, would I?' said Slider.

'That's true. What can I do for you, sir?'

'Just have a look at this photograph. Is that the young woman that Dick Neal brought with him that last night he was here?'

Doyle took the photographs, but began his caveats before he'd even looked. 'It was dark in here, you know. Well, it's always dark in here. You'd hardly know your own mother if you served her a snowball. I don't know that I'll—'

'Just take a look.'

Doyle looked in silence. 'Yes, it looks like the same one. F'what I can see from this. She wasn't dressed in a shroud then, o' course.'

Slider took the picture back. 'Are you fond of the theatre, Mr Doyle?'

He grinned suddenly. 'Every Irishman's interested in the theatre. It's in our blood.'

'Do you ever go?'

'Only to local stuff. I haven't time to be going up to Town.'

'Ever go to the plays the Fire Brigade puts on in Hammersmith Town Hall? I hear they're very good.'

Doyle looked puzzled for a second, and then the lovely light of intelligence shone in his eyes. He touched the photograph with his forefinger. 'Ah, so that's it! D'you know, I thought I'd seen her before somewhere, but I couldn't quite pin it down in me mind. Of course, it'd be the costume that was unfamiliar.'

She wasn't in her shroud then, Slider thought. To live a life half dead, a living death. A nice civilised murder in theatreland. He was beginning to feel very tired, but he knew that was just his mind trying to shy away from what it didn't like.

Norma met him at the door of the CID room. Her face was full of suppressed questions, and her eyes were full of sympathy. 'I've got it all sir, what you wanted.'

He took hold of the door jamb and leaned against it lightly. 'Well?'

'Eleanor Forrester's date of birth was March 28th, 1962. Marsha Elspeth Raskin married Gilbert George Forrester on September 13th, 1961.'

'She was already pregnant when she married him.'

'Yes sir.'

'And the other thing?'

'I asked Jacqui Turner. I thought it would be more tactful than asking Mrs Neal in the circs. Turner cried a lot, and said Richard Neal had a very slight deformity of the fourth toe on both feet. It was nothing much, she said, just a crookedness. You wouldn't even notice unless you were really looking. He said he was born with it.'

Slider said nothing for a very long time. It was Norma who broke the silence. 'Would you like me to check with Catriona Young, sir?' she asked gently. 'If it was hereditary, it would probably—'

'No,' Slider said. He drew himself upright, leaving the door jamb to stand on its own two feet. 'You'd better come with me,' he said. 'She'll probably need you.'

'You'll probably need me,' Norma said. 'She's a big, strong girl.'

'It won't come to that,' he said.

She opened the door to them, and for a moment the cat looked out from under the hedge, wild, wary, self-confident. Then her eyes went from Slider to Norma, and a remarkable change came over her. Her face drained of what little colour it had, her eyes seemed to bulge, and she looked both very young, and very, very frightened, like a child caught out in some misdeed by a feared and brutal parent.

He forced himself to begin, though he felt he had been cast against his will as Mr Murdstone, a part not natural to him. 'Eleanor Mary Forrester,' he said as sternly as he could, 'alias Helen Woodman—'

'Don't!' she cried. She lifted her hand like a policeman halting traffic; and then the other one, too, so that it became a warding-off gesture. 'Please don't!'

He felt a confusion he didn't understand; but Norma was there behind him, solid, strong, unemotional. 'I have to,' he said, and it sounded as though he was pleading with her. 'I'm obliged to warn you.' Norma stirred like waiting nemesis, and Eleanor's eyes flickered to her and back to Slider.

'No, please,' she said. 'I'll tell you everything, I promise, only please don't say that. Afterwards, if you must, but not now. I want to tell you properly first, as a friend, not a policeman.'

'A friend?' he said doubtfully.

'You like me,' she said certainly. 'If this hadn't

happened, we could have been friends.'

If this hadn't happened, he thought, as though it was just an accident, an act of God, something she couldn't have helped. Well, perhaps she couldn't. He had better find out, in whatever was the easiest way for her.

'All right,' he said. 'I'll hear you first, if it's what you want.' Sentence first, verdict afterwards. Where did that come from? She backed away from the door, and then turned and led the way in. Slider followed, feeling Norma's curiosity and – was it? – disapproval like a weight on his neck.

It was always easy to spot the orchestra coming through – not just the instrument cases, but the rapid and directed gait of the regular traveller marked them out. Lots of them knew him now, and smiled or said hello as they passed. Friendly lot, he thought. He liked musicians, they were a lot like policemen.

Joanna came through in the middle of the early bunch, with her small travelling bag – specifically chosen to fit under the seat so that she didn't have to wait at the carousel – over her shoulder, and her fiddle-case in her hand. She was talking to a tall, bearded trombone player, who had his arm round her waist as they walked. Slider sternly thrust down a twinge of outrage that raised its head. He found it very difficult to cope with the way artistic people touched each other so freely. At least, he wouldn't have cared a jot if they touched each other all over the place, as long as they didn't touch his woman like that.

She spotted him, and her face lit up like a pinball machine. She detached herself from her companion with flattering (to him, not the trombonist) haste and the next minute was giving him a fierce one-armed embrace, and the sort of kiss that two years ago would have embarrassed the pants off him in public.

'Hello, darling inspector! Have I missed you!' She released him only sufficiently to look at him, and her face slithered from rapture into concern. 'What's the matter?

270

You look awful!'

'Lack of sleep, that's all,' he said.

'No it's not,' she contradicted. 'Something's happened.'

'It's the case – we've made an arrest.'

'You've cracked it? Oh brilliant! But why aren't you happy? Have you got the wrong man?'

'Come and have a cup of tea and I'll tell you.'

'Here?'

'Yes. Please.' There was nowhere safer, or more anonymous, than an airport terminal. Just at the moment he found that reassuring.

'God, it's awful,' she said at last. 'No wonder you look so grim. All of them? She killed all of them?'

'Not Hulfa. According to her that was suicide after all. She was still working on him when he jumped the gun. He had been treated for severe depression.'

'But the others—?'

'One by one, planned and executed. And that's what it was to her, of course – an execution. They had let her Daddy die, so they had to be punished. Saving the best till last, as Norma put it.'

'But did she really believe Neal had murdered Forrester?'

'It's hard to know what she really believed. I don't think it's very clear to her any more, she's been living with it for so long.'

'Do you think Sears really told her that story, though?'

'No. I think Sears probably said that he and the others felt guilty about Forrester's death, and she made up the rest for herself. It didn't really matter, though, whether it was an accident or not – they were morally responsible in her eyes.'

She had cried in the end, sobbed like a child – the child she really was in one part of her mind, hurt so much by what had happened that she had shut that bit off from the rest to protect it. Schizophrenia, absolutely classic, Norma had said afterwards. But she had flung herself weeping into

271

Slider's arms, and what he had held was a hurt and pitiful child.

'You don't think – it's not just one of those mad confessions?' Joanna said suddenly. 'You know, people confessing to things they haven't done, for the notoriety.'

He shook his head. 'She has a notebook – she gave it to me up in the flat. Names, dates, every detail. Things she couldn't possibly have known if she hadn't been there. She's been keeping it, waiting for the moment when I'd come for her.'

'But how could she—?'

'Me, or someone else. Once it was all over, there was nothing left for her to do but confess, and die.'

'Well she won't die, will she? What will happen to her?'

'They'll put her in a psychiatric unit for a few years, then decide she's not dangerous and let her go. It's at times like this that I wish we hadn't abolished hanging. Oh, not for our sake,' he added, seeing Joanna's surprise. 'For hers. She'll have to go on living with it for the rest of her life.'

'So you think she wanted to be caught? Then why didn't she tell you the first time you interviewed her?'

'She tried to help me along. She told me she was on duty the night Neal died, which wasn't true. As soon as that was checked, we'd be bound to be back. But I suppose she felt she had to go on trying as long as the curtain was up.'

'She was acting a part?'

He paused, waiting for the right words. 'Not just that.' She was trapped in the inevitability of a situation. 'Once she started along the path, she had to go on. At least, I think that's how she felt.'

'Like a Greek hero. The plaything of the gods, in the grip of Moira.'

'Moira?'

'Fate. Or like the chap in the limerick, you know:

> There once was a man who said "Damn
> It is borne in upon me I am
> Just a being that moves
> In predestinate grooves
> I'm not even a bus, I'm a tram." '

272

'Oh, Joanna!' An unwilling smile tugged his lips.

'Sorry. But I can't bear to see you hurting so much about this. It isn't your fault, or your worry. And why so much sympathy for her? Think of all the misery she caused.'

'That's part of it.' He thought of Mrs Webb, left to bring up her children in so much ugliness. Of Mrs Neal, watching the door like the faithful dog that will never understand he's not coming home any more. Of Jacqui Turner, brooding over her precious, pathetic notes.

'And poor old Gorgeous George, caught up in her plans. Your Head's going to take some convincing that he was just being used by her.'

'It's a funny thing about that,' Slider said. 'Her original plan was to kill Neal at the flat. It would have been much easier for her, and less risky. But at the eleventh hour she changed her mind, cleared out from the flat, and made Neal take her to a motel.'

'Why d'you suppose she did that?'

'I think, so that she wouldn't mess up Gorgeous George's flat. Because at the last minute she realised she liked him.'

Joanna grunted through a mouthful of tea. 'It's nice to know she had some human feelings. And talking of the motel, why did she take Neal's car keys away?'

'Because she'd left her suitcase in the boot of his car. She had to retrieve it.'

'And his wallet and credit cards?'

'She wasn't clear about that. I think it was to rob him of his identity, to leave him with nothing. She wanted him brought low, utterly destroyed.'

'And all for Gilbert Forrester's sake. He must have been some man.'

'There were a whole lot of reasons mixed up. So mixed up it's going to be hell trying to put them in any sort of order anyone will understand.' Love, jealousy, fear, hurt pride, a child's defiance which, once begun, was hard to leave off. 'Self preservation, for one thing. She had to adore her Daddy because otherwise she'd have to admit to herself that Neal was her father, and she hated Neal for betraying

Forrester and sleeping with her mother.'

'How did she find out about that?'

'She walked in on them once. She says that's when it suddenly came home to her, as well, about his funny toes.'

'My God, it really is like a Greek tragedy – Oedipus, only in reverse.'

'But she must have guessed it subconsciously a long time before that.' He remembered the photographs, the eternal and indivisible happiness. 'I think they all had a pretty shrewd idea of the truth.'

'Dear Lord, though, what a frightful thing to do! To seduce her own father – and go on seducing him over a period of weeks – while she plotted his murder. How could she bear to do it?'

'Because she loved him, of course. That's the whole point – you have to understand. A little girl's crush that gradually got out of hand. She must have been horrified when she found out he was her father. And she hated him for loving her mother more than her. There was a whole seething cauldron of emotions building up between those four people over the years. Three of them at least were too intelligent for their own good. If they had been dull and stupid, none of it would have happened. Dick and Marsha would probably have married straight out of school—'

'And be perfectly normally divorced by now,' Joanna added. 'Shall we make a move? I'm longing for a bath and a decent drink.'

'All right,' he said, standing up automatically. She heard from the dullness of his voice that there was more to come, that he needed to talk it out. It was all hurting him too much, the horror of it, which he hadn't yet fully communicated to her. Well, walking would help the words along. It was quite a distance to the car.

'I think it's Mrs Forrester I feel most sorry for,' she said when they had found a trolley. It ran along jauntily in front of them, looking for a slope down which to misbehave. 'She must have known that Eleanor knew about her and Neal.'

274

'Eleanor said not, but I agree with you. I can't believe in all those flaming rows they had about her wanting to be a firewoman that she didn't throw that at her mother.'

'Do you suppose Mrs F suspected about the murders?'

'I don't suppose we'll ever know. She's not the sort to give us even a supposition to use against her daughter. My guess is that even if she did, she wouldn't let herself believe.' If she had, she'd have had to begin to wonder whether it would be her turn next.

'And what about Lister? Do you think he'd worked it out?'

'I think Lister probably thought it was Marsha. If he'd worked out the why, then the who would have seemed obvious, as it did to us. Marsha had the motive and the skills. He wouldn't have thought of Eleanor, who was only a child when it all happened.' A child, watching and listening in the background, knowing, probably, that her mother blamed Red Watch for her father's death. Was that when the seed was planted? The soil was well-prepared by then, and what a tropical-sized tree had flourished!

'Why didn't Lister go to the police, I wonder?'

'I suppose he must have thought it was imagination after all. If he said to Neal, beware of Marsha, and Neal said, I haven't spoken to her in years, he might have felt there was nothing to worry about. Then when Marsha phoned him up to say Dick was dead, the shock was too much for him.'

'Why *did* she phone? To find out how much he knew?'

'Maybe. Maybe.'

The car park, grey and echoing. He had first set eyes on Joanna in a car park – at the Barbican, oh occasion of blessed memory. The instant recognition of his mate in her had made even a multi-storey seem briefly like heaven. Not this one, though. Even having her beside him was not enough. He wanted to get out of here. Where the hell had he left his car?

'So the Neary connection was purely coincidental?' she said.

'She was looking for a way to be near Webb so that she

275

could get to know him in her Helen Woodman persona. She got the job at the Nearys' pub because it was live-in, and of course, being a noticing sort, she got to know that Gorgeous George had a place in Hammersmith, and stored the information away. Later when she wanted to get near Neal, Gorgeous's flat was just what she wanted.'

'And Webb didn't recognise her?'

'Why should he? Why should any of them? They'd last seen her when she was twelve years old, and they hadn't seen all that much of her even then. You don't particularly notice other people's children, not to recognise them twelve, thirteen years later.'

'No, I suppose not.'

'And as Gorgeous George said, it was clever makeup – theatrical makeup, designed to deceive.'

'Yes. I suppose she must have been a clever actress, to take so many people in for so long.'

'She lived her parts. All things to all men – what's that saying?'

Out in the sunshine now, thank God, and the green verges of the M4, heading towards London, Chiswick, Joanna's flat. He remembered her saying she'd once told a man she'd met in Wales that to find her place he should go straight down the M4 and turn left at the first lights.

'Her father was mad about the theatre – that's why his nickname was Larry, after Olivier. Being stationed at Shaftesbury Avenue put him in the heart of theatreland—'

'Must have been heaven for him.'

'And of course he shared his passion with his little girl. Took her to plays as soon as she was old enough to understand. Got to know all the stage door keepers, took her behind the scenes. She starred in all the school plays, and then went on to amateur dramatics. Acting was a way of life to her.'

'Especially given all she had to hide.'

'Yes.' Shadows chased each other across green fields where cows and horses grazed. A pretty approach to

276

London, he always thought: a nice first impression for the tourist.

'It explains why there was the long gap before the killings started – school, and then VSO. And I suppose in Israel she heard the word revenge in many a conversation.'

'It wouldn't have been an impossible concept to her, by the time she got back.'

'So then she got to know her victims socially, seduced them, and then murdered them? Reproducing the circumstances of her father's death – suffocation, hanging, burning.' He nodded, watching the traffic. 'You were right about Neal's death having the appearance of a ritual killing,' she mused.

'But how could Dick Neal not recognise her?' she added after a long silence. 'I mean, I can understand the others, but he'd virtually watched her grow up. She must have given herself away in a hundred ways in those three weeks of intimate contact.'

'I think he did,' Slider said. 'I think he probably knew all along who she was.'

'And still went to bed with her?' Joanna sounded shocked.

'Think of his life, what it had become,' Slider said. 'Think of what we know of his desperation and hurt. Maybe he didn't know the very first time he went to bed with her – not for certain – but afterwards, once he did know, what was he to do? Turn from her in disgust? Denounce her? A lot of men commit incest, you know, and they aren't all evil brutes. A lot of them do it because they love their daughters.'

'Love,' she said. It was so without inflection that he didn't know if it was ironic, derisive or doubtful.

'He loved her. He was lonely. And she was Marsha's daughter. She looked a lot like Marsha.'

'Yes,' she said thoughtfully, 'all his women were tall redheads, weren't they? He was searching for his lost love in all of them.'

'That's why Eleanor wore the red wig, I think. And why

it worked.'

'So he loved her, and she killed him. Like a lamb to the slaughter—'

'He knew,' Slider said, staring blankly ahead through the windscreen. 'He knew that last night what was going to happen. Lister had warned him – told him about the others. He wasn't stupid; and he of all people knew what she was capable of, how much she was hurt.' She was Larry's daughter. She was following in father's footsteps, following the dear old dad. But which one to follow? That must have been something of a poser for her.

'But surely—'

'No. He said to Collins that last night, "I'll never leave her as long as I live". He knew it was coming. Eat, drink and be merry, for tomorrow we die. But he went willingly to his death. It must have beckoned to him like quiet sleep, after all he'd been through.'

'Oh God,' she said. 'Oh God, Bill, I'm sorry.'

'Sorry?' He was surprised.

'For you. It's been so awful for you. And I wasn't here. Darling, it's all over now.'

'Not for her,' he said.

The bath had to wait – his needs were too urgent. As soon as they got inside the door he took hold of her, and she put down her bags and received him into her arms, and then backed with him to the bedroom, understanding more than he was probably aware of. He made love with pent-up passion, and she with a tenderness so acute that afterwards when he lay panting against her like a spent rabbit, tears ran sideways out of her eye corners, and she let them, rather than sniff and let him know she was crying for him.

But then afterwards it was all right; afterwards he was just tired. She ran a bath and got in, and he sat on the floor beside her. Two tall gin and tonics sat in the soap dish, and the steam condensed prettily on the cold glass.

'Well, anyway, it's a good result, isn't it? And you were right all along, and Head was wrong, and that's something

278

to celebrate,' she said, soaping an arm.

'Absolutely,' he said, his eyes fixed on her. How comfortable this was. Just looking at her fed something in him. She looked tired, too, he thought. There was a greyness about her skin, and the lines at her eye corners seemed more marked. She was no mere girl, of course. A vast surge of tenderness for her passed through him from the head downwards, and his penis stirred slightly like someone half asleep who thinks they've heard their name called. Not now, lad. Later. Plenty of time. He wasn't going home tonight.

'What would you like to do? Go out for a meal?' he asked.

'We'll have to go out a bit, at least – there's no food in the house,' she said. 'But we can get some stuff in and cook, if you'd prefer.'

'Yes,' he said, a nice idea blooming in his mind. How did it manage it, when he was so tired? Must be the gin. 'How about we pop down to the shop on the corner and get the makings, and then I'll cook you a huge pot of spaghetti bolognese.'

She smiled. Blackpool illuminations. 'Terrific idea! And if we get one of their small French loaves, I can make garlic bread to go with it. And there's that special bottle of chianti left from my Italy tour last year.'

'You wouldn't want to open that, would you?'

'Why not? It's a special occasion. You've solved your case, and you're staying the night.'

Oh dear. He saw the thought come into her eyes at the words, and she saw him see it. Now they were both thinking about it, and it would have to be said, and maybe the evening would be spoiled.

'Bill, you said when this case was over, you'd sort things out.'

'Yes,' he said.

She made a movement of irritation, not easy to do in a bath. 'What does that mean, yes? Are you going to talk to Irene?'

'Yes, I will, but the thing is – well, I don't want to do it just now.'

An unlovely hardness came to the lines of her mouth. 'And why not now? What's the excuse this time?'

He was nettled. 'It's not an excuse, it's a reason. Look, she's doing this special thing at the moment – she's involved with a gala charity performance at Eton, and she's so happy about it all, I don't want to spoil it for her. When it's over, then I'll talk to her. It'll only be a few weeks.'

'A gala charity performance,' she said in a dead voice.

It sounded idiotic on the lips of an outsider, someone who didn't know Irene. 'Yes,' he said defensively.

'At Eton. And for that, you want me to go on waiting?'

'It's the best thing that's ever happened to her, at least in her eyes. It would be cruel to ruin it for her, when just a few more . . .'

His voice trailed away. He looked at Joanna apprehensively. Her eyes were very bright, her lips were pressed together tightly, her tail was lashing. She was ready to spring. Now it would come, he thought miserably, the torrent of anger, fear, hurt, resentment – the ultimatum, the shutdown, maybe the tears.

Her shoulders started shaking. Tears then, he thought. That was the worst of all. He had never seen her cry, and the thought of it was terrifying.

Then her lips burst apart and she almost screamed with laughter.

'Oh Bill! Oh God, you're priceless!'

'I don't see what's so funny,' he said at last, crossly, as she went on laughing.

'A gala charity performance!' She was sinking dangerously back into the water now, hitching for breath, tears of laughter squeezing out between her eyelids.

'It's not funny,' he said, half resentful, half shamefaced.

'Not to you,' she agreed, and then went off again. 'Oh you are a lovely man!' she whimpered. 'If you didn't exist, it would be impossible to invent you.'

'Careful, you're going to go under,' he warned. And then, from sheer contagion really, he started to smirk too.